TO MOM: YOU INSTILLED IN ME THE VALUE OF "WHY,"
THAT IRREVERENT CURIOSITY FOR SCIENCE, NATURE,
HUMANITY, CREATIVITY . . .

I'M NOW CONDEMNED TO AN HONEST LOVE FOR
THIS WORLD OF OURS, AND IT'S YOUR FAULT.

ALSO BY S. L. HUANG

S. L. HUANG

null

set

TOR

A TOM DOHERTY ASSOCIATES BOOK · NEW YORK

This is a work of fiction. All of the characters, organizations, and events portrayed in this novel are either products of the author's imagination or are used fictitiously.

NULL SET

Copyright © 2019 by S. L. Huang, LLC

All rights reserved.

A Tor Book
Published by Tom Doherty Associates
120 Broadway
New York, NY 10271

www.tor-forge.com

Tor® is a registered trademark of Macmillan Publishing Group, LLC.

ISBN 978-1-250-74990-1

Our books may be purchased in bulk for promotional, educational, or business use. Please contact your local bookseller or the Macmillan Corporate and Premium Sales Department at 1-800-221-7945, extension 5442, or by email at MacmillanSpecialMarkets@macmillan.com.

First Tor Edition: July 2019
First Tor Mass Market Edition: October 2020

Printed in the United States of America

0 9 8 7 6 5 4 3 2 1

null set

one

My name is Cas Russell.

Except a little over a year ago, I found out it isn't.

That night a woman named Dawna Polk stood over me and melted my brain, filling it with scenes from a mislaid life, flashes of a past I'd forgotten to miss. She'd cracked the window into shredded fragments I'd only glimpsed in dreams, negative spaces where I'd never noticed the blank emptiness of what was gone.

In the scattered time since then, I'd been shocked to discover that everyone else had memories of a coherent existence. Memories of being a child, of growing up. Of a life before becoming a supernaturally mathematical retrieval specialist who drank her way from one job to the next.

Yeah. That would be me. Cas Russell.

Right now, however, I was unfortunately not drunk. Right now I was crouched on top of a metal shipping container in the Port of Los Angeles with a high-powered rifle in my hands. Five people stared up at me from a rough semicircle on the ground, all clad in black to match the moonless night, and all more than ready to kill me if I took my eyes off them for the least split second. They were the first break we'd had in finding their shitstain of a boss, and I was going to make them tell me.

Even if I had to do it without torturing them. Because torture would piss off the tall black man who'd decided to become my conscience, and who was currently forcing a sixth trafficker up alongside the rest with the business end of his Glock.

"Okay?" I called to him.

"Okay," Arthur called back. He started roughly patting down his prisoner.

"Here's how it's going to go," I addressed our standoff. "The first one of you who tells me how to find Pourdry gets to live. The rest get to see how well their organs can withstand the hydrostatic shock of a .308 round. Clear?"

"Fuck off," snarled the guy whose hands Arthur was zip-tying, which was stupid, because I twitched the rifle over and pulled the trigger. The shot whizzed by and buried itself in the ground behind him, so close it grazed his neck. A dark line of blood welled up, and the guy froze.

From less than a foot away, on the other side of him, Arthur glared at me. He didn't like when I was cavalier with guns, even though he knew I could predict exactly where I would hit, probability one. Whatever had Swiss-cheesed my memory had left enough skill at instantaneous mathematics to hit a penny falling behind a wall from a mile away through a windy hailstorm.

The dudes below me, however, did not know I breathed superhuman knowledge of velocities and forces. They only saw me fire a shot that would have killed a man if it had been an inch over—and all a foot from my own backup like a goddamned maniac.

"Hey, that was lucky," I said. "Next time my aim might not be so great."

Everyone stayed very still, except for Arthur, who finished securing the guy he'd brought over and moved on to the rest. His eyes kept flicking up to me with just a little irritation. Okay, more like a lot.

I ignored him and very obviously adjusted my rifle to the next person in line. Quickly rising to the ignominious title of largest human trafficker on the West Coast, their boss was the scum of the earth, but somehow he inspired devoted allegiance in his rank and file. Which meant I had to make these people more afraid of me than they were loyal to Jacob Pourdry. "I'll ask one more time, and then this gets violent," I said. "Tell me where—"

The back of the guy's head shattered, and a rifle report rang out just as his body slumped to the ground.

"Russell!" yelled Arthur.

"Not me!"

The other goons scattered and started clawing for weapons. A second one went down, jerking as if on a marionette string before he hit the dirt almost right next to Arthur. I tracked the kinematics of the trajectories back, measuring against speed of sound, the math blasting clarion in my head, and dove off the shipping container.

I protected my rifle in a perfect shoulder roll to come up by Arthur's side and grabbed the back of his leather jacket. "This way. We need cover!"

One of the traffickers tried to track us with his sidearm as we ran. My rifle took him out before the sniper could. We dashed around the corner, out of their line of sight.

But handgun rounds would punch right through the shipping containers like they were made of butter, let alone the rifle rounds the sniper was using. I sprinted through the maze, skidding into sharp turns and putting as many layers of 14-gauge steel as possible between us and anyone with a gun. Arthur followed without question. He knew to trust my math.

I slapped at my earpiece as we ran. "Pilar! Surveillance, now!"

"On it," chirped a perpetually cheerful voice in my ear. "Checker says he doesn't have eyes on who's shooting at you yet. Four of the goons are down though."

"We gotta get to the kids," said Arthur.

Right. The whole reason we were here in the first place—to rescue the shipment of children these assholes had been trying to smuggle into the city for the worst of purposes. Arthur had wanted to get them out first, but I'd insisted we take the chance to try for intel on the man behind it all. We'd been after Pourdry for months, but he was a fucking ghost.

No matter how many kids we pulled from the trafficking ring's clutches, it wouldn't make a difference if we couldn't behead the operation. And now our best chance had exploded in front of us. My hands tightened on my rifle.

"Hang tight where you are," Pilar said in my ear. "Checker's taken some of the drones up to see if he can get a— Oh. Whoever it was just shot one of them down."

"Okay, now I'm mad," came the voice of Arthur's business partner and LA's top computer-expert-slash-hacker. "Who would shoot a perfectly nice robot like that? No manners."

"Pilar, tell Checker to shut up unless he has something useful to say," I said, so harshly I practically heard Pilar wince.

"Pilar, please tell Cas this is not the time for her little grudge against me," Checker said back with perfect cattiness.

"Shove it up /dev/null, you dick," I shot back.

"Both of you, stop it. And remember, I used to work for a tech company, so I speak geek." Pilar was a recent hire of Arthur and Checker's, though her usual job was admin in their private investigations office. Since being hired she'd also taken it upon herself to pressure me into teaching her to shoot a gun, which may have endeared her to me slightly, and tonight she'd been recruited as dispatch. A good thing, too, because I didn't know how much longer I could keep being professional.

"You said you'd pegged the kids down near the water?" Arthur said into his own earpiece, ignoring our byplay.

"We did get a thermal read—" Pilar paused, then spoke like she was reading off the numbers. "Cas, it's bearing three hundred and forty-one degrees, a hundred and ninety-four meters from you. But we still don't have eyes on whoever that sniper is, so stand by—"

"Forget it," I interrupted her, and took off, not waiting to see if Arthur agreed. I did take us on a roundabout route that would at least keep us hidden from the sniper's last known position—I wasn't totally reckless.

We hurried under a line of cranes, their struts rising in looming silhouettes against the starless night sky. The water spread inky and black to our left. I kept us at a jog, Pilar's bearing fixed in my head along with a constantly updating map of how far the sniper or the goons could have gotten on foot. Unfortunately, both those numbers had intersected with our position long before we got there.

We crouched among the struts of the last crane. The number Pilar had given led straight to a lone shipping container just at the water's edge. No confirmation yet that it had people inside, but if it had lit up the thermals, it probably did.

Fucking Pourdry. I was going to get those kids out of there if it was the last thing I did tonight.

I turned to grab Arthur and make a dash for the shipping container, and for the barest instant I couldn't find him. Instead, another man was next to me, a bronze-skinned man with wavy hair, and I was yelling to him, *I'm going to get those kids out if it's the last thing I do*—

"Russell?" said Arthur.

I shook off the vision. "I'm fine. Let's go."

We edged out along the water, at an angle to each other so

as to cover more of the surrounding darkness. I was acutely aware of how much height the Port of Los Angeles had. Cranes, scaffolding, shipping containers stacked four or five high—plenty of places for a mystery sniper to hide. Who might it be? One of Pourdry's rivals? Then they'd definitely want us dead, too. Law enforcement? Not exactly their MO, but if so, that was even worse for us than an enemy. Of course, they could always be dirty vigilantes like us, but Arthur was right that most people didn't shoot that close to someone if they cared about the person staying alive.

We crept closer. Only a few meters out, I glanced back toward our destination—and immediately held up a hand.

Arthur stopped behind me. "What is it?"

"The lock's busted. Someone beat us here."

Arthur cursed softly.

A dark blade of a shadow appeared around the edge of the shipping container, at the minuscule strip of dock before the drop-off into the water. A shadow holding a rifle.

"Well, hey there, Russell," he drawled.

The silhouette of a long coat, and a tall Asian man who moved fluidly across the young brunette in front of me. The spray of blood smacked my cheeks as her eyes went glazed and vacant. The man stepped back.

"Hello, Cas," he said.

"She wasn't going to hurt me," I said through stiff lips. I was holding a handgun, but it dangled at my side.

"What she knew could have," said the shadow.

"Rio," I whispered.

Pain blossomed in my bicep. Arthur had unobtrusively grabbed my arm, so deep bruises were forming, but I'd needed it. My hands had gone slick on the rifle.

"What did you say?" asked the man in front of us. The man who wasn't Rio, wasn't part of my swamp of a past, and who currently had his own rifle raised and pointed directly at the center of my face.

I'd just lost it in the middle of a job. I couldn't lose it while in the middle of a job.

I *didn't* lose it while in the middle of a job.

And why Rio? He was off somewhere on the other side of the world, reveling in blood while he brought the Lord's justice down on those he deemed deserving. Lately, however, he wouldn't stop bringing his massacres into my dreams . . . and now my waking life as well.

Rio was my oldest friend, but even I didn't like dwelling on what he was capable of.

"You going to point that thing somewhere else?" Arthur called across to the sniper. I had the distinct impression he was covering for me.

"That depends," the man answered. "Are you?"

"Malcolm," I growled, my mind finally dredging up the correct name. "What the hell are you doing here?"

"I could ask you the same question," Malcolm said lazily. "Would've expected you to be on the other side of this. Aren't you the gal who'll take any job for the right price?"

"They're children," I said with disgust.

"Glad to know you have a line somewhere."

Malcolm was one of the best snipers I knew—like most people in LA's criminal underground, we'd both worked together and tried to kill each other a few times before, which put us on reasonably friendly terms. The minus side was that he worked for the LA Mafia, who I didn't currently have the greatest relationship with. On the plus side, his appearance here probably showed his bosses' demented protectiveness over their city if they were this keen to stop human trafficking.

"What does the Madre want with all this?" I demanded. "Madame Lorenzo's in the business of rescuing children now?"

"Somebody's got to," Malcolm said.

An all-too-familiar guilt stabbed. Arthur and I had been

doing our best to wrench up Pourdry's operations the last few months, but we kept running face-first into brick walls. The powerlessness had been suffocating. But if the Mafia was getting involved . . . I revised my initial reaction that their brand of protection could be a positive. If they took over here, it would either lead to all of LA getting burnt to the ground or the whole city under mob control.

I had flexible morals when it came to criminal enterprises. But the idea of them taking over completely . . . maybe it was Arthur's influence that made the bile rise in my throat. Or maybe the fact that I felt responsible for it all.

I'd chosen this future, after all.

Malcolm seemed to make a sudden decision and slung up his rifle. "You two can head. This situation's been handled."

"You shot the guys who were going to lead us to Pourdry," I said, even as I reluctantly lowered my weapon too. "Fuck you very much for that."

"They weren't going to give anything away," Malcolm said. He pulled out a pack of cigarettes.

"What's going to happen to the kids?" Arthur asked.

"We'll call the police, of course, like good citizens, and get them taken care of." Malcolm gave us the grin of a Cheshire cat as he lit up, the flame lighting the hard planes of his face. The Mob owned good portions of the Los Angeles Police Department, I remembered.

We own you, whispered a voice in my head.

"Come on, Russell," someone said in my ear. Arthur. "We're done here."

We weren't even *close* to done. We had to make sure the port was clear of any more of Pourdry's people—and search whatever ship they'd used; I was a shit investigator but Arthur was a goddamned PI. Not to mention that I wanted to stay horned in on this long enough to ensure that the Mafia kept their fucking word, and they actually did get the kids we'd been trying to rescue to safety. . . .

Rio splashed someone's blood across my brain again, and

the world schismed in front of me for just long enough that I lost my bearings.

What the *fuck*.

"Give my regards to the Madre," I managed in Malcolm's direction, and followed Arthur away into the night.

two

Arthur said something quietly to Pilar and Checker and stopped the call. I'd stuffed my earpiece in a pocket without telling them we were out and okay, which probably broke some kind of team etiquette. I hated working with people anyway.

"Well, that was fubared from start to finish," I said, kicking back in the passenger seat of Arthur's SUV. The thing was built like a tank—he'd splurged after his last few cars had gotten blown up or shot at.

Arthur's friendship with me hadn't been good for his car insurance bill.

"We're still alive. Kids are too," Arthur said, nosing carefully down the predawn streets toward the freeway. "Not as bad as it could have been."

"Pourdry's making LA into his own little fiefdom. And what, the LA Mob is going to sort him out? The last thing this city needs is the crime syndicates warring for control."

"You almost sound like you approve of law and order," Arthur said.

"I'll give you some law and order. I'm going to find Pourdry and put him in the ground."

That shut him up for a minute.

"I'm surprised *you've* been so willing to go all vigilante lately," I said, maybe just to needle him. Arthur was usually the one lecturing me—call the cops in, stop carrying so many illegal weapons, stop stealing, stop killing so many people. But the past few months, he'd been the one bringing in most of the intel on Pourdry and looping me in on the rescues.

"Sometimes you gotta make exceptions," Arthur mumbled. "Seems like it's more and more necessary these days."

"You mean because it's our fault?"

"Maybe some of that, too."

Guilt spiked in me again. Just over a year ago we'd been jointly responsible for hamstringing the organization known as Pithica, an international conspiracy bent on making the world a better place—though run by literal telepaths who accomplished their good deeds through murder and brain-washing. And as we'd dreaded, without their influence, crime had been burgeoning slowly ever since.

I'd sat with Checker, staring at a computer screen that held the key to defeating them, and we'd wrestled with ourselves over whether we should push that button. Take down Dawna Polk and her gang of psychics and let the world spin on as it would, free of their puppetmastery, or let them be and let the results of their machinations make most people's lives . . . better. Even if those people didn't know why.

I'd self-righteously taken on that decision for the entire global population.

Now I was seeing what I had wrought. Over the past year and change, criminal activity had gone from a slow ramp-up to an exponential explosion. Los Angeles had never been a particularly friendly city, but now it was becoming a nerve center for gang violence, for organized crime, for kids OD'ing in squalor and drive-by shootings in neighborhoods that had so recently bragged of safety and revitalization. Los Angeles wasn't the only place, either. But in LA, we saw it up close and personal.

I'd be lying if I said I wasn't second-guessing the decision we'd made. And I was pretty sure it was even harder on Arthur than it was on me. He'd cared a lot more to begin with.

The night was late enough for even Los Angeles's preternaturally frustrating traffic to have died down, and Arthur sped up the freeway toward the Valley. Instead of heading to drop me at my current hidey-hole in Santa Clarita, however, he swung off onto the streets to pull up in front of a dim dive bar that was still open despite having zero other customers.

"What are we doing here?" I said.

"Gonna buy you a drink."

I suppressed a sigh. Arthur had an annoying tendency to go all worried-parent routine on me. But with the job over I wasn't about to turn down hard alcohol.

Arthur ensconced me in a booth at the opposite side of the room from the bar and then came back a minute later with a beer for himself and a glass of something stronger that he set in front of me. I knocked it back all at once. The burn felt cleansing.

"Sounds like you and Checker are still fighting," Arthur said after a minute. He hadn't taken a sip of his beer yet.

That was a subject I definitely didn't want to discuss. "If Checker wants to be friends again, he can stay the hell out of my past. I told him I don't want to know, end of story. He has no right to get all hacker-y and try to dig it up anyway."

"He's stubborn. And he's worried about you. He cares." After a pause, Arthur added, "He's not the only one, either."

"I'm *fine*," I snapped.

Arthur studied me, his expression unreadable.

"What?"

"What happened today?"

"What do you mean, what happened?" I said it too loud. *Rio murdering someone in front of me. The darkness shifting and changing to places and times I didn't know.*

Arthur spoke slowly, picking out his phrasing. "Never seen you get . . . distracted like that before. Scared me."

I tried to tell him it had been nothing, but the lie stuck on my tongue. I pushed up out of the booth instead. "I'm getting another drink."

I persuaded the grubby bartender to give me the whole bottle, mostly by waving a C-note at her for a fourteen-dollar bottle of whiskey. When I came back, I slid onto the booth's bench and chugged from it.

Arthur watched me with what was probably disapproval, but he didn't try to stop me.

"You and me are supposed to be watching each other," he said instead. "Remember? Making sure Dawna didn't do anything permanent?"

Right. Watching each other's brains. I wasn't the only one Dawna Polk had psychically attacked in a last-ditch effort to save her global string-pullers. Arthur hadn't had an easy time of it either, but he also didn't seem to be suffering any residual effects. Whereas I . . .

Dawna had almost ended me that night. The whole on-slaught was still a prickly jumble, parts of it intermittently remembered and forgotten, other parts only the shapes of a memory. But since then, my nightmares had begun slowly bleeding into my waking life.

At least I was pretty sure she wasn't still influencing me, though. She'd just scarred me badly enough for my brain to start chewing on itself.

I'm doing very little, said the echo of power. *Picking at threads, as it were. Your brain has the most inventive ways of trying to destroy you.*

I gulped some more whiskey, grateful for the slight edge it took off my senses, and then leaned my elbows on the table so I could press my head against my hands, conveniently burying my face behind my forearms and avoiding Arthur's gaze.

If I was screwing him over in the field . . .

I had to tell him. Shit. *Shit.*

"I saw things." I tried to spit it out in one go, without hearing the meaning behind the words. I'd never planned to say it aloud, even as more and more of Dawna's attack resurfaced, haunting me—

I forced myself on. "When *she* was in my head. I saw . . . things from my past, I think. And this."

I reached into a pocket with a hand that felt like it was pushing through molasses and drew out a folded piece of paper. It had crumpled and gone ratty around the edges from being carried with me. I put it on the table and slid it to the middle, slowly, as if it were dangerous.

I thought it might be.

Arthur reached for the paper and unfolded it. Read it. Glanced up at me. "This is your handwriting."

"Yeah."

"You don't remember writing it?"

"Nope," I said. "Dawna played that note for me in a vision. And then I found my own grave."

"Show me," said Arthur.

WE PULLED up outside the cemetery just as the sun rose, washing out the city in pale dawn light as the day figured out whether it wanted to stay chilly or turn scorching. We were just moving out of Los Angeles's version of winter, which meant it was still jacket weather but now mixed with increasingly frequent ninety-degree heat waves.

The note was back in my pocket. *Do not try to remember under any circumstances,* it read, the precise math of the handwriting analysis leaving no doubt I had penned it.

And my signature underneath. *Cas Russell.*

I saw my own hands folding the note, the paper crisp and white—

"Just in case," a male voice said. "We won't need it."

I turned to pass it to him—

"Russell?" Arthur touched my shoulder.

I shook myself. "This way."

The smooth asphalt of the paths shimmered in the morning sun. We headed down between the soldiering lines of headstones and well-manicured lawns.

I remembered exactly where the columbarium was. Dawna had shown me the location of the note in my own head, and somehow my hindbrain had grabbed on to it and *yanked,* pulling me to drive, drive, drive here one night and then push inside the door until I stood *here,* in this building, surrounded by the soaring slant of wall plaques, each a human life burned down to a few pounds of ash—

I was panting slightly. Arthur waited next to me, a steady presence.

"There." I pointed.

Arthur moved over to the wall. I joined him. "Cassandra Russell" read the carved marble. The hand of death felt like it crawled up the back of my neck.

Arthur ran his fingers over the cover stone and found the fine cracks in it. "Your doing?"

"I broke it," I said. "To get the note. I guess they repaired it."

"You knew it was here," said Arthur. It wasn't a question.

I swallowed. I didn't know why I wanted to cling so hard to not saying anything, to not admitting the mounting trouble I was having with my own goddamn brain. But a good part of me—most of me—wanted to run. Hide. Ignore. Bury myself elsewhere, somewhere I'd never have to face anyone who might guess how much I was teetering.

I pressed my hand flat against the marble wall as if it would anchor me here. "Today, at the port," I made myself say. "You asked what happened. I saw—I think it was a memory."

Arthur straightened toward me. "You saw something?"

"It was—I don't know. Some guy. I was talking to him." I didn't mention the other memory, the one with Rio. Arthur already didn't like Rio. He didn't need to know I was hallucinating the man's murders. "It was . . . I was there, for just a second, and then I was back."

The door to the columbarium pushed open. I spun away from the wall like I was guilty of something.

Arthur, who was a lot better at undercover work than I was, merely turned toward the noise as if it were the most natural thing in the world. An elderly caretaker with a full beard and a haircut that rivaled Einstein's had come in carrying some gardening and cleaning tools.

"Morning," Arthur said.

"Good morning," the man answered genially, and moved to cross past us, going about his duties.

"Excuse me," Arthur called. "This wall niche, any way I can contact the next of kin?"

"Oh. Oh." The man patted down his coverall with his free hand, as if he were looking for a phone number to pull out and give to Arthur but had forgotten where it was. "You'll have to ask in at the office about that. They open at nine today."

"Thank you, I'll do that," Arthur said.

"That's the one that got vandalized, isn't it?" The man squinted past us. "Yes, I know they called the family about it. Such a shame, what kids will do these days. . . ."

Called the *family*?

My senses dulled, the world closing in on me. Who the *hell*—

"Hey, Russell. Russell."

Arthur had a hand on my shoulder. The caretaker had shuffled off.

"What the *fuck* did he mean by that?" I ground out.

"I take it you didn't get a call," Arthur said.

I moved my head in a stilted shake. I'd put that note in the wall. *I* had; I was sure of it. And the cemetery had called someone else.

"This is so fucked up," I said through a hoarse laugh. "Dawna pulled some batshit scrap of something out of my head and then I go to find it and the fucking thing tells me *not* to remember. . . ."

My hands twitched, my fingers recalling the tactile memory of dragging a pen into the shape of words. *Do not try to remember . . .*

The ballpoint snagged against an irregularity beneath the paper, making the *r* turn topologically inequivalent.

"I'm telling myself not to," I said with an effort. "That's the core of it, right? I need to trust myself. I need to *stop*."

"Sounds to me like you might not have a choice," Arthur said quietly. "If this is happening . . . you can't erase the memories of your life at will, right? Lord knows I've tried."

"It's not my life, though," I said. "It's someone else. Someone not me. I don't care, I don't want it, I fucking warned myself not to—"

I stopped.

"What is it?" said Arthur.

My breath hitched in my throat. "I just—something Dawna—"

You might have a chance at fighting me. If you weren't already fighting yourself.

"Russell? What'd she do?"

"Dawna—she—" How had I forgotten? How? Dawna's words reverberating through every corner of my mind as she'd taken me apart . . . "I thought she just left some sort of—some sort of injury, or mental scarring, but that's not it. That's not it." My voice sounded hoarse, as if I'd been screaming. "She's the one who told me. She *told* me to . . ."

"Told you to do what? Russell?"

"She said—she said *remember.*" I swallowed. Uncontrolled

nightmares made real, invading my waking consciousness. Dawna had made it so. She hadn't stabbed me in the psyche; she'd merely opened a door and ordered me to look.

That was all. That was everything.

"She told me to remember," I whispered. "And now . . . I think I am."

three

ARTHUR CAME with me to the Hole, probably because he was afraid I would chicken out.

The Hole was technically Checker's converted garage-turned-hacker cave, but at this time of morning and after the night we'd all had, it was marginally more likely he was in bed in his house rather than online. We tromped up the ramp onto his porch, and I pounded on his door loudly enough that I probably woke several of his neighbors. When he didn't answer right away, I pounded again.

It took six and a half minutes, but finally we heard the deadbolt slide back and a skinny white guy with a goatee swung the door open. He blinked up from his wheelchair at us in the morning light as he shoved his glasses onto his face; his hair was tousled with sleep and he wore pajama pants and a T-shirt with a picture of the Milky Way on it and the words, "You are here."

"Cas," he said, after a good eight seconds. I couldn't tell if he was glad to see me or not.

"Hey," I said.

He couldn't seem to think what to say back. I crossed my arms tightly and looked at the worn floorboards of the porch, trying to ignore how long I'd been refusing to talk to him. .

"Can we come in?" said Arthur after another highly awkward fifteen seconds.

"Okay. Right," said Checker, and moved back from the door, pulling it open the rest of the way for us.

We followed him into his living room. Arthur sat back on the couch; I remained standing, shifting from foot to foot.

"So what are you doing here?" said Checker.

"Cas has something to say to you," Arthur answered.

"Yeah," I said. "I'm having . . . I'm having a problem. I think I . . ."

"You got something to say before that," interrupted Arthur firmly.

"I do?"

"You do."

"What?"

Arthur just kept looking at me meaningfully. The awkwardness ratcheted up a couple more notches.

"Oh, for the love of Tesla," said Checker. "Arthur, stop it. He's trying to get you to apologize," he said to me.

"Oh."

"She doesn't have to. Cas, I forgive you for being such an asshole to me, okay? Done. Now, what's going on?"

Some of the tension in the room bled out. I moved over to sit next to Arthur on the couch. "The memory thing," I said. "I think . . . it turns out it might be an issue." I braced myself for a sarcastic *I told you so*.

"What happened?" Checker said instead. He wasn't a person I would have generally characterized as "gentle"—brilliant, cheerful, voracious, slightly mad, but not *gentle*—but he sounded that way now. As if he wanted to protect me.

Which was ridiculous, of course, since I could have

kicked his ass and Arthur's together without breathing hard, but I was suddenly, incongruously, reminded of how much I missed spending time with him.

I cleared my throat and tried to focus. "I don't know if looking into it would make things worse or not," I ground out. "But I feel like . . . I don't know."

Checker digested that. "I'm still willing to help you track down your . . . whatever your previous life was," he said. "Maybe understanding more would help? We could take it slow."

"I don't know," I said again, more belligerently. "I still don't think I should." I'd *told* myself not to . . . but what was the alternative? Do nothing?

"She's started getting flashes," Arthur said. "Since Dawna."

Checker's eyes got wide. "Oh. Crap."

"Since then, but . . . worse lately." I rubbed at my face. "She broke something. In my mind. And then *you* being all 'Cas, you have to find out who you were,' like picking a goddamn scab—"

"I'm sorry," blurted Checker.

"Yeah, well, you should be."

Arthur made a small sound beside me.

Checker took a breath. "All right, I'm asking you. What would you like to do?"

Like I had an answer for that. I opened my mouth. Shut it. Opened it again. "I want to stomp out this crime wave."

"What?" Checker said.

"Dawna's not the only one with a superpower. If she could do it, I should be able to, too."

He snorted a laugh. "Only you would decide to fight crime because you don't want to be shown up." Then he looked uncertain, as if he wasn't sure if it was okay to take the mickey with me again yet.

I pretended not to notice. "It's only a matter of time before LA's being run by warring organized crime rings. We're not going to let that happen. There's got to be a way to cut them down."

But Dawna was a psychic. How to leverage mathematics to do it instead? What was a supernatural math ability good for? I'd need to merge it with some sort of technology. . . .

"Pilar," I said aloud. "I need to talk to Pilar."

"Russell, we were talking about you," Arthur murmured.

Right.

"How about this," Checker said. "If you really feel like you don't want to know . . . why don't I take the lead for you? If you're comfortable. I'll ask you questions, and try to find out where you came from, and if I find a good reason not to tell you what I find, I won't, but at least we'll know if there's anything, anything dangerous, or if there's any way we can help you. . . ."

Despite having been the one to come here, I still felt inclined to snap at his suggestion. But then I'd have to answer his question about what I *did* want.

Putting my history in Checker's hands . . . it felt vulnerable, too trusting. Even though I'd been trying to make a conscious choice to trust more, to force myself to believe in the people I now called friends . . . this was a hell of a lot to ask.

Besides, Dawna had been the one to tell me to *remember*. The last thing I should be doing was listening to her. But Arthur was right: whatever chaos she had pried open inside my head, ignoring it was no longer an option.

The only choice remaining was to change a variable.

I hunched into the couch, curling around myself. "I reserve the right to put a stop to this at any time."

"Unless—" started Checker.

"No. I say stop, you stop."

He waited until I looked up, then met my gaze seriously. "Okay. It's a deal."

I was tempted to stop right then, tell them we weren't going anywhere with this. In fact, something in me was already screaming about what a bad decision this was, some intuition lambasting me that this was wrong, wrong, wrong—

I forced myself to nod.

Checker and Arthur exchanged a glance. "All right," Checker said. He reached over to pick up a tablet off an end table. "We'll go slow, okay? What's the first thing you remember?"

"I can't answer that," I said. "My memories aren't a well-ordered set."

"You mean you don't have a definite earliest memory?"

"No." I was staring at the floor now.

"Can you remember anything from before you lived in Los Angeles?"

"No." That wasn't strictly true. "I only have— When I think of being a kid, I see . . . all people who look like me. Brown skin, black hair. Lights. Bright colors. And then some other image—a classroom, I think. That's it."

"Didn't think it was likely you're from the US," Arthur said. "The way you talk. You mix your dialect."

"I don't have an accent," I objected.

"Well, you do—General American, or close to it. But I'm not talking about an accent. Your vocabulary's a mix."

Checker frowned. "Yeah, I think I noticed that, too; I just didn't think anything of it because I watch so much British television—but you're right, Arthur. You use words like 'mobile' and 'lift,'" he added to me.

"Flat," said Arthur. "Washroom. Ground floor—"

"Okay!" I cut in, feeling uncomfortably scrutinized.

"But the American versions, too," continued Arthur. "Like you got extra synonyms or something."

"Enough. I'm done for the day." I was already sick of this. I stood up and pointed at Checker. "I'm going to go get drunk and pass out. You—when I wake up I want a statistical analysis of the recent increase in crime."

"Way to be specific. What kind of statistical analysis, pray tell?"

"Any numbers you can get your hands on. Get me the data, and run your stochastic programs."

"You realize that it's not as easy as—"

"I have every faith in you," I said, and stalked out the door without looking back.

I didn't wait for Arthur to drive me home. I stole a car off the next street over instead. The shadows yawed and writhed at me as if a million eyes drilled into my back, but I paid no attention.

I DIDN'T sleep well.

As usual lately, my dreams were a confusing mass of colors and images, realities I thought I might be able to understand if I only had a second to look closer. I saw a dark boy with curly hair and a thin black girl. I saw mountains, and some type of aircraft, and a desert, and a jungle, and I screamed and I died.

When I woke up, tangled in blankets and empty liquor bottles, I didn't feel rested. Unfortunately, I did feel sober, and I couldn't indulge in more alcohol because I'd assigned myself this stupid crime-fighting job. At least working kept my brain busy enough that it staved off the need to self-medicate.

I fought traffic down to Arthur's private investigations office, which was a clean and respectable hole-in-the-wall in a terrible part of town. I knew for a fact that Arthur and Checker could afford a better location for the business; Checker had let slip one night that he wished Arthur would move to Beverly Hills but the idiot insisted he preferred "fighting for people who needed it"—whatever that meant. Checker never came into the office himself, doing his information-gathering via telecommute, so Arthur had veto power on the location.

Today, however, something itched at my awareness as soon as I got out of the car. I stood on the street for a minute and let my surroundings seep into my senses, the inputs dropping through functions into outputs, cause and effect. Everything fell within error margins, mundane and safe.

What the hell?

I took one last look around before dismissing whatever vibe I'd had as a subliminal outlier and climbing the outside stairs to the heavy door stenciled with "Arthur Tresting, Private Investigations." I pushed it open into a pleasant, professional office.

Arthur had renovated and expanded since the place had gotten shot up. Now the door opened into a bright reception area with Pilar's station in it. I expected to find her at her desk like usual, but instead the small front room had been taken over by two young teenagers who were brandishing their phones at each other like swords.

"Ah hahahaha, I got you!" the girl cried, and then did an honest-to-goodness somersault to come up on the other side of Pilar's desk.

"Ya got me!" the boy yelled dramatically, collapsing to the floor. A loud series of clangs sounded from his phone speaker as he let his hand fall.

"What the hell is this?" I wasn't annoyed, just puzzled. I didn't really understand kids, but I generally liked them more than adults, and if Arthur wanted to let them run roughshod over his office having fake sword fights, that was his business.

The kids' heads whipped over to me and they scrambled up. The girl looked defiant, the boy scared.

"Pilar said—" started the boy, his eyes darting to his partner in crime, but at that moment Pilar herself came out of Arthur's inner office, toting a stack of files. She wore a bright ruffled blouse and looked as chipper as if she hadn't been up half the night running dispatch for us.

"Cas! Hi!" She gave me a huge smile—and a genuine one, as far as I could tell. Almost as short as I was but quite a bit heavier, Pilar was charming and cheerful and one of those people who basically personified the word "cute." Arthur and Checker had snatched her up after meeting her on a case, and she was one hell of an office manager.

And a good shot. Arthur was still mad I'd taught her firearms.

"I see you met Katrina and Justin," Pilar continued, waving at the teens. "Guys, this is Cas. She's been helping Arthur fight back against Pourdry."

I blinked. Why would these two know about— But they both shrank back upon hearing the name, and Katrina spit a blue stream of cussing that beat even my usual discourse.

And then I saw what I hadn't noticed right away. Despite their smartphones, these kids weren't out of a cushy suburban home. Katrina's hair was tangled and lanky, and needle scars crisscrossed her forearms under a profusion of cheap bangles. Justin's clothes were cleaner than hers, but threadbare at the seams, and his sneakers had been worn flat.

"They aren't some of the kids we pulled out last night, are they?" I said.

"We can hear you, you know," Katrina spoke up rebelliously. "You can talk to us directly."

"No," Pilar answered me. "But they and their friends had some trouble with some of Pourdry's guys a little while ago. Arthur's been helping them out."

Katrina thrust her head up and stuck a hand on her hip. "Think of us like clients."

"Sure," I said. "Tiny clients."

"Who're you calling tiny?"

"Okay, okay, no fistfights," Pilar said, hurrying to shepherd Katrina and Justin to the visitors' chairs. She also shot me an exasperated look, though I didn't know what she thought *I* had done. "Cas, Arthur's not in yet. D'you want to come back later?"

"Actually, I came to see you." I swung over and sat down on the edge of her desk. "Your ex-employer. Arkacite Technologies."

"You used to work for Arkacite?" broke in the talkative Katrina. "Whoa, man! They, like, made my phone." She waved it at us.

"And now they're bankrupt and dead," Pilar said. She still sounded cheerful, but her smile was starting to strain a bit. "What about them?"

I searched my memory. Pilar regularly brought up weird tech she'd seen while working there, from biotech to AI software. Technologies for people in comas that could literally read minds, or gadgets that could help law enforcement . . .

"I'm looking for information on a specific kind of technology," I said. "But I'm not sure what yet. Start with anything you knew about that was being tested for police or military applications."

"Cas, I'm happy to talk to you about this, but I'm really very busy right now—"

"Aw, man, Velasquez," Justin chimed in. "You worked for the Five-Oh? I thought you was one of us."

Pilar put down her files and heaved a sigh. "If it makes you feel any better, Justin—most of it didn't work. There was a thingummy for police to remote-disable cars, but they could never get it functional. Or some frequency generation stuff to break up mob violence, and ditto. Most of the stuff they did manage to make was for the military—they did get some really sleek robots off the ground for sensing and then disabling IEDs, and lots of spy stuff that was actually pretty cool, like little cameras that would attach themselves to bugs—you'd like it—"

"Go back," I said. "What was the frequency generation thing? You mean something that would calm people down? Make them less aggressive?"

"Hey, no one's making me less aggressive," Katrina called. "It's like that white woman always said. We women gotta *lean in*." She made a gesture with both fists that looked vaguely obscene. I wouldn't have pegged Katrina herself as not being white, but with her dark hair and olive skin, I guessed she was probably an ethnic mix. She leaned back in her chair, crossing her arms over a tank top that read, "I'm not a bitch, I just act like one."

"I like her," I said to Pilar.

"Lady, I told you, I can hear you," Katrina said.

I gave her a grin and tapped the middle of Pilar's desk, on top of her files. "Frequency generation?"

"All right, all right." Pilar put aside her other work and turned fully to me. "This is actually something important? You're not just making conversation?"

"Since when do I ever make conversation?"

"Yes, very true. I guess we'd better go back into Arthur's office, then." She stood up, led me back through the inner door, and shut it over Katrina's good-natured objections at our unfairness in taking the conversation elsewhere. Pilar gave me a wry smile and took Arthur's chair while I dropped into one of the client seats.

"Now what is it you need?" she asked.

"This frequency generation tech. You were saying they wanted to use it to stamp out aggression?"

"Not quite." She cocked her head to the side and thought for a minute. "I mean, I suppose that was the result they were going for, sure. But what it really did was break people out of, um—'deindividuation,' that was what they called it. Which in practice meant—"

"They were looking to disrupt mob mentalities," I guessed.

She nodded. "Exactly, that was a big part of it. The Signet Devices—that was the project code name—they emitted a frequency or something that stops the brain feeling . . . you know how people can get in crowds? They lose control, they get all overwhelmed and sucked into the group . . . 'crowd psychology,' that's another thing they kept saying. How people feel swallowed into the masses and lose their sense of personal responsibility. They found a frequency or something that stops that from happening. The idea being that when they get swept up in those situations, people do all sorts of awful things they wouldn't ordinarily if they'd just been able to think about it."

I thought about the riots LA had been suffering. A lot of people who weren't ordinarily violent, escalating into layer upon layer of savage destruction. . . . From what Pilar was saying, the Signet Devices could stop such chaos before it ever sparked.

These things might be able to calm war zones. Or take down cults. Or, heck, even undercut the power of schoolyard bullies.

"It *was* something the police and military were all sorts of interested in," Pilar continued. "Really interested. Like, Arkacite had a bajillion meetings with important government people through the whole fiasco."

"So why isn't it out there?" This sounded like exactly what I wanted. But she'd just called the project a fiasco . . . "What went wrong?"

"They couldn't calibrate it right," answered Pilar. "No matter how much money the Defense Department piled in. It turns out people's brains were real sensitive to it. Either it was too low to work, or too high, and—well, then it made the test subjects *too* individual, made 'em distrust each other and start fighting because of *that,* instead of mobbing together. So the point was to stamp out aggression, and it ended up causing aggression for a different reason. And there was a sweet spot where it worked, but they could never maintain it reliably, and they especially couldn't do it evenly over a large area."

Hmm. "How easy would it be to get more specs on these things?"

I expected Pilar to say I'd need to ask for Checker's help, but instead she grinned and started logging onto Arthur's computer. "I'm betting we already have some of it. At least the testing data. Remember how I ended up working here? Checker pulled everything out of Arkacite that wasn't behind a military firewall, even if it wasn't relevant at the time, and he never throws any data away when he hacks a place."

Of course. The very case when Checker had recruited Pilar to work for them. Fabulous.

She started typing, her eyes scanning down the screen. "Wow, yeah, there's a lot. Like . . . everything. This is going to take me a while to sort through, but I can send you whatever there is on the Signet Devices. What do you need it all for?"

"Calibration's just math," I said.

"Wait, you want to *build* one?" Her voice rose into a squeak.

"No," I answered. "I want to build a lot of them."

"What *for*?"

"The crime in the city lately. I'm looking for a way to axe it, and this sounds like more than a good start." The possibilities kept expanding in my head. Combating deindividuation would potentially be a sweeping blow against gangs and organized crime, at the very least. I thought of Pourdry's goons and their blind loyalty and was angry all over again. Devices like these might not be able to stop someone like Pourdry himself, but if they gutted his organization, how powerful would he be then? These things might keep all the big criminal rackets from getting out of hand. "Let's see how brave these assholes are without their armies to hide behind."

"You mean you want to put these things around LA?" Pilar's face stretched itself into a bizarre combination of incredulity and horror. "Cas, don't take this the wrong way, but that is a terrible idea!"

"Why? I'm not going to do it unless I can get the calibration right, which I bet I can."

"They barely did any human testing!" she protested. "I don't even know if it's something people could take long-term. You could make things way worse—"

"And I could make 'em way better," I said.

She leaned away from me, shaking her head over and over. "It's too risky. This is so dangerous. You're talking about—"

"This could save a lot of lives."

"I don't know," she said. "I want to make LA safer, too, I do, I *do,* more than anyone. But if this went wrong—think how bad it could go. If you didn't get it right, people would start tearing each other apart. Normal people. I saw the test results."

I crossed my arms. "Does that mean you're not going to give me the files?"

Pilar wavered. "I mean . . . you do seem to do the impossible on a regular basis. Checker and I have conversations about it, you know. Did you really lasso the wing of a fighter jet one time and—"

Not technically, and certainly not how she was describing it. "I'm good at math," I interrupted. "That's all."

"That's what you always say! If this were anyone else asking, and I mean *anyone* else . . ." She pursed her lips and thought for a moment. "Promise you're not going to do anything unless you're sure it's going to work?"

"Sure. I can promise that."

She looked down at the desk for a minute. "I've got a lot of family here, you know."

"I know," I said, confused by the non sequitur. Pilar mentioned her family a lot.

"One of my cousins joined a gang a couple months ago," she said. "My aunt is devastated. There was no reason, you know? He's a good kid, good family—and my baby brother's still in high school, and you know what an LA public school is like. It was a jungle when I went through and now . . ." She trailed off and cleared her throat. "My mom tells me he comes home with black eyes sometimes. From high school. Can you believe it? It's not fair. My folks don't even live in a bad part of town."

As much as Pilar talked about her family, I tended to forget they actually existed as people. But hey, if they were going to help my cause, I was okay with that. "That's why I want to do this."

"I know," she said, the earnest trust in her voice assigning me more goodwill than I probably deserved. She flapped a hand despondently toward the outer office. "And then you look at people like Katrina and Justin . . . All they want is a chance, you know? And everything's against them, all these jerks who just—who want to tear everything down so nobody gets that chance."

"Yeah," I said. "Exactly."

"Okay. All right. All right, I'll send you whatever I can."

I felt pretty satisfied as I walked out, enough to be good-humored about Katrina flicking what I was pretty sure were spitballs in my direction as I passed. I flipped up the back of my hand with the right moment of inertia around the pivot point of my wrist, and Newton's third law bopped them back to hit her in the face. She squawked.

I smiled to myself and stepped out the door.

The pleasant feeling lasted until the sole of my boot hit the sidewalk below—then spooled abruptly away, everything around me jarring, *wrong.* The sensation of being watched tugged hard at the hairs on the back of my neck.

My hand went to the Colt in my belt, and I glanced back up at Arthur's office, then around the street. The sidewalk was empty save for one pedestrian, a dark-haired man who shuffled by without taking any notice of me.

The feeling that someone was following still crept up around me, throttling.

What the hell. I didn't get *feelings.* I saw quantifiable data that translated into probabilities. I tried to push it away, to tamp it down, but instead it smothered me, stuffed me in darkness, and I saw one of the people from my dreams.

"You're dead," he said to me, his face blurred in the throes of either hallucination or memory. "You're dead. This is only borrowed time."

four

YOU'RE ON the job, I reminded myself as I stumbled to my car and drove home, trying to keep my mind from cleaving along fault lines. *You can't afford to lose it; you're on the job: Attain technology. Do math. Fight crime.*

Was it really a job if I'd assigned it to myself? Had I ever successfully been able to do that before?

I needed an objective, now. Something to dig into and stop myself from slipping. Usually I turned to liquid medicine when things got this bad, but—

I'm working, I tried to insist. *I don't drink while I'm working. I don't . . .*

I got through the door to my current apartment and stumbled to my computer like a parched person groping for water. But neither Pilar nor Checker had emailed me anything yet. Nothing to grasp onto. Nothing to keep me—here—

I flipped over to an academic journal website. Pulled up a new modern algebra proof that had been making a splash.

Sometimes that was enough, when combined with the promise of a pending case.

This time, the lemmas and equations stared back at me mockingly. *You used to be able to do this,* they seemed to say. *You used to. And then you forgot.*

Just like everything else.

No one knew how much of a mathematician I wasn't. I might have been able to do mundane calculations faster than a supercomputer, but somewhere along the line, any true higher mathematical intuition had been burned out of my brain. The emptiness festered, a blistering hole I'd never be able to bridge.

Compared to that, having lost pointless episodic memories was an insignificant nothing.

I started aggressively scrolling through the proof, as if I wanted to tear the virtual pages through the screen. It wasn't even *right*—the authors had made a fundamental error propagating through the whole pack of nonsense and pretending to truth, and nobody had caught it. Suddenly angry, I scribbled an obscene note mocking their attempt and tacked it into a comment. I signed it with the name of a legitimate computational theorist I'd met through Arthur—served them both right for reminding me of everything I wasn't.

Do you really think this will improve anything? jabbered a voice in my head.

There are two kinds of improvement, answered another. *The type that makes things better, and the type that puts us in control.*

My email chimed.

Fuck, I needed to get a grip. I unclenched my fingers from the edge of the table and navigated over to my inbox with enforced calm.

The message was from Pilar. She'd sent me access to a server folder instead of links or email attachments, and once I logged on I could see why. An impossible volume of data unfolded before me, a massive, overwhelming computational problem that sprawled to the edges of the earth. One I could lose myself in.

I took a shuddering breath. Thank Christ.

WHEN ARTHUR knocked on my door that night, I had printed out and fitted together zoomed-in satellite images all across my floor, until one huge map of the greater Los Angeles area carpeted the space. My sparse furniture was pushed to one side, and I perched on the table, gazing down. My brain had calmed, momentarily, swallowed into submission by the breadth of the problem at hand.

Pilar had not only gotten me the qualitative reports, she'd found gigs and gigs of testing data, actual numbers I could manipulate and adjust and use to answer the question of whether I'd be able to adapt the technology in reality. She'd also traced the location of where the prototypes had ended up after Arkacite Technologies had disintegrated— breaking in and lifting one would be the easy part, as long as the mathematics told me a smooth overlap of the devices' influence would be possible in the first place.

Thousands of inputs. A two-dimensional surface function that undulated above the differentiable manifold of Los Angeles, mapping and combining, the colors striating and then smoothing as I tweaked each point source. A delicate spider-web over the city, each thread tugging at every other in a massive, continuous constraint satisfaction problem.

"Russell? You there?" Arthur called.

I reached down from the table and unlocked the deadbolt. "Come in."

He opened the door to step inside and stopped short, taking in my floor full of paper. "Hey. Whatcha doing?"

"Differential geometry."

"Sorry I asked." He sidestepped against the wall to avoid walking on any of the sheets. "We got another one."

My head snapped up. "Another what?" Relief at more to do collided with the dread that pooled in my gut. I was pretty sure I knew the answer.

Arthur had his hands shoved in his pockets, his shoulders sloping with fatigue. "Think it's Pourdry again."

"Tell me it isn't kids this time."

"Don't know yet," said Arthur. "You in?"

"Of course I'm in. Just let me gear up."

Ten minutes later we were speeding down the freeway. I took the passenger seat of Arthur's SUV again, making sure my spare magazines were all topped off.

A set of headlights poked at my consciousness from one of the side mirrors, a driving pattern that wasn't taking advantage of the traffic properly. I jerked.

"What is it?" Arthur asked.

"Are we being followed?"

He slowed and changed lanes, as if about to take an exit. The car sped past.

What the hell was wrong with me? At least that time it had been something quantifiable, but the driver had probably just been drunk or something. Going into an operation, I needed to be clearheaded or I'd get us both killed.

I tried to slam the demons out of my head. I didn't have time for them. "Give me the lowdown," I said to Arthur instead. "What do you know?"

"Not much. Just a location. Heard Pourdry's trying to replace his shipment from last night."

His shipment of people. Teenagers. Children. Kids like the spirited Katrina, abducted and ground down and hollowed out because, in the eyes of these lowlifes, they were nothing.

Arthur was clearly thinking along the same lines. "No one wants to admit we still got slavery going on in this country."

"The strong will always prey on the weak," I said. It came out more severe than I meant to be. "That's human nature."

"So—what? We gotta accept they have the power?"

"No. We make *them* weak."

Arthur's grunt didn't quite sound like agreement.

We pulled over a block out. Arthur's location was a multi-arch bridge that spanned the river and freeway as well as a few city blocks, raising the city into three dimensions. Side streets ran parallel, ramping up onto the raised highway level or slanting down off it. The local roads below became a jungle of concrete in the darkness, a no-man's-land of pillar and tunnel and shadow.

We kept our footfalls quiet as we jogged forward and ducked under the darkness of the bridge. We both had handguns out—me my trusty Colt, Arthur a Glock .45. I'd ragged on him for carrying a Glock since I'd known him, but he continued to insist it had never given him a hiccup of trouble in the field.

I also had an HK416 carbine looped around me on a sling. Best to be prepared.

Arthur held up a hand.

"What?" I whispered.

"Hear something."

He sidestepped farther into the shadows, his gun steady. I followed.

The sound rose and fell, tickling the edges of my hearing. A jagged, bleeding sound. The sound of a kid crying.

Ahead of me, Arthur moved steadily toward it.

"Wait," I said.

He froze.

Up and down. Up and down. Sob, breathe, sob.

"Russell?" Arthur's voice bowed with tension, tight as a guitar string.

Sob, breathe, sob. The same frequencies, as clear as if it were graphed out on an oscilloscope. Periodic.

"It's looping," I said.

He didn't try listening for it—he probably couldn't have discerned it anyway; the cries weren't distinctive enough from each other for the loop to be obvious to anyone else. But Arthur trusted me. "A recording?"

I half turned to cover our six. "Where did you get this intel?"

"Info on crime lords, it's not like I'm talking to folks with tons of vetting. Think it's a trap?"

"Well," I said. "Yeah."

"Back the way we came?"

I considered. If I were setting a trap here and I had an infinite number of goons at my disposal, the first thing I would do was close off escape.

"We cut sideways," I said. Not back to where they'd be closing the gap, not forward where they'd be expecting us.

Arthur rotated on the spot and slid into following me as I took point. I headed deeper under the bridge, the alley we were on becoming a tunnel. The air reeked of stale sewage and human urine.

"We keep going this way, we'll hit the freeway," Arthur murmured.

"That's what I'm counting on," I answered. Arthur thought the freeway wall would box us in. Hopefully the bad guys would, too, and wouldn't bother trying to cut us off that way. If we could get to it before the trap sprung, they'd never know how we slipped their noose.

"How's your climbing?" I said.

"You gotta be kidding."

"I'll give you a boost."

We angled into the darkness, toward the deceptively distant sounds of whizzing traffic, slipping from one edge of cover to the next. Arthur kept his vision and gun barrel sweeping in a wide arc behind us as he followed me, and I stayed alert for a whisper of movement, a glint of metal. . . .

We almost made it.

It's hard to beat me in a gunfight if I know where you are. But if you're smart, if you're the type of person who shoots before revealing your position . . .

A suppressed report echoed against the concrete at the same time Arthur went down like he'd been kicked in the chest by a mule.

My Colt roared and smacked my hand, and somewhere out in the darkness there was one less goon.

"Arthur!" I stayed covering him, not daring to take my eyes off our surroundings and look down. I swung up my carbine with my other hand and let loose a volley of suppression fire into the darkness while I scanned. There: a rustle, a flash of skin. I fired again, and this time I saw the body sprawl out of the shadows. "Arthur, get up!"

Arthur was an ex-cop. I was pretty sure he'd been wearing a vest. And that he'd been hit where the vest was covering.

Asshole. He better have been wearing a vest.

I popped off some staggered suppression fire again, and two more unlucky would-be assassins gave away their positions by trying to fire back. They didn't get anywhere close, and signed their own death warrants by trying. I yelled at Arthur again, and he finally answered by joining the fight, his Glock barking as he stumbled to his feet. His gun wavered in wide figure eights and he almost fell into me, but someone behind one of the bridge pylons screamed as one of Arthur's bullets found its mark.

"Back!" I suited action to words as I pushed us into a reverse stagger. Reaching any decent cover would take us toward our assailants, and the freeway wall was only a short open stretch behind us . . . but now we'd be easy targets for the seconds it took us to go over.

And Arthur would be slower after taking the kinetic energy of a bullet. Shit.

"Change of plans!" I called the words between bursts of gunfire as we reached the wall, backs against the barrier. "You're giving me the boost first. Cover me!"

I'd been counting down and knew he needed to reload. I let off a few more rounds while he slapped a new magazine in, then dropped the carbine to dangle from the sling, said, "Brace yourself!" and ran into a jump.

One boot levered off the wall, rocketing me high enough to drive the other down on Arthur's shoulder. He grunted and half buckled, but his gun didn't drop, keeping up the cover fire. My free hand smacked against the unyielding roughness of the top of the wall, and my fingers clamped down through the pain and became a pivot. All of my momentum went angular to swing my feet in a quarter circle and let me flip onto my stomach as I hit and balanced. The six-inch thickness of the freeway barrier socked me in the sternum.

Ow.

I swiveled to sit up and let loose with both weapons again. My left hand was bleeding all over the carbine, making the trigger slick. "Grab on!" I yelled at Arthur, kicking my boot at him above his head.

"Are you *kidding me!*" he yelled back, but he was already holstering his Glock. Arthur didn't hesitate when under fire, even when I was telling him to climb me like a jungle gym and pitch himself into traffic.

The wall might make us an easy target, but it also gave me a good vantage point. Even with a hundred-seventy-five-pound man using my leg as a ladder, I picked off another two goons I'd pinpointed by sound while climbing. Then I let go of the carbine and reached down to help haul Arthur over the top of the wall. He folded over it inelegantly, scrambling with his legs against the stone so he wouldn't fall on his head on the other side. The traffic on the freeway was a roar beneath us, beckoning us into the vortex.

A man straightening from the shadows in my peripheral vision snagged my senses. I shot him, but too late—at the same time I pulled the trigger, Arthur jerked and almost slid off the wall.

I heaved at him before his weight could drag us back the way we'd come, and instead sent us both tumbling over the other side into the dark roar of headlights, a tangled sprawl of limbs. I dropped my Colt so I could grope with my right hand as we went down. The wall took off five layers of my palm and two fingernails as I dragged for a crack of purchase to push our tumble halfway upright. I controlled us enough so I hit first, the force compressions crushing my flesh with bruises but any breakable bones angled out of the way. Arthur's upper body landed on top of me, and I clenched his jacket in a death grip to keep him from spilling off and into traffic.

There was almost no shoulder here. Horns blared as cars screamed by, the slipstream of their passage a violent maelstrom.

"Arthur!" I rolled us into the wall, away from traffic. *Fuck, fuck, fuck, fuck*—"Arthur, how bad are you hit?"

His eyelids fluttered. "'M okay—'m okay."

Relief sandbagged me so hard I almost choked. I scanned him—the seat of his pants was soaked with wet red that was almost black in the darkness, but not enough to mean an artery. Flesh wound. Thank Christ.

"Get up. We have to move." If I were Pourdry's gang, I'd be racing toward a car to take around to the nearest on-ramp and run us down into so much bloody road jelly. How long would that take? I ran estimates, error bounds expanding in my head. Not long enough.

I knew without looking where my Colt had gone down— gravity only pulled in the negative y direction. I scooped it up and got a shoulder under Arthur's arm. "Come on. Up you get."

Between me and the wall, he managed to stand, but leaned all his weight on his left leg.

Shit. With both of us ambulatory, it was no problem to time the cars and race us across. Now . . .

A semi came barreling down in the right lane, its headlights blinding us. "Stay here," I said, and started running parallel to the freeway. As the truck thundered by, I jumped.

Smacking against the door of the cab felt like running face-first into a tornado. A sixty-mile-an-hour wind tried to tear me off and my bloody hands almost slipped. I found purchase where I could jack in a boot and establish an unstable equilibrium, balancing the vector diagram so I had space to move. I got one hand into the door handle and used the other to swing my carbine around into the glass of the passenger-side window.

The truck swerved when the pane went, but by the time the trucker realized what had happened I had the door open and was falling inside, that same carbine pointed straight at his head.

"Hazard lights and stop," I said.

"Yeah! Yeah! Okay!" His hands scrambled around to find his blinkers, and he slammed his foot down on the brake with an alacrity that pleased me. He was an older guy, probably someone with a family and a lot to lose. Good.

The truck's brakes squealed. Velocity squared over twice the deceleration—the stopping distance would still bring us almost three hundred feet down the freeway. With a leg injury, Arthur would be too long catching up.

"Stay stopped for one minute, then you can go," I said to the trucker. "If you start moving before then, I swear on all that is holy, I will shoot you in the back of the head. Got it?"

He nodded as fast as he'd slammed on the brake. "Got it. Got it."

"Don't be a hero. One minute." I half fell, half jumped out of the cab before the truck's velocity had quite hit zero.

Traffic in Los Angeles is blessedly predictable, even in the middle of the night. The semi had started to cause a jam as soon as it began to slow. Cars behind it hitched into a halting staccato as they tried to angle out into moving traffic, and the right lane quickly dragged to a crawl, the lane next to it clogging as drivers from behind the truck moved to cut in.

I pounded back to Arthur. He'd started to limp after me,

but he hadn't gotten far. I made it back in less than ten seconds and skidded against the nearest vehicle, a nice big Ford pickup that was now rolling along at four miles per hour.

I didn't even have to break the window. The driver threw his hands up and braked, half veering out of his lane before he stopped. By the time I made it over to the driver's side he was already tumbling out of it, trying to keep his hands absurdly high the whole time.

A large African American guy in hospital scrubs, he babbled, "Take it! Take it, mama!" over and over again.

I took it.

Traffic was close to a standstill, but not quite, and people are pleasantly willing to get out of your way when you bulldoze toward them in an F-150 with no compunction about bashing them aside if they don't move first. I shouldered our way across the slowing swamp of traffic before Arthur had even gotten the passenger door shut, and we popped out into the fast lane, where I rocketed up to freeway speed. Within seconds we had passed the semi, its lights still flashing, and left the traffic snarl I'd caused behind us.

Arthur kept his gaze on the mirrors. "Good. Someone picked him up."

"And here I thought you were watching our six," I said. "Any sign of them?"

"Don't think it matters. Pretty jammed up now, no way they're getting past that."

"LA traffic, better than a roadblock," I said. The humor fell flat. "How bad are you hit?"

"Don't know." He had both hands pushed up under the top of his leg, and every line of his posture was tight with pain. "Think it's just the flesh."

"On the scale of 'hospital' to 'call your doctor friend' to 'I pour whiskey on it and sew you up,' where are we?"

"GSW in a hospital means I got a lot of explaining to do to the cops," Arthur said. "The drivers are gonna remember you. Won't get away with saying I was on my lonesome."

I knew all that. "Whatever. Checker and I can handle it. Now, will you fucking answer me? Do you need an ER?"

Arthur thought for another minute. "My DNA's at the scene anyway, and I'm in the system as an exclusionary. Best to report right away on this one. I can tell 'em you were one of the bad guys."

"Great."

"Or maybe a Good Samaritan. I can come up with something. Lie low for a bit while they poke around."

Good Samaritan was probably even less fitting than goon-for-hire. I followed signs for the next exit ramp and twisted off into local streets.

Pourdry would pay for this.

Jesus, I hoped Arthur was all right. As complicated as it made things, part of me was glad he'd chosen the hospital.

Arthur had his phone out, its screen a bright rectangle smeared with red. "Keep going straight. Right in about five blocks." He nodded at the blood painting the steering wheel. "You okay?"

"It's just my hands." They stung like a motherfucker, but abrasions always looked worse than they were. All the important bits of me were intact—I just wished I knew that were true about him. Anxiety coiled in my throat; I tried to ignore it. "Turn here?"

I pulled up outside the emergency room's ambulance loop. Arthur levered himself out with a grunt, hopping a little as he landed on his good leg. I felt like I should say something, but all I could come up with was, "We'll get him, Arthur."

"Yeah," he said.

I waited for him to limp up the sidewalk before speeding off to ditch the truck. God, he'd better be all right. If he wasn't, I would kill him.

My current burner phone was in my pocket. I called Checker as I switched cars, my still-bleeding hands making the keys stick.

"Cas? Is everything okay?" He didn't sound like I'd woken him.

"No." Something shifted behind me, out of place, and I whipped around, the carbine coming up again. But it was only shadows.

I was going out of my mind.

"Cas? Cas, what's going on? Are you guys all right?"

Goddammit, focus. "I'm coming over," I said to Checker, crushing the words to diamond hardness. "And I want everything you can give me on Jacob Pourdry."

five

"JACOB POURDRY," Checker said, fully dressed and alert when I entered the Hole an hour and a half later, "is a piece of trash of the highest order. Law enforcement knows all about him, but hasn't been able to touch him because he keeps his hands clean on paper. What's with the gloves?"

The scrapes weren't serious enough for me to have burnt time bandaging them yet, but I'd swung through a convenience store to pick up some work gloves so I would stop bleeding on everything. "It's nothing. They'll heal. Keep going, but tell me how Arthur is first."

"He'll have trouble sitting down for a few weeks, but if you have to get shot, apparently the gluteus maximus is the place to do it. They left the bullet in and patched him up, and I'm tracking the police investigation. Are you sure you're okay?"

"Yeah. Keep going on Pourdry. I know he's a scumbag; everyone knows he's a scumbag. Tell me what I don't know." Pourdry's was a name even I hadn't been willing to work for, long before I met Arthur and started getting a conscience. But this was becoming a war, and I was going to need more than common knowledge and urban gossip.

A lot more.

"Okay, well, do you want his history?" As usual, Checker worked as he talked, scrolling through documents I didn't recognize as he recited the litany from memory. "This is stuff I've already run through with Arthur, so stop me if you've heard it. Pourdry is a privileged sociopath who got bored making millions on Wall Street. I'm not kidding. He was born vanilla and middle-class in Toronto, blew his peers out of the water academically, and ended up at Harvard Business School, where he was apparently so bored he started running a drug ring for all the jacked-up over-pressured grad students. Allegedly. He dropped out halfway through to go be an asshole in the financial sector, wrung what he could out of New York, then decided that wasn't enough of a playground and expanded his business into one of the most sprawling criminal enterprises in the southwestern United States."

"This is all public knowledge?"

"If you know where to look. I'm telling you, this guy is like Al Capone: the only way they're going to get him is if they find a misplaced decimal on his taxes. Everybody knows what he does but no one can charge him."

"That's okay; I'm going to put a bullet in his brain."

The skin around Checker's eyes tightened, and he swallowed, still studying his screen.

"Come on," I said. "This guy traffics in *children*. He doesn't get second chances."

"Yeah, just— I'm helping, but give my conscience some plausible deniability, please."

I didn't have the patience for his squeamishness. "His guys shot Arthur tonight. They could've killed us both. I need to know where I can find him and what'll happen to his network if there's a sudden power vacuum." If only Pourdry had the charm and skill to keep the ranks following him, maybe beheading the snake would be all I'd need.

Checker blew out a breath. "I can't help you with those. They don't write that sort of thing down on paper, or, you know, in digital files. But I can tell you he runs things through a bunch of fronts and shell corporations—Arthur's had me trawling his financials for a while, and I'm kicking it into high gear for you. Would a list of addresses for the front companies help to start with? I want to make sure the police investigation isn't snapping back on you and Arthur first, but I can email it."

"Do that. And remember, you still owe me statistical data."

"I'm working on it. You didn't give me much to go on. What's your plan?"

"Remember Pilar's old employer?" I said. "They were developing some sort of frequency generator that would disrupt people's brains so they wouldn't succumb to peer pressure or go all mob-like. I want to finish it and then distribute them around LA." Hopefully their problem had only been the mathematics. "It won't solve everything, but I'm hoping to filter out at least some of the mindless violence."

Checker froze. "*That's* how you're planning to fight crime?"

"Yup. With math and tech. Smart, huh?"

Checker spoke like he was choosing his words very carefully. "You want to mess with people's heads?"

"Only when they're getting sucked into groupthink," I said. "Think how much violence goes on because of gangs, or because of people following along and getting their pleasure centers activated by joining the herd. I'm hoping to counter that." Checker didn't look as excited as I expected. "What?"

"Changing people's brain chemistry that way, without them knowing—it's, it's not right. Please don't get mad at me for saying this, but—isn't what you're proposing exactly what Dawna Polk was doing, with all her 'fixing' people into world peace? And we decided she didn't have the right."

And had we really made the correct choice?

I pushed the thought away. "Dawna was killing or brainwashing innocent people. The whole chaos effect thing. She didn't care if they were being violent, as long as their deaths flapped enough butterfly wings to make the world her version of a better place. I only want to affect people when they *are* becoming dangerous."

"But it's still not—"

"We caused this situation!" I cried. "We have to do something about it. We took down widespread influence with Pithica—picking off these assholes one at a time is never going to match that!"

Checker folded his lips together.

"Come on," I said. "Arthur just got *shot* and you still don't want to help me? What will it take? Will you help after *I* get shot? After you do? After Pilar is walking down the street by the office and gets mugged?"

"That's not fair—"

"Of course it's not fair! That's the whole reason we need to do this!" *Of course it's not fair,* mimicked a voice in my head that wasn't mine. *We were born to it.* I squashed the phantom and spoke over it. "I'm trying to *make* it fair. And you won't help me."

"Because I'm against this. I wouldn't want my brain messed with, and I'm not going to help you do it to anyone else."

"Oh, you think you're likely to get caught up in a mob, do you?"

"Not the point."

"It fucking well is the point," I said. "Because if you *were,* and you temporarily lost your ability to reason, I guarantee the thing you'd want most in the world would be for something else to beat that feeling back." I knew the argument was going to work as soon as I started it, and I tried to keep the egotistical triumph off my face. "Crowd psychology is like a drug. This is going to help people *not* be affected by something that would otherwise make them feral and amoral against their will."

He hesitated.

"It's not a pacifier, and it's not messing with people's brains," I insisted. "It's preventing the deindividuation from doing it."

Checker leaned his elbows on his desktop and dropped his face against his hands. "Screw you, Cas."

"You should know by now. I'm always right."

"That is not even *close* to being true." He sat back up, taking off his glasses to rub his eyes. "Dammit, I'll *think* about it, okay? But I want you to leave out the Hole. I don't care what you say; I don't want my brain affected by this."

"Fine," I said. "Your delicate little neurons will be spared."

"And if this thing starts making people so peaceful they want to lie down and die, I'm holding you personally responsible—"

"You watch too many movies," I said tiredly. Suddenly feeling every inch of the bruising from tonight, I hitched myself stiffly up to sit on Checker's desktop between monitors and leaned back against a computer tower.

I felt Checker move closer to me. He picked up a keyboard off the desktop and slid it on top of one of the towers so he could prop his elbows next to me. "Cas. Hey."

I curled my gloved hands loosely against my knees. Blood was starting to seep through along the seams.

Checker nudged my legs with his shoulder. "You know, only you would assign yourself the problem 'fight crime' and then try to come up with a general solution."

"General solutions are the only ones worth anything," I said.

"Nah," he answered. "For instance, I think we're going

to find a kickass particular solution to the Cas Russell recombination problem."

I huffed out a breath of air that was something like a laugh.

"I'm working on tracking you back," he said softly. "Talk to me about some of your clients. The regular ones, or the older ones."

"Don't you have a police investigation to follow?"

"I'm waiting on CSU. We have a minute."

God, everything hurt. I wanted to go and sleep, but moving would hurt, too. "I can't tell you what I do for them," I said to Checker. "Discretion is part of the job."

"That's okay. I don't need that."

I sighed. "There's Tegan. Yamamoto. Dolzhikov. The Lorenzos, before I pissed them off." I'd done a few jobs for a few Mafia members back in the day, before I'd tangled opposite them a time too many and Mama Lorenzo had started giving me the evil eye. I had to admit, not wanting them to take over LA notwithstanding, I did miss working for them—they'd paid well. And I got along with people like Malcolm, at least most of the time. "What do you want, the whole list? How does this help?"

"Just tell me about meeting them. Whatever you remember."

"Yamamoto got my name from Anton, I think. I don't know what Anton told him, but he put together a ridiculous display the first time he met with me. Huge array of power, lots of guards with guns, a spread that was practically a banquet. I've never met someone who tried so hard to impress me."

"From what I hear of Yamamoto, that doesn't surprise me," said Checker, the ghost of a smile in his voice. "How did you meet Anton?"

"Anton was—he and I went back pretty far." I swallowed. Anton's death still stabbed. I hadn't known him all that well on a personal level, but the big, gruff man had left more of a hole than I had expected. And his death had been my fault—his and his daughter's deaths both. "I needed an information guy, and Rio told me—no, that's not right. I asked. Rio gave me his name but he couldn't exactly give me a referral." Not many people worked with Rio willingly. Anton had been too good of a man to have considered it.

"How long ago was that?" asked Checker.

"Oh, uh . . . five years, or thereabouts? Maybe a little less."

"Did you have an information guy before Anton?"

"No, I did most of the looking up myself before that. But I was sorely in need of someone—I can't do much beyond basic search engines."

"Trust me, I know," Checker said.

"Shut up."

"And how about, uh, Rio?" Checker asked. "How long have you known him?"

"Oh, forever," I said. "We go way back."

"How far is way back?"

"I don't know; years. Forever."

He paused for a moment. "Will you tell me how you met?"

He sounded surprisingly neutral, and I wondered if the hesitation had been to make sure he'd leached the judgment out of his voice. Checker felt the same way about Rio that Arthur did.

I couldn't say I blamed them.

They have sinned in the eyes of God. The echo was spattered with blood and death. "He saved my life."

"From what?"

"From . . ." I squeezed my eyes shut, my brain crackling behind my eyelids. "I don't want to talk about it." I swallowed. "Jesus, I was shot at and almost run over tonight, in case you don't remember. Can we not do this now?"

Checker paused for just long enough that I could tell he

wanted to say no. "Of course. We'll pick it up later. Thanks, Cas, this helps."

"Helps whom?"

He ignored me. "Get some sleep, okay? I promise I'll think about the data thing. You're right, it might save people in a way that they'd want, I just— I have to think about it."

"Think fast," I grunted, not entirely graciously.

But he was right about one thing. I did need sleep. My body had stiffened enough that I briefly considered asking Checker if I could kip on his couch, but I figured I should go to my apartment and peel off the work gloves before they started sticking so I could properly dress my stupid hands. I levered myself out of Checker's workspace and left the Hole.

On the sidewalk in front of his house, I stopped. The night snapped into numbers and data structures. I breathed them in, slowly.

Something was wrong.

I'd left my carbine in the car, but my Colt still rested against the small of my back, edges and vertices of the metal frame forming my awareness of its precise, deadly shape. I'd checked it over after delivering Arthur, and the drop had banged up the finish in a way that pained me more than my hands, but all the tolerances were still tight and solid. My brain and muscles teetered on the edge of pulling it, of drawing and firing at the threat I knew was out there, if only I could pinpoint it—

"Please," said a voice. "Don't."

I spun and dove, conjecture becoming reality as the Colt swooped out of my belt and into my gloved fingers.

"Please!" cried the man, the bronze-skinned man with the dark curly hair, the one I'd seen lurking outside Arthur's office and hadn't even *noticed,* the man who'd been following me—me—for most of the day. The man I'd seen even before now . . . over and over, haunting my dreams. He raised his empty hands, palms out, and stepped back. "I'm not going to hurt you, Cassandra."

I kept my gun trained right between his eyes. "Who the *fuck* are you?"

six

"CASSANDRA, PLEASE," he said. "Put the gun down."

"You've been following me." *Nobody* was able to follow me. Not like that. "And what did you just call me?"

The dark-haired man took a slow, cautious step forward, but not as if he was afraid—more like one might approach a frightened puppy. I felt like I was seeing his outlines properly for the first time: a handsome face with well-defined features, a medium build in nondescript casual clothes, a little taller than average but not enough to be remarkable.

"Cassandra," he said. "It's your name, remember?"

What the hell? "I know that," I said. "I want to know how *you* know it."

He let out a breath that sounded like relief. "It's okay. We knew each other a long time ago. You wouldn't remember."

I scrabbled at the disordered mess of my mind, at every memory I could muster up. Every time I'd felt like I was being watched, seeing his blurred shape out of the corner of my eye . . . the impressions crossed with my dreams until I didn't know which had actually happened. The dark man running with me through a forest, crouching together in a hidden place, afraid . . .

"Cassandra, what's wrong?"

I tried to reach back, strained for something solid, and suddenly he seemed horribly familiar, like someone I'd known in another life. But I still couldn't *remember* him—

"Cassandra, stop! Stop trying!"

He had closed the distance between us and was gripping my shoulders, heedless of the gun that was now in his face. And I—I hadn't seen him do it. *Somehow I had missed the movements of a potential threat while in the middle of a standoff.*

I tore back from him, away, tightening my grip on the Colt, making my aim straight and sure. "Don't touch me. Don't fucking touch me!"

"Cassandra—"

"Stop calling me that!" Who was this man, this . . . apparition? And the only person I'd ever known who used my name every other sentence that way was Rio—

Rio.

I saw Rio and this man standing together, talking, backlit against a deepening twilight—

"Cassandra! Stop! Come back to me!"

He'd come up and grabbed my wrist this time, pressing my gun down. I twisted out of his grip, shoving him back. My heart slammed in my chest, my adrenaline spiking. "What the hell are you doing to me?"

He didn't seem to have heard my question; his eyes were crawling slowly over my face like he was surveying me as a home furnishing. "Oh—oh God—what happened?"

"What do you mean, what happened? *Who are you?*"

He blinked very fast, his forehead knitting, and his eyes fastened on mine again. His gaze was arresting, a dark magnetism that threatened to pull me in. I choked on it.

"Cassandra," he said softly. "I have to ask you something."

"Tell me who the fuck you are first."

"My name is Simon. Like I said, I knew you. A long time ago."

"That doesn't tell me shit."

"Maybe not," he said. "But I have to ask something of you. It may—it may seem crazy."

"How were you following me?" My voice was hoarse. I didn't bother trying to raise the gun again.

"When I try not to be noticed, people usually don't notice me. It's nothing nefarious, I swear to you."

"You're doing something to me. My thoughts. My memory." Fuck, I'd met other people like him before—or at least, one other person. Dawna Polk.

Dawna Polk, psychic extraordinaire, who'd had me betraying Rio, Arthur betraying Checker, and her minions so brainwashed they believed entirely in her cause.

"Holy shit," I said. "That's why I can't— You're from Pithica. We had a deal!"

"No! No. I'm not Pithica. I swear."

Buzzing filled my brain, as if it wasn't getting enough oxygen. "You say you're not them, but you know who they are. You know that name."

"Yes. And I see you do, too." He searched my face.

"You, you're . . . you're like them." A psychic. Another bloody psychic.

We stared at each other. I needed to escape, or kill him, or break his bones until he told me everything he knew about me that I didn't.

I wasn't going to do any of those things. This was Dawna all over again. Shit. Shit, shit, *shit*.

"Cassandra, I'm not trying to— I won't make you do anything against your will, I wouldn't. I promise. I haven't been, and I'm not now. I tried not to be noticed, I admit, and I'm, I'm effective at that, but I wasn't doing anything to you. I swear."

"That sounds like a distinction without a difference." I lifted my Colt back up, slowly, cautiously. "If you're not doing anything to me, why does it feel like I couldn't shoot you no matter how hard I tried?"

His head straightened back and his hands hitched higher. "There are some things— I'm not doing anything consciously, but— Cassandra, please, it's not an exact science."

"You just can't help brainwashing everyone around you, is that it?"

"No! That's not— I'm not."

"I'm probably going to forget this whole conversation, aren't I."

"No." His eyes stretched wide and scandalized. "Cassandra, I wouldn't. I won't. That's why I'm standing here asking you; I wouldn't have to if I didn't . . ." His expression crumpled. "Cassandra. You trusted me once. Please."

That seemed unlikely.

He ran a hand through his curly hair. "Cassandra, I'm begging you. You're in danger, and I don't know *what,* or how, not unless you let me—" He bit his lip again, cutting himself off.

"Let you *what*?"

"I need to . . . look closer. Please."

"You mean read my mind."

He closed his eyes. "Yes, but—"

"No way. No way in hell."

"Only to figure out what kind of danger you're in. That's all I'll look for, I swear."

"The only person I'm in danger from right now is you and your twisted brain-screwing powers."

He sucked in a breath. "Then tell me—what happened with Pithica? How do you know that word?"

"How do *you* know it? How do you know *me*?"

"Cassandra—"

"Stop calling me that."

"Please!" He reached out to catch my arm. "Please let me—"

I snapped my hand over his wrist this time instead, so fast

it was a blur, and wrenched. Simon yelped, his body following his arm to stumble to the side as I let go.

"I said don't touch me," I said. "And I never, ever, ever want you in my fucking head."

Adrenaline and fear punched through my system. If he was really like Dawna, he could make me give him permission—whatever he felt he needed it for—and I would do it gladly. Who knew why he hadn't forced me to his side already, but Dawna's machinations had been games within games, twisting my logical processes around until I'd lost which way was up.

I backed away, edging toward where I'd left my car.

"Cassandra!" he called again.

"What did I say?" Raising the Colt was probably useless, but I did it anyway. "Get away from me and stay away. Don't follow me. Don't ever come near me again. Ever."

I got to my car, drove away, and kept driving. I switched cars and drove some more, crisscrossing the city half a dozen times before going to a hole-in-the-wall I hadn't stopped at in months.

I didn't sense anyone behind me, but that didn't mean anything, did it?

Fuck.

I finally pulled over and leaned my head against the steering wheel. Every muscle ached, and the work gloves pulled at my scabbing hands every time I shifted my fingers.

I should probably tell Checker what had just happened. That a man from my past had appeared. That a man from my past had appeared, and was a . . . was one of *them.*

Heck, I should probably tell Checker and Arthur both, and Pilar, and Rio—anyone Simon might approach and attack with his powers.

Rio—

Try Los Angeles. It's a big enough city. America will be easier to disappear in.

I closed my eyes and breathed. My pulse was racing.

Shit. I'd left Simon outside Checker's house. I hadn't even been thinking about it. And I'd seen him outside Arthur's office—he knew everyone I associated with, could approach any one of them, find out whatever he wanted, turn any of them into his puppet.

Was Checker's inane crusade to figure out my secrets already a part of this Simon person's master plan? How much could I trust anyone?

Or maybe he wants you not to tell anyone. Maybe that's his plan, to convince you to keep him a secret, like a tree that's fallen with nobody to hear it, an unobserved particle, until he's gotten whatever he wants out of you.

This was the trouble with psychics. I never knew which decisions were my own.

But come on, what would I even tell Checker anyway? That a psychic man from my past had followed me and then demanded *permission* to read my mind? It was starting to sound mad.

This isn't a joke—Cassandra, listen to me, please, you'll go mad—

I jerked.

You're in danger, I heard Simon say again. He overlapped with the memory of Checker, pushing at me to look into my past, telling me I could have other enemies—

Enemies. For all I knew, Simon might be one of them.

Christ, I didn't have time for this.

I texted Checker to make sure he was okay, and he confirmed right away, which I supposed I could trust as much as anything right now. Then I toyed with the phone, considering, trying to weigh the pros and cons of what to do about Simon without fucking second-guessing myself. But after less than three minutes, I was interrupted by Checker texting again:

GET 2 HOSPTL
JP GOING AFTER ARTHUR

I didn't wait to ask how he knew. I accelerated so fast I took a layer of rubber off the tires.

Fuck, fuck, fuck. This was what we got for going to a hospital, for reporting to the police like good citizens. Pourdry didn't just have the game of evading law enforcement down. He had informants.

If anything happened to Arthur, I'd burn Los Angeles down to get to Pourdry. Hell, I'd do that anyway. I was out of patience.

Whoever Simon was, he and his stupid, bizarre, frightening pleading could wait.

seven

Hospitals don't have great security, but they tend to frown on people with guns. I left my carbine and carried my Colt concealed.

I dashed into the ER, phone to my ear. Checker had been trying to reach Arthur but hadn't been able to get through—he didn't know whether Arthur was still in the middle of being treated or the hospital just had bad signal, but he was tracking medical updates in real time. "He's in exam room four. Straight down the hall from the entrance, through the door in the back right corner of the waiting room, past the nurses' station, third room on the left."

I snapped my senses into the mathematical overlap of visual fields. Every set of eyes became angles that stretched from vertical and horizontal meridians, constantly shifting and crossing in rough elliptic cones. There were too many people crowding the ER to make myself completely invisible, but I could at least dance around the staff. People who weren't in authority generally wouldn't speak up.

I slid between peripheral fields of view like I was dodging

lasers, ducking and sliding through the door and then crab-walking by the nurses' station. In order to stop me they would have had to see me, and not a single person in scrubs or a white coat did. A patient or two caught the edge of my antics and frowned my way, but then they looked to those in charge, assumed they must have noticed me, and shrugged it off to go back to their own business.

I escaped the crowded areas and sprinted down the hallway. Exam room 4, third door on the left—

I burst in, my gun raised. Arthur looked up. He was on his feet, but still in a hospital gown, and leaning heavily on a gurney. A wiry white guy was sprawled on the floor with a needle stabbed in his neck.

"Oh," I said, brought up short. "Nice job. Are you good to get out of here?"

"Lord yes," he said. "Just gotta get some clothes on. Two minutes."

I turned my back while Arthur got dressed, keeping half an eye on the goon on the floor. He was breathing, but shallowly.

Part of me was sorry I was too late. My helplessness against Simon was still bitter in the back of my throat, taunting me. The aggression I had wanted to wreak against him coiled in every nerve.

I briefly fantasized about introducing this guy's face to my boot, letting the crunch of bone reassure me of my own power over myself. How much would I be pushing it with Arthur if I did?

"Probably not worth the time to ask for crutches," Arthur mused. "Give me a hand?"

I took a moment to clear my expression of any of my dangerous mental wandering and then came over to duck under his arm. He leaned heavily across my shoulder. I cast one last glance at the unconscious man on the floor, then helped Arthur limp over to the door, where we cracked it and peeked out.

Hospital staff and patients flowed by intermittently, unaware.

"Get ready," I said.

The moment the hallway had a lull in traffic, I pulled the door open and supported Arthur's hobble out. We hoofed it away from the waiting room and its many eyes, toward the emergency exit at the end of the hall, the one labeled, "Emergency Exit Only—Alarm Will Sound."

"Wait! Sir?" a woman's voice called behind us.

"Time's up," I said, and pushed open the emergency door. We spilled out into the parking lot, the alarm blaring after us into the night.

"I got the detectives' number," Arthur said. "I can call 'em and straighten this out, soon as we're safe—"

The spattering pop of gunfire sounded off to our right, and the brick wall of the hospital spit back, bits of stone and masonry pelting us across the shoulders.

"Get down!" I yelled, tackling Arthur. Already off balance, he toppled to the asphalt. I had my Colt out, tracking the night.

"You got another piece on you?" Arthur huffed from below me.

The caustic insecurity I'd been feeling crackled down my limbs, twisting my face and making every nerve tingle. Every self-doubt about what I hadn't been able to do to Simon buzzed against my fingers, making me itch to prove myself.

"Take mine." I stuffed the Colt into Arthur's hand and dove straight toward the shots.

It was dumb. I'd pinpointed the position of our attacker in the first instant. In one extra second I could have taken out whoever it was and covered Arthur if there were any more, instead of pretending he needed my only weapon for self-defense. But halfway across the parking lot was too late to question myself.

I zagged between the parked cars and rushed the gunman.

He saw me coming, but only at the last second. His eyes widened from where he was hunched over a car hood aimed at the hospital's back entrance with some variant of AR-15. He tried to bring the rifle around, but only managed to turn about three degrees before I smashed into him with pure ballistic force.

I was wrong. The sound of bone crunching against me did not make me feel more in control.

More gunfire behind me. Pourdry's men shooting, and the supersonic crack of my .45 answering them. Arthur. I had to help Arthur. . . .

I staggered back from the dead man. His neck was broken, what had been his face a mess of fleshy pulp. Had I hit him more than once? Why couldn't I remember?

I reached down to take his gun, my limbs shaking. But not from the killing. *What will Arthur think?*

Images crossed each other in my head, a scene from a year ago, months ago, a day ago: Checker's house. Through my eyes, as I stood off to the side with a glass of whiskey, neat, lurking in the shadows. Checker and Arthur, and some other people—their friends—Pilar; Checker's friend Miri; and Arthur's friend Sonya, the math professor, laughing as they got out board games—no, this wasn't right, this wasn't real; this had never happened.

Their faces went skeletal. The demon mathematics professor turned to me and stretched out a hand burned down to the bone.

And then she was someone else, someone with a scar down her face—

"Russell! Russell, come on!"

I fell against the hub of a parked car. Where was my gun?

The hand plunged into my chest, numbers and equations flowing down it, in both directions, carving me out and giving back a power I didn't want.

"Russell!"

Arthur was yanking at me. The night crashed back, drenched with shouts and sirens.

"It's getting worse," I gasped out.

"Never would've guessed. Let's go."

"I brought a— My car is over there. Are you okay?"

"Yeah. One of the hospital staff was hit. Better for everyone if we get gone."

I managed to scramble up, and Arthur leaned his weight on my shoulder again. We made it to the car and piled in. Trying not to show how unnerved I was, I flattened the accelerator, zooming us away toward one of my bolt-holes. Arthur would need a place to lie low. Yes. Pourdry was coming after him—coming after all of us, and I couldn't protect—

I kept an eye on the rearview mirror and backtracked, changed directions, turned onto a different freeway. How many people could Pourdry have sent? I flipped through my mental file of safehouses in my head—Arthur would need one without stairs. Fortunately, since knowing Checker I'd acquired a few of those. . . .

I could do it. Get him somewhere no one could find him.

Unless my telepathic stalker had stumbled across every one of those addresses in my brain.

Dammit! Did Simon have that kind of power, to pull locations straight out of my head like that? Or would he have had to trick me into telling him, while the whole time I thought it was my idea?

Maybe I *had* told him and forgotten. Panic flitted in and out of my thoughts. My senses flickered across the headlights of the expressway, searching for ghosts, but I didn't trust myself.

"Keep your eyes out," I warned Arthur.

He held a finger up to me—he was on the phone, presumably with Checker. "Did you talk to— They're safe? You sure? Okay. Good man. No, it's best if I don't know for now.

Thanks . . . Don't know yet. You talk to Pilar? Yeah, best to be safe. Tell her I'm sorry."

"Pilar knew what she was signing up for," I said. Of all the things to worry about right now . . . as far as I was concerned, occasionally needing to keep her head down from bad guys was in her fucking job description.

Arthur shot me an annoyed look and spoke back into the phone. "Yeah, I'll be in touch. You be careful, too, son." He hung up.

I drove faster.

"Pilar's gonna stay with Checker," Arthur told me, even though I hadn't asked. "He keeps his digital tracks pretty clean; don't think anybody would track me to him."

"Then they're fine." I needed to believe that. I couldn't be everywhere at once. Jesus, I was even failing at being in one place at once.

Just how far was Pourdry's reach? Had he only tracked us to the hospital, or did he know everything about Arthur now?

"No one should have to worry about getting shot at just 'cause they work with me." Arthur sounded tired.

"Probably no one should get shot at *period*. In a perfect world. Pilar and Checker are grown adults, and they wanted to be in on fighting Pourdry. They knew what it could mean." I sounded pretty sure of that. I didn't have to take on responsibility for fucking everyone, did I? They'd taken this on of their own free will, right alongside me and Arthur.

"Don't gotta like it," Arthur said.

"Didn't say you did."

He sighed. "Seems Pourdry's gone on offense. What's the plan?"

"Checker's doing some more research into his front businesses," I said shortly. "Once we get a lead, we'll offense right back."

"Your MO, always so elegant."

"When did you get so sarcastic?" Jesus, I wished it were more elegant. "Elegance would be fighting back at the god-damn root. One bad guy here, one there—it's ass-backward. On the scale of . . . we're doing fucking *nothing,* you know that?"

I expected Arthur to argue back that at least we were making a difference to the people we helped, as paltry as that number was. Or gently tell me off for biting his head off when he wasn't the one I should be mad at.

Instead, he said quietly, "I know."

The anger and powerlessness that had been building in me deflated just a little. At least I wasn't the only one who saw the fucking problem.

And Arthur was a smart guy. "All those maps you were looking at," he went on. "That got something to do with this?"

I studied the road. "Yeah."

There were plenty of good reasons not to tell Arthur what I was working on, the first and foremost of which was that there was a better than even chance he'd side with Checker and try to stop me. Arthur had tried to stop me from doing things a couple of times in the past, and I'd always plowed right through his moral stance with a nice fuck-you and done them anyway. It usually resulted in people getting killed.

He was a hard man to read, but I was pretty sure he wasn't going to keep tolerating it. I'd promised him I'd try to stop doing that shit.

But more than that . . .

Everything was wrong, nothing I did made a damn difference, I didn't trust my own mind, and for the first time in my life I wanted to hear someone say this was a good idea before seeing it all the way through. I was unmoored in space with my brain folding in and a telepath lurking in my rear-view, and God help me but I wanted Arthur to tell me we could do something about it.

I licked my lips. "I think . . . I think I might have a way to clothesline the crime rate."

"Yeah?"

I explained.

Arthur let me talk without interruption as I outlined the plan: Arkacite technology, my math, and metropolitan Los Angeles as a testing ground. I kept my eyes on the road, steadily framing out his reaction. If he said we shouldn't—if he shot this plan down the way Checker had—what other options did I have to fight against all this? What was left to try?

"And I think Pilar's right," I finished out my summary. "The technology, they had it functioning. It was just a matter of the mathematics."

"How does it work?" Arthur asked. I couldn't tell yet from his tone what he thought.

"I don't have the technical specs yet, but I can give you the report summaries." I made an effort to keep my voice calm. Reasonable. "First, they discovered the unique brain pattern that comes from the deindividuation state. You know about brain waves, right?"

"Know they exist."

"We've been able to categorize brain waves for a while— what they look like in the normal waking state, for instance, or what they look like in deep sleep. But the researchers figured out the unique Fourier series—or rather, the narrow range of Fourier series—"

"English, Russell."

"They managed to pick up what the brain is doing when you hit that deindividuated state. The mathematical characteristics of the brain waves."

"And then what?"

"It turns out brain entrainment has been around for a long time," I said. The science was making the explanation easier. I concentrated on the black and white, the facts that existed outside of morals or responsibility. "People have discovered all sorts of ways to get a subject's brain frequencies to align with an imposed frequency. Like, they'll play beats in the subject's ears and get their brain frequencies to slow down to a more meditative state."

"Subject," said Arthur. "You mean a human being."

"Yeah. We're all math inside."

He shifted in his seat. "Go on."

"It's only recently that the social psychologists and the neuroscientists started to cross over and talk to each other more. They did heavier research into the neuroscience of different psychological states, and somewhere along the way someone with funding got wind of it."

"Arkacite Technologies."

"Or the military grants, or some combination. The important part is, they figured out how, when someone is in that deindividuated place—they figured out how to use a combination of audio and electromagnetic frequencies to realign the brain out of it."

"Side effects?" Arthur asked. "Is it dangerous?"

"No more dangerous than listening to music." That wasn't strictly true. After all, as Pilar had said, when it hadn't worked properly it had caused some . . . unexpected behavior. "As long as it's working the way it's intended, it's not dangerous," I amended reluctantly. "All it's doing is realigning brain frequencies to a more normal level, taking them out of that state. It's returning people to normal."

"What about people who aren't doing the mob thing? What kind of effects does it have then?"

"None."

"You sure?"

"I'm sure. It's mathematically impossible for it to take people out of a normal brain state."

"Thought you said we have more than one normal brain state. Like when people sleep or meditate."

"It won't affect those either. It's, uh—" I thought about how to explain. "It's too far off. Have you ever seen the thing where people break glass with a resonant frequency?"

"Like opera singers? That happens for real?"

"It can. But it's not like any frequency does it. It has to be resonant with the glass. This isn't quite the same thing, but—mathematically, what they put together, it's too far off anything else to affect states other than the particular range of waves they wanted it to."

"Then what's the catch?"

I laid out for him how they hadn't been able to figure out a way to blanket a large area evenly. "The short version is, they could do it if the experiment subject was one person standing still—they tested it on people playing video games and such—but in real-world mob scenarios, that's never going to be the case. It's always going to be a lot of people over a big area, and they couldn't get the right combination of frequencies to stay constant enough over a large field." When people had moved out of the sweet spot and into the places where the frequency bands weren't correct anymore—that was where any trouble had sparked. "And for what we want, well, we want an even bigger scale. We want a consistent impact and we want it everywhere; we don't want people to wander in and out of the effects."

"We don't?" said Arthur dryly.

"For two reasons," I argued. "This isn't going to have a large-scale impact if the people in vulnerable situations"—I leaned on that, thinking of Katrina and the old track marks scarring her skin—"if they're just going to get indoctrinated once they wander over to the next city block. Think of people fighting addictions. Or kids in gang neighborhoods." Like Pilar's cousin. Christ, there were way too many people's lives at stake here. "Second, we want to be able to see if there's actually a statistically significant effect, and for that we need to test it out over a substantial enough area—"

"Hey, calm down, Russell. I'm hearing you out."

I counted out the median seconds in each breath, forcing it to moderate itself.

"So, what, you suggesting all of LA?" Arthur continued after a moment. He spoke as if he were feeling through. Digesting. "That's a lot of ground to cover, isn't it?"

"I did a back-of-the-envelope. Setting enough of them will take some time, but it's doable. Especially if Checker and Pilar will help."

If they would help. I thought of Checker's reaction and it mixed with my rapidly souring feelings.

"But you say the math, it works out," Arthur confirmed.

"I can *make* it work." I wasn't there yet, but the computation was so close I could taste it. I was going to be able to adjust the devices precisely and position them around the whole city, and it would *work,* and there would be no more nights of Arthur getting shot or Pourdry's men shooting up a hospital or all of us depending on the fucking LA Mafia to keep other crime lords in check. I'd be able to blanket the whole metropolitan area evenly, so everywhere would be within the right frequency band, and I'd watch the violence fall and know that I had solved it.

Arthur coughed. "So let me get this straight. You're saying a racket like Pourdry's, or the kids in South LA who get sucked into the life . . ."

My breath caught. I'd started to brace for his objections, dug in so hard I wasn't even sure I was hearing him right at first. But the optimism in his words—he was agreeing. He was *agreeing.*

Adrenaline began tingling through me in the other direction, like fireworks under my skin, as if I wanted to laugh at the sheer relief of it. Every emotion tonight felt forged extreme and too raw.

"I—I'm going to get Checker to run simulations," I managed to answer him. "But yeah. It should have a non-trivial impact."

"Right. Okay. Russell, I realize you're not asking my

permission, but . . . I worry, you know? About what we haven't thought of. But if this has got even a chance of help-ing . . . you say it's only gonna affect people who are caught up already, right? No one else?"

"No, no, no one else."

"If that's the case, then—I don't think we've got a right not to do it, just 'cause we're scared of what might happen. But I want us to think this through every step, right? Nothing hasty. Anybody sees anything concerning, we call it off."

"Yeah, of—of course."

"And I want you to explain it to me in more detail. Want to see their studies and the like."

"No problem."

"After that, if it seems like this is gonna do what you say, I want to help."

Holy shit. I didn't even know how to react. This was—this was excellent, and freeing, and suddenly I had a goddamn ally and I didn't understand how that could feel like every-thing.

"Don't know that I'd be much help right now, of course. . . ." Arthur gestured down at his leg.

"Oh, bullshit." I did laugh then, giddy and sharp-edged but absolutely genuine. "I don't need you for a gun hand. You're useful for the things I'm bad at." Namely, any inves-tigative or undercover work. Suddenly, taking on all of Pourdry's operation—and anyone else we'd managed to piss off—by myself didn't seem so overwhelming. Not when Arthur had my back on the rest of it. I'd get control of my goddamn mind, and we'd fix the city.

"One condition," Arthur said then. And I wanted to feel sandbagged, but his voice was so gentle I couldn't. Gentle, and open, and nonjudgmental, which was ridiculous, because Arthur was one of the most self-righteous people I'd ever met.

He shifted around to face me fully from the passenger

seat. "Tell me what the heck happened between when you dropped me off and when you came to pick me up."

Arthur always saw more than I thought he did.

I swallowed and told him about Simon.

eight

INSTEAD OF trying to calm me down, Arthur was flat-out shaken. Much more than I'd expected him to be.

"We need to find out more about this guy. Stat," he said, as I helped him up the walk and into a ground-floor apartment. Somewhere close by, I heard sirens going again. Not related to us this time.

Except in the way everything was related to us. The way every new death was on our heads.

"I'd like to punch his face in, but I think we have higher priorities, unfortunately," I said to Arthur. I ran the algorithm for the flat's key location and stabilized Arthur for a minute to pry the key out from beneath a slat of the building's warped siding. Now that I'd calmed down, I could be an adult here. "The way he came at me was creepy as fuck, but if I step back from it—objectively, I was probably overreacting."

"What? No. No way in hell you were overreacting. That's what people say to excuse—" He cut himself off, then gusted out a sigh and put his hand back on my shoulder to limp inside. "Russell. I saw how you were acting out there. He had you scared bad."

"Yeah, well, maybe I was being a baby about it. He never even tried to come at me physically, and he clearly wasn't influencing me much if I still want to bash his skull against cement. Let's file him under 'annoying wet noodle' and move on."

"Russell? Think through what you said just there."

I shut the door behind us, puzzling through Arthur's words. What . . . ? Oh.

Oh.

"You're saying he might have influenced me to say that," I said slowly.

"Even if he was being honest about not reading you—if he made us not notice him without trying, he can probably do some kind of, I dunno. A harmless impression. Something that's making you doubt your suspicions of him."

I was a suspicious person by nature, but when it came to someone who could manipulate minds . . . Arthur was right. If I took Simon's "not an exact science" comment on good faith, every gut feeling I had about him was probably manufactured.

And Arthur was also right that I didn't even have one singular gut feeling about him. Impotent fury collided with rabid fear, which was now smothered by this newfound determination to ignore him as irrelevant, and when had that even crept into my brainspace?

I sank down on the threadbare futon that was the studio's only furniture. "I hate psychics."

"At least it sounds like he's not gone full-on aggressive yet," Arthur said, stretching out the leg on his injured side to sink down next to me. "Unless he isn't as strong as Dawna. Or unless he's got some larger plan."

"Aren't you pleasant."

"We gotta find him again."

The fear and anger lifted their heads again. I wasn't sure

if finding him was the last thing I wanted to do or if I wanted to dog him into the ground until I could take disproportionate revenge for his power over me.

"He'll probably find me," I admitted reluctantly. "I got the sense he wasn't going to take no for an answer." The impression that he wasn't going to give up may even have been a bleed-through thought he'd accidentally projected, which meant I was definitely right. "But even if I do see him again, it's not going to do us much good, is it? He's not going to tell me anything he doesn't want to."

"Hmm. I'd like to look into him, and not to his face. You get a last name?"

"I'm not sure 'Simon' is even his real first name."

"What about how he found you?"

"Well, he knows me. Apparently."

Arthur scoffed. "You switch phones every few weeks and don't even keep a driver's license. Knowing you isn't the same as finding you."

That was a good point. I thought for a minute. Could he have tracked me through my clients . . . ?

Arthur snapped his fingers. "I got it. The cemetery."

"What does that have to do with Simon?"

He tilted his head at me, as if I were being worryingly slow. "I went back to talk to 'em about your note, the one you found in the wall niche. Somehow, the cemetery folk couldn't find any records on that wall niche, even though they were *sure* they'd called the next of kin when it got vandalized and all. Totally sure. Said it was a real nice gentleman, too. I'm betting it was him, Russell—pretending to be your family and all."

The realization punched through me slow and heavy, with the speed and inevitability of an oil tanker. How had I not seen what Arthur meant immediately?

Because Simon hadn't wanted me to, probably.

"I'm betting they called him all those months ago when you broke the stone," Arthur went on. "He comes running back to LA, and then . . . how long did you say he's been following?"

"A day or so," I said numbly. "That's how long I've felt like someone was behind me."

"Could be he was here in town trying to find you, but then that damn caretaker saw us this morning. Probably gave this Simon guy a call without even knowing he did."

I pushed my fingers against my temples, an ache pulsing through them.

"I'll keep digging at the cemetery," Arthur said. "They've got to have some kind of records I can get at."

"Track down Pourdry first," I said. "He's the more dangerous one."

"Russell, *you don't know that.*"

Fucking psychics. Everything around me was fracturing, and the feeling was swamping me again that I might not have enough time or resources or sanity for any of it. "All right, then we put Checker on Pourdry, you on Simon, and I get Pilar."

"What are you gonna do?" Arthur asked.

I stood up. "I'm going to break into an old Arkacite warehouse and steal a bunch of top-secret prototypes."

That, at least, was something I could do without second-guessing myself about telepathic influence.

ARKACITE TECHNOLOGIES might have gone bankrupt and died a fiery death as a company, but the detritus of their empire was still everywhere. Large chunks of their technology had been bought out by other corporate behemoths, all of their old brands now carrying a subtitle marking them with whoever the new overlord was, from their operating systems to their smartphones.

Some of the tech that had dead-ended had been bought up wholesale with everything else, but some had been wallowing in limbo, particularly the research sensitive enough to be mired in legalities with the government or military. Pilar had located the old Signet Device materials locked up in a well-secured warehouse that nobody wanted to pay for anymore.

"You need Checker for this," she'd protested when I called and commandeered her help. "I can't cut feeds and sensors for you. I mean, he's been teaching me some things, but this is way, way, way, *way* beyond me."

"I've been breaking into places long before I knew Checker," I said.

How long? whispered a voice in my head.

"I don't need anyone else," I insisted over it. "Besides, this is a defunct storage space getting passed around between people who don't want it in their budget. The security isn't exactly going to be airtight. I just need some information— floor plans, specifics, how things get tripped. You can get me that much, right?"

"Um," she said. "I guess I'll try."

Checker himself had sent me a long, *long* email that went into digressions about the Holocaust, the Nanjing Massacre, the Khmer Rouge, and the Congo Wars, among other atrocities of the twentieth century. *For serious, I've never been able to wrap my head around stuff like this,* he wrote. *I've seen violence up close in my life, but brutality on such a wide scale . . . how the fuck does that happen? How do they get people to go along with rounding up anyone who freakin' wears glasses and literally hacking them to death with pickaxes? How do doctors go along with injecting syphilis into people or raping countless women to experiment on their fetuses and then say they were "just following orders"? I don't get it, Cas. And I look around today and see these hosts on cable news willing to shit on other people HARD and even worse, they have an audience . . . but I'm also stubborn enough to keep believing that most people are fundamentally good. So I don't fucking know. Don't get me wrong, I still think your idea is a shittastically bad one, but*

I keep coming back to what you said about evil in the world being what's messing with people, and wondering what kind of person I'D be if things went really bad, and if I got scared or managed to rationalize something to myself or . . . I don't know, maybe THIS is me rationalizing. But then I think about looking at today's or tomorrow's horrors and knowing I might have helped you prevent them, and whether it's only intellectual arrogance that's stopping me . . . Point is, I might change my mind, but I'm willing to help. FOR NOW.

By the end, I'd started skimming—I was torn between mocking him for sending a doctoral thesis and feeling self-conscious I hadn't dug as deeply into the possible effects of my tech as he had. I'd been considering violence as an abstraction, with maybe a helping of guilt for what I saw here in my own city, but I hadn't connected to thinking about specific historical barbarism.

Not that Checker's examples were all that historical. He was right—we weren't exactly evolved past such things. Maybe . . . maybe this could make a real difference.

And at least I'd be able to count on having Checker's computing skills, once he'd dug up all he could on Pourdry.

Meanwhile, after all her protestations about not knowing whether what I'd asked of her was even in her wheelhouse, Pilar texted me the next day to come meet her where she'd been staying at Checker's house. She opened the front door and immediately thunked a three-inch binder into my hands, complete with a full table of contents and neatly organized colored tabs.

"Holy shit," I said. "What the hell is this?"

"I'm an admin! It's what I do," she said. "Besides, I wasn't sure what all you'd need."

"So what, you branched out into tax law?"

She wrinkled her nose. "Well, I haven't had much to do, what with the office closed and all."

I pushed in past her to come drop onto the living room

couch. "Speaking of, I take it everything's been quiet on this front."

"All quiet," Pilar confirmed.

"I brought you a shotgun. It's in the car."

"I almost, um. I almost brought Arthur's from the office," she confessed, "but you know Checker. He wouldn't like having that in the house."

"He can deal," I said. "You'll need more than a handgun if Pourdry's goons come around. You've got your CZ?"

I'd bought her the pistol. Pilar's color heightened and she patted her sweater behind her hip self-consciously. "Yes."

"Good." I hefted the binder. "Now give me the short version of this monstrosity."

Pilar sat down next to me and proceeded to talk me through two hours of details I didn't really need. Checker came in from the Hole right after the eleventh time I told her to move on.

"Hey," he said. "How's it going?"

"Great!" Pilar chirped, at the same time I said, "Kill me now."

Checker snorted a laugh. "Cas, you could do with not flying by the seat of your pants for once."

I ignored the jibe. "What have you found on Pourdry?"

"He's got a hell of an enterprise. I'm unearthing it, slowly. Following the money and all that."

"And what about the cops? What've they got on the shootout?"

"Arthur's down as a witness, and they're after you as one, too, but nobody has a good description of you or any good forensics—you're welcome, by the way; you left your fingerprints on some of the shell casings."

"That's what I've got you for."

"I'll add it to your tab. You could stand to be a little more careful, you know. I'm not a magician."

"You're admitting electronic fallibility? You?"

"Excuse me while I go find something to throw at you."
He headed off into the kitchen. "You guys want some food?"

"No," I said, at the same time Pilar called, "Yes, please!"

I imagined slowly banging my head against the multi-
tabbed binder. "Most of this is an easy job. There's no infra-
red and they don't keep the lights on inside, so the only
place I can't avoid the security cameras is going over the
fence. It's too bad they log that, or it would just be a matter
of knocking out the guard watching the monitors."

Checker poked his head out of the kitchen. "I said I'd
help, you know. You need something looped?"

"It's a Rachnid system," Pilar said. "It's wireless, but an
intranet."

"Oh, that's easy. You carry a dongle close enough, I can
piggyback onto the signal and edit whatever we want."

"Can you also get her the keypad codes?" Pilar asked.
"That's the only piece I couldn't—"

"I can just bust it open," I said. "Unless there's something
we haven't gotten to yet in your magnum opus here, their
security isn't good enough to sense the damage."

"Isn't it better if they don't know you've broken in,
though?" Pilar asked. "I mean, that's why I looked up all
their inventory procedures and whatnot. Don't you want to
hide what you're taking? 'Cause then nobody will be looking for it, or looking for the effects."

Checker had ducked back into the kitchen, but he hol-
lered out, "Cas Russell, put the explosives away. Keypad
codes are not a problem."

I thought for a minute. "What's the range of your dongle?"

"Fifteen feet, give or take a few," he called back.

I flipped to the blue tab marked "floor plans" and mentally
drew out the radius intersecting the security grid. "No, total
stealth is a no-go anyway. I have to take care of the security
guard or I'll cross multiple cameras before Checker's signal

is in range to knock them out." Checker could edit the footage after the fact, but not a person's memory.

Human memory is infinitely malleable, someone sang. *Like painting over a canvas . . .*

"Why not just *distract* the guard?" Pilar asked, hauling me back to the present. "Then your heist goes undetected and nobody has to suffer a head injury. Win-win!"

"I liked you better when you were afraid to talk back to me," I grumped, shaking off the cobwebs and trying to sound normal. I pushed away creeping doubts that I'd be able to do this job at all. I should be able to control my own brain; I just had to *focus.* "That wouldn't work anyway," I said too loudly. "Mathematically, I can't be in two places at once. I can't reliably draw the guard's attention somewhere else at the same time I'm going over the fence. Unless I use an explosive or something to do it, and then we're still talking about leaving behind evidence, so there's no advantage."

"What about asking Arthur to do it?"

I considered. He *had* offered to help. And though force might be easier, more efficient, and my overall preferred way of doing things, Pilar had a point about stealth helping the cause.

Checker came back out to the living room, balancing a tray of sandwiches. "Don't you dare ask Arthur to do field work injured, Cas Russell. Don't you dare."

"It's not like his condition would impede him on this," I said. "He can limp in and out just fine."

"And if something goes wrong? Wait till he heals. I'm putting my foot down."

"If Arthur's safety is your worry, getting our hands on this technology might help a ton against Pourdry and anyone else we've pissed off," I said. "We need to get the brain entrainment going as soon as possible. Does one of you two feel like going in? I didn't think so. If you don't want me to ask Arthur, then we're back to the quick-and-dirty route inside. You can tell me something else to steal so they won't notice the Signet Device stuff missing."

"They'll still notice," Pilar said. "If you look in the green section on inventory—" She cut herself off at the glower on my face. "Never mind. But anyway. Could I help? What would you need me to do?"

"What?" Checker said. "No!"

Pilar's eyebrows drew together so fiercely Checker rocked back in his chair.

"I just mean, you don't have the experience!" he squawked. "You're talking about stealing a highly secretive piece of technology—if Cas gets caught, you get arrested. This isn't a game!"

"Thanks," said Pilar. "I know that."

I leaned back on the couch, putting my feet up on Checker's coffee table and suddenly enjoying the spectacle.

"Unlike the rest of us, you have a clean record, and Arthur and I would both like you to keep it," Checker said. "We're *not* asking you to do this."

"You're right," Pilar said. "You're not asking; I'm volunteering."

"Wait," I cut in. "Checker, you and Arthur have criminal records? Since when?"

"Since none of your business, that's when," Checker shot back. He turned back to Pilar. "I don't want to have to play the boss card, but when Arthur and I hired you, it was not to get you in trouble as an accessory to burglary! You're not getting involved."

"This isn't part of my job," Pilar said. "It's for Cas, not for you. So you can't pull rank."

"Do you want to do it instead?" I asked Checker.

"I *can't* if you want me editing and looping the security footage in real time! And besides, I'm not good enough at that sort of thing anyway, and I'm smart enough to know it. Wait for Arthur!"

"I'm a girl," Pilar said. "The guard won't see me as a

threat. I'll say I had car trouble or something and just chat with him. Or her."

"Hey, she can carry the dongle," I said. "That way I won't ever appear on the monitors at all. Totally safe. No chance of anyone catching on."

"There's always a chance! Newton save me—Pilar, why on earth are you humoring Cas on this? Arthur will be better in a few weeks; there's no need!"

Pilar hunched her shoulders. "A lot can happen in a few weeks. People can get hurt in a few weeks. If this is going to work the way Cas thinks it will . . ."

One of my cousins joined a gang a couple months ago, Pilar had said. Arthur wasn't the only one with kids he cared about.

"This won't be a panacea," I suddenly felt the need to warn her. "It'll help. It won't wipe out every problem."

"So maybe it'll help enough for a good family to balance things out," Pilar said, not looking at either of us. She stood up. "I'm going to make some tea. Cas, I'm in if you want me."

"I want you."

She nodded and went into the kitchen.

"Don't do this," Checker pleaded in a low murmur once Pilar was out of the room. "Don't. She doesn't know what she's getting into."

"Yes, she does," I said. "She's worked for you guys for a while now. She knows. Stop patronizing her."

He flushed. "I'm not. It's an issue of experience—"

I scooped up half a deli-meat sandwich and took a bite. "Yeah, about that," I said with my mouth full. "What illegal activities did you and Arthur ensnarl yourselves in? Other than with me."

"I did some dumb shit as a teenager, that's all. As for Arthur, it's seriously not your business. I shouldn't have said anything."

"Oh, and my past is *your* business?"

"I am dead begging you here—don't bring this up to him," Checker said, staring at his hands. "It's done, it was years ago, and you'll only hurt him. Just don't."

"Fine. But I get Pilar tonight."

"Tonight?"

"Why wait? What, do you have a hot date or something? Or were you just hoping to talk her out of it?"

He covered his eyes with one hand, not answering for a moment. "I'm not trying to patronize her."

"You're not *trying* to."

"I still say it's a stupid risk. She's never done anything like this before."

"Only one way to learn," I said. "This is an easy job. Good thing to start with."

"I don't like it."

"You don't have to."

We sat in tense silence for a moment. I finished my sandwich and brushed the crumbs off onto Checker's couch. He winced. "Can you at least spare my coffee table?"

I let my boots thunk back down to the floor. "If you're thinking about backing out of your part of the gig tonight, we'll still find a way in without you. Only it won't be as clean."

"God, Cas! I said I was in, as shitty as I feel about all this. I don't like what you're doing and I don't like you involving Pilar, but that doesn't mean I'm going to go off and sulk and let you get yourselves caught."

"We still wouldn't get caught."

"Sure." He groped at an end table behind him and came up with a tablet. "Speaking of people's pasts, let's hop back on yours. Arthur's digging into this Simon fellow; he needs intel."

"Oh, look at the time." I got up. "I'd better prepare for the heist."

"Prepare what? You're just walking in and walking out. Pilar and I are the ones doing all the work. Sit yourself down."

I tried to rustle up a comeback to that and failed. I sat down.

"Right," Checker said. "So. We were talking about . . . um." He cleared his throat. "How you met Rio."

My irritation slammed up against a massive wall of weighted memory, a black tar seeping up over the present.

The Lord guides my hand—

Cassandra. We picked the name Cassandra. Remind her.

I flinched.

"Cas? Cas, are you all right?"

"No."

"Do you . . . are you remembering something?"

Cas. Do you recall who I am?

One of the people who killed me—

My mind cringed away, the stabs of image and sound leaving my thoughts speckled red.

"I can't do this right now." The words came out steadier than they had any right to, as if it were another person talking.

"I've been thinking," Checker said. "I've been thinking, um . . . maybe I should talk to Rio."

The sentence whiplashed me back to the moment like I was a drunk who'd been dropped into a freezing lake. My eyes snapped into focus and I stared at Checker for a full four seconds, my jaw working. *"What?"*

He fiddled with his tablet and didn't drop eye contact with me. "Well, I've been putting this together since the last time we talked. It seems like you've known him a long time, longer than anyone else you remember, and you keep dodging my questions about it."

"Because I don't want to answer them," I said. "It doesn't mean anything."

"I think it might." Checker's expression softened. "Cas, I'm not sure you even know you're doing it, but it's like a . . . a reflex with you. Every time I ask you something that might get close to what you did before this, you deflect."

"No, I don't."

His mouth twitched. "Then tell me how you met Rio. Or give me a phone number or email address so I can ask him."

That concept was still derailing my brain. "You. Want to talk. To Rio."

"Want? No, no, no. 'Want' is far too strong a word." He flailed his hands and swallowed visibly. "What I *want* is to help you, and in order to help you, I am willing to attempt some extremely delicate inquiries of your friend who also happens to be the pure embodiment of blood-curdling evil. That's just how good of a person I am."

"Or you have an obscene level of curiosity and are like a pit bull when you want the answer to something. I can't believe you want to talk to *Rio*."

I expected Checker to snark back at me, maybe something about how obscene curiosity was the best kind, but instead he winced away and turned the tablet over in his hands. "Cas," he said, without looking at me, "if you don't mind, this is really rather a terrifying thing for me, and I wouldn't do it if I weren't trying like hell to help you, so please give me the damn contact information before I lose my courage entirely."

There wasn't much I could say to that. I wrote down Rio's phone number for him.

nine

I HALF EXPECTED Checker to call Arthur and try to get him to thwart my plan for the night, but he didn't. Maybe he was worried enough about Arthur's injury that he didn't want to be responsible for him volunteering to take Pilar's place.

I didn't care which of them served as my diversion. It was an easy part to play, and even if things went wrong, I didn't anticipate any danger.

Unless my central nervous system decided to go out on me again. I weighed the chances of that happening. But even if I collapsed in the building, it wasn't like Pilar would be in trouble, was it? Checker could pull her out, the mission would be a bust, and I'd get myself out somehow too.

Fear of my own mind couldn't keep me locked inside, unable to take the smallest action. I refused to let it. Besides, if I stopped working . . .

That was a bad idea even under normal circumstances. I didn't want to know how much worse my brain might get if I ended up at loose ends right now.

When I came back from making a run for backup gear, Pilar met me in front of Checker's house. While I'd been gone, she'd changed into a black cocktail dress with tasteful cleavage and more makeup than I was used to seeing on her.

"What on earth are you wearing?" I said. "We're committing robbery, not going to a wine-tasting party."

"And my role in your robbery is to be as trustworthy and vulnerable a person as possible. I was coming from a party when my car broke down, for your information."

I pointed at her heels. "You can't run in those."

"Cas, honey? I know you have way more experience than me when it comes to pretty much everything involved in this. But you gave me this job because you thought I could do it, so trust me when I say I know *way* more than you do about how to make someone want to help me."

To be perfectly honest, I'd recruited Pilar because she volunteered, not because I'd given consideration to her capability of looking nice in a dress. Maybe Checker was right, and I hadn't thought this through.

Or maybe *I* was more right than I knew, considering that Pilar clearly *had*.

I sighed. "Where's your sidearm?"

"In my purse." She lifted her sleek clutch.

"That's not the best place for it."

"The dress is worth it. Trust me on this one."

I supposed I'd already made that decision. I jerked my head at her and got back into the car. She trotted after me and slid into the passenger seat, opening the clutch to take out a few gadgets.

"From Checker." She handed me a cell phone, an earpiece, and a small plastic stick about the size of a flash drive. "I've got a dongle of my own on me, but here's one for you, too, just as backup."

I snugged in the earpiece. "Checker?"

"Here," he said.

"Don't sound so excited."

He harrumphed at me.

The warehouse was several hours outside the city. Pilar didn't sleep on the way, but she didn't seem nervous, either—she sat with her hands folded loosely in her lap, staring out the windshield. When I finally pulled over a few blocks from our destination, she took one steady inhale through pursed lips and then got out of the car.

"You sure you're ready for this?" I said.

"Yeah. I am."

"Good, because it's too late to say no."

She looked around. "I—I'm not oriented; I'm sorry."

I pointed. "That's San Alvarez Street. Turn right. You should see the guardhouse. Are you with it now?"

"Yeah. I got it."

"Tell me what you're telling the guard." We'd been over this earlier in the evening, but the last thing I needed was Pilar freezing up on me.

"That my car broke down, and I'm waiting for Triple A but I didn't want to wait out on the street, because it's dark and dangerous and all, and can I please hang in the guardhouse for a few minutes. And then just chat. Chatting I can do."

"What's your signal to leave?"

"Once you're out, Checker's going to call me saying he's the tow truck."

"Good." I popped open the hood of the car and reached down to unscrew the distributor cap and pull it off. "Just in case the guard tries to be gallant, your pretend car now will truly pretend to not start." I tossed her the keys, which she caught clumsily and tucked into her clutch. "Now go."

She paused for long enough to take one more deliberate breath, then started swiftly in the direction of the intersection.

"You're at least keeping half an eye on her, right?" Checker said in my ear. "This plan only makes sense because this is a deserted and scary neighborhood. If Pilar gets mugged or assaulted because she was walking around there alone—"

"I'm following, I'm following," I groused, and hurried after her, keeping to the shadows. I couldn't help wondering if this area had been so deserted and scary a year ago, when Pithica still had their fingers everywhere . . .

Pilar's heels echoed on the pavement. She turned the corner and made a beeline for the guardhouse. I lurked, out of range of the warehouse's security but still within sight of her. Once she was on the security cameras, she didn't pause. She approached the guardhouse with a half wave as whoever was inside saw her, and hugged her arms as she leaned to converse through the sliding window.

"She's close enough," Checker said. "Taking control of the security cameras in three, two, one. You're set for as long as she's in range."

Nodding and smiling, a white-haired man in a security guard's uniform opened up the door and ushered Pilar inside with him.

"You can see her on the cams, right?" I said to Checker.

"Yeah. She's in. He's facing away from you and talking to her. Go."

Good. As long as my psyche held out on me, this would all be fine. I turned toward the warehouse—

And ran smack into Simon.

"What the *fuck*!" I barely managed to keep the exclamation to a hissing whisper.

"What are you doing?" he asked.

I drew my Colt on reflex. Not that it would do me much good. "What am *I* doing? What are *you* doing!"

"I'm sorry, Cassandra," he said, hugging himself. "I didn't want to follow you again, but you don't know what I know. I'm concerned. And now I'm more concerned. After putting yourself in so much danger the other night, and now—what

are you doing here? What are you involved in?" His forehead wrinkled in worry.

He must have followed us from Checker's—I realized I'd
forgotten to tell Arthur that Simon knew where Checker
lived. I'd forgotten to tell any of them.

*Or maybe I hadn't forgotten. Maybe he'd made it so I just
wouldn't think of it.*

If I had, would it have made a difference? Would we have
been able to figure out a way for me not to pick up a fucking
tail again?

"Cas!" Checker's voice in my ear grounded me. "Cas,
what's going on?"

"Nothing," I said. "Nothing at all is going on. Is Pilar still
keeping the guard busy?" I reholstered my weapon and
pushed past Simon.

"Yes. I think he's showing her pictures of his grandchil-
dren. Who are you talking to?"

"You're about to see," I said. "He's following me."

"Holy shit," Checker said. "Is it that Simon guy? Tell me
it's not the Simon guy. Abort. Abort right now."

"No," I said.

"He's going to blow the whole thing! Cas, you're probably
not thinking clearly—call it off!"

"No," I repeated. I was closing in on the chain-link fence.
Simon scrambled behind me, every few breaths pleading for
me to stop and talk to him.

"This isn't right," Checker said. "I'm pulling Pilar out of
there."

"You do that, and you'll expose me," I said.

"Dammit, Cas!"

The metal of the fence was chilled to the touch, and my
scabbing, bandaged fingers curled stiffly, the links digging
into the still-healing flesh. But chain-link fences were easy
to climb even without mathematics, and the horizontal lines
of barbed wire at the top only required a careful shift of my
center of mass before I was over.

My boots landed lightly on the pavement of the other side. I tried to ignore the noises still coming from the top of the fence. Simon deserved it if he got skewered.

But he was also going to crash my whole operation if he kept it up, and I didn't trust a nickel's worth that he'd help us get out of the consequences if he did. I unslung the empty backpack I wore and took off my jacket to throw it in a swooping parabola, the air resistance catching it neatly to drape on top of the barbs. Simon flailed over it and tumbled next to me, hitting the pavement in a heap. I didn't make a move to break his fall.

In fact, after jumping to pop my jacket off the barbs, I kicked him in the stomach.

It pleasantly surprised me that I was able to.

"Cassandra!" he coughed, his eyes filling with betrayal. "Why?"

"Because you're stalking me and trying to blow my cover," I said. "Now get up and out of view of that guard-house." I dragged him upright by the collar and then marched for the main building. Somehow I knew he would hurry after me.

"Cas," Checker tried again. "Please listen to me. You are being stupid and dangerous and dangerously stupid. You cannot take this guy on a mission to steal a top-secret proto-type. Are you hearing the words I'm saying? Stupid. Dangerous. Top secret. Cas, I think—I think you might be compromised. And Pilar's in the middle of this with you. Will you please listen! You have to abort!"

"Keep distracting me and I'll mute you," I said.

"You know you can't do that. That would be even *more* stupid than what you're doing right now, which is—"

"Five. Four," I said. He shut up.

I reached the heavy metal security door and pulled out a set of lock picks. Not my usual MO, but the plan had been not to leave a trace. I picked the lock with algorithmic preci-sion, the pins dropping neatly onto the edge of the shear line one after the other, and pushed open the door into the darkness of a cavernous hallway. The LED flashlight I snapped on just after the door closed revealed a cement floor large enough to drive trucks down, flanked by enormous metal roll-up doors on each side that gleamed in the slashing beam. Almost like a storage facility, except bigger and way more oppressive.

"What is this place?" Simon's question echoed off the concrete and metal.

Now that the guard couldn't see or hear, I spun around, grabbed him, and shoved him against the wall hard enough for his body to ricochet like a rag doll. "I am not letting you interfere with my life," I said. "You hear me? You are a ghost. A nightmare. I don't care what you think you know about me. You have no claim on me. If you keep following me, I will work my ass off until I figure out a way to kill you, and in the meantime maybe one of my enemies will shoot you for me. Now stay out of my way."

I strode off down the corridor without looking back. No footsteps sounded behind me.

I paused and took a second to breathe, trying not to let Checker's reaction shake me. At least my brain was still quiet.

At the second-to-last vault on the right, I entered the code Checker had looked up for me earlier and hauled the door up high enough for me to duck under. The Signet Devices had been listed as lots 466 to 487, and it took less than four minutes of searching for me to find a working model. It was a bit large and cumbersome, with a scattering of additional pieces outside the main casing, but I managed to stuff everything in my backpack. I also found what looked like the technical specifications in the next file box over and jammed those in, too. They'd save me a good deal of reverse engineering.

"Checker," I said. "Are the dongles traceable to you?"

"No," he answered instantly.

I hadn't wanted to leave anything behind, but the dongle was probably a lot less obvious than a creepy, bruised psychic. I had no doubt Simon could get back out past the guard, but he wouldn't be able to erase himself from the security cameras . . . which meant Checker was signed up to cover his exit, too. *Total stealth,* I reminded myself, *leave them no reason to take inventory.* Too bad—under other circumstances I would have enjoyed blaming him for my little theft.

I tucked the dongle in the bottom of a file folder fat with design specs for a different project and put everything else back the way I had found it. "Checker, if you're picking up my signal for the cameras, pull Pilar out now."

"What about the guard? Your exit—"

"You keep me off the monitors; I'll worry about the guard. Now pull her."

"Pulling her."

He kept the line open, and I caught the low murmur of him faking the tow truck call to Pilar as I jogged back through the dimness. It took him longer than I expected—I gathered the guard wanted to walk her out after the third time Checker had to assure her he was right down the street at her car—but he ended the call about the time I reached the outside door. I shined the LED flashlight around, but Simon was gone.

"I'm headed back outside. Where's the guard's line of sight right now?"

"He's looking at his monitors. They'll stay blank."

Good. At least one thing I wouldn't have to worry about.

The guardhouse bisected the front section of chain-link fence. I had a vast open area of pavement to cross, and it would only take the security guard lifting his eyes unexpectedly to nail me. And I had to go through the front—behind me the warehouse property abutted buildings with even tighter security, and to the right the fence divided the property from a blind alley that had been built over at the ends. No egress that way.

No egress, but maybe still a better way out . . .

There's no escape from a one-way function, laughed someone who sounded like me.

No. *No.* I was so close. The alley to the right. Built over on both ends but with the chain link running along it.

I cut sideways, sprinting faster than I should have, as if I could outrun my own past. I hit the fence against the alley and scaled it, my loaded pack bumping my shoulder blades. But at the top, instead of swinging over to the other side, I kept running straight up the links like they were a ladder, up the links and then up the strands of wire between the hooked barbs, my momentum bringing me up and up and straight up and stretching me to the heavens in direct opposition of forces until I stood balanced on the barbed wire. The strand pressed through the soles of my boots, swaying gently below me. I let my muscles compensate, shifting my weight minutely so the vectors lined up equal and opposite.

I waited for a hairsbreadth, almost expecting another mental spiral to rear up snarling and tear me down off the top of the world. Anxiety bit into me like the barbed wire beneath my boots. But the night was quiet again, taunting me with uncertainty.

Go, I ordered myself.

I ran.

The barbs were spaced five inches apart, and the soles of my boots were almost twice that. I ran between them on the balls of my feet, a springing prance, the wire absorbing and rebounding against the vertical component of the tension as it rocketed me down my knife-thin path. The front corner had a tall, fat brick pillar interrupting the chain link, but just before I reached it I leapt diagonally, cutting the corner and turning my skipping dash so I was running along the front side of the fence.

I was almost right on top of the guard, but I was playing the odds that he wouldn't notice. People never looked up.

As I neared the guardhouse I fed in some deceleration, braking myself until I'd hit the barest tiptoe when I stepped onto the guardhouse roof. Less than a minute and I'd be out of here. I only had to hang on for a few more seconds.

"Is the guard looking away?" I whispered into my earpiece.

"Still on the monitors," Checker said.

I crept to the edge of the roof and dropped. On the street side of the guardhouse, I stayed curled below the windows for one more moment, listening, and then moved away at a crouch.

"Am I good?" I asked.

"He's looking up at the building now. No way he sees the street."

I straightened up and ran.

I'd made it. We'd done what we came here to do.

Then why did I feel like I was leaving pieces of myself scattered on the ground behind me, with Simon cackling among them as he watched me crack?

Pilar was waiting inside the car, in the passenger seat. She jumped a mile when I knocked on the window and immediately groped for the unlock button. "Oh, thank God!" she said as soon as I opened the driver's door. "I didn't see you coming. I was so worried. You were supposed to be out ahead of me."

"It got hot," I said.

Her eyes widened. "It did? Oh my gosh, it's probably better I didn't know that. What happened?"

"Keys, Pilar."

"Oh! Right!"

She dug them out and handed them to me. I tried to start the car, but when I turned the key, nothing happened.

"You forgot to fix the engine," Pilar said.

Fuck. I must be even more rattled than I thought.

Or maybe Checker had it right, and I wasn't thinking straight at all.

ten

I HUNG up with Checker and took out the earpiece, over his protests. I didn't want him ranting at me, especially if he was right. Once I fixed the car and got us on the road back toward LA, Pilar started asking me questions about what had happened, her hands twisting with way more nervousness than she'd exhibited before the operation. But I put her off.

I didn't feel like explaining. Even to myself.

Especially to myself.

I dropped Pilar off at Checker's house and sped away without going in. Avoiding Checker forever wasn't an option— I'd need his help on the devices soon enough—but I could be petty for tonight.

By early the next morning, however, I was sitting on the floor surrounded by pages of technical specs and the guts of the model Signet Device, and feeling like I'd just thumped my head slowly into a wall about three dozen times. In order for my calibrated net to work, I needed to deploy hundreds of the things all over LA in extremely specific locations, which meant miniaturizing the one I'd stolen from the warehouse. I'd been able to figure out how each component worked without much trouble—circuits were little more than Boolean algebra made exponential—but making the pieces themselves *smaller*—

My hands tightened on the pieces. I had to be able to do this. This was my superpower. My realm.

Except that I was a mathematician, not an engineer.

I'd even given in and emailed Checker a copy of the specs in the middle of the night, but morning had rolled around without a reply from him, which was . . . unusual. Very unusual. His responses tended to be improbably instantaneous.

I half wondered if he was ignoring me. Maybe it was comeuppance for me ignoring *him* for so long and then contradicting him during an operation. That didn't seem like him, but what did I know?

I pushed the gutted hardware aside and picked up the specs again. The logical pathways were so clear to me, including their loops and redundancies. I *should* be able to condense it all. I *could* condense it all, theoretically, but the theory wasn't good enough. What I wanted to do was possible according to the laws of physics, but the necessary knowledge of circuits and wires just wasn't in my head—hell, the components I'd need might not even exist, for all I knew about electronics.

A skinny black girl handed me a box the size of a cigarette pack, circuits and wires splaying out the sides.

"What does it do?"

Laughter from her, with a savage edge. "Go find out."

I tried to shake off the apparition; it clung for a moment before fading back into nothingness. Christ. I needed to figure out some way to make this stop.

Fortunately, just then my phone buzzed, distracting me. *Finally.*

NOT A HWARE GUY, Checker's text said with uncharacteristic terseness—yeah, he must still be mad. CAN ASK ARND IF U WANT.

Damn. Checker was good enough at basic hardware that I tended to forget he identified way more on the bits-and-bytes side of things. And I wasn't keen on involving someone else.

I tossed my phone in my hand, frustration burning through me.

Wait. *Wait.*

My whole focus went to the mobile phone in my hand. I examined it closely, then got up, walked over to the wall, and smashed it against the corner. The case broke open neatly along the seams.

I looked back to the pieces of the Arkacite device strewn on the floor. A massive jumble of circuitry, hiding the simplicity of what it did. Arkacite had used it to deal with the design problem in a language they understood—but I didn't need *their* language if I could translate it into mine.

The heart of the hardware was simple. All I needed was the ability to send signals—a lot of signals. The Arkacite device had ponderous engineering in place for the directionality and calibration problems they'd been trying to counter, but I didn't need any of that—*if* I had enough point sources in my grid.

A dense enough net, with every device able to reach out and sense the position of every other one . . . a net that was able to adjust itself according to what it found, according to its place in time and space . . . and all that was left was math.

Not programming or hardware. Just math.

I gazed down at the split-open cell phone for another few seconds, then laid out its guts next to the pieces of the Arkacite device and pulled over some old academic journals to scribble on the backs. If I cut all the inputs to a subliminal audio frequency and then fed in the density of smartphones in Los Angeles . . . almost everyone had smartphones these days, even homeless folks, or kids lacking any good support like Katrina and her friend. Pseudocode spiraled out from my pen, structuring the logic my app would need. GPS variables, density of other phones as a proxy to population . . . raise or lower the signals instantly, according to a hair trigger . . . I sat and wrote, sprawled and wrote, wrote and wrote and wrote. The algorithm was mathematically complex enough Arkacite never would have jigsawed it together from their testing data, but it would be beautifully simple from a coding point of view.

I hoped.

Shit. I scrawled a box at the end of the completed program outline and sat back on my heels. Now I didn't need a hardware guy, I needed a software one—someone who could transform my mathematical outline into actual programming and then, well, package it into an app, or whatever software engineers did.

I needed Checker. As I'd known I would, in some fashion. I needed to give him all this and discuss it with him and ask what he needed to make it happen, which meant I had to go to the Hole, where I was going to get an earful of a lecture about the night before.

It was midafternoon. I put my phone together and checked in with Arthur via text rather than calling so he couldn't gnaw at me with questions about Simon—I had no illusions about Checker keeping the previous night's incident to himself. Then I grabbed my stack of pseudocode and reluctantly drove back to Van Nuys. I was fully braced for Checker to lay into me immediately about stupid risks, possibly mixed in with a scolding about not telling Pilar what had gone down, and for me to sit there and deliberately not tell him it was worse than he knew.

Instead, he jerked around when I came into his computer cave as if he hadn't already seen me coming on his security cameras.

"Cas," he said, his hands slipping and dropping the tablet he'd been holding. It clattered to the floor, but he didn't seem to notice. "Hey. Hey."

"Uh, hi," I said, thrown. "I have a plan. Can you build a smartphone app out of this?" I tossed the sheaf of pseudocode on his keyboard.

I was expecting more objections to the brain entrainment, but instead he just pushed up his glasses and started reading. "This doesn't look too bad, actually. Is it—um. You figured out how to use cell phones for it."

It wasn't really a question, but I answered anyway. "I did. Brilliant, huh? Los Angeles has so many phones; I can lose all the other junk the Signet Devices needed. This can run in secret on everyone's smartphones—*everyone's*, everyone who has one—and it'll adjust in real time according to the algorithm and blanket the whole city. Keep everybody safe and calm."

He twitched at that, and I waited for him to protest again, but he didn't. He also wasn't looking at me.

The silence stretched out.

"I'll start working on it," Checker said, still avoiding my gaze. "How, um. How are you going to get this onto the phones?"

"I need some way to hack the cell network. I figured you were the one to ask about that."

He seemed to get some of his sarcastic vigor back then. "You know, usually when people use the word 'hack' they're *way* oversimplifying. Sadly, in the case of our cellular network, these days it actually is that easy."

"Really? How?"

"You want something that will eventually reach almost the whole LA population? Probably the best way would be baseband hacking—hitting the phone radio processors with a fake tower signal. This used to be a lot harder, but now it's as simple as buying some hotspot boxes and reconfiguring them. Still, in order to make it remotely feasible to engage a critical density of cell phones, you'll have to set a lot of the things—I'll get you all the numbers, but you'll have to figure out for yourself if you can place enough of them to reach download saturation as people's phones move in and out of range."

"Sounds good," I said. "What *is* the range?"

"About two hundred meters, if I remember right?"

The estimates slotted in for me lightning fast. I wouldn't be able to cover close to all of LA, but I wouldn't have to. I just needed enough high-population areas. Heavily used freeway interchanges, where people would be sitting in traffic while their phones downloaded my program . . . the canyon roads, the airport . . .

"Doing this sort of thing is highly illegal, of course, but it's ridiculously straightforward," Checker continued. "It's the same tech the government uses for StingRay surveillance—did you know the LAPD alone has used that to spy on hundreds of citizens, all without a warrant? Anyway, we'll have to think about power consumption, but I'm guessing what with you being you, that's not going to be a huge stumbling block to steal. Depending on how many you want, we can probably rig them for you in a weekend."

"Cool," I said. "Thanks. Sounds perfect." It was, in fact, exactly what I needed.

But Checker was neither celebrating such an elegant solution with me nor arguing with me about why I shouldn't do it.

We had fallen into an awkward stillness again. I didn't know what to think. When Checker fought with me, he *fought*: he was loud and blunt and opinionated.

Not this stilted, muted interaction.

"What happened with Simon?" I said, when the silence had become too uncomfortable. "Did you track him on the cameras after I left?" I didn't *want* to invite a lecture, but I did want to know—and Checker was acting way too strange for my tastes.

Was this the sort of thing Rio had noticed in me, after Dawna had influenced me? Could Simon have gotten to Checker in a way I was able to notice? Rio had turned out to be immune to telepathic influence, though. . . .

"What?" Checker straightened and became a little more animated again. "Right. Simon. Right. Uh, it's totally weird.

He didn't appear on any cameras at all after I saw him with you."

"That's impossible," I said.

"I know. When you left him, it was dark where he was. I watched for the rest of the night for him to pop up elsewhere, but nothing. Then once the sun rose, I checked everywhere. He wasn't on any of the cameras at all."

"Impossible," I said again. "Those things covered the whole property." The security map rose in my mind's eye, the cameras' fields of view overlapping.

"I *know*," Checker said. "But then I thought, well—he didn't know you'd directed me to cover his exit. We assumed he'd sneak out and maybe modify the guard's memory or whatever, but . . . he didn't know he wasn't on the monitors."

"So? Why would he care either way if he was?" It hadn't been *his* heist to protect, and the man had superpowers, so it wasn't like he would've gone down for the crime by accident.

"Maybe he just wanted to avoid questions? I don't know. But if he can make himself unnoticeable—Cas, what if that's what he did after you left him? Just made himself unnoticeable?"

"They're *cameras*," I said. "He can't impact cameras. It's human psychology these guys are experts in."

"And I think he's on the cameras," Checker said. "I think he's on the cameras and *I can't see him*."

My gut went leaden.

"Run some sort of program or something that recognizes humans," I said. "Have the computer analyze the footage."

"You think I didn't try that? I get three results, since I scrubbed you. And when I try to bring them up, I get Pilar, the guard, and an empty hallway. Cas, I don't think he's tricking the computer; I think whatever he's doing is tricking anybody who looks at the footage before we can see him. You told Arthur he kept going on about permission, right? What if he didn't want to alter the guard's memory directly,

and this was his way of taking care of both the guard and
the cameras?"

"This *is* altering us directly," I said. "I don't buy that 'not
an exact science' bullshit—he just brainwashed the guard
and you *and* me!"

"I don't claim to know how it works," Checker said. "I'm
just telling you what I know, okay?"

He trailed off. The room got quiet again.

Checker *never* got quiet.

"What is wrong with you?" I said.

"What? Nothing!" He moved his hand so fast one of his
keyboards banged.

"Okay," I answered, chewing the word slowly. "Okay. So
you'll get everything we need for the cell phone hacking for
me? And translate my program into computer-speak?"

"Yeah, uh. Sure."

More silence.

"So, what annoying past-life questions are you going to
pester me with today?" I tried, as a last resort.

"Oh. Right," he said. "Um, none. I mean, I'm not. Take
the day off."

"You're not? You've been prodding and prying every
chance you get and now you've got nothing? That's a nice
change."

"Cas," Checker said. He was looking down at the keyboard now, but didn't seem to see it. "I—I think I made a
mistake. You told me to respect your wishes on this, and I
just kept pushing, and—I think that was, was wrong of me.
So if you still want me to, I'll drop it."

Of course I wanted him to. I opened my mouth to say so.

His hands were shaking. Checker's hands were shaking.

"Holy crap," I said, everything about his odd behavior
collapsing to a conclusion at once. "What did you find?"

"What? Nothing!"

"Bullshit. What did you find?"

He looked me square in the eyes. "I swear to you, I didn't find anything."

The man was a fucking asshole. He wouldn't stop looking into my past no matter how much I asked him to, and now he was suggesting we drop it when I knew he was lying to me?

I thought about letting it go. I wanted to. But the way he was acting . . . if I was in danger, or if he was in danger for looking into this—*It would serve him right,* some part of me thought. But it was only a small part.

"Checker," I said, and I hoped I was the only one who heard the slight tremor. "So help me God, if you don't tell me what you found out, I will start shooting up the Hole." I drew my Colt and pointed it at the nearest computer tower. "Now what. The hell. Is going on?"

Checker paled. "You wouldn't."

"Watch me," I said. I carried in condition zero and the gun was ready to fire, but I lowered the hammer and recocked it for dramatic effect.

"Hey, *whoa*!" cried Checker. "I want to tell you; I do! I—I still might. The reason I didn't—I'm *scared,* okay? I'm not like you."

I brought the gun back down. "What are you talking about?"

"I—I can't say."

"If you came across something dangerous, we can deal with it."

I spoke more confidently than I felt. But if I didn't know what we were up against, then I definitely couldn't protect against it. . . .

Checker sniffed loudly and turned away. He wasn't just scared. He was *terrified.* Holy fuck. "No, that isn't— I told you, I didn't find anything. I was telling the truth. It isn't just me, either. I don't know what's going to happen if I tell you. I don't. To anyone."

"Hey. Whatever happened, whoever scared you this badly, we can figure it out." My mouth was dry. I wasn't sure if I was saying it more to convince him or myself. "We can. I promise. I'm very good at finding people and rendering them impotent, and so is Arthur, and so is Rio—"

Checker choked.

"Come on, I know you don't like Rio, but this is the exact kind of situation he's good in. If there's someone who's a threat to us, I can think of no better—"

Checker's whole posture had knotted up as if he were about to have a seizure.

"Oh my God," I said. All my senses contracted and hardened. The room went flat and unreal.

"Cas—"

I couldn't string thoughts together. Logic scattered like dry leaves. "Tell me you're kidding," I said. "Christ almighty, tell me you're kidding! Tell me it was someone else!"

"I didn't say anything!" Checker shrieked.

Fuck, he'd *told* me he was going to call Rio— "No. No. I refuse to believe this. You must have misinterpreted. Rio doesn't come after people like you. He doesn't. He can't. He wouldn't. You're—you're lying, or you imagined it, or—"

"If it makes you feel better," Checker said in a strangled voice, "I think he's trying to protect you."

"Protect me from *what*?"

"I don't know!"

"I'm perfectly capable of protecting myself!"

"I know that!"

We both stared at somewhere that wasn't each other. Checker sniffed hard again, and knocked over a few things on his desktop to find a pack of tissues.

"Cas," he said hoarsely, "I'm really, really scared right now."

"He won't come after you," I said again, wondering why the words felt hollow. "He won't. He doesn't do that."

"He told me he would." His voice cracked. "I don't know

why you trust him the way you do, but he said—" His mouth worked.

"What did he say?"

"He said he was going to destroy everything I held dear and then—and then kill me, he *said* it—Cas, he was serious, and I don't know if he meant Arthur, or—"

I pulled out my phone. My hands were stiff.

"What are you— Are you crazy? You can't call him! Tell me you're not calling him!"

"I'm going to get to the bottom of this," I said. I had to. I had to.

"If he finds out I told you—that's what he was threatening me about! To keep you from knowing! If he finds out I told you what he said, *he is going to kill me,* do you understand? And—"

I closed my eyes. "Checker. I promise. I will not let anything happen to you."

"He could do it in a way that you don't know it's him! Do you understand what I'm saying? Please, please, *please,* if you have any regard for me whatsoever, *please* do not call him, and do not tell him I told you any of this!"

I curled my fingers around the phone. "Why did he threaten you in the first place?"

"To stop me from looking into your past," said Checker quietly. "He knows something for sure."

Rio knew something. About me.

"Cas," said Checker. "Whatever he knows, he thinks it's best if we don't find it. I think he's trying to protect you. Maybe—uh, maybe we should let him."

"What happened to 'knowing is always better than not knowing'?"

"Maybe there are exceptions."

Rio wanted to keep me in the dark. With Simon stalking me, and voices in my head, and notes in graveyards and Rio threatening Checker and my whole fucking past hurtling forward to crush me. He didn't want me to know.

Which felt . . . just fucking fine with me, because *I* didn't want to know. Since all this had started, every fiber in my being had been screaming about how much I didn't want to. I wanted to run. I wanted to push away, and forget, and take the helm of my own destiny. Bury everything else if I had to give myself a head injury to do it.

Rio apparently thought I should run, too.

A woman with short, steel-gray hair frowned down at a clipboard. "Have they told you—"

"Yes," I said.

She nodded. "I agree. Giving up is for those who would have us fail. We will never do something great if we run."

Too bad for whomever had just slithered out of my hidden memories, because in this case I was going to do my damnedest to try.

eleven

I LEFT Checker's place and walked back to my car. I sat down on the curb, holding my phone. A light breeze blew around me, and the sun wandered across the sky.

After the initial shock, my brain had recalibrated to believe what Checker had told me. It was hard to imagine him having any motivation to lie about this. Unless he was trying to put me off Rio, but he'd always been open about his discomfort with Rio's and my friendship—and he wasn't the type to play games.

Besides, I did know what Rio was. I knew what he was capable of. What Checker had claimed . . . wasn't out of the question.

What *was* out of the question was Rio going after someone innocent of real wrongdoing—someone like Checker—in a way I couldn't persuade him to stop. I was as bone-sure of that as I was about the type of man Rio was, the type of pleasure he derived from doing unspeakable things to people. After all, I'd known him a hell of a long time.

How long?

I ignored the question.

"He doesn't go after innocent people," I said aloud. "He doesn't." His faith prevented him, a religious faith that guided him to channel his proclivities into being judge, jury, torturer, and angel of death only to those he weighed as sufficiently evil.

That didn't include Checker. It couldn't. It would violate every axiom of understanding I had. Rio wasn't going to come after Checker or Arthur unless he thought he had to, and I was going to make sure he didn't ever feel like he did.

I dialed Rio's number.

The message from his permanent voice-mail box played, the one set up the same way mine was. "Call me back," I said. My throat was dry.

I hung up the phone and sat, and waited. The evening drew on and got chillier. I got up and drove back to the apartment I was using, watching for tails I couldn't see.

I'd made it back and was pushing open the door when my phone rang with a blocked number. "Hello?"

"Hello, Cas," said a flat baritone. Rio.

"Hi," I said. The word was tight. It was hard to know what to say.

I'd never been good at hiding anything, however, especially from someone who'd known me as long as Rio. "He told you."

"I guessed," I corrected. I shut the door and leaned against it, staring at a spot on the carpet. "You scared him. Badly."

"I meant to."

"Why?"

"Cas, it's important you not look into this. Will you trust me?"

"Of course," I said. "We'll stop. We already have. I didn't want to in the first place."

"I would have expected."

"Checker assumed you had a reason, you know. In between being petrified, he said he thought we should give it up anyway. You could have made your point without threatening him."

"Evidently."

"Rio . . ." I swallowed. "Please don't do that again."

He was silent.

"Checker is . . . important to me. I don't know if you can understand that, but—please at least remember it."

"I shall take it into consideration."

"I don't want to go back to . . ." I cleared my throat. "Before Checker and Arthur were in my life, I was— If something happened to either of them . . ." My voice rasped. I felt oddly naked saying this out loud, weak and maudlin, but I had to make him understand. "If it did, I'm not—I'm not sure what I'd do. I'm not sure what it would do to me."

Rio paused. "Understood."

"You're not going to come after him, are you?"

"No. Not this time."

"Not *any* time!"

He paused again. "I can't promise that, Cas."

"Yes," I said. Anger started to burn in me, hot and furious. "Yes, you can."

"Cas—"

"I can't be worried about this," I said. "This is not negotiable. Promise me, Rio."

He was a long time in answering. "All right."

The tension and frustration leaked out of me. I sank to the floor, my back against the door. "Thank you."

"Cas, how have you been?"

The change in topic threw me. "Fine," I said automatically. "What do you mean?"

"This . . . sudden interest in past events. Was there a reason?"

"I . . . I realized I . . ." I tried to steady myself. "I used to think it was normal, not being able to remember. It's not, is it?"

"No," he said. "But you should not look into it."

"Okay," I said. I trusted him.

"Good."

"I didn't want to anyway."

"Good."

I pressed my lips together. It was on my tongue to tell him about Simon, about the visions, about how I felt like I was starting to lose myself. But I didn't. Rio had said to ignore everything from my past, and those were all squarely out of my past.

I'd have to direct Arthur to stop looking into Simon, in addition to halting the investigation into me. Who knew what I'd do about the man himself. Maybe I *should* tell Rio about him, come to think of it—Rio was unaffected by telepaths, as far as I knew, and given what he'd said to Checker, I was willing to bet my Simon problem would swiftly cease to exist.

I opened my mouth, reconsidering, and then shut it again, reticence squirming through me at the idea of aiming Rio at Simon in what amounted to cold-blooded murder. . . .

That was weird. I didn't usually get squirrelly about killing people. At least not people who were so clearly a threat. I remembered the way I'd tried to convince Arthur out of going after him . . . not to mention the way I'd felt like I couldn't shoot Simon myself.

And I felt like vomiting.

Fuck. Simon had influenced me not to kill him, and telling Rio would effectively bust that, so I couldn't.

It really, really made me long for my enemies to take him down in a crossfire. Fucking *psychics*.

ARTHUR DIDN'T want to be dissuaded from investigating Simon, especially when I didn't give him a reason for calling it off. He'd been doing a lot of legwork for a man with a fucked-up leg. First, he'd kept his promise to keep questioning people at the cemetery and discovered that not only had a next of kin been listed, on a record that had mysteriously gotten lost somehow, but that someone had been doing periodic check-ins by phone. When Arthur had pulled the records, the numbers all snaked back to countries on the other side of the world—Greece, Bahrain, India, Sri Lanka, Malaysia.

The people Arthur had spoken to at the cemetery had all enthused about how this person whose name they couldn't quite recall was such a nice man, who cared so much, and they were happy to keep checking on the wall niche for him. Some of them said they were sure he'd stopped by, or maybe been there when my urn had been entombed in the wall . . . but none of them could agree on either a description of his features or the year it had happened. Or what relationship he was supposed to have had with me.

Simon had made himself well liked and yet unmemorable, and gotten what he needed without technically brainwashing anyone. After all, people helped out likeable folk all the time, and forgot unmemorable ones.

"I'm surprised he didn't just make *me* decide he was my friend," I said to Arthur. I'd come to the apartment I was lending him to tell him to quit his Simon efforts, and Arthur lounged back on the futon on his good side while I sat on a folding chair.

"You're not predisposed to it," Arthur said. "You'd be wary of him whether he made himself likeable or not. But Russell, you know you're mixed up about him, too."

I knew. I pressed my fingers against my forehead as I remembered something. "He saw where Checker lives."

"*Fuck*, Russell. I'll get them out of there." He picked up his phone. "See, this right here is why when you say stop, I hear red alert. We gotta keep looking into this guy. Even if he messed you up in the head—especially if he messed you up. Can you see that, at least?"

He didn't wait for an answer before dialing Checker. A fair amount of profanity ensued from the other end of the line.

"I should've known, I should've known," I heard Checker say more than once. I also definitely caught my name.

They were right. I should've seen Simon's knowledge as an immediate, actionable threat, and I hadn't. Only one logical explanation offered itself for *that* kind of oversight.

Of course I'd trusted a telepath when I shouldn't have.

Belated guilt washed over me. I might not be able to prevent Simon from messing with my neurons, but I was the one he was targeting. I was the reason Arthur and Checker and Pilar were getting tangled up with a psychic. Again.

We'd get the brain entrainment up and running, and then, if Simon was still dogging my heels, I'd leave town and give him the runaround for a while. He could chase me until he got tired of it. Or until the strange images rising in my head won and drove me insane.

We stood on the roof of a silo, farmland quilting the land around us to the horizon, and Simon laughed. "We're here; we're alive; we're free!"

I'm not, I thought, but I didn't tell him. Time enough for that later.

Fuck, I needed to get a handle on this.

Arthur hung up the phone.

"It's not Simon who's making me tell you to stop," I said, hoping that was the whole truth.

"You can't know that, Russell."

"It's not." I braced myself. "It's Rio."

Arthur stared at me. I was pretty sure he'd momentarily stopped breathing.

"I know you have a hard-on for Rio," I said. "Quit it. He's telling me we should stop, and I trust him, and you and Checker fucking promised me that you wouldn't keep going if I told you no."

"We did, but—"

"But?"

"Russell! You got another psychic after you. You saw what the last one did. This isn't a matter of preference anymore!"

"Wait, you two digging into my past is a matter of *preference*?"

He glared at me. "Not what I mean, and you know it."

"We already know this Simon guy's a wuss. Objectively, Arthur; we know it *objectively*. He could've gotten whatever he wanted from all of us without anybody knowing, and he didn't, because he's a wimp. Rio's a lot more dangerous than he is."

"You don't know that. Maybe this Simon fellow just doesn't have enough telepathic-type skill to do what you say. But he could still—"

"He can erase himself from security cameras!"

"And maybe that's Telepathy 101. You don't know what's easy for him and what's not."

He had a point. I didn't like it when that happened. "Rio said stop, so we stop," I said. "You really want to get you and Checker on his bad side? This is *Rio* we're talking about."

I hoped he wouldn't press the issue. I didn't want to tell him Rio had explicitly threatened them. Arthur was the martyr type; it would probably make him even more stubborn.

"Look into this instead," I said, pulling out a sheaf of printouts. "Checker got me that list of Pourdry's businesses and connections. If we shut him down, you and Pilar won't have to be looking over your shoulders anymore. And you guys can be manual labor for me on all the hardware stuff I'm about to need, too. There's a ton of shit to do without making extra work for ourselves."

"This conversation isn't over," Arthur said.

"But you'll stop looking into him for now?"

He hesitated.

"Arthur. This is important to me, and it's important to Rio. You do not want to piss *either* of us off."

"There's stuff you're not telling me, isn't there?"

My lungs clenched. "Yeah."

He made a face and reached out a hand. "Give me the Pourdry stuff."

Feeling victorious, I handed it over. It was kind of nice that Arthur's and my relationship had progressed to where he'd go with my word, even if it took a little convincing.

I should have known Arthur would consider any respect or trust he might've ever had for me to be utterly compromised when it came to a psychic being involved. And I should have remembered he was a very good actor.

twelve

THE NEXT two weeks were a thankfully Simon-free flurry of activity. Arthur and I went out almost every day trying to track down Pourdry's operation, but it was so well hidden by layers of legitimate-looking fronts that we kept hitting dead ends. From what we could determine, Pourdry never even showed his face personally anywhere, but instead was a mastermind from behind the scenes—we couldn't find a single person who'd admit to having met him.

So far, though the voices and nightmares still lurked and snapped at me with increasing and exhausting frequency, at least I hadn't fallen apart in the middle of a dangerous situation again. Either I was fooling myself, or I was getting better at ignoring the mental lapses when it mattered. Maybe Rio was on the money about the right path being denial.

And in between times, the little army of Arthur, Checker, Pilar, and I got a crash course in cell phone hacking. Checker was right: it was shockingly, terrifyingly easy. I'd calculated I needed at least two hundred and eighty-three of the fake cell tower signals to saturate LA effectively, and Checker had acquired our little hotspot boxes from various online companies through anonymized accounts and then had them overnighted to us. Each was about the size and shape of a wireless router, and even the power question turned out to have an easy solution—the boxes were low-draw enough that it had taken Checker about five minutes to sketch out a way to rig them to a solar panel and a rechargeable battery.

I could put them on top of roofs, telephone poles, overpasses . . . anywhere people wouldn't be likely to notice them. I had a lot more flexibility with placing them than I would have had with the Signet Devices themselves, because all I needed to do was get to people's cell phones, not solve a delicate constraint satisfaction problem. After all, the app itself would be doing that part—Checker had already coded up my algorithm for deployment, and I didn't even bother QA-testing the software. I knew the math was right.

The ease of it all would have been discouraging from a national security standpoint, if one were more worried about national security than I was.

With Arthur and me out investigating Pourdry, Checker and Pilar stayed at one of my crappy apartments and did the lion's share of the deployment preparation, reprogramming and waterproofing the hotspot boxes and wiring them up to their new power supplies. The construction was monotonous enough for me to be glad to get out, even for our frustratingly fruitless field trips.

"How are you going to set them?" Pilar asked, on the evening she, Checker, and I sat exhausted and stared at the monstrous stacks of rigged-up boxes. Arthur had taken off on some sort of personal errand. "I mean, are you just going to climb up and superglue them on top of lampposts and stuff?"

"Yeah," I said. "I'll do that part of it. Some of the places might be hard to get to." That, and I had to follow the proper mathematics for reaching my critical population density, hitting the spots with optimal and maximally independent mass flow rates of people.

Pilar giggled. "I just got an image of you swinging from a traffic light over the PCH. Okay, so once these are all set, they put your app on everyone's phones, and done?"

"Sort of," I said. "There'll be a small delta. The app will download automatically whenever a smartphone comes within range, so it'll keep downloading to more and more until we're saturated, and from there all the affected cell phones should start coordinating with each other to put out the subliminal audio signals."

"I'm just looking forward to everything getting back to normal," Pilar said. "Normal but with less crime, we hope, right?"

"Yeah. And if we're lucky, these things will start weakening all the big criminal organizations, including Pourdry's. Once we can get to him, you won't have to play musical apartments anymore."

"There's still—um," Checker said.

"The telepath who's stalking Cas?" Pilar piped up cheerfully.

"Oh, right, him," Checker said, which probably should have tipped me off but didn't. "Him and . . . other loose ends."

He meant Rio. I'd reassured him multiple times that Rio had promised his safety, but he didn't seem to entirely believe me. It irked me. "Simon hasn't shown his face in weeks," I said. "Maybe he finally listened to me and is leaving me alone. If so, we're well shot of him."

"We can't keep living our lives like he's around every corner," Pilar said. "Like Cas says, maybe he just . . . left. I say, once you and Arthur get this Pourdry dude arrested, we go back to our lives."

That *also* should have tipped me off, but didn't. Pilar was a better liar than Checker was.

"Get Pourdry arrested?" I scoffed. "What has Arthur been telling you? That's not *my* plan."

"Checker and I will start putting together evidence on him," Pilar continued brightly. "Right, Checker? So the police will be able to put him away instead of him wiggling out because he's got things sorted out so well."

I rolled my eyes.

There was a knock on the door.

I went over and opened it to reveal a tall Asian man in a long duster. There was a yell and a bang from behind me.

"It's *fine*," I said without turning around, then added to Rio, "I didn't know you were in town. Hi."

From the sound of it, Pilar and Checker had rapidly vacated the front room of the apartment and escaped into the kitchen or one of the bedrooms, but I couldn't help a slight sting of guilt—I'd forgotten to mention to them that I didn't mind Rio knowing where my safe houses were. I stepped out into the hallway and shut the door behind me. "What's up?"

"Cas," Rio said. "Where is he?"

"Where's who?" I asked.

"Simon."

A funny clang sounded through my head. My worlds colliding.

Rio, how is she?

As well as can be expected.

"I don't know," I said, through stiff lips.

"But he has contacted you."

"Yes," I said.

"He is now missing."

"I—I don't have anything to do with that." The last time I'd seen him was at the warehouse. Maybe security had gotten him after all.

"Your friends do. They did not include you?"

The ground shifted underneath me. His words weren't making sense. "What? No, you're wrong."

"Am I?" Rio had raised his voice slightly, and before I could answer, Arthur spoke from behind him.

"She was compromised." He limped into view from down the hallway, still using a crutch to keep his weight off his injured side. "We didn't have a choice."

He and Rio stared at each other. "Take me to him," Rio said.

"What the fuck," I said. "Take *me* to him."

Arthur sucked his breath through his teeth. Then he did what I never would have expected. He turned to Rio and said, "You're immune to these guys, right?"

"I am given to understand that, yes."

"Then find out what he wants, and fix this," Arthur said. "You seem to be on Cas's side, Lord only knows why, but if you are, *fix this.*"

"It is far more complicated than you know," said Rio.

Arthur snorted. "I don't care, man. Do it."

"Take me to him," Rio repeated.

THEY'D LOCKED Simon in an empty warehouse Arthur maintained as a temporary bolt-hole. Checker, Pilar, and Arthur had all been in on it.

I decided I hated all of them.

Of course, Arthur insisted on updating Checker and Pilar before we left for the warehouse, and he came back out to tell us both of them were coming, too. I was suspicious the real reason for that was Checker wanted to be near enough I could protect him, rather than waiting it all out in a location Rio knew about and might come back to without me.

I'd *told* him that wasn't going to happen. I'd have to yell at him again later.

Rio had a black Hummer. I drove with him, as I was still too furious at the rest of them. Of course, I couldn't decide whether I was furious at Rio, too.

He knows something for sure, Checker had said.

And now he had come asking about Simon. He had *known* to come asking about Simon.

We pulled into a deserted parking strip off an alley that would fit about five cars and was well hidden from the street. Arthur pulled in next to us with Checker and Pilar and got out to unwind the heavy, padlocked chain over the warehouse door. He hauled the door open.

The inside was cold and utilitarian, with not even a mattress, just a pallet of bedding in one corner. Simon had been sitting cross-legged on the blankets. When we came in, he scrambled to his feet, his face going slack with shock.

And then his expression clouded over, and he marched straight at Rio.

"You hung up on me," he accused. "What did you think was going on here? You don't ever hang up on me! Not about this!"

Well, *that* was not what I had been expecting.

Simon jabbed a hand at Arthur, the gesture encompassing Checker and Pilar, who had piled in behind him. "None of you have the slightest idea what you're playing at! Your friend could die, and I'm the only one who can help her, and none of you will get over yourselves enough to see what's staring you in the face!"

"Wait," I said. "What friend?"

"*You,* Cas," said Checker.

Right.

Simon poked a finger right up a few inches from Rio's eyes. "I *do not contact you* unless it's an emergency. When I contact you, you take it seriously, no questions asked. Do you understand!"

"I'm here, am I not?" said Rio, with a small bite of humor.

"So you two know each other," I said.

"Yes," answered Rio.

"Unfortunately," spat Simon.

Rio raised an eyebrow at him.

"You call this protection?" ranted Simon. "Her job?

Where did she learn to do that, huh? And you halfway across the globe—"

"If that's what you're concerned about, she's fine," said Rio. I again didn't connect what he was talking about until he continued, "Cas can take care of herself."

"Hold the phone," I said. "Stop talking about me like I'm not here, and explain before I start shooting."

"Cas does what she likes," said Rio. "If that is what disturbs you, then you have wasted my time."

"And why does she like it? I suppose you're the one who called her Cas in the first place, aren't you?"

"It's what *I* prefer." I raised my voice and waved my hand in between them. "What the hell are you two on about? And why do *you*," I added to Simon, "think you have any say in the way I live my life, or what Rio calls me, or anything else?"

"Apologies, Cas," said Rio. "I believe I traveled here in error. If you have time for a meal before I depart, your company at dinner would not go amiss."

"Yeah," I said. Dinner would give me a chance to pick his brain and get some questions answered. "I'll see you then."

"*Wait,*" said Simon.

Rio paused in the midst of turning to go.

Why would he still care what the man had to say? Why had he cared in the first place?

"I swear to you this is serious." Simon's voice was so intense it shook. "Something happened, didn't it?"

I was about to mock the ridiculous vagueness of his question until Rio answered, "Yes."

"I'm standing right here," I said.

"We need to talk," said Simon to Rio. "As soon as possible. Now."

Rio didn't say anything, but he turned his head a fraction back toward Simon and then swept out the door, his duster swirling as he left. Simon took the invitation and hustled to catch up. None of us tried to stop them.

I considered following, but even I couldn't track Rio if he wanted to lose me.

"I think we might be out of our league," murmured Checker.

"You want to know what I think?" I said, whirling around to them. "I think every single fucking one of you needs to stop messing with my life. I *told* you—"

"You're not the only one who was in danger," Arthur cut in. "We didn't know what this guy would do."

"So what was your plan? Keep him locked up here forever?"

"Well, we hadn't figured that out yet," Pilar said. Checker glared at her. "What? We hadn't!"

"If someone can manipulate minds, you're always going to second-guess what you do with them," Checker pointed out, in his I'm-trying-to-sound-reasonable voice. "For the record, we kicked ass kidnapping a psychic. It took some ingenuity. A little respect might be in order."

"Right now you're lucky I'm not pitching you out a window."

"We were just worried about you," Pilar said.

"And ourselves," added Checker. "Don't worry, we didn't try to interrogate him about anything that—about you, or anything that would bother you, or, uh, anyone else." His eyes darted at Arthur. By "anyone else" he definitely meant Rio. "But having this guy out there following you? Poking in on all of us? Acting like he has some kind of interest? Look at the life you lead, Cas. You can't ignore something like that. The fact that you were willing to is—it's suspect."

"So just the presence of a psychic turns you all against me," I said. "He doesn't even have to do anything."

They all shifted uncomfortably.

"You might think I'm a weak-minded idiot, but these guys can't get to Rio," I said. "Whatever he says to do about Simon, you listen."

"It's not about being weak-minded," Arthur tried to argue. "Dawna got me doing all sorts of—"

"Whatever Rio says to do, you listen," I repeated. "And don't you *ever* go behind my back like this again. Not unless you have concrete, iron-clad evidence I'm being manipulated. I was in perfect possession of my faculties when I said to *stop looking into Simon,* and you did it anyway. Don't feed me that line about thinking the rest of you were in danger, either, because that would necessitate one of you actually having to be *in danger* from him. I was the only fucking person he talked to."

"We don't know that—" Checker tried.

I glowered at him.

"Cas," Pilar said soberly. "Whether that's true or not— and you might be right—but it doesn't change us all being super worried about this. Worried for you, *and* worried for us. You can't blame us."

Even if she was right, I wasn't about to admit it. "I sure as hell can," I said.

thirteen

RIO AND Simon came back in. Simon was pale, and his arms were wrapped around his body as if something had scared him badly. I really hoped that something was Rio.

God, I was furious at everybody right now.

Well, except Rio.

"Cas," said Rio. "Please allow this man to read you."

And there went the last person I didn't want to punch in the face.

"What?" I exploded.

"It has been brought to my attention that Dawna Polk's attack on you last year may have been more harmful than we knew at the time."

A sick uneasiness sloshed through me at the reference to Dawna Polk. I'd barely been able to acknowledge the true strength of her attack to Arthur, let alone myself. I definitely didn't want it confirmed by some two-bit telepath with no claim on my life. "I'm *fine*," I insisted. "Why would this guy have anything to do with that anyway?"

"As I believe you have already deduced, he is like her," said Rio.

"Which is why I'd like very much to smash his head in for following me," I said. "Only he won't let me."

"Cas," said Rio. "I do not believe him a threat."

"Rio—"

"Besides which," he continued, "he could already have examined you without your permission, and has refrained. I do not like him, but he is no threat."

I was suddenly, acutely embarrassed that Arthur, Checker, and Pilar were in the room. *You were the one who said you'd go with whatever Rio suggested,* I reminded myself mockingly.

But I hadn't expected *this.*

"Rio," I said. "I don't understand."

He looked down at me, his expression unreadable. "Trust me."

It was weird. I'd never had Rio ask that of me before. I *did* trust him, but . . .

I looked back at Checker. He ducked his face away.

"Wait," said Pilar.

Rio turned to her, very slowly, the way a mountain might reposition itself before it falls on someone. Pilar swallowed and backed up a step. "I just. I wanted to ask, um—why can't Cas have an explanation? Why so, uh, so mysterious?" Her back hit the wall, and she swallowed again. Rio hadn't moved.

He turned back to me. "Cas. Trust me."

Fuck.

"Fine," I said. I turned away from Checker and Pilar and Arthur and looked Simon square in the face. "You do anything other than what Rio says you can, I will fucking end you." I ignored the fact that I had no idea either how I would know he was overstepping or how I would make good on such a promise.

Trust me, Rio had said.

Simon inhaled deeply, and his eyes drilled into mine. Intense. Liquid. The weight of a thousand years in his gaze. I tried to break the stare and couldn't—

A cottage in the woods, a desert sun, cold and darkness. Stars, pain, danger, a crowded city, racing through the night until our lungs burned—

"Rio," I choked out.

Rio's arm whipped around Simon's throat, and he levered the other man around and slammed him face-first into the cement floor of the warehouse like he was pile-driving him. Then he stood over him.

"Cas," said Checker behind me, urgently. "Cas, are you all right?"

I didn't answer. Strong hands gripped my shoulders supportively. Arthur.

"Cas?" ventured Pilar.

Simon coughed, curling on the floor. He didn't seem to be able to form words. "Done?" said Rio.

"What—the hell—" Simon spat out. Drops of blood sprinkled the ground. Rio must have busted his nose against it.

"Walk with me," said Rio.

"Rio, I want to know—" I started, but he shook his head. "Trust me, Cas."

Simon pushed himself to his feet. None of us helped him.

"What the *bloody* hell was that!" he screeched at Rio. Flecks of blood spattered his shirt as he shouted.

"Did you see what you needed to?" asked Rio.

"You don't lay hands on me, you hear? You do not—"

Rio drove out one arm and grabbed Simon's throat. His words cut off in a strangled choke.

Rio didn't even try to push him backward, just stood there with his hand on the man's neck like a vise, almost blandly. Simon pawed at his arm, but it was like pushing against an iron bar. His face went pale. His eyes flickered to me for a moment.

I said nothing. I trusted Rio.

Simon's movements started to lose articulation. His hands fell. The lids of his eyes got heavy.

Rio let go.

Simon fell again, gasping, his hands shaking a few inches from his bruised throat. "Good," Rio said. "You passed."

What? "Rio?" I said.

"Cas," he said. "This is important. Did you feel any urge to stop me?"

"What? No. Grind his fucking face into the ground."

"Good," Rio said again.

"You—you—" Simon's voice rasped. *"You—"*

Rio raised an eyebrow.

Simon stopped trying to talk. He pushed himself up, still coughing, and barely staggered upright before he wheeled to find the wall and braced his hands against it, trying to breathe. Eventually he slid back to the ground and sat.

Rio waited. I followed his lead.

Simon buried his face against his hands. "It's bad," he murmured.

Rio stiffened. Then he swept down, yanked Simon up by the elbow, and dragged them both outside again.

"Fuck," Checker said weakly.

It's bad. What did that mean?

"He was testing him, wasn't he?" Pilar said. "Seeing if he would get Cas to, uh—interfere or something? Save his life."

That did seem like something Rio would do.

"What did he mean by 'it's bad'?" she asked.

"Pilar," growled Checker. *"None of us know."*

He'd said that for my benefit, I was sure. We might not know, but we could suspect.

Fifteen months ago, Dawna Polk had royally fucked me up. Even more than we'd known.

Well, wasn't this fun.

Checker must have been thinking along the same lines.

"Doesn't this invalidate the deal she made with, um, with Rio? She was supposed to—supposed to—"

"Put everything back where she found it?" I said, with a heavy dose of sarcasm.

"Yeah," he said quietly.

"You mean as part of the 'she doesn't come after you, you don't go after her' thing?" Pilar asked.

"It was more like 'she doesn't come after us, Rio doesn't go after her,'" I corrected. She'd beaten us handily. Of course, we'd beaten her, too. The reminder gave me a jolt of good cheer.

Until I remembered what our victory had cost the world. I thought of Pilar's cousin and brother, and wondered if she would have agreed with the choice we'd made.

Maybe we should never have gone up against Pithica at all. So what if they murdered a few innocent people every so often? After all, so did Rio. So did I.

"Well, if this guy's like Dawna, maybe he can, uh—fix you, or something," Pilar ventured.

I took it as a mark in the "better person" column that I didn't punch her. She quailed back from my expression anyway.

Arthur was markedly silent. I avoided his eyes. After all, Dawna had fucked with him, too.

Rio and Simon swept back in. Or rather, Rio swept, and Simon stumbled at his side. Rio still hadn't given up the grip on his elbow. "Cas," Rio said.

"Yeah."

"How is your sanity?"

I choked. "My *what*?"

"I told you," said Simon, "even if she hasn't noticed it yet, this is a problem—"

"Cas," Rio said again.

I shifted my weight from foot to foot.

Failing, was the honest answer.

I wasn't sure anyone but Arthur suspected that yet.

Checker and Pilar might know something was wrong, might know I had a defunct memory with more shreds tearing through all the time, but they didn't know how dangerous those shreds felt. How much power they had to fracture me . . . or how scared I was of losing to them.

"Cas?" Checker asked, and Jesus, it sounded like he was about to cry.

"What does this guy want?" I said to Rio.

"To help you," Rio answered.

"Help me how?"

"You know what he does," Rio said. "Cas. You need assistance."

Stay with him, whispered a stray memory. *He'll help you.*

I ignored it.

"You want him to go in my head," I said slowly. "You want him to . . . to what, rearrange me?"

"You aren't well," Simon said earnestly. "It's all— It's going wrong. Please. Let me fix it."

"It," I echoed. "You mean my brain. Me."

Simon winced. Rio simply met my eyes, his gaze level.

"No," I said. *"No."* The world was collapsing around me, the warehouse too cold and too empty and too full of watching eyes. The prospect of hands reaching into my brain, wrenching around the pieces of me I was having so much trouble keeping a hold of already—

I was barely keeping my snarling past at bay, the memories that wanted to erase me and twist me into a different person and a different place. Now Simon wanted me to let him do that *willingly*—submit myself to being warped into something else, when I'd been fighting so hard against exactly that? The horror of it ballooned inside me.

The violation.

"Cas," Rio said. "As I said, I do not like this man, but this may be the only way."

"You have to understand." Simon's too-earnest voice dug under my skin, sprouted parasites and turned me inside out until I was no longer me. "Cassandra—Cas—this isn't going to stop. I saw enough to know—this is going to—it's going to kill you eventually, if you don't let me help you."

"Then it kills me." My voice felt disconnected. Already dead.

"Cassandra," Simon gasped, and it was almost worth everything to see him so crushed by that.

This was my life. My mind. Not Rio's, and sure as fuck not Simon's. They wanted me to address an inconvenient breakdown of my sanity by rewriting me, and that wasn't a solution.

That would never be a solution.

Dying was preferable to ceding control to this man.

fourteen

SHE WON'T LAST, predicted a woman's voice.

It's flawed, but I believe—

This will work. We'll fight them. We'll save ourselves.

Half images and the shapes of sounds sprayed through my thoughts, as if seeing Simon had cracked a high-pressure pipe. Trying to push back against them all, I stole Arthur's SUV and drove back to the apartment where we'd been making the fake cell signal boxes.

I can't save me. Neither can you. Nobody can.

What do you want me to do, disappear?

No. Die.

I loaded up all our little homemade electronics, cardboard box upon cardboard box filled with the things. My compact devices that would deploy my program stealthily, silently, until it was everywhere.

"They're everywhere," someone said, and started laughing. *Cold filled my mouth and I tried to scream, but only gulped it into my lungs—*

I stacked the final load into the SUV and slammed the door. If I did one fucking thing before I fulfilled Simon's predictions and went insane and died, it would be this. I would save LA, and make that my fucking legacy.

I'd done the calculations: hitting everywhere I needed to would take me more than a hundred hours, even if I mostly avoided bad traffic. But that was okay. A hundred hours was nothing. I was perfectly okay with not seeing anyone for a week, anyway.

Arthur tried to call me, but I didn't pick up. He was probably pissed I'd left them alone with Rio—well, both Rio and a telepath. But I trusted Rio not to attack them, and I'd run out of patience for their squeamishness about him. As for Simon . . .

Cassandra, this is the best way. I only want to help you.

Well, I'd told them we'd let Rio decide. Rio could fucking decide.

He clearly didn't think Simon was a threat, anyway, if he was telling me to let him—

Fuck.

I flattened the gas pedal with my foot and then stabbed the brake as I got to my next location. The SUV jerked like it wanted to tumble over to protest the way I was handling it.

I broke into buildings, scaled utility poles, hung out over the side of bridges. Climbed walls and tall decorative palms and art installations. Drive, set, drive. The monotony boiled my brain and fatigue made my eyes ache, but I kept going. Better that than thinking about the phantoms flitting through my brain, or Simon, or Rio, or whatever the hell was happening to me.

Eventually some of these boxes would stop working, or be found and removed, but by then everyone's phones would have the app anyway. I'd just keep checking on where I'd planted these, keep knitting my net together wherever a tiny tear appeared, so every time someone brought a new mobile into the network it would become part of the grid.

Rush hour flooded the streets along with the dawn, and I pulled over and slept in the SUV for two hours before continuing. Drive, rinse, repeat.

Arthur tried to call again. Then Checker. I got a text that said, WORRIED ABT U. AT LEAST TELL US UR OK.

I'M FUCKING WORKING, I texted back, and kept going.

Her heart can't sustain this. The words slithered in my ear like they were real.

I understand the tradeoffs, said someone else. *We're still within the realm of acceptability, if we can finish.*

If only I could finish this . . .

Then who cared what came next.

RIO CALLED on the fourth day.

I picked up for him.

"Cas," he said. "Are you well?"

Health is not the determining factor. Usefulness is more heavily weighted.

You've transformed me into a utility function.

We're all utility functions. Didn't you know that?

"I'm perfect," I gritted out over the noise in my brain. I was seventy-two percent done.

"I would like to talk to you, Cas. Will you meet me?"

I closed my eyes. Wind blew behind my eyelids with the echo of hail and fear.

"Cas?"

"Yeah," I said. "I'll meet you. But about your psychic buddy, the answer's no. I don't want to have to keep saying it."

"Very well," Rio said, after only a hitch of a pause. "When and where?"

"I'm finishing a project," I said. "What day of the week is it?"

"Friday."

"I'll meet you Monday."

"Very well. Until Monday." He hung up.

As exhausting as everyone else was being, thank Christ at least Rio respected my decisions.

I never got to Monday. Sunday night, as I was down to the last handful of wireless devices clattering in the bottom of a box, I got six texts in a row from Checker.

GOT INTEL ON POURDRY
ARTHUR CANT REACH U
WONT WAIT
CALL ME
NOW
CAS

I hit the button to dial him back. "You'd better not be making this up to force me to call."

"What? Cas! We wouldn't do that."

"Just like you wouldn't kidnap someone from my past without telling me?"

"Cas!"

"Where's Arthur?"

"Pourdry's organization is already choking. Everyone's is. Anyone who relies on any sort of structured criminal organization is seeing it collapse out from under them. I know you're setting the boxes, I mean, we figured that's what you've been doing—but I still don't understand how this could be working so quickly."

That was faster than I'd expected, too. A fierce pride bubbled up—it was working, and even better than we'd hoped. "It's the people who had doubts," I conjectured. "The ones who wanted to quit but were too scared or swept up. They woke up and just did it, almost all at once this week."

"I don't know what kinds of consequences this is going to have," Checker said. "I really don't. I've been running every predictive algorithm I have, but none of my priors apply anymore—this could be good, or it could be—I don't know."

"Stop with the hating," I said. "It's good. I told you it would be good. We're already having an impact."

"I hope so, but—what if there's retribution? What if this destabilizes LA in other ways? What if—"

"What if nothing. What's going on with Arthur?"

"All those dead ends on Pourdry you two were hitting last week suddenly aren't dead ends anymore. Arthur wants to take advantage, jump as fast as possible. He's been going out, questioning people—and now— I keep telling him to wait for you, but he said it doesn't make sense to wait. And he got tangled up in helping some of Pourdry's former associates after they ran, and tonight they want to go take down one of his smuggling rings. Cas, he needs you. He still isn't all the way healed."

"Tell him to hang on," I said. "I only have a few more of the boxes to set. I'll be done within two hours. Tell him I'm coming."

My phone beeped.

"Two hours, Checker. Tell him I'm coming. I gotta go." I hit the button to switch calls, trying to remember who else had my direct line right now. I'd used this phone for some of the Pourdry inquiries the week before, so it was a decent handful. "Hello?"

"Cassu-san!" effused a far-too-enthusiastic voice in my ear. Yamamoto, one of my most frequent regular clients. He had a heavy Japanese accent I was pretty sure was faked— I'd heard he'd grown up in Detroit. "Cassu-san, I am so glad I still catch you at this number. There's something going on in LA, yes? Something big. Something bad. You have heard the things?"

"LA always has big, bad things going on," I answered. That was the whole point of the brain entrainment, after all.

Wait. From what Checker had said, Yamamoto probably *meant* the brain entrainment. Holy shit.

"It doesn't sound like that big a deal to me," I said, the lie brittle. "I guess? I'm not fussed about it."

"No, no, you should be. This is huge. Is happening to everybody. So strange. Trouble in the ranks. People gone, poof, no loyalty. Profits down. Do you hear me, Cassu-san? Profits down!"

"Well, you know me—as long as *I'm* still making money, I'm good." I winced. That sounded too cavalier. "Do you think it's going to get worse?" I tried.

"Worse! How can it get worse!"

"Okay," I said.

Yamamoto seemed stymied I wasn't joining him in outrage. Shit. I'd never been good at playing a part.

"Um," I said. "So. What do you want us to do about it?"

"I think we take drastic step," Yamamoto said. "I think we all meet. Talk. Compare the things happening."

"Who's 'we'?" I said slowly.

"We who work for ourselves, of course," Yamamoto exclaimed. "The real men—and women, gomennasai—who do not submit to the authority of a fascist government. The brave ones who carve our own path!"

"Let me get this straight," I said. "You're trying to get all the criminals in Los Angeles to sit down at a table and work together? And do what?"

"We figure this out. We show the man it cannot keep us down. Cannot take our business!"

"You think what's happening is the *government's* doing?" I said.

"Who else? Who else has the sneaky power in the shadows? The CIA maybe—or the black groups, the ones they do not tell us about. And it is just Los Angeles. The other cities, my business there is not affected, but Los Angeles, this city is very large part of my operation. It is terrible problem."

"Yeah," I said. "Uh, yeah."

"It keeps up, I will be drove to other cities. All of us will. LA will be ghost town. Collapse!"

"I doubt that," I said dryly. "You don't really think criminal enterprise is propping up the whole economy, do you?"

"Cassu-san! You must take me seriously! The CIA may expand to other cities as well. Maybe other countries. The whole world. They will destroy our business!"

I liked Yamamoto. He hired me a few times a year for a lot of money, and I didn't want to see his little empire destroyed. But . . .

Unintended side effects. Yamamoto *did* run a criminal racket. If the worst side effect of slashing the crime rate in LA was that Yamamoto had to find a new career, then I wouldn't lose very much sleep.

Maybe a little. But not much.

On the other hand, if every criminal enterprise in Los Angeles suddenly banded together . . .

That would be a *very bad* unintended side effect.

"When are you having this meeting?" I said.

"Tonight!" he crowed. "Eleven o'clock. At Maddox pub. You know the place."

I did know the place. I was banned from it, in fact, thanks to a shootout with none other than the Lorenzo crime family. Who would probably also be invited. Fantastic.

"I'll be there," I said.

"I know you help, Cassu-san," Yamamoto enthused. "I see you then!"

Unbelievable. Now I wasn't going to be able to give Arthur an assist. Nothing was ever fucking easy.

I hung up and dialed Rio.

"Hello."

"Hey," I said. "How would you feel about helping bust apart a human trafficking ring?"

Arthur was going to murder me.

fifteen

ARTHUR THREW a fit at me at the prospect of working with Rio, as expected. Which was why I'd set it up first. Easier to ask forgiveness than permission, and all that.

Better than Arthur ending up dead because he was injured and didn't have proper backup.

I finished placing the two hundred and eighty-third signal box and then drove straight to Grealy's pub, a greasy oyster bar owned by Cheryl Maddox. It was a regular meeting place of all manner of shady characters—I'd missed it tremendously since being persona non grata.

The place had remodeled since I'd last been around. Like Arthur's office, that probably had something to do with it getting destroyed in a firefight. Now the large front window was gone, replaced with an aggressively bricked-over wall sporting an angry mural of jagged red and black that made it look more like an underground club than a bar.

I pulled open the door, the "Closed" sign rattling on it, and ducked into the darkness.

The inside was a little newer-looking, but still just as

seedy as I remembered. Various disreputable types hunched over drinks at the wooden tables. Nobody seemed to be talking to each other yet, but that was normal for Grealy's. What wasn't normal was that they'd all arrived with the express purpose of eventually talking to each other.

We don't have to like each other. We just have to be effective, someone observed, in a different time and place.

"Ah, hello again, Russell," said a voice back in the present.

I pulled myself back to reality with an effort. "I'm still pissed at you for fucking up our operation on the docks," I said by way of greeting.

Malcolm gave me a half smile. "I only do the Madre's bidding."

"And how is Mama Lorenzo?"

She probably still had her sights set on me. The head of the LA Mafia hadn't declared open war on me or my dealings, but she hadn't only put her own family off hiring me—for a while now I'd heard whispers she was blackballing me for work. I didn't know exactly why, but I could guess. It wasn't like I hadn't had it out with her men more than once—including here at Grealy's—and Mama Lorenzo didn't seem the type to forgive and forget.

There were a lot of reasons I didn't want the Mob to control Los Angeles. Hell, they'd already expanded to control large chunks of the police, the media, and the entire criminal underground. They needed to learn to stay in their own fucking corner.

"The Madre is well. Concerned, like all the rest of us," Malcolm answered. He squinted down at me. "I wouldn't have thought you independent operators were as affected by this."

I thought fast. "Well, I do mostly work alone. But my clients are big fancy crime families like yours."

"True."

Damn. Despite everything, I did miss working for them.

A buxom bleached-blond woman with more tattoos than the last time I'd seen her came out from behind the bar and stood in front of me, arms crossed against her ample chest. "Thought I said you was banned, Russell."

I raised my hands. "Just here for the meeting, Cheryl, I promise."

She cast aggressive eyes on Malcolm. "You're a Lorenzo, ain't you? You two planning on shooting at each other again tonight?"

"No, ma'am," Malcolm said.

She snorted. "On good terms again, are you?"

"The Madre deeply apologizes, again," Malcolm said. "Like Miss Russell, I'm only here for the meeting."

Cheryl huffed. She clearly hadn't forgiven any of us. I couldn't say I blamed her.

"You two got a day pass," she said. "The minute this nonsense is over, you're out. You hear?"

Malcolm and I both meekly murmured our acquiescence. "Thank you, Ms. Maddox," he added.

"I don't wanna make this harder for everyone else, is all," she said. "You still ain't welcome here. But, Russell, I'm glad to see you're still kicking." She stalked away.

"Someone try to kill you lately?" Malcolm asked me.

"No, she's still talking about you guys."

"It wasn't personal, you understand," Malcolm said.

"Water under the bridge. I've ended up on the other side of a lot of folks in town at times." To be honest, it was a relief to be talking to someone where I felt like I had my footing, even if he was a trained assassin. And at least Malcolm could be professional about it, unlike his boss. Some people never got over it if you tried to kill them.

Malcolm pulled out a chair for me at a nearby table and then took one for himself, next to me but one table over. I appreciated it—he wasn't trying to signal that we were together, but to make a sign of respect and indicate we knew each other. In this company, the smallest action was taken with political weight, and it wasn't a gesture I had expected.

I really did like Malcolm when we weren't pointing guns at each other.

He scanned the room. "Strange bedfellows."

"Yeah." I recognized most of the people here. Most of the ones I didn't were wearing colors: the Carrion Boys, Los Pícaros, the 4X8s . . . street gangs who ranged from mixed bags of loyalty and survival to ones that were dregs of society who preyed on teens.

And there was also Pablo Roldán of the Fuentes crime family, and two people from the Russian Mafia, and, of course, Malcolm from the Lorenzos, who represented Sicily here in town. Yamamoto hadn't gotten representatives of every interest in Los Angeles here—or even the majority of them—but I was seeing a nontrivial-enough chunk to worry me.

Before now, I wouldn't have bet on catching some of these guys dead in the same room as the others. Come to think of it, if anyone got twitchy, Cheryl might end up redecorating her bar again.

As if to prove my point, a guy from the Grigoryan crime family glared at me from across the room.

I blithely ignored him. "Hey, Malcolm. Who's the blonde?" She was one of the few women in the room and also one of the only people I didn't recognize. She was also sorely out of place here—she wore a navy blue business suit and carried a briefcase, as if she had just stepped out of a boardroom.

"Lauren Vance," Malcolm answered me, keeping his voice low. "She works for Pourdry."

"*Pourdry's* fucking in on this?" The man was gobbling territory every time I turned around.

"He's no worse than the 4X8s," Malcolm said.

"That's not a high bar. Come on, you were the one sniping his minions."

"I guess we all choose our own code, Russell."

Vance sat with her legs crossed and let her blue eyes wander around the room. They didn't snag on me. Either she had a great poker face, or Pourdry hadn't made me as the person who'd been with Arthur. After all, they'd tracked him to the hospital via the gunshot wound, but given the darkness, the distance, and the fact that I'd killed most of them, they probably only had the vaguest description of me: short and brown and deadly.

That *would* narrow it down pretty drastically, but maybe not enough yet.

I scooted my center of mass forward so I was on the edge of my seat. I couldn't be the only one here who had a current tab open with someone else in the room. Making things worse, as I scanned the crowd it occurred to me that almost everyone present was in the secondary ranks—no big bosses had shown up, only their assistants and attack dogs. Smart on the leaders' parts, but people were a lot more willing to off the cannon fodder. This meeting was a bloodbath waiting to happen.

I kept my weight even, alert and ready. I couldn't help feeling like I owed it to Cheryl to do my damnedest to prevent Grealy's from turning into a crime scene again. If this became a massacre, however, there wasn't going to be much even I could do to prevent it.

It's only a massacre if the news reports say it is, boasted a shadow from my dreams. *Otherwise it's a victory.*

I clenched one hand against my thigh, my fingernails digging in hard. I had to *stay ready*.

Yamamoto breezed in. "Cassu-san!"

"Taku, hey," I tried to check him, "hang on a second. Look around; are you sure this is such a good ide—"

"We talk later, yes? So glad you came!" he gushed, before sweeping past to work the room, shaking hands and bowing extravagantly at people. A little, slimy, sleazy fellow who always wore cheap suits that made him look like a used car salesman, Yamamoto had a finger in just about everything and made an appearance of trying to get along with everyone—at least on the surface. His entourage of bodyguards and yes-men crowded into the bar behind him like a huge, silent herd of buffalo, not one of them under six-four.

For an instant their images crossed each other, reminding me of people I'd never seen.

"That man is either very savvy or very stupid," Malcolm murmured beside me.

"Maybe both," I answered with an effort. "We did all come, didn't we?"

"Which might only mean we're not any smarter."

"Hullo, everybody! Hullo. Hullo!" Yamamoto had finished his rapid and enthusiastic round of the room. Now he waved his arms above his head to get our attention and hopped up on a barstool. "Thank you for coming!"

A Latino guy who was about nineteen or twenty stood up, hitching his jacket importantly and sneering at the rest of us. "What is this bullshit? I ain't working with any of these fucks."

"Now, now, Miguel," Yamamoto said. "We have such grave happenings in common at this moment. Someone is acting against us. We must find them, and eliminate." He clicked his tongue.

"And how you plan to do that?" shouted a belligerent woman. I vaguely recognized her colors as a crew out of South Vermont Avenue.

"You're welcome to leave," one of the Grigoryans sneered at her. "Take the rest of the street trash with you."

The half of the room in colors surged forward simultaneously, somehow all edging away from each other at the same time.

"Whoa! Whoa!" cried Yamamoto, waving his hands overhead again. "I ask you, peace, please! You would not insult our host this way, would you?" He gestured expansively at Cheryl.

Cheryl, for her part, had been standing with her arms crossed, but once all eyes were on her she reached forward with great deliberation and drew a Mossberg pump-action from under the bar. She pointed it in the general direction of the room and racked it, the *chu-chunk* more expressive in the silence than any words would have been.

"We must all stand together on this," declared Yamamoto. "We must."

"How do we know you ain't the one screwing all the rest of us?" demanded the combative Miguel.

"The horror!" cried Yamamoto, putting a hand over his breast. "How could you expect that of me? I! The one warning you all of this threat!"

"I want to know what you expect to do about it," said a young East Asian guy with a close-shaved head. I didn't know him either, but he was sitting with Kevin Fong, and that pegged him as attached to the Chuntianjie bikers.

One of the Russians at the next table grunted in agreement.

"Oh!" cried Yamamoto as if he had not expected to be called upon for anything but hosting. "The first thing, I say, is we must find out what is causing this. We all see the effects, but what has happened to deliver us to this malice? We must pool our knowledge."

The bar was silent.

"Nobody has a fucking clue," the same Grigoryan finally shouted. There was a chorus of agreement.

"You accusing one of us, man?" Miguel was on his feet again. "You wanna make some *accusations,* you come right out and say it!"

"I do not accuse anyone!" Yamamoto raised his hands in a gesture of surrender, but two of his bodyguards inched closer, and a few of the others edged toward Miguel and the Grigoryan. "I want us to find this! Together! It is bad for business, for all of us!"

"Maybe you're the one who's bad for business!" someone in the back called out.

"Yeah!" cried the woman who had spoken earlier. "How we know you ain't brung us here to get us in some scheme of yours? We ain't trust you!"

More shouts of agreement. Discontented shuffling.

"I say you tell us what's happening!" shouted the heckler from the back.

The bodyguard to Yamamoto's right moved his hand an inch closer to the edge of his coat.

"Hey!" shouted Miguel, and tried to go for his piece first.

I was faster. My Colt thundered in my hand and Miguel shrieked and dropped his cheap-ass pistol. I hopped up onto the chair I'd been sitting on in one move.

Behind me, one of Yamamoto's bodyguards—a huge black man named Cesar whom I really liked—pile-drove the Grigoryan into his seat.

But nobody else twitched.

My momentum stalled out like I'd tripped over a pile of bricks. I'd expected to be shooting half the room. I'd shot Miguel's gun instead of him because I'd wanted to keep the peace here for Cheryl's sake and leaving corpses wasn't the best way to do that, but I hadn't expected the luxury to last more than a second and a half. This room, with these people, should have erupted into violence.

It didn't. Everyone sort of shuffled their feet and looked at their drinks.

"I owe Cheryl," I declared into the silence, totally un-nerved and trying not to show it. "Nobody shoots anybody, okay?"

The Grigoryan spat in my general direction, but he didn't try to get up again.

Miguel was shoving the kid next to him in the same colors, reaming him out for not backing him up. The subject of the rant just sort of sat there and let himself get shoved, not looking at his comrade.

What the *fuck*.

And then it hit me, much slower than it should have: I was seeing the brain entrainment work in real time.

I rewound the sequence. The various factions had pushed and shouted and surged, but nowhere near to the degree they should have, and a lot of people hadn't joined in when I would have expected them to. In a meeting like this, all seconds and stooges, where no one was worried about accidentally executing someone at the top of a crime pyramid—except maybe Yamamoto, whose bodyguards were half the mass in the room anyway—this easily could have erupted into a gang war.

With my little app, I had just single-handedly prevented one.

"Everybody go home and cool off," I said.

The people who hadn't moved to violence didn't need telling twice. They all avoided eye contact with each other as chairs scraped back and the various factions shuffled out, leaving as much air space between themselves as possible.

"You all think about this!" Yamamoto shouted after them, flapping his hands. "You go home, you think! We come back and talk again, yes? We fix this!"

"In your dreams, man," muttered one of the Carrion Boys, but a few of the other folk—especially the older ones, or the ones from the crime families—gave Yamamoto subtle little nods.

I'd shut down the gang war, but I hadn't shut down Yamamoto's little crusade. Well, shit.

At least I'd ensured I'd be invited next time, I supposed.

I kept a close eye on Lauren Vance as the last of the invitees filed toward the exit. She stepped over to Yamamoto for a moment and exchanged a few quiet words with him. Then she squeezed his arm, picked up her briefcase, and headed out.

I wanted to follow her. I hopped down off the chair.

"Cassu-san!" Yamamoto hailed me.

Great. I wheeled around. He was talking to Cheryl and

waving me over as if he wanted to break his arm with the vigor.

"An odd sequence of events," Malcolm said in my ear.

For a second I thought it was another deviant recollection, and I had to stop myself from reacting. But almost worse that it was reality—it meant Malcolm had noticed something.

I turned and squinted up at him. Did he mean the way all the mobsters and gangsters had behaved, or the way I had? Or both?

"What do you mean?" I asked, trying to sound careless about it.

"Odd all around," he repeated, almost to himself. "Good day to you, Miss Russell." He produced a fedora—I almost laughed, but I honestly wasn't sure whether he was trying to be ironic or not—tipped it onto his head, and stuffed his hands in the pockets of his coat as he left. I had no doubt he was ready to draw down on anyone out there who still felt aggressive.

I hopped over the intervening chairs to where Yamamoto and Cheryl stood. Cheryl had laid down the shotgun on top of the bar, but Yamamoto's bodyguards had edged around us in a circle that was either protective or intimidating, depending on your perspective.

"Congratulations," I said to Yamamoto. "That was a terrible idea." Maybe, just maybe, I could get him to keep from repeating it, get him to leave the brain entrainment alone to do its job.

"I gotta second Russell on this one," Cheryl said. She sniffed. "Thanks, by the way."

She didn't look my way as she said it, so I had to assume she was talking to me. "You're welcome. Do I get my ban lifted?"

She snorted. "Not a chance."

It had been worth a try.

"Come on, you have to admit it," I said to Yamamoto.

"Even if something *is* going on, there's no way to get people together on it. We'll just have to deal. Shit happens."

"Since when do you give up, Cassu-san? No, no, I have just gone about my plan wrongly. We will figure out a way. And you are with me, yes? None of this foot-dragging. I do not know where this comes from."

Oh, wonderful, at this rate I was going to give away the brain entrainment just by acting out of character. "I gotta go," I said. "Uh, keep me in the loop, okay? You guys all good?"

Cheryl nodded, and Yamamoto waved me off with grievous words about how sorrowful it was to part with my company. Jesus Christ.

I pushed out onto the street, still hopeful I could scan for Vance, but she had rabbited. A minute later I thought to check the cars—this wasn't exactly a posh area, and Vance seemed the type to drive a BMW to a meth carnival—but I didn't see any likely vehicle. Chances were she'd been gone before I'd escaped Yamamoto's clutches.

My phone rang. Arthur.

"Hey," I answered, keeping half an eye out in case Vance strolled back by. "Everything go okay tonight?"

"Yeah." He didn't sound entirely happy about it, probably because of the working conditions I'd imposed on him.

I decided to ignore it. "I've got some new intel on Pourdry. There might be somebody else we can track him through."

"Later," Arthur said. "You and me need to talk. 'Bout Rio."

"Not *again*," I said. "I told you, Rio is not open to discussion. You don't like him. Fine. End of story."

"Not that. Some things he said tonight . . . Russell, he thinks your brain entrainment's Pithica. Or something like 'em."

"Oh." I'd forgotten I hadn't actually told Rio what we'd all been up to lately. "That's easy to straighten out. I'll just tell him it's us, and not to worry."

"Russell . . . I'm not sure you should."

"Why not? If he thinks it's someone like Pithica, he might start working against us—"

"'Cause I don't think that's gonna change if he finds out it's you."

"What are you talking about?"

"I don't pretend to understand this weird . . . thing you got going on with him. But he's dead bent on slamming down whoever's responsible for messing with the people in LA. He doesn't talk much, but he sounded—he's got a crusade. He says it's all wrong and ungodly. Russell, he's gonna try to stop you."

Oh.

Shit.

sixteen

RIO HELD me to our Monday talk.

I felt awkward around him. First of all, I was hiding something from him—which I didn't do, as a matter of course—and second, Simon loomed between us like an enormous telepathic elephant.

Halfway through our meetup, I couldn't stand it anymore.

"Where is he?" I asked, as I pushed around my steak and eggs in the diner we'd met at.

He arched an eyebrow in a distinctly Rio-esque fashion. "You are referring to Simon."

"Yes, *duh*. I left him with you and Arthur and Checker and Pilar. What happened after I left?"

"Your friends attempted to interrogate us."

"Did you answer them?"

"No." Rio was blessedly predictable, at least.

"And then what?"

"I recommended to Simon in the strongest possible terms that he cease to bother you, and I sent him on his way."

"You did?" I sat up. "I thought you wanted me to bend over for him."

"I would not put it in precisely those terms."

"*Rio.*"

He considered. "I judged his methods to be counterproductive. If you are to be convinced, it will not be the way he was attempting."

"I'll say," I said. "Are *you* some sort of psychic now?"

"No, Cas. But I have known you for quite some time."

How long?

I picked more at the eggs. "I might be going insane," I said. "But it's still *my* mind that's going insane, you get it?"

Rio cocked his head at me.

"I let Simon start pawing around in there—he's going to change me. Remake my brain. I'll be a different person."

"I don't believe that will be the case."

"What, you're denying he'll alter me? Wipe clean the person I am right now, pervert me into something else?"

"I would not put it in precisely those terms," Rio said again.

I threw down my fork with more force than necessary. "Then what terms would you put it in?"

"When a surgeon knits flesh together, to cause it to heal in the correct pattern, it is not a perversion."

I barked a laugh. "You're calling this guy a surgeon?"

"He could be considered similarly, yes. In . . . certain circumstances. I believe this to be one of them."

"The answer's no, Rio."

"It is your decision." He sipped from a paper cup of tea.

"But, what? You're going to keep trying to convince me?"

"Yes."

"The answer's still going to be no."

"As you wish."

A flat in an infinitely tall apartment building, one that reached for the sky. "I can't keep doing this," someone said in my voice. "I don't care if it's the safe thing."

Rio's profile against the light. "As you wish."

I lashed out against the versions of us in my head. When I spoke again it came out forced and brittle. "What, are you just waiting until I start to go off the deep end? Going to stand back until I'm a babbling idiot, and then you'll shove my addled brain in Simon's direction?"

"I hope there will be no need for that, Cas."

I stared at the remains of my meal.

I wasn't hungry anymore.

"I have business to occupy me in LA anyway," Rio said.

It took me a second for my brain to settle and catch up. When it did, I tried to stop the self-conscious hitch to my posture—because I knew what Rio was talking about. Crap.

"Oh," I said aloud, and tried to moderate my tone so I wouldn't sound so goddamn obvious. "What's that?"

"Doubtless you have noticed there is some new power in the city."

Playing dumb would probably be too dumb. "A lot of people are pretty unhappy. I met with some of them last night."

"They will not be able to counter this," Rio said. "This is a force of widespread strength."

"And you think it *should* be countered? The people it's affecting aren't ones I'd consider saints."

"It is wrong regardless, Cas," Rio answered, perfectly serene. "Just as Pithica was wrong. The ability to make our own choices is God-given. No man can be judged a sinner or saint without his free will intact."

"You think this, uh, you think this is Pithica?" I said. "I thought your deal with Dawna was that you had to leave them alone."

"It is not Pithica. The methods do not match closely enough. But the aim is the same, and the sin is just as grave."

Shit.

"Cas, it seems you know something about this. I would be grateful for the intelligence."

Double shit.

"Right," I said, way too fast. I'd have to work on avoiding Rio for a while—I wasn't a good enough liar for this. "Okay. Um. You might run into some people." Grateful I had something to tell him as a cover, I related Yamamoto's meeting the night before, keeping it as vague as I dared.

"And nobody seemed to know the provenance?" Rio asked.

"Nope," I said.

"Perhaps I should speak to Mr. Yamamoto."

"Knock yourself out. I can give him your number. He probably knows who you are, though." Not many people who did were willing to talk to Rio by choice, and he knew it.

Rio nodded. "If you would attempt the connection, it would be appreciated. Otherwise, may I depend on you to pass on any information that might be of help in combating this?"

"You want us to work together?" I blurted. Oh, *brother*.

"If you like. I would not refuse the help, but it is your decision. I would ask for any data you happen across regardless, if you do not mind the imposition."

Rio wanted to work with me, against me. Only he didn't know it.

"Sure," I said. "I'll, uh, relay your interest. Um, as for anything else, let me—let me think about it. I've got some . . . things going on right now."

There was no way Rio didn't know something was up with me, but he let it pass. Maybe he thought it was just my mounting madness. "Of course, Cas."

"What are you going to do when you figure this out?" I asked.

"I shall find whoever is responsible, and allow God to be the judge of their souls."

Rio continued sipping his tea, and I sat back, my appetite entirely lost.

RIO'S OBLIVIOUS threats and Yamamoto's efforts to start a multi-family mob war against me notwithstanding, I couldn't help but celebrate a little when I stood in Checker's Hole a few days later and admired screens full of crime statistics. The line graphs tripped and tumbled over cliffs into statistically significant abysses. Violent crime. Property crime. Organized crime.

"It's only been about a week," Checker said, sounding disturbed. "But this . . . okay, Cas, I have to admit. I still don't like it, but it's staggering. I think it's been having a knock-on effect, too—I mean, obviously not all crime is caused by what you're preventing, but this has caused such a shake-up everyone's chasing their tails. Hopefully we won't see them reacclimate. . . ."

"Yeah. Good," I said.

And hopefully we wouldn't end up dead if anyone found out this had been us.

"I've still got my doubts," Checker said. "But . . . wow. Job well done?"

"Well, Arthur's strong-arming me into cleanup mode," I answered. *Thank Christ.* My worries about more breakdowns in the field notwithstanding, I needed to keep my mind occupied with work more than ever. Like always, it sharpened me, dulling the lapses in lucidity.

"We're chasing the bad guys while they're chasing their tails, as you said," I continued to Checker. "Hey, have you found anything on Lauren Vance?"

"Oh, yeah, I was going to update you on that. As far as I can ascertain, she's both Pourdry's very genteel attack dog and one of the more public faces of his operation. Assuming you can hang around here a while longer, I'll have a summary on the server for you and Arthur by this evening."

There'd been no sign Pourdry was after Checker, but he'd still asked me to come back to the Hole with him to collect some additional laptops and do some work that required more processing power. "Where is Arthur, anyway?"

"I thought he was off on some PI thing today," I said. "He's not?"

Checker half smiled. "I am incredibly flattered you think that with all the work we've been doing for you, we would still have time to have a case on."

"Well, Pilar said he had some emergency with, um, a couple of kids I saw hanging around the office. Katrina and . . . Jason, maybe? Justin? They're not a case?" I did hope Katrina was okay. She'd been a hoot.

"Oh, that must be some of Arthur's lost kids," Checker said. "Huh, hopefully all this'll be a help to some of them. Arthur would be ecstatic."

"What do you mean, Arthur's lost kids?"

"Cas, what do you think *we* are?"

I looked at him blankly.

"Come on, you didn't realize this?" Checker said. "Arthur's got a weakness for troubled kids. Almost an obsession. He's not happy unless he's trying to fix someone." He frowned. "That sounds bad. I don't mean it that way. Heck, Arthur saved me, him and—" He coughed.

"We're not kids," I said. I wasn't sure how I felt about being someone's project. On the other hand, it wasn't like I hadn't known I was one; I just hadn't known he had others.

"Yeah, well, it's all relative, isn't it?" said Checker brightly. "Arthur does a lot of good for people. He's pretty swell at it."

We built you. You're something better, now. The prideful croon came with an oily stain of violation, fingers reaching forward into my present and future. I didn't know who had said it. Maybe a hundred people. Maybe nobody.

My mood soured. "I'm goddamn sick of people trying to fix me."

Checker turned from his computers, the movement slow and deliberate as he gave me his full attention. "We're not talking about Arthur anymore, are we?"

I didn't answer.

"Do you . . . want to talk about it?" asked Checker.

Do you want to see what you can do? one of the ghosts whispered.

"No," I said to both of them. I tried to focus on Checker. "No, I don't. Unless it's to tear you a new one for fucking *not telling me* you had decided to blunder face-first into my business and kidnap the person I told you to stop looking into—"

"You know what we did made perfect sense." Checker sighed. "So can you stay? If you can, I'll get Pilar over here and we'll finish this double time."

Dread closed in on me as I realized something else: now that I was done here, I didn't have anything to do anyway, at least until Arthur had finished his thing or I had some intel on Vance to chase down. It was exactly what I'd been stalling against. The lull from work, the lack of focus that historically had never gone well for me.

Buck up, Cas, I ordered myself. I had to face it eventually. At least riding it out here would be better than doing it locked up alone in one of my apartments. "I can stay, as long as you have some tequila in your kitchen," I told Checker.

"Yeah, uh. Knock yourself out." His face twisted up a little. "Cas, seriously. With so much going on, we haven't talked about— They said you aren't— Is it true you aren't okay?"

"They" meant Simon and Rio. "We've known I'm not okay for a while now," I said.

"Cas . . ."

"What?"

I could tell Checker was steeling himself to say something I would hate by the way his hands clenched and his whole posture tightened. "The, um. Not just your memory stuff, but the, uh, the math thing—about you not being able to do, um, proofs and stuff anymore. If this guy really is a 'good' psychic, maybe he can help you with—"

"What, and *you'd* trust him?" The dig about the mathematics stabbed. The reminder that I wasn't whole, that grasping after anything beyond raw computation would leave me only with a phantom wisp of forgotten wonder . . . I could solve any problem known to humankind, but the unknown ones were forever closed to me, my brain stunted and seared off. It was the only part of my whole messed-up brainspace I'd give anything to fix, and Checker knew it. He was the only one I'd ever talked to about it, and I regretted having told him at all.

Fuck my memory; if I could get the math back . . .

Would such a thing be worth considering? Was there even a chance?

No. I couldn't let myself think along those lines. My broken mathematical intuition might be the only impairment I wasn't in denial about, but nothing Simon had said suggested he had any interest in helping me with it. Letting myself hope for that was like staring into the sun—it would burn me to the core before I saw anything.

Black resentment bristled in me at Checker even bringing it up.

"Simon seems to think the problem here is all down to what Dawna Polk did a year ago," I reminded him acidly. "Whatever messed up my brain initially, whether it was her or Pithica or someone like them, it happened long before then. And you seem to be forgetting that Simon keeps telling me *not* to try to remember things, so he's clearly not interested in fixing my memory or—or anything else, only whatever *she* knocked apart, and why he's even interested in *that* is highly suspicious bordering on disturbing—"

"Is it so strange to you that you might have had a friend before you lost your memory?" Checker asked.

"So he's a friend of mine now instead of a dangerous enemy you helped abduct and hold prisoner for weeks? You wouldn't want him in your head either, admit it!"

Checker shifted uncomfortably. "Well, no, but—I'm just saying. Not to underrate Pilar and Arthur and me or anything, but this guy's thing about not influencing people without asking—to be perfectly fair, I'm not sure we *could* have held on to him if he hadn't been sticking to it. Which makes me think . . . I don't know. Maybe at least ask some questions? Find out more about if you're in trouble from what Dawna did or—"

"Sounds like he did influence you," I said cruelly, and Checker flushed, though I wasn't sure whether it was from annoyance at me or real fear that what I said might be true. "I'm going to go drink. Come get me when you're done here."

I stomped out of the Hole and through the back door into his house, where I found the tequila and slouched on the couch with a bottle. I'd self-medicated earlier in the morning as well, but the buzz that took the edge off my senses had already started to fade. Blurred scenes I didn't want anything to do with pried through the cracks, invading my consciousness.

Did you take your medicine? someone taunted.

"*I had to do it. They were killing you,*" begged someone else.

My mouth bent in shapes it had never made, ugly and malicious. "*How were they killing me if I'd never been so alive?*"

God*damn* it.

Checker was right about one thing—if only one thing. I deserved some answers from Rio and Simon. I'd told Rio I wouldn't look into my past, and still didn't want to—but we weren't talking about my past anymore; this was my present. The two of them were fucking up my life without offering the slightest explanation.

My mood folded in further. What with the brain entrainment and Yamamoto's meeting and finding out Rio was going to try to stop me and working on finding Pourdry, the fury I'd felt about the whole thing had been piled over by other priorities. Now it came flooding back, burning in my gut until the edges of my mood charred and curled. I drank more, but it didn't help.

"There's no limit to this type of power."

"That doesn't scare you?"

"Why would it?" I stretched my fingertips to the sky, my skin crackling with possibility, probability. "I'm the one in control."

I jumped off the edge of the world, and the land flew by below me, sea and sky and space and stars, and I laughed and laughed and laughed.

My hands had contorted into claws. I swiped for the tequila bottle, my fist tightening enough that I could feel the pressure building against the atomic bonds of the glass, stretching and stretching until they were on the verge of pulling apart and shattering.

This time, instead of drowning me, the shards of unreality fissuring my consciousness stoked my anger until I wanted to hit something.

Kill something.

For more than a moment, I considered destroying Checker's house. I was still angry at him, and fuck, smashing things would be cathartic. But then I had a better idea.

I texted Rio. I'd been planning to avoid him, but we wouldn't be talking about Los Angeles. Besides, I was feeling reckless.

Then I texted Checker: I told Rio and Simon to come over to your house. Happy now?

My phone buzzed with a reply immediately. Then another.

The general gist of the next seven text messages was FUCK U, CAS.

I gave the phone a bitter smile and put it down. Then I sat, drank tequila, and waited.

seventeen

CHECKER AND Pilar insisted on being in the room when Rio and Simon showed up. I had expected that to be the last thing they'd want, and I had the bizarre impression they were doing some weird imitation of wanting to protect me.

Which was, of course, absurd. I tried to ban them, but Checker and I got in a shouting match in which he pointed out I'd invited a dangerous killer and a possibly dangerous telepath to *his* house without asking him first, and therefore he was fucking going to be in the room.

I thought about leaving just to be spiteful, but at that moment Checker's security system pinged at Rio and Simon's arrival. I yanked open the door.

Rio, of course, was perfectly equanimous, standing relaxed in his long tan duster. Simon hunched half behind him, hugging himself as if he wanted to disappear.

"Hello, Cas," said Rio.

Simon nodded to me, but kept his mouth shut this time.

I ushered them inside. Rio's gaze crawled over Checker and Pilar, who had retreated to the far side of Checker's living room, against the wall. As far away as they could get without actually leaving the room.

"Ignore them," I said.

We sat down.

"Cas," Rio said. "May I take this as a sign you are reconsidering your decision?"

"No," I said. "You may take it as a sign that I want some answers."

"I am given to understand it would be dangerous to you to satisfy such curiosity." Rio flicked a glance toward Simon.

"You mean telling me why I'm crazy will make me crazier? Yeah, he's implied as much. But I'm calling bullshit. This isn't buried in the past anymore, Rio, and you can tell me *something*. First of all," I said, turning to Simon, "who are you, really?"

Simon and Rio exchanged a glance.

"Hey. *Hey*." I snapped my fingers at them. "I'm over here."

"Cas," Rio said. "As I have told you, this man is on your side."

"I'll determine that, thank you very much."

They looked at each other again, as though surprised I wasn't just going to take Rio's word for it. Rio shrugged slightly and said, "She is her own person. It seemed important."

"Over. Here," I repeated.

"Cassandra," Simon said, "the more you can keep blocked, the better it will be. Whatever we tell you will start breaking down those barriers. Even my presence here, it's not—it's not good for you, but I don't see the alternative."

"Well, if you don't give me some answers, I'm just going to have to remember as much as I possibly can," I said.

Simon paled. It was disturbing. Not that I *wanted* to remember—I definitely didn't; I hadn't from the beginning—but I also hadn't expected my threat to have so much of an effect.

Someone hit me. "You see? That is what it means, to have an effect."

I hit them back. "I understand now," I told the corpse.

I tried to keep my face blank despite the interruption.

"Can you tell one of us instead?" Checker ventured the question from the side of the room. "If Cas would trust us to be, um. An advocate? For her?"

I knew Checker was only trying to help, but I wasn't fond of that idea, either. "Rio," I said. I pointed at Simon. "I need to know who this guy is. To me. Broad strokes aren't going to kill me, and I need to know."

Rio glanced at Simon, whose mouth was pressed in a tight line. "You and he knew each other," Rio said. "A long time ago."

"Less broad," I said impatiently, when he didn't add anything else. "I'm not going to let you do *anything* if no one tells me what the hell is going on."

"This has to do with what Cas can do, doesn't it?" Pilar said.

I whipped around to face her. She tried to back up but ran into the wall. "I'm sorry! It's just, it makes sense. You guys and Dawna, you all have these, like, superhuman powers, and we know some of them involve memory, and—that can't be a coincidence."

"We're not the same," I ground out.

"How do you know?" Checker asked.

Show each other what you can do.

Good girl.

The flash of faces and feelings dazed me. Was it only my imagination, or were they hitting me harder? Becoming more real?

I tried to reorient, concentrate on logic. "You're talking coincidence," I sneered at Pilar. "Well, isn't it a hell of a coincidence that I would *happen* to run into Pithica years later if they had something to do with—"

My thoughts screeched to a halt. Pithica . . . they hadn't known what I could do, at first. They had only been interested in me because I knew Rio.

Because Rio had been trying to take them down. Had been tangling with them for a long, long time. Since before I had met him.

Or maybe *exactly* since I had met him.

Call me Rio.

Fuck.

"Rio," I said. "How did we meet?"

"I can't tell you that, Cas."

He saved me. . . .

Had saved me from where? From somewhere I had known people like Dawna and Simon, from people who had mind-wiped me to keep me from remembering them?

From people who had broken my ability to do real mathematics and left my computational prowess in its place—a poor substitute for a human mathematician, but an excellent bonus for a living weapon?

Pithica had originally been a government project, or at least linked to a project code name. We knew that much.

Halberd and Pithica, something echoed and chanted in my head. *Halberd and Pithica . . .*

Halberd was—what? Another project? A missing piece of my life? I opened my mouth to ask, but the question strangled me. Dawna's prohibition against learning more about Pithica meant no matter what guesses I had, I wouldn't get any of them confirmed. "God*dammit!*"

"Cas?" Checker said, his voice shot through with worry.

"I think Pilar's right," I said. "I think I was . . . associated with Pithica, or something like them, and I think—I think they did this."

"It makes sense." Pilar was babbling a little. "I mean, considering your amnesia—how many bad guys could there possibly be with real-life psychic powers? It would be totally weird if there were a bunch of unconnected sets of people walking around with the ability to muck with people's brains, wouldn't it?"

"Pilar," I said.

"Yeah?"

"Good job. Now shut up."

"Okay. Right. Okay. Sorry."

I turned back to Simon. "Somehow, in the past, you and I were both connected to Pithica." Maybe we'd decided to turn renegade and fight them, and that's how we'd hooked up with Rio. I was feeling it out, but it made sense. "We got out, but before we did, they fucked me in the head. Of course, you're not going to confirm or deny this." If I thought he would, I probably wouldn't even have been able to say it, thanks to Dawna. Pithica had fucked me twice now.

We appreciate your loyalty, murmured the voices in my head.

"Will you let me help you now?" asked Simon.

I almost laughed. "Help me? By doing what, screwing around with my brain on top of whatever fun mutilation someone else already did? Yeah, that seems like a good idea. And you and I might have worked together against Pithica, but that means nothing. I've worked with a lot of people who were scum of the earth. For all I know we were allies of convenience."

Simon sucked in a breath as if I'd stabbed him and wrapped his arms around himself again. "It wasn't convenience."

I raised my eyebrows at Rio to see if he'd confirm that, but he gave me a half shrug, as if to say, *What do I know about human relationships.*

Well, true.

"Please," Simon said. "This isn't going to go away. I can help you repair—"

"What?" I challenged him. Checker's suggestion from a few minutes ago tugged at my consciousness. Impossible. Simon couldn't repair the math; this wasn't about that. It didn't stop the fleeting, aching hope from wringing through me. . . .

He saw it, the asshole.

"I can't do what you want," he said hoarsely, and disappointment lanced through me hot and bitter, for all my resolution not even to imagine it. "I'm sorry. But I can mend what Daniela—what Dawna, I can reverse what she did. I won't do anything to hurt you. I promise."

"I wonder if the person who scraped all my memories out said that to me beforehand, too," I said viciously. "Isn't Pithica all about making the world a better place? They were probably making me a shiny new person, just like you want to."

"Cassandra—"

"Stop calling me that."

"Cas," he amended. "This is serious. The symptoms you're having are going to keep getting worse. Please, you have to let me help."

"No. I don't."

There are limits here, babbled one of the voices. *Limits such as death.*

"You don't understand," Simon pleaded. "You could die."

"I understand perfectly," I said. *Such as death.* "What *you're* not understanding is that I am *fucking done* with people reshuffling my neurons. Pithica, Dawna Polk, you, anyone else." *What is death, except utter unending unconsciousness?* I couldn't tell if it was my own thought. "I'll find another solution."

"I don't know that there is one." Simon had started to sound panicked. "Cas, I know what happened to you; I know your mind; I can— This isn't something you can snap yourself out of!"

"She's right," I said, jabbing a thumb at Pilar. "I have superpowers too. I'm as good as you *or* Dawna Polk. I can fix LA, and I can fix my own goddamn brain. I'll figure it out."

The room stopped dead.

I can fix LA . . .

"Cas?" Rio asked, with the moral weight of centuries.

Shit. Shit, shit, shit, *shit.*

I'd been planning to avoid Rio for *exactly this fucking reason.*

Rio considered me. "You."

I pointed at Checker and Pilar. "You two. Out."

Checker opened his mouth like he was going to try to protest, but Pilar just hustled them out of the room.

I turned back to Rio. It was no use trying to lie to him after a slipup like that; he'd see right through it. "Are you going to try to kill me?"

Simon jerked and almost fell off his chair. My gun hand twitched a little, as if I wanted to defend myself, even as another part of me wanted to laugh in hysterical disbelief at the idea.

"No, Cas," Rio said. "I would not harm you. But I am going to stop you."

Fuck.

eighteen

RIO DIDN'T insult me by trying to ask me any questions about how I'd done it. I wasn't going to answer, and he, apparently, was not willing to attempt the application of his . . . usual methods.

Given that, we didn't have much more to say. I swallowed any of my own doubts about the effects of the brain entrainment, forcibly reminding myself of the statistics we'd seen cascading out of Checker's programs. It was working. I would *make* it work. Rio or Yamamoto or anyone else—if they got in my way, I'd plow through them and win.

As for Simon, I made him leave with Rio. He kept swiveling his head back and forth between us as if he wanted to plead with me but was forcing himself not to because he knew it wouldn't do any good.

Smart man. Or maybe just telepathic.

Once I was satisfied they'd gone, I went out and found Checker and Pilar right where I expected—in the Hole, watching a feed of the living room from one of Checker's security cameras.

"We should abort," Checker said immediately. "If we reprogram the hack—"

"What? Not a chance in hell!" *Checker* wasn't going to stop me either. "You've seen the statistics. We've got a real chance to change the city here—we're not going to fold the instant someone tries to throw up an obstacle. Not for Rio or anybody else!"

"I—I think I'm with Cas," Pilar said. "If we're making a difference—Cas, as long as you're sure this guy can't, um—"

"He *can,* that's the point," Checker said shortly. "You don't understand; you haven't been in this world long enough. There are times you cut your losses and run, and when someone like *him* targets you . . ."

"Since when have you been the cut-and-run guy?" I said. "You're the person who wrote me fifty fucking pages about how this could prevent another Nanjing or Hitler. And now we have proof it's saving LA and you want to wuss out?"

"I was also against this from the beginning," Checker snapped. "And even though we're seeing an effect—shit, maybe *because* we're seeing such an effect, it's gotten goddamn frightening. Cas, you're the one who doesn't want anyone so much as *touching* your brain even though it would be helping you—how can you feel like this is all okay? Are you really fine with saying we should have this much power?"

"It's not the same thing," I gritted out.

"*Rio* thinks it is," Checker shot back. "Arthur told me what he said. I may not be religious, but I have a moral system, and I can't believe I'm on his side on *anything,* but his reasons here make sense. You can't tell me they don't!"

"Why can't both sides make sense?" Pilar was studying the ground like she wanted to disappear into it. "Why can't what we're doing be a little bit wrong but also be right? It's not like life is black-and-white. I know you guys think I'm naïve on a lot of this stuff, and I know I am—but you two are trying to draw lines where there just, there aren't any. You're so invested in what's right or wrong always making some sort of nice logical sense, but real life is, it's messy, and sometimes you can't draw nice perfect boxes around it and know what to do." She hunched her shoulders.

"Bullshit," I said. "If there's illogic involved we just haven't defined enough axioms for the system. Or the proof is fallacious."

Checker laughed. It sounded a little hysterical.

"Cas," Pilar said. "Your friend, um, this guy—what's he going to do?"

That was a very good question.

Rio didn't know what our methods were. He did know about Yamamoto's effort to rally LA's criminal element, thanks to me—if he wanted to, he could tip them off and slingshot the entirety of Los Angeles's underground around to land right on top of me.

But if he did that, there was the very real possibility I'd get killed. Speaking of logic, I didn't think Rio differentiated between hurting me himself and weaponizing all of LA to do it for him.

"I don't know," I said. "I guess we'll find out."

"Then why don't we wait and see?" asked Pilar. "Would it be so bad to—to see how things play out? As long as he's not, um. Not threatening you?"

"Or us," Checker added darkly.

"I told you, I talked to him about that," I said. "Yeah, I vote for wait and see, too. Whatever he's planning, I bet I can beat him."

Checker mumbled something that sounded suspiciously like, "I didn't sign up for this" and moved over to one of his computers. "Cas, there's something else you should hear. It doesn't sound like this is going to change your mind at all, but Rio and Yamamoto aren't the only people noticing something. This popped up in my alerts earlier today."

He clicked at the mouse a few times and then held down a

key to turn the volume all the way up. A blustering man's voice filled the room from the computer speakers.

"*. . . and something's going on in this city. You can feel it. Something is wrong here in Los Angeles, and I promise you, patriots, I will get to the bottom of it. Bombs aren't the only way for the terrorists to strike against this greatest of nations. We've long known how vulnerable we are to a biochemical attack, but did our mewling, terrorist-appeasing president take even one step to prevent it? No, of course not. And now you and me are the ones paying for it. Let's talk the water supply here in Los Angeles, for starters. Do you know how easy it would be for someone to . . ."*

Checker dialed the volume down again until it was muted.

"I've heard that guy before," I said. "Who is he?"

"Reuben McCabe," Pilar answered. "Isn't it?"

"Yup," Checker said. "Radio host, political shit-stirrer, and professional troll. And one with a hell of a reach."

"Oh, yeah," I said. "Him. Likes to inflame people or something, right?"

"Understatement of the year. But this time he's onto something. He's always been on about suspected conspiracies, but now he's revving it up, and he's got specifics. He knows there's been a change."

"Hey, maybe what we're doing will axe his audience. Stop people from being lemmings or whatever." It was an appealing thought. "Do his listeners really take him seriously anyway? He sounds like an idiot."

"He's a *charismatic* idiot with a nationwide show, and yes, a lot of people—" started Checker.

"My dad loves him," put in Pilar. "I mean, he says he could do without some of the, um, inflammatory tone and stuff, and he doesn't always agree with everything, but he says McCabe is the only news person willing to say what he thinks."

"The important point," Checker said loudly, "is that in this case McCabe is right. Nobody in the mainstream is reporting on the drop in crime, other than mentioning it in passing and praising the mayor's policies, because anything else would sound like a conspiracy theory. But McCabe doesn't care, and he's going whole hog on it. People are starting to pay attention."

"So what?" I said. "What can they do? Complain about it on the radio? Let them."

"Not just complain. I was listening earlier, and there are some militia groups who've been calling in to his show and making noises about coming to town. Setting things right, that kind of talk. These are the type of people who take it upon themselves to patrol the border like it's a video game, or stand their ground to Feds armed to the teeth. They're dangerous."

"Okay," I said. "They still won't know where to point their guns. If they come to LA and start making trouble, I'll deal with them. Heck, once they arrive the brain entrainment will probably neuter them for me."

"Take this seriously!" Checker said. "People are getting mad about this, and I can't say I blame them! Can you please hit pause for a minute and consider there might be a good reason they want to stop you? Stop *us*?"

"So you're saying you think Rio and McCabe are the good guys here?" I scoffed. "You?"

"And you're trying to tell me I should think they're wrong because, why, because I think one's a destructive moron with too much power and the other legitimately scares me shitless? That's a logical fallacy and you know it!"

We glared at each other.

"This is what I was talking about," Pilar said into the silence. "It's messy. I don't think the right solution is to try to make it not-messy, because it *isn't*."

What makes this so charming is that we all get to pass responsibility up the food chain, whispered someone, about *something dangerous and far away. Nobody has to take the blame for anything.*

I jerked away from it. Whoever the voice was, I wasn't like her. I wasn't plunging my hands into people like they were sculpting clay and squashing them around until they either turned into something satisfactory or died or—or whatever she had been doing—whoever she was—

I wasn't like that. *Was I?*

"Where's my info on Vance?" I said. That was at least one fucking thing that was clean and clear cut.

"It's done, but I thought you were waiting for Arthur," Checker said.

"Arthur's got other priorities, apparently." And the mood I was in, Arthur probably wouldn't approve of how I wanted to play things. "Did you figure out how I can find her?"

Checker heaved a sigh. "Yeah. She doesn't stay in the shadows like Pourdry does. In fact, she's pretty easy to track; she pops up on the grid regularly."

"I don't care about the rest of the intel," I said. "Just get me a location. I'll take it from there."

I FOLLOWED Lauren Vance for the rest of the day. Checker was right—she moved around in a surprisingly ordinary manner, using ATMs and stopping to buy overpriced coffee. She also walked into meetings in some of the seediest areas of Los Angeles as if they were glass-and-steel corporations, always standing with perfect posture and carrying her brief-case. I didn't know if she was depending on Pourdry's reputation to protect her or if she was capable of protecting herself. Either way, she was making a statement by going alone, especially dressed like a New York banker—a statement about either her own power or Pourdry's.

She didn't go to reconvene with her boss in person at all, and after watching how openly she moved around, I was starting to suspect she never would. I'd have to grab her and convince her.

That was okay. I'd almost been hoping I'd have the chance to beat the shit out of someone.

At least being back on the job did seem to be helping my dissolving sanity stay pasted together. Not as much as it had in the past, not by a long shot, but the stray intrusions had mostly retreated to a disordered susurration. I could only hope I'd be able to keep them there . . . especially as I was about to make things a lot more dramatic.

I waited until after the sun set and I had followed Vance's fashionable little convertible—I'd been right about her car choice—into the type of area you had to pay off the local gangs to spend any significant time in. Then, on a nice deserted street, I rammed the accelerator into the floor and ran her off the road.

She must have seen the headlights grow huge in her mirrors, because she tried to swerve and speed away, but I was ready. I pulled the e-brake, juked the wheel, and countersteered to slam into her back rear panel at over fifty miles per hour. The crash was deafening, and her car imploded with a shattering of glass and polymer. I kept my foot on the gas, spinning us out of the skid and against a closed medical marijuana shop so the back of Vance's car was crushed between mine and the storefront.

I'd purposely been driving a tank of a sedan, and it hadn't suffered more than a little hood crumpling. Perfect. I got out, my gun drawn.

Lauren Vance got out, too, clawing the airbag out of the way and pulling her briefcase with her as if it was attached to her hand. Her face was scraped and burned from the airbag, but she still held herself with that rigorously straight posture and seemed rather too collected for someone who had just been run off the road and was facing an attacker with a gun.

She raised her free hand slightly. "What do you want?"

"You," I said. "Hands on your head and get over here."

Very slowly, she bent her knees to set her briefcase on the ground.

And closed her eyes.

The world flashed pure white fire and my vision went blank. I reacted before registering what had happened, doing instant trigonometry to lower my gun and fire blind. Vance screamed.

"I want you alive," I said, blinking rapidly. Nothing but blackness—she must have used some sort of flash grenade. I stretched out my other senses—scuffling noises against the ground, ragged breathing—she probably hadn't expected me to shoot. I let my mathematical awareness lean on what my ears and memory told me, let the numbers draw my surroundings. "But believe me when I say I can kill you without being able to see you, and if you do not—"

The sound thundered into me like a herd of rampaging bison, trampling my eardrums, clobbering me in the sternum and putting me on my ass. I managed to hang on to my Colt, and I twisted against the maelstrom, unable to see or hear or sense a goddamn thing but depending on the lines of sight and minutes of angle I'd already spun out to guide me—and I put five rounds straight into her fucking briefcase. The Colt twitched in my hand as I pulled the trigger, but with the world taken over by Vance's sonic weapon only the sting of the recoil told me I'd fired.

I could tell I'd disabled the weapon because I was able to move again, but my senses were a dark and echoing box, and any equilibrium provided by my inner ear was dead gone. I leaned into my proprioception instead and put my faith in the mathematics, flipping up to my feet even as the rest of my brain was convinced I was falling sideways off the planet.

Vance only had one smart play to make, assuming she hadn't been knocked out by her own weapon. I pivoted through the correct angle and fired again to take out the front tire of my own car and then bulldogged straight toward where I knew the driver's side was.

Metal slugged me two feet before I got there—Vance had swung the car door out to body-slam me. I shot out one hand and grabbed the top of the door as I ricocheted, the new data giving me enough points to extrapolate a partial picture. I used my grip on the door to rebound my momentum and swung around it to smash the side of my gun into Lauren Vance's face.

I pushed her head down in the street and straddled her, my gun barrel against the back of her skull. The car engine vibrated next to me. She'd been so close to getting away.

My vision was starting to clear, fuzzy shapes oozing through the dimness, and my hearing had gone from an empty void to a rising, high-pitched ringing. Interpolation filled in enough blanks that I estimated I could still drive like this. I'd limp out of here on the rim of my wheel and then tie Lauren Vance up somewhere until I could recover and interrogate her.

I felt in my pocket for a zip tie and trussed up Vance's wrists behind her, and then tugged off my belt to tourniquet her leg above where I'd shot her. I started out doing it by feel, but my vision had mostly returned by the time I finished, albeit with fuzziness around every outline.

Vance stirred weakly against me.

I belatedly noticed she had some kind of fancy earplugs in. That accounted for the delay in her briefcase flashbang bomb—she closed her eyes for the flash, stuck in the plugs, and then escaped while everyone else was incapacitated. I ripped the earplugs out.

"Hi," I said. My ears still rang, painfully enough that it stabbed all the way to the back of my throat and made me want to throw up, but I could hear myself in a muffled, tinny way. "You're coming with me."

And better to skedaddle sooner than later, just in case we'd attracted any cops.

Or this neighborhood's version of the cops.

I realized my peripheral vision was still compromised when dark shapes solidified out of it to show us surrounded. Dark shapes in colors.

Shit, whose colors? Which neighborhood was this?

The lead silhouette detached himself from the rest and approached us with a swinging, loping gait, full of ego and scorn, and cemented into none other than my rowdy friend Miguel from Yamamoto's meeting.

He said something.

"You're going to have to speak up," I called back.

He came closer and raised his voice. "You on our turf, lady." The words were still wrapped in muffling layers of sensory loss, but I could understand them. "And this here's our prize, we been looking for her all night. Hey, you that chick from the bar!"

Shit.

"The one that shot me! I gonna learn you real good, woman."

I tensed my muscles. If I could delay a little, till my inner ear wasn't trying to bowl me over at every step . . . "What do you want with Vance?" I said. "Maybe we're on the same side here."

Miguel howled with laughter. "Same side? Woman, you on drugs? You fucking shot me!"

"Only your gun," I said. "I've got money. Let's talk about a deal. I get what I want out of Vance, and then you can have her."

"And then you get the credit? Nuh-uh. The Blood Skulls are the ones taking her down, and all those fancy gangsters the little Chinaman got together, they gonna be eating out of our hand."

I had no idea what he was talking about until Vance shifted below me. "It's not us," she called. "You've been misinformed."

"You shut your pretty mouth," Miguel said, and turned

back to me. "And you, why don't you put that piece down nice and slow."

"Wait." My brain felt like it was working only in skips and halts. "You think Vance and Pourdry are the ones who've been shutting down LA?"

"It's not us," Vance repeated, more urgently. "Whoever told you that lied. They're trying to start something. We got word today the responsible party is the Grigoryan brothers."

What?

"Piece on the ground, sister," Miguel repeated. "No sudden moves, neither."

I had one round left before I needed to reload. My vision had recovered enough to count: Miguel plus six other guys, most of whom had guns out already.

But Miguel had gotten closer so I could hear him, confident his boys were backing him up, and there was no doubt he was carrying as well, which gave me potential to gain another weapon. Of course, just to make my life difficult, he hadn't drawn yet. And I couldn't see well enough yet to figure out where he might be concealing.

"What happened to your gun?" I taunted. "What, did I scratch the finish on it? Afraid you'll get it messed up again?"

It worked. It fucking worked.

Miguel went for his piece and I rocketed up from the ground right into him. His boys all hesitated, not wanting to shoot their boss, and by the time they started to react I'd brought my hand up past his shoulder, wielding Miguel's own pistol. With my Colt jammed up under Miguel's chin, I shot all six of his guys in less than a second and a half.

I could hear the last body slump to the street through the ringing.

Miguel squeaked and went wild, his hands going for my gun. It was a stupid move on his part, because I pulled the trigger. Heat and wet spilled against my face and neck as he went down.

I wiped at the mess with my sleeve and turned back to Vance, tucking away Miguel's weapon and reloading my empty Colt, though it was so sticky I wasn't sure it would function right. I studied Vance as I did it. She didn't look scared; she looked calculating.

My equilibrium was still off, but I didn't let my senses relax. Something in me warned I shouldn't appear the least bit weak in front of her. I kept an iron grip on my mathematical perceptions of gravity and my own bones and limbs, and I was steady as a rock when I muscled her into one of the gangsters' cars and drove away.

nineteen

"YOUR INFORMATION is wrong," Lauren Vance said, from where she was sitting on a mattress, tied to its metal bed frame. Her voice was tight, the only display of the pain she had to be enduring—she hadn't made a sound even when I'd slapped a field dressing on her leg. The woman was sculpted from ice.

I sat at a table eating some processed meat out of a can and drinking cold coffee, still waiting for my ears to stop ringing entirely and my headache to go away. Vance's flash-bang had been a motherfucker.

I'd wiped off my face, but Miguel's blood still stiffened my shirt and jacket, the collar poking me every time I shifted. Reminding me.

I hadn't gone there to kill anyone. In the new Los Angeles I had created, would taking out seven members of Miguel's street gang lead to more violence, or less? Would there be retaliation, or would this just become part of the cleanup?

And if I hadn't fired, if I'd solved the night another way, would Miguel's guys have drifted off eventually from their places in the Blood Skulls, the brain entrainment freeing them of feeling trapped by gang control? Or had I killed young men who were loyal for life of their own free will?

What about Miguel himself?

Sure, I'd been halfway incapacitated, but maybe there had been another way of stopping them, of giving them that second chance. Until this moment, I'd been thinking of the brain entrainment as being in place to help *victims* of crime . . . but the massive dropoffs were making me start to see the perpetrators as victims, too. Especially ones as young as Miguel and his lieutenants had been.

I thought of Pilar's cousin. The probability he was one of the boys I'd shot out there was so slim I wasn't actually worried about it, but in theory, he could have been.

I closed my eyes briefly. I almost wished my decaying mental state would rear back up and confuse everything. It might be more comfortable than the choices I'd made tonight.

"I don't know who is spreading the lie that we are responsible for the behavioral changes in the population of Los Angeles," Vance tried again, drawing my attention back to her. "But they are either misinformed or fabricating the information. We have nothing to do with it."

"Right," I said. I was still thrown by the sudden slew of rumors flooding the streets. "You say it's the Grigoryans."

"After what happened, I'm beginning to suspect that information is unreliable," Vance said. "Someone is pitting us all against each other."

If she was right, that was an even worse turn of events than the criminal elements in LA banding together. An all-out war would hurt a lot of people. That scenario had been one of the things I'd been trying to *prevent*.

God, my head hurt. I finished my coffee, left Miguel's gun on the table pointed vaguely in Vance's direction, and started taking apart my Colt. Miguel's blood gummed every surface.

"I'm willing to pool information," Vance said. She must remember me from Yamamoto's meeting. "We want this stopped as much as you do."

"That's not why you're here," I interrupted. "I don't care. I want your boss."

I could almost see her brain click and whirr as she switched gears. "What do you want him for?"

"To kill him."

"I see," she said. "Is this a business dispute, or a personal one?"

"I want him in the ground," I said. "I don't care how much money anyone pays me. Your only concern is whether you go with him, or you help me."

"I see," Vance said again. Her gaze sharpened. "You're one of the people who's been interfering with our operations. The dark girl from the bridge."

"Me and my colleagues, yeah." I grinned wolfishly. Rio had been out working against Pourdry the other night, too—combined with the difficulties the brain entrainment was causing them, we had to be making the higher-ups frantic, even if Vance wouldn't show it. "And we're not going to stop until you're finished."

Vance nodded. "If I help you, I'd like to be taken to a hospital, and then given enough time to leave town. Can you guarantee me that?"

I blinked. Given the slavish devotion Pourdry's people were famous for, I hadn't expected this to be so easy. But then, maybe this *was* her way of panicking. Her exceedingly calm way of panicking.

Or maybe the brain entrainment was working on her, too.

"Talk and we'll see," I said.

"There's no advantage in me lying to you," Vance countered. "I saw what you did tonight with my own eyes, and in any event the other reports had been making me reconsider our organization's position. I'll tell you whatever you wish to know about Jacob, on the condition I have time to move aside before the fallout."

"I want to know how to find him," I said. "Convince me you're telling the truth, and you'll see the inside of a hospital before they end up needing to take your leg."

"All right," she said. "You will believe my motivation once you understand what kind of person Jacob is. If I may?"

I knew what kind of person Pourdry was, but I waved her on with Miguel's gun anyway. As long as she kept talking until she told me where to find him, I didn't care.

Vance nodded and continued on. "He and I met back at HBS. Jacob was the type of intelligent other people didn't even try to compete with. And more than smart, he was confident. Half the time I think he won because he went in assuming he had won, and everyone else ceded to him without thinking. But he always wanted a challenge."

"A challenge like selling kids into slavery?" I said.

She gave me a tolerant tilt of her head. "You have to understand. It's a game to him."

I snorted.

"I don't mean that the way you're taking it. He's not a sadist. He's . . . moving pieces on a gameboard to wipe everyone else out at Monopoly. It's not even about the money to him—or perhaps it is, but not the money itself. It's about being the person who has all that money. He'd burn it afterwards on a whim, but he likes being the person who owns everything."

"Does he own you?" I said.

She shifted her leg slightly, and winced. "Jacob is a genius. He's the best businessman I've ever met. My talent is picking a winning horse."

"He's not winning. I'm taking him down."

"All right."

"That doesn't bother you?"

"One thing about picking horses is you know when to collect your winnings and look for a new race. If people like you are after Jacob, it's time for me to cash out."

"So, back to Wall Street then?" I said.

"Maybe."

I raised Miguel's gun and pointed it at her. "Maybe I just shoot you instead, you don't back any more horses."

She gazed at me coolly. "I thought you wanted my help. Now that you know our history, understand this. I have no loyalty. I calculate what's best—for me—and that's the way I tack my sails. So if the way out of being hunted down by the likes of you is to help you and then leave the state, I am all too happy to do that."

So it wasn't the brain entrainment. This was just how she was. Wow. "You're not afraid Pourdry's goons will come after you for betraying him?"

She lifted one shoulder in half a shrug, the movement somehow elegant even tied to a bed with a bleeding leg and a face full of airbag burns. "Like I said, I pick winning horses. I have no interest in who wins this vendetta of yours, but whichever way the wind blows, I expect Jacob isn't going to be doing much chasing down of anyone by the end of it."

"If you're so fickle, why would Pourdry trust you with anything?"

"Because I'm very good. And it's not like Jacob doesn't know this about me. I'd even venture to say he respects it. He's always been confident he'll continue to win, and that *would* have kept my loyalty."

"You're disgusting," I said.

"After what I saw tonight, I suspect some might say the same of you," Vance replied evenly. "Our morals are simply different."

Different morals my ass. Vance *had* no morals. "Tell me how to find him."

"Jacob does not see people. He conducts his business from his home office, always."

"And do you have an address?"

"He doesn't know it, but yes."

I almost laughed. She was so axiomatically *selfish*. "What is it?"

"I'll agree to tell you. After I've left town."

"You'll tell me now, or you'll never make it out of town."

We were both aware we were negotiating, and where it would land. "Take me to a hospital," Vance said, "and I'll give you the address. Guarantee me forty-eight hours before you move."

"Twenty-four," I said, and she nodded.

I was cautious of a trap, of course. But if the information did pan out, it was nice to have something go right for once.

Or at least, I thought that until I dropped Vance off outside an emergency room driveway. She told me what I wanted to know and waved off my threats of what I'd do to her if she'd lied, and then she added something.

"You were at Yamamoto's meeting. It would do you well to figure out who is trying to set us at each other's throats. I'm sure someone was whispered your name as the likely culprit."

And as Vance limped out of the car, it hit me.

Nobody had been whispered my name as a target. Because I knew who was doing the whispering.

I sped away from the hospital so fast the tires almost broke static friction, my fingers stabbing the buttons on my cell phone.

"Hello, Cas," Rio said blandly.

"You're pitting everyone in LA against each other?" I said. "You know what a gang war will do to this city!"

"I do," he answered.

"What, is this some messed-up way of trying to convince me this isn't worth the trouble, because you can just boost the violence back up to the same level?" I ranted. "That doesn't even make sense—it's not exactly going to convince me this is less necessary. And you know how many innocent people are going to get hurt!"

"So do you," Rio said. "Collateral damage. You can make it cease."

His statement took my breath away. He wasn't trying to make the brain entrainment functionally useless—this was extortion, plain and simple. If I stopped what I was doing, he'd stop setting people up to die. "You're blackmailing me by provoking violent criminals into destroying Los Angeles," I said.

"Yes."

"That's not fair."

"I do not mean it to be."

"I'm not backing down," I said. "I'll figure out a way to keep this from happening. People aren't going to start shooting each other just because you tell them to."

"You have a far more optimistic view of human nature than I do, Cas."

Someone put a hand on my shoulder. "The definition of humanity is far more flexible than most people believe."

Goddammit. This was the last time I needed my stupid brain acting up on me again.

"Good luck to you, Cas," Rio said. "Let me know when you change your mind. I hear a militia is coming to town."

Right. He'd probably paid for their plane tickets.

I hung up and slammed my palm against the steering wheel. Well, at least I had Pourdry's address. I debated whether to wait the twenty-four hours I'd promised Vance or if I should just drive there now and get some fucking satisfaction.

My phone jangled. "What!" I barked into it.

"Cassu-san!" howled Yamamoto. "You remember our meeting? Someone is trying to tear us down. We must be on the right track! They are trying to divide us!"

"I've heard," I said. Hopefully he didn't catch the black irony.

"So you know, you do not believe anything you hear? Is bad, is very bad. I tell people, do not listen! But they are blinded by anger. The violence, it is happening already, and once it does is the retaliation—Cassu-san, I tell you, if some of our friends at that meeting make the move, there will be no coming back. It is grave."

"Hey, ironically, the 'problems' here are probably stopping them," I couldn't resist pointing out. We'd see how long my brain entrainment could counter Rio's machinations. It would give me time to hit on a better plan.

"Cassu-san, for shame. We do not need some CIA power to stop us from acting like animals. I am calling everyone, telling them—no one is to raise a hand against anyone else in our little group of friends. We work together, yes? Until we find out the true culprit, no violence! Or that person is no longer welcome. We work together or it will not work. You understand, yes?"

Shit. "I have a . . . personal matter with Jacob Pourdry," I said. "It doesn't have to do with this."

"No violence, Cassu-san! Your personal matter, it can wait. Until we find and stop these shenanigans! Now I must call the rest. You are big help, Cassu-san, I hope you stay our friend." He hung up.

My good night had suddenly been fucked over. Not only was Rio screwing the entire city of Los Angeles unless I gave in to him, but I'd finally gotten intel on Pourdry only to be told I couldn't use it without being thrown out of Yamamoto's coalition. And if I burned my welcome there, I'd lose any insight into what they might be planning, and thus possibly end up shooting myself in the back of the head.

Fuck, fuck, fuck.

twenty

I GOT back to the apartment I was using as my base to discover I had a bigger problem.

The brain entrainment was set and done—anything I might do to defend it would be a response to actions other people hadn't taken yet. My hands were tied on Pourdry. And I'd tried texting Arthur to see if he had any other vigilante jobs lined up, but he was still caught up with whatever problems had taken him away earlier.

Which meant that once again I had nothing to do.

Murmurs fragmented through my consciousness, swelling back up. People I knew and yet didn't, faces who were only just in shadow.

"This plan will take years to bring to fruition."

"How many of them have years? This is a large investment."

"Oh, some of them will die. We've accounted for it."

"Fuck you," I muttered to the voices. They sneered in response.

The data sharpened around me, razor edges snagging and

stabbing at my senses. I tried to stay still, to sit on the thin mattress and freeze myself in time and space, but of course it didn't work. Gravity, fucking gravity, drawing infinite arrows downward, and an equal infinity of normal forces pushing back—and no, not down, but toward the center of this ball called Earth, every crushing beat of physics bouncing down the radius and back.

"Is sensory overload a problem?" Clinical fingers pressed against my skin.

"Yes, it will be. But not the most dangerous one."

I tried to force the bleed-throughs away, slam a lid on their grasping tentacles. I had so much to concentrate on, to be alert for. I had to focus. Stay on top of myself.

I couldn't afford distractions.

My breath buzzed in and out, counting the moles of oxygen, nitrogen, argon. Every molecule was a barb against the tissue of my lungs. And this time accompanied by other breaths taken other places, running through a forest, crouched against a concrete wall, lying on a wooden floor that smelled of citrus and lilac. . . .

Jesus Christ.

I only lasted one pathetic minute before I was groping for the whiskey bottle I knew was close to hand. The alcohol was so cheap it scoured my throat raw, but at least it dulled my senses.

Not enough, of course. It had ceased to be enough ever since my mind had decided it needed to throw echoes of another person's life across my reality. Ever since Simon's presence had pushed me into scraping at those mental walls, ever since Checker's prodding had nudged at the cracks in them, ever since Dawna Polk had broken down any protection from my past I'd once had.

Fortunately, I had other things in this apartment as well.

Part of me wished mixing pills and alcohol was more dangerous for me. It might have helped to feel a touch of recklessness. But, I reminded myself, I didn't want to take too much anyway—after all, within a few hours I might have to be able to function well enough to fight again. God help me, but an ugly, selfish bit in the back of my self-pity hoped enough would go wrong in LA that I'd have to be.

At least the cocktail finally knocked me into fitful unconsciousness. My last thought before blacking out was that maybe I was sauced enough not to dream, but I knew it was only a false hope. Especially as my subconscious had more and more to choose from.

Of course, of all my myriad problems, the one that invaded my dreams that night had to be Simon.

Some part of me pushed against his image, even asleep, but he'd been stalking my unconscious mind for years and apparently wasn't about to stop. Only now his face was clearer, and instead of disorganized glimpses of memory, my nightmares had become the future, a future in which he *helped* me. . . .

We sat by a window, the surf crashing in the distance outside.

"You have to," he said. "You have to let me."

"No," I answered. The intonation wasn't my own. "No, I don't want to—"

"This is the only way." His face was close. Uncomfortably close. His voice hitched.

He was crying, for some reason.

"You're wrong," I said. "It can't be the only way. It can't." I sounded like I was pleading, and hated my dream-self for giving him the satisfaction. Why would I do such a thing?

"I'm so sorry," Simon whispered, and reached for me.

No—

I screamed. The scream went on forever, echoing through time, consuming me from the inside out. I blacked out and dissolved, every sense of self crushing to nothing. I tried to hang on, to cling, to stay, but it was no use.

I broke into pieces.

Melted away.

Died.

I woke, and jerked upright, the blanket tangling around my legs. *No no no* no—I needed to run, run run *run*—

How fast can she run?

All of the physical skills are at the upper limits for a human.

I spasmed. My head hit the wall and my pulse banged against my throat like an out-of-control drum set.

"I'm awake," I growled. I was awake, and in control, and I wasn't going to allow this. I had a choice. I could figure this out.

Figure everything out.

I drew my knees up and dropped my head between them. *You can handle this,* I reminded myself. *Remember what you can do. You're as powerful as Simon or Dawna or any of them, and more powerful than Rio. You can win.*

If my own brain didn't fuck me over first. I cast about for the whiskey bottle.

Someone rapped loudly on my door.

My hand had shot up with the reassuring grip of my Colt against my palm before I'd fully registered the sound. I got up quietly, twitching to the side just in case. "Who's there?"

"Miss Russell? It's Sonya Halliday."

"Who?"

"Professor Sonya Halliday. Arthur's friend."

I marched over and yanked open the door. "I know who you are. What the hell are you doing *here*?"

Sonya Halliday was a tall, African American woman whose uniform of choice included sharp skirts and rimless spectacles, and she was, to my everlasting annoyance, a mathematician. A real one, unlike me. If Arthur had told me he was childhood friends with a math professor back when we first met, I probably would have walked out of his life and never looked back. Of course, I had a sneaking suspicion that he might not have put up with me in the first place if I hadn't reminded him of her.

Unfortunately, being a computational theorist meant Halliday had cottoned on to how not-normal my abilities were, but I'd studiously avoided all her prior attempts at calling me to talk about research.

"I always so enjoy your eloquence," Halliday said now, with disturbing calm. "You humiliated three of my colleagues and signed my name to it. Did you really forget?" Completely ignoring the fact that I was holding a gun, she thrust a piece of paper in my face.

Right. My ill-advised little mathematical commenting spree right before this job had started. This job that had obligated me to the whole world, that had worked but made me a target, that had succeeded but caused Rio to try to smash an entire metropolitan area if I didn't reverse it.

And Arthur's friend wanted to talk to me about *math*. It was all too absurd.

"I was right," I said. "They were wrong. Take the credit for it; I don't care. Now go away."

"I don't want credit. I want you to sit down and go through the proof with me. I've asked you before to collaborate—"

"And I said no." I tried to shut the door in her face, but she showed an astonishing lack of self-preservation and pushed into the gap. "Get out or I'll hurt you."

She just pushed in further. "You more than said no! You spat on the idea—and now you upend all of mathematics and sign my name to it? Do you realize what you've done? Two of the authors of that paper are Fields Medal winners, and they're claiming it's still correct. Half the math world doesn't even fully understand what you were trying to say, including me, which I will freely admit because modern algebra isn't even my field—"

"And what do you want me to do? Go beat them into submission?"

"I want you to either walk me through it, or, preferably,

sign your own name to it and tell these idiots who you really are!"

The sentence rang in the musty air of my decrepit living room. Like something dangerous.

Something deadly.

Who you really are.

"What did you say?" My lips barely formed the words. I tried to move away from her, but my body had gone thick and slow, as if my blood had turned to clay.

"I don't care how young you were; you still have credibility in this field," Halliday went on, oblivious. "Your proofs—people remember. You can pass things through me if you want, or if you decide to keep staying out of it all that's your decision even though I think it's a tragic waste—but don't you *dare* try to make me the L'Hôpital to your Bernoulli."

I barely heard the last of her words as memory forcefully unraveled itself.

"Think of the wealth and fame we could claim." The man spoke from behind me, about me, but I ignored him. My pen flew over the paper, unspooling pseudocode. "The technological possibilities alone. We could be rich."

"We could," answered a woman. "But this will be better."

My hip hit the table and I almost fell. I'd stumbled back, into the room. The planes of reality slid and closed inward, the edges of my vision darkening.

"Miss Russell?" Halliday stepped over hastily and reached out, but her hand hovered by my elbow as if she were afraid to touch me. "Miss Russell, are you all right?"

"I see you've managed to keep them alive. Are they still human?"

"More than human," the same woman answered. "Superhuman, if you will."

"I, uh—" Halliday's grip was on my arm now, helping me fall into a chair. She fumbled out a mobile phone. "I'll call Arthur. Or—do you need an ambulance? Are you ill?"

"No." I lashed out a hand. Her mobile clattered against the opposite wall in the sharp angles of gravity and elastic collisions.

"I didn't mean to— I never brought this up because I thought it might be a sensitive, I mean, I didn't know why you— I haven't told anyone."

She was so *earnest.*

"Are you in some kind of danger?" Halliday asked.

"You don't know what it is anymore, to be in danger," someone taunted me.

Every neuron, every cell, every enzyme and protein receptor and biochemical nuance—they sparked in a million interactions, and I could feel every one. Everything. I controlled it all.

"Precious. Not all."

A spasm bubbled up from my diaphragm, a hiccupping laugh, strangling me until I couldn't breathe.

"Miss Russell?"

The hysterical laughter wouldn't stop, shaking me from skull to knees. I hung on to the edge of the table so I wouldn't slide off the world.

"All this time . . ." I panted. "You knew. All. This. Time . . ."

Halliday straightened with a slight frown. "It would be more accurate to say I only suspected, but the pool of people with your caliber of mathematical ability is a vanishingly small group. I didn't think you were seriously trying to hide it from me." She'd started to sound like someone who'd opened the door to a washroom and found a house of mirrors instead. "Are you telling me—does no one else know?"

For some reason, that struck me as even funnier. *"No one* knows," I gasped out between the hyperventilating giggles. "No one at all. Null set. Empty. Until . . . until you."

Not many other people would have gotten what I meant by that, but Halliday's eyes widened. "Are you saying—

Wait a minute. Are you saying you lost your—your own identity? You have some sort of amnesia?"

"The null set's not right," I babbled on. "There's Rio, and fucking *Simon,* and you and apparently everyone else with a cursory understanding of anything above calculus, so really it's everyone, the set of all sets, except they can't be members of their *own fucking selves*—"

I wasn't even making sense anymore. A living Russell's paradox. Someone who had less access to her own history than a complete stranger.

twenty-one

"I'M SORRY," Halliday kept trying to say. "If I'd known . . I didn't know you'd lost your memory—"

"Neither did I." I shoved back from the table and almos fell. My hysterical laughter had cut off as abruptly as it ha come, hamstringing me into a blackening morass in it wake. "I have to go."

"You don't want me to tell you—?"

"No. I don't."

You're not entitled to know.

Really? What does this entitle me to?

Blood, blood and bone—

Only he has that information.

The jumbled chunks collapsed against my reality, faste and faster, strobing my senses with faces and colors and remnants of excitement or despair. I pushed past Halliday and out of the room, then out of the building. Onto the street where the over-bright sun stabbed me in the eyes. Passing pedestrians shied away from me.

We have to run.

Run away—run—

I need to be here. I'm not leaving. Not leaving, not leaving, not leaving . . .

I ran for a long time, the pavement pounding through the soles of my boots. Ran and ran and ran, as if I could escape my cracking memories.

Run. Run or die.

Die.

Where are you?

Someone shouted at me. A uniform—police? Hired security? I ducked between buildings and cut into a park. Run, run, run, he couldn't stop me.

They'll find us, wherever we go.

They won't find you if you don't exist.

The path dead-ended against a bricked-up archway between two buildings. I smacked my palms against it, pressed my forehead against the roughness. Turned and leaned into the corner. Cold sweat shrink-wrapped my skin, but not from the running.

She has to believe me. It was Simon's voice. *She has to believe until we're done—*

My legs crumpled and I pressed myself into the shadows of the corner, my body forming three directional cosines, three coordinate planes trapping me in this quadrant of reality. Whispers smothered me, flashes of fire and jungle and rain, and people who didn't seem real but were. I struggled against them, building my coordinate system into cylindrical and then spherical and then a four-dimensional parameter space.

Footsteps scuffed against the pavement. Here or in my head?

A shadow above me. Arthur.

He sat down next to me, back against the wall, arms loosely across his knees. "Hey."

His voice knifed me. I hunched away.

"Sonya called me."

I forced my mouth to form words. "I figured." *You'll lose*

everything, something babbled inside of me. "How did yo
find me?"

"I'm a PI, darling," he said. "You . . . wanna talk abou
it?"

"No."

I'm telling you they lied.

And I don't believe you.

The last voice I recognized as mine. It dizzied me, lik
looking into a mirror of a mirror of a mirror.

"Halliday—she's got to be wrong," I said to Arthur. The
sentence gnarled hoarse in my throat. "She could still be
wrong. Checker couldn't find—he didn't find anything
he would have found something, found *that,* if—if wha
she said—"

"Can't find what's been erased, but Sonya, she's been i
her field for decades. She remembered."

"You're saying I met her before? Do you know how coinci
dental that would be? The odds—"

"Of two mathematicians knowing each other? Hear tell it'
a smaller world than you're making out."

"But I'm not a mathematician." I couldn't call myself one
not except as convenient shorthand, but even if I granted my
self the description, I'd never been in the field as a researcher
Never frequented universities or conferences. Never shake
hands with the people making the discoveries.

"Mathematics will never know what hit it. If our only
limitation is time—"

"Ah, but that's not the useful part."

Were they the same people who had been talking in my
head before? The same ones who'd been watching me as if I
was their prize livestock? Their pet mathematician? I
couldn't remember.

"Well, Sonya, she thinks maybe you were one once," said
Arthur. "She tells me—more'n once before, she's told me I
don't get it. She says what you can do, that it isn't . . . I think
the word 'impossible' might've come up."

"I'll take that," I said, trying for normalcy and belly flopping.

"Anyhow. Just now, when she called, she explained—" Arthur cleared his throat. "Said one day something reminded her of a child prodigy she'd heard of. Ten, fifteen years ago. Kid was writing papers at eleven years old. Like a Mozart or someone."

Or Gauss, for a more relevant example. "Well, that's not me," I said. Relief bubbled through me, an almost hysterical reversal of emotion. "I wasn't a child prodigy. She got it wrong."

"Russell," Arthur said. "How do you know?"

I gazed up and up, from the height of a child, as a man's silhouette filled the doorway.

"Introduce me to your tutors?"

A sudden ringing filled my head, like someone had bashed a gong, a vibrating clang. "No—no. It doesn't make sense. It's—it's stupid. I might not know who I am, but I'm not *that*." Child prodigies were people you read about in the news or in biographies: improbable savants who would shine so brightly they'd blind the world before they hit puberty. Reconciling that idea with the violent, practical brutality of my own life—it didn't compute.

Halliday was wrong.

Talent? It's only logic, sang a child. *Other people are dumb.*

"She said it was a Bahraini girl," Arthur continued, inexorable. "Had the math world all a-buzz. Sonya read the papers with everyone else, couldn't wait to see what the gal did when she grew up. Then the girl drops off the face of things. Sonya said she forgot about it altogether, maybe mentioned it once in a while with colleagues, idle curiosity. And she says the next time this got brought up in passing, after she met you—she said she knew, all of a sudden."

"Oh, yeah," I said. "Yeah, gut feeling. That's never wrong."

Arthur ignored my sarcasm. "She went and did some

research. The girl, seems she dropped off the planet when
she was still just a kid. Disappeared. Sonya poked more
and . . . well, party line is the girl went off to some board-
ing school and then died a few years later, but Sonya didn't
believe it. She always figured . . . well, she figured you were
keeping your silence for a reason, 's why she never mentioned it to us. And Checker . . ." Arthur hesitated.

How's that fancy school of yours?

Fine.

"Just now Checker, as soon as he heard, he looked it all
up, and he says Sonya's onto something, that those records,
they're all fishy. Faked files, not a lot, just fishy enough
that—he thinks she could be right."

"She's not," I said.

"Russell, if she is . . . it's not just about knowing your
name. If she's right, then . . . then you got a mother and sister,
still alive."

All you do is study!

Because I'm smarter than you are.

"She's not right," I said again, louder.

"We could look them up," suggested Arthur, very softly.
"See for sure—"

"No."

"You could have family out there. Can't ignore that."

*The same man again, in a suit and a broad-brimmed hat,
his face still in shadow, briefcase in hand—tall, so tall, like
the giants in stories, his voice low and gravelly—"Is this
your daughter?"*

"Watch me," I spat out, loudly enough to drown out the
voices in my head. "I'm very good at ignoring things."

"Russell—"

"LA's going to go nuclear."

I hadn't meant to say it. Hadn't decided yet whether I
should share.

"Say what?" Arthur asked.

"It's Rio." The words tumbled out, misshapen and desperate. "Like you said. He's trying to stop the brain entrainment. He . . . he's setting up the city to implode."

I updated him on what I'd learned since we'd last seen each other. I left out the part about killing Miguel and his friends.

Left out how I'd shot Vance, too.

"Well," Arthur said, when I'd run out of words. "What are we gonna do about it?"

I didn't think I'd ever been so grateful to him.

The alcohol was metabolizing out of my system, but I was starting to get my focus back. There *was* a next step here—brainstorming with Arthur and Checker and Pilar, and solving this. We'd done it before. We could do it again.

My fingers touched skin, pale and soft, and so fragile. Human frailty. I would make him hurt for this, take vengeance for them as no one had done for me.

How to start? Mathematics gave me so many options.

I came back to myself. My hands were over my face, and my breath hitched raggedly against them.

"Hey. Hey, Russell. You okay?"

"I think I'm losing my mind," I whispered. I couldn't solve anything if my brain went out from under me. I needed my brain. Without it . . .

Oh, Jesus. Without it, I was going to lose.

This couldn't be what defeated me. For fuck's sake, I should be able to handle a few scary memories. I was going to pieces over nothing more than the shadow of a nightmare.

A man screamed, a wild, unearthly sound—

I jerked.

My hands pressed against my eyes, my fingers a crisscrossing spiderweb trying to keep my brain inside my skull, keep me sane. Useless.

"Tell me," Arthur said gently.

"They're pushing me out," I mumbled. "The memories. Like I'm going to wake up one morning and be someone else, someone who is—" My jaw clenched so hard it locked;

I pried it back open. "I'm not that person. Whoever she is. I can feel her. She's—she's not *me*, Arthur. I know it sounds crazy, but I swear it's true. And I keep—I keep losing track. . . ." My grip on reality was slipping; I would dissolve into the abyss and be nothing but scattered atoms, emptiness. . . .

I didn't want to go. Didn't want to die.

Arthur moved closer to me and wrapped an arm around my shoulders, pulling my head against his shoulder the way a father might with his child.

I thought about what Checker had said, that Arthur had an obsession with fixing people. I decided I didn't care. Fuck, our current conflict notwithstanding, I considered myself Rio's friend and had for years, and he'd never pretended his concern for my welfare extended an inch beyond religious obligation. People had all sorts of reasons for helping each other. It didn't change anything.

In fact, it made me feel better about the logic of it all to think Arthur might have a fixation with hard-luck cases as one of his axioms. His concern for me made a lot more sense that way.

I leaned my forehead against his shoulder. The fabric of the button-down he wore was slightly rough, like canvas, and smelled of clean sweat and old leather.

"You have twenty-three seconds," said a voice, and I jumped—

Arthur felt me flinch.

"I don't like to say it," he said softly, "But maybe . . . if you got no other options . . . this Simon guy, he might be able to help you."

My stomach twisted like I wanted to be sick.

"I don't know," Arthur admitted. "God knows I understand why you don't want to talk to him. But this . . . might be he's the one you need." He sounded despondent, as if it were his fault I had no other option. "He says he won't do anything you don't want him to, right?"

"And you believe him?"

I felt Arthur shrug slightly. "He could've already, and he didn't. Guess that's a point in his favor."

I pulled upright and sat back against the wall. "It doesn't matter. Even if he got a signed agreement from me every other fucking second—it doesn't matter." The fear loomed, a black, ugly cloud, and I struggled to confine it to words, to articulate it so Arthur could understand. "I'd be letting him into my brain. *Letting* him. There's no way I can know what the fallout from that could be—there's no way I could ever, possibly, in a million years, understand it well enough to say I'm okay with it. And what if he does something accidentally? Or that he *thinks* is the right thing, and . . ." The words felt disconnected, floundering, islands of meaning with no continuity between them.

"I get that," said Arthur, and Jesus, it sounded like he did.

"Too many variables," I murmured.

"Thing is . . . what if it's the only way?"

The impending nightmare settled on me like a thousand dusty cobwebs, stifling. Doing nothing, continuing on, descending into madness until I lost myself—it wasn't an option, was it? Especially if I wanted to be functional to do what I really needed to, to save the city I'd signed up for protecting only to lead it toward its downfall.

Or even if I only wanted to save myself.

Then why did part of me still want to cling to that suicidal dive instead of submitting to Simon?

"Sometimes a thing's needed," Arthur said. "Like what we got going right now in LA, nudging people's brain waves. A little help isn't always a bad thing. Not even for you."

I tensed away from him. I didn't want to think about Simon *helping* me as being in any way parallel to the brain entrainment. One was a benign crime-fighting measure; the other was the most personal violation.

What I was doing wasn't the same. Not the same thing at all.

But what Arthur had said . . . sometimes a thing was necessary.

I hated it when he had a point.

"I can be there, if you want," Arthur continued. "Make sure nothing goes wrong, or happens on accident. If this guy's aboveboard, he isn't going to be throwing anything my way, right?"

Rio was the more logical choice, given his immunity, but I didn't want to see him right now. I twitched my head in something like a nod.

"You got a number for Simon?" Arthur asked gently.

I didn't, but I was more than certain Rio would send him to meet me, even if he was currently trying to screw me over in every other way.

"We're gonna get you taken care of, Russell," Arthur said. "And then we're gonna go and fix the rest of it."

I let him help me up.

I should have known it would never be that easy.

twenty-two

ARTHUR GOT a call as he was helping me back to his car.

"Hello? Justin, hey, did you get her—" He listened for a long minute. "Easy, kid. Uh—I'll be there as soon as I can, but it might be a few minutes, I got someone else with an emergency right now. Can you call—"

"Go," I said. "It's okay." I was a fucking adult. I appreciated Arthur trying to support me, but I'd feel worse than stupid if he tried to treat me like spun glass above kids who actually needed him.

If Katrina and Justin had gotten stuck in a bad place, I could only hope that Checker's optimism was true, and that what we had done would make it easier for them to get out of it. I could feel good about that, at least.

Arthur covered the phone with a hand to turn to me. "I'm not okay with you going to this guy alone anyway, Russell. Just in case, you know? Even if you feel like you gotta do this, you should have someone with you."

"I'll call Checker, then," I said wearily. "Go take care of your kids."

He nodded reluctantly and spoke back into the phone to tell Justin he'd be there in half an hour, which I thought was ridiculously optimistic for the time of day no matter where he was going, but whatever. Then he insisted on calling Checker himself and waiting with me while I texted Rio. He probably suspected I would have chickened out otherwise.

He might have been right.

Checker told me to come back to his place—Simon already knew where it was, after all, and there was no point in burning the safe house Checker and Pilar had been staying at. I drove to Van Nuys alone like I was driving to the gallows. As I walked inside, I couldn't help swiveling my head, taking in the trees and grass, the slight scent of smoke from someone's barbecue . . . the layers of mathematical data edging every stone and corner, shimmering with measurements and reflection coefficients, curvatures and spatial relations.

I couldn't help feeling like I'd never see it again. Like this was the end.

My lungs twisted tight in my chest. I walked up to Checker's door and knocked.

He was the one who opened it. I was grateful for that, and that he didn't say anything really, just let me come inside. Simon was already there, sitting on the edge of the couch.

"So how does this work?" I said.

"It's nothing . . . invasive. You don't have to worry." Simon gestured, and I forced myself to sink down across from him. He half raised his hands as if he were about to lean forward and touch me, but thought better of it. "I'm just going to talk to you, and have you talk back. That's all, I promise. You'll be aware through all of it."

Cassandra? Talk to me. Talk to me!

I tried to shake the apparitions away. "I want to know what you're doing," I said to Simon. "Every step of the way. I want to know when you're influencing me."

"I . . . I can do that. It will be a little less effective, but I can, if you want me to."

"I don't care if it's less effective," I said. "Tell me."

"All right."

"Are you going to bring her memory back?" Checker asked.

The sun stabbing through clouds onto the cobblestones, the scent of roasted nuts and blood—I clenched my teeth, working to anchor myself.

"No." Simon was studying me worriedly. He also looked faintly annoyed Checker was there and talking, but I didn't give a fuck. "Cas, believe it or not, the amnesia is protecting you. You had some—uh—some trauma—"

"That you can't tell me about, I get it," I said.

"Yes," he said. "I could reverse your memory loss, but it might—it *would* kill you."

"Peachy," I said. "So this is just about shoring up whatever Dawna did to me."

He shifted a little. "Essentially. I'm afraid that will mean reinforcing your—um—your mental blocks."

"You mean making sure I can't remember anything."

"I'm sorry." He looked it, too, his face drawn and strained. "I wish I could do more."

I took a breath. Tried to be mature about it. If I was honest with myself, I wanted nothing more than to keep my prior self safely behind thick black walls, forever. If Simon had said we were going to let her out, I wasn't sure I could have gone through with it. Whatever Pithica had done to me—whatever anyone had done to me, back in the distant past—I was better off not remembering.

The status quo was much preferable. Well, the status quo without going mad and dying.

"Are you ready?" Simon asked.

"Fuck you," I said. "Of course not."

His jaw worked a little. "I, I won't start until you feel—"

"Simon, I swear to God, if you don't get this over with—"

"Right, all right, I just wanted to make sure." His breath hitched. It occurred to me that this seemed to be as unhappy a process for him as it was for me, and took some vindictive pleasure in it. "Try to relax," he said.

"Fat chance of that," I muttered.

Simon leaned forward.

Simon leaned forward—

My vision doubled, two versions of the man in front of me staring earnestly into my eyes. I recognized the second version from my dream, the nightmare in which every fear had coalesced. But this time I noticed he looked younger—

"No," I said. "No—"

No—

"I have to." Tears flooded his cheeks, his expression stretched with pain. "I have to—we have to—"

He reached for me, and resistance folded in my brain with a dying whimper, even as I fought to cling to it, fought to live . . . I didn't want to go. Didn't want to die.

"I'm sorry," Simon wept, "I'm so sorry. . . ."

And I ceased to want anything at all.

I jerked back and up, stumbling to stand, stumbling away.

"Cas?" Checker's voice.

I'm sorry, Vala.

"Cassandra!" Simon leapt to his feet as well.

"You . . ." My hand had come up of its own accord, my finger pointed, trembling. "You!"

"Cassandra—Cas—don't—"

"Don't what? *Don't try to remember?* Why, because I'll know what you *did*?"

"Cas!" Checker's voice again, high with alarm. "Cas, what is it?"

"Admit it!" I screamed the words, spat them in Simon's face. "It wasn't a dream, was it? You—it was real!"

He won't be remaking you, Rio had said.

Rio had lied.

"This was never about protecting me, was it?" I was hyperventilating. Oh, God. "You telling me to block it all out—not to try—"

"It *was* to protect you!" interrupted Simon. "It *is*. Cassandra, I was not lying, I swear. This will kill you—"

"This will kill you," pleaded Simon, somewhere dark and close and far away. "You must let me—it is the only way—"

The world seesawed.

"Cas!" Someone grabbed my arm. I shoved him off violently before I realized it had been Checker; he flailed as his chair tilted but managed to catch himself against the wall before he fell. "Cas!"

"Pithica didn't take my memory," I said. "It was you. It was you."

Simon's face was stricken. He didn't reply.

The room fell into a silence so complete it was as if all the air had been sucked out of it.

Checker broke it. "He did *what*?" he whispered.

"He's the one," I said. "He erased me. Admit it. Admit it!"

"It was— I had to, we had to." Simon's eyes darted desperately between Checker and me. "I can explain—you were dying—"

"I was someone else, wasn't I?" My throat closed. "I was a— I was somebody, and you destroyed her. You killed her, and she didn't want to, she didn't want to go. . . ."

Simon was breathing raggedly. "You have to understand—"

"I can feel her." Suddenly everything made sense, too much sense, stampeding through my head like it wanted to take me over. "She wants to come back. You killed her and she didn't want to die, and now she wants to come back."

"Not *her*, Cassandra, *you*. You! We were saving your life!"

"No! You weren't!" Certainty surged in me, the certainty of voice and memory and knowledge creeping through into my own goddamn brain. "You killed her, and you wiped her brain, and you made me on top of it. Don't tell me I'm not fucking remembering it right, because *I am*."

"You *what*?" Checker was leaning forward in his chair as if he were about to physically throttle Simon. I'd never heard him sound so dangerous. "You overwrote her like a fucking hard drive? You utter *piece of shit*—"

"Stop!" I thrust out a hand, my other one cradling my forehead as if it could keep my brain from fracturing.

Waves crashing—
Glass breaking—
Wood splintering—

"Thank you." Simon ran a hand through his hair and gestured limply at Checker. "He doesn't understand. I'm trying to explain; we had to. You were—it was killing you, and I had to do it, I had to save you—"

"Shut up." I took a step forward, putting Checker behind me. "I didn't tell Checker to stay out of this because he's wrong. He's not. But this is between you and me."

The certainty in Simon's face faltered.

"You erased my memories."

"To save your life! It was the hardest thing I ever did!"

"You?" My mouth twisted, going crooked and ugly. "The hardest thing *you* ever did? Please, try to convince me this is about you. I'm just rabid to hear it. Go on, try."

"That's not what I . . ." His dark skin went paler, the color draining from behind it and leaving it brown parchment. "Don't you get it? You were going to die!"

"Oh, I get it. You did what you thought was *best*." I was biting out the words, each a sarcasm-coated pill. My voice had started trembling around the edges. "You went into my head and you took the most important parts of me and you want me to thank you."

"Did she even get a say in it?" said Checker from behind me.

"I told you, stay out of this," I snapped at him without turning around. I stayed focused on Simon. "Whether or not you *asked* to blank out everything I was—" I stopped. Simon's features had gone tense and taut as if some too-large emotion were trying to burst through; he folded his lips together deliberately and looked away from me. "Fuck you. You didn't ask me, did you."

"I did!" he insisted. He sniffed. "I did—I tried to convince you. It was the only way! You said, you kept saying that you—it would mean forgetting me, never seeing me again, forgetting *us,* and you said you couldn't bear that. We were in *love,* Cassandra, do you understand?" He was blinking furiously against tears; they spilled over and slid down his cheeks and over his jaw, dripping onto his collar. "You wanted to keep on going together until you destroyed yourself and died, and I couldn't watch you do that! Even though it meant losing you. Even though it meant going into your thoughts when I had told myself I would never—when I had promised—and even when I knew it meant I would never be able to see you again, that seeing me might remind you—" His voice broke. "I gave up everything I had told myself I stood for, I broke every rule I had, I gave up *you*—because I had to save you. Even if it meant I lost everything!"

I slugged him.

The punch was so fast he never saw it coming; his head snapped halfway around and yanked his body after it. He staggered and fell against Checker's couch.

"*You* lost everything?" I cried. "You?"

He cowered away from me. "I'm trying to explain!"

"And I don't like your explanation." I crossed my arms, keeping my fists trapped in my armpits. I wanted to do a lot more than sock him one.

We were in love, he'd said, as if he'd expected the words to break me. As if he had some claim on me.

Instead, it only cemented my revulsion.

He's a challenge, giggled the ghost in my head. *I like challenges much more than I like men.*

I scrabbled to cling to my fury, clawing to keep myself in

the present. "You keep bleating that you did this for my own good," I said to Simon. "You know who else says that? Dawna Polk."

He drew into himself, hunching down and leaning on the arm of Checker's couch like it was holding him up.

"You took everything I was. Everything." He had been the one to take the math from me. Not Pithica or Halberd or whoever else lurked behind me. Simon.

I didn't know how I was certain, but I was. My fractured memory knew.

"You took everything, because *you* thought it was right. And you stand here, and you whine about how painful it was for *you,* and you tell me the only reason I wasn't fully on board with it was that I was so in love I needed a few more minutes of *your* magnificence—that's the only reason my former self would have for not having her personality erased, is that it? I'm sure she had no other objection at all." My voice rose, cracking over the space between us. "You're a raging egotist, you know that? And whoever I used to be, you murdered her."

"Vala would have understood," he mumbled. His shoulders shook. "We were in love. I did it for her."

"God save us all from your brand of love," I said.

Of everything I'd said, that was what defeated him. He hugged his arms around his chest, shrinking into himself.

"Get out," I said. "I never want to lay eyes on you again."

He half turned back to me, like he wanted to argue. But then he looked at my face, and whatever his psychic ability saw there, it made him curl back and close himself away and stumble for the door without another word.

I sank down on the couch and dropped my head into my hands. Faces crossed and blurred, irising in and out of darkness—a tired older woman, Simon, a girl who looked like me but wasn't, Simon, a scarred woman in a white coat, Simon . . .

Valarmathi. Be polite.

I don't like being touched, but then, you don't like touching people.

It works, right? Ignore everyone else.

Valarmathi might get her wish and come back to life. Or maybe she'd kill us both in trying. I wasn't sure she even existed anymore—but then, I wasn't sure I did, either.

"Hey," Checker said. He'd come over next to me.

I didn't answer.

He moved a hand as if he were going to reach out, and then thought better of it. "Do you want to talk—"

"No."

"Okay."

I squeezed my hands against my face until it hurt, as if I could hold myself together. I thought about the shattered bits of memory and emotion that belonged to a dead woman, the pieces of feeling that I now knew echoed from someone who hadn't wanted to leave. And the life that had taken her place, my own half-life, bereft of any real meaning . . . even the proofs I'd tried lay impotent, dangling threads of elegance I knew had to mean something, but didn't.

Simon had no idea what he had taken from me.

Even worse, I only existed because of his clumsy attempts at playing God. Valarmathi and Cas Russell were completely different people. Did that mean I owed every part of who I was to Simon?

The question festered in me, turning me inside out and making me question every part of who I was, and I hated it, because nobody except me should have had the slightest claim on myself.

"Do you want to be alone?" asked Checker.

Even if he left I wouldn't be alone. Valarmathi lurked in the shadows, mocking, making me wonder if I wasn't a creature born entirely of Simon's own making. I thought about Rio and his belief in a deity who had brought all of creation into being, a God responsible for who we all were at our cores. Some being who had *made* us. How could he believe in something so violating?

Checker moved his chair a little closer to me and sat back, his hands relaxed in his lap.

"Thanks," I said.

We sat that way for a long time.

twenty-three

I STAYED at Checker's place that night. I didn't even ask—he ordered in food and brought some sheets and blankets out to the living room to stack beside me on the couch. I didn't say anything, but I was grateful.

Arthur came and joined us late in the evening. I got the sense he already knew what had happened—Checker had asked me quietly if it was okay if Arthur knew, and now I belatedly connected that when I'd seen him on a tablet he must have been sending an email version.

That had been considerate of him. I didn't want to relive it, even by hearing someone else relay things.

"How are you feeling, Russell?" Arthur asked, sitting down next to me.

"Losing it," I said baldly. There was no use putting up a front anymore.

Valarmathi snickered.

"He erased me," I whispered. "He . . ."

Arthur put a hand on my back, gently supportive.

"And Rio knew." He had to have.

A girl my age tugged at me, laughing. Somehow I knew she'd be dead by morning, that I'd wake and trip over her corpse.

I dug my hands into my thighs hard enough to hurt. "I'm living in someone else's body. I don't even know if I'm a real person."

"Hey," Arthur said sharply. "Stop that talk now. Doesn't matter what they did to you, you got the same worth and value as anyone else."

"Even the woman whose life I stole?"

"Wasn't your doing," Arthur said.

"Sure. After all, I didn't exist when they killed her, did I?"

"Cas . . ." Checker said, but he didn't seem to know what to say after that.

"I don't know what to do," I said. After all, nothing had changed, had it? I was still going to go insane and die, unless I let Simon violate me, *again*. He and Rio hadn't lied about that; my own mind was bone-certain.

And Rio was still going to tear Los Angeles apart at the seams if I didn't do something to stop it.

Checker and Arthur didn't say anything. Somehow it was comforting, that they offered only weighty silence instead of platitudes.

"I don't want to die," I said.

Arthur's hand squeezed my shoulder, hard.

"I'm—I'm not trying to be the false-hope guy," Checker said, "but maybe there's still a third option. Something we haven't thought of."

"Yeah," I said unconvincingly.

"Your vitals are not improving," a clinical voice informed me. *"The current course is unsustainable."*

I flexed my fingers against my palms, skin singing. "What will it take for you not to inform them?"

My lungs contorted in on themselves, and my breathing wobbled like I'd forgotten how. "If there is a third option, it's got a deadline," I got out. "And I don't think it's a very long one."

Arthur squeezed my shoulder again.

We sat in silence. My body felt like it was vibrating along every seam, my skin too tight, the air too shallow, my brain squeezing and popping against my skull until it wanted to fracture in oozing cracks.

After a minute, Arthur said, "If it's a psychic you need, maybe more of 'em are out there. We met two already."

"One not connected to Pithica?" I said hoarsely. "Good luck."

"It's worth a try," Checker put in, reaching for his tablet, but I could tell he was lying. There was no way we'd find another telepath to help me.

"Maybe we should talk to Rio," Arthur said. "He knows this world, seems to me."

In all my life, I never would have expected a solution like that to be coming from Arthur. "I'll give it a shot," I said. In spite of everything, I still trusted Rio. He wouldn't have supported Simon's decision to . . . delete me. The only reason he even talked to Simon seemed to be in an effort to keep me from dying, and it wasn't like he was wrong about that.

I was viciously glad to remember how he'd beaten up Simon in the warehouse. Rio was still on my side. In this, at least.

Simon's voice shouted, dictating, insisting—

"No," said Rio, with a ringing flatness that cut off every possible argument.

I wrenched myself away from the abyss so ruthlessly it felt like something tore.

"Russell?" Arthur said softly.

"I shouldn't exist at all. He should have let her die."

"I—um, not in any way excusing what happened to you, but—selfishly, I'm kind of glad you do," Checker said, shrugging a little. "Exist, that is."

"Same," said Arthur.

I sucked in a breath. "Are you sure about that? I'm pretty sure I'm more trouble than I'm worth."

"You *have* saved both of our lives." Checker gave me a lopsided smile. "So, you know. I wouldn't write you off so quickly."

"Eh . . ." Arthur said, and despite everything, half a laugh bubbled up my throat.

They sat with me, both of them, until I fell asleep on Checker's couch. I woke up in darkness, covered in a blanket, and knew what I had to do.

JACOB POURDRY awoke with my gun in his face. Even in the dead of night, tousled with sleep, he had the look of an animated Prince Charming—slick and handsome with conniving eyes and a con man's grin.

"You got past my security," he said. He didn't seem concerned.

"Hey, Vance told me you were smart," I said. "I woke you up because I wanted you to know. I'm about to kill you."

"I could use someone like you." He gave me a lazy half smile. "How much will it take?"

"No one's ever told you no, have they?" I said.

"Not yet." He sat up. "How much?"

I shot him in the knee.

The inhuman squeal that ripped out of him as he went down was extremely satisfying. I raised my Colt back up and pointed it at his left eye.

"Please!" He cringed behind his hands, the confidence finally gone. With his skin pale and tight with pain and the bed spattered with blood, he suddenly looked so young. Like a boy who'd only wanted to play a game. "Whatever you want, just tell me, whatever—"

"I wanted you not to traffic in kids," I said. "I'm going to kill you now. I'm telling you so you have a few seconds of abject self-loathing to contemplate the fact that you lost."

He tried to plead through the sobbing.

"Bye," I said, and shot him.

I was Los Angeles's avenging angel.

I pulled out my phone and called Yamamoto. "I just shot Jacob Pourdry," I said. "You call everyone else and tell them. Anyone makes a move, they join him. You know how good I am, Taku. I am not fucking around, and I am not going to let this city devolve into a war. If I have to clean up Los Angeles by wiping all of you from the face of the planet, I will fucking do it."

"Cassu-san—"

I hung up on him.

Vengeance! someone cackled, and I wasn't sure whose voice it was.

I thought back through everybody who had been at Yamamoto's little meeting. Maybe I should pay them all a visit myself, just so they knew I could.

MALCOLM WAS the only one who got the drop on me. In the ensuing fight he threw me through a plate-glass door. The shattering panes burst around me along crack patterns that rained data, forking and fracturing, useless numerical constants spraying the night with conclusions about strength and impact. I let it all shower down around me as if in slow motion and regretted nothing.

"You got one minute, then I let the dogs loose," Malcolm called from inside the estate house I'd tracked him to. A sawed-off was dead-steady in his hands. "Now get out."

RIO MET me at the same diner we'd eaten at before. He raised an eyebrow at the blood and dirt streaking my clothes and skin.

"Your move," I said.

The words reverberated through when my lips had said

them a dozen, a hundred other times, over gameboards or in smoky gambling dens or holding a knife to someone's throat over a thousand-foot drop.

I hitched a bit as I turned to go.

"Cas," Rio said.

I forced my feet to move. Started walking away.

"Cas," Rio called again. "I have spoken with Simon."

I froze.

twenty-four

"I WOULD kill him for his sins, if you did not need him," Rio informed me.

I closed my eyes. "I'm not going to let him help me. It's off the table."

"All right."

I remembered what Arthur had suggested and reluctantly turned back to face him. "Do you . . . do you know of anyone else?"

"Another with his abilities, you mean?" Rio asked. "Yes. But all would be even less advisable to invite into your life."

So there were others.

"Simon attempts to sin no more. It does not excuse him, but the Lord is forgiving. More so than I."

"And I," I said.

"Understood." He stepped closer to me, and his voice went quieter. "Cas. Stop this."

I blew out a breath that was almost a laugh, and didn't dignify that with a response.

"You must know. This is not the way."

"I don't know anything, Rio," I said. "I don't even know who I am. And hey, I'm dying." My lips twisted into a devil's grin. "Once I'm gone, the secret of what I've done to LA dies with me, no matter how many innocent people you kill. I just have to wait you out."

"Cas." Rio said my name with as much anguish as I supposed someone like him was capable of.

"There won't be any point once I'm dead or insane," I said. "You'll just be helping more people get hurt, and I know you won't want that, so you'll stop. LA will go on and be better, and so maybe all this is okay."

"Do not do this, Cas."

"Which? Save LA, or die?"

"Either."

"That free will you're so fond of, right?" I said. "My choices. My decision."

Rio didn't usually have much expression, but he tensed as if he didn't want to go forward with what he said next. "Cas, three militia groups arrive tomorrow."

Of course they did. "You can't let me fucking have this, can you?"

"I'm afraid not."

"Well, then I'll fight them, too. And if it doesn't work, you'll be stuck with the cleanup." I started to push past him, but he caught my shoulder very gently.

"Cas."

I didn't look up. "This is the only thing I give a damn about right now, Rio. I'm going to keep at it until I can't anymore. That's it."

"So be it," he said, and let go.

"THIS IS what life should feel like," he said, but I needed blood, so we went out and found knives and guns and a crusade. Then we traded riddles until the sun set and I beat him at chess.

Maybe this is your chance to be normal.

I didn't know you were so good at making jokes.

"Cas. Cas, are you with me?"

I struggled to dig back into reality. "Yeah. What's going on?"

We were in Checker's Hole. Now that Pourdry was out of the picture, Checker had moved back home, apparently finally taking my word for it that he didn't need to worry about Rio.

I wasn't sure how many days it had been. My sense of time kept eliding the hours, leaving blank chasms and collapsing spans of consciousness. Not more than two weeks had passed, probably—I'd looked at a calendar a few days before and been surprised to find it had only been ten days since I'd thrown out Simon.

Without discussing it, most nights I'd been staying on Checker's couch. I'd punched him twice when he'd woken me from nightmares. For some reason, he kept doing it.

"Do you want to hear the latest on McCabe's show?" Checker asked. The various leaders of the militia groups kept popping up as radio guests, under pseudonyms. Three men and two women were the most common ones. We hadn't yet been able to figure out who they were or where they were camping out in Los Angeles, if they were even basing inside the city limits at all.

The mainstream news shows had started dropping line items on the situation, though they acted like they were reporting on conspiracy *theorists* rather than reporting on a *conspiracy*. Small favors.

"Summarize it for me," I said. "Anything new?"

"They're convinced it's the water system," Checker said. "The way they're talking . . . I worry about an attack on the DWP."

LA was in the middle of a desert. If someone knocked out the Department of Water and Power in a misguided attempt at justice, it would cripple the city. I thought back to when an

EMP had fried every circuit in Los Angeles—that had been my fault, too, and a lot of people had died.

If I go back there, I'm going to kill them all.

It was my voice. Or her voice. Valarmathi's.

"Are they still threatening the government?" I asked, with an effort.

"Honestly, I think the only thing that's stopping them from marching on City Hall with guns is the brain entrainment," Checker said. "My stats programs are still all over the place, though. There aren't enough priors for them to have predictability. And there are some really odd things happening, like the drug numbers."

"What do you mean, the drug numbers?"

"I'm seeing evidence the various cartels have been hit hard, as you'd expect. But then there's other data suggesting recreational drug use is *up*. I mean, a lot of this is drawn from correlative factors, and who knows, those correlations might have been made obsolete for some reason, so I'm not sure if there's a useful conclusion to be drawn. And I don't know; if we somehow manage to have higher recreational drug use without the negative impacts of the drug *trade,* is that necessarily a bad thing, or just neutral? My libertarian soul is inclined to say the latter."

"Bottom line?"

He flung out his hands. "I don't know? There's not really enough firm statistical data to draw solid conclusions on the overall domino effect of secondary and tertiary impacts. We'll have to wait and see."

"But the primary effects are still good? The gangs and big criminal organizations are feeling the impact still?"

"Oh, hell, yeah. Did you know Los Angeles has been heretofore known as the gang capital of America? Almost fifteen hundred active criminal gangs with hundreds of thousands of members. I didn't know that till I started trying to run data on this. That's staggering."

"Only if you're bad at estimation," I said. It was about in

line with what I would have expected. "Have those numbers changed nontrivially now?"

"The jury's still out until I can get some more solid correlations, but from what I've seen so far, I suspect the answer's going to be 'yes,' 'absolutely,' and 'to great effect.'"

So all I had to do was keep them from falling for Rio's instigation and firing the first shot, at least until that sort of provocation wasn't worth it to Rio anymore. In other words, until I went insane or died.

I hadn't told Checker and Arthur that part of my plan.

"This isn't working," Simon said. He was crying. He *opened the door and left.*

I turned to Rio. "Who was that?"

"Cas?" Checker said. "Are you okay?"

"What? Yeah."

"Did you hear what I just said?" I didn't know how he made the question as patient as he did.

"No. Go again."

"Going back to McCabe's show for a minute, he had someone new come on this last time. Anonymous, again, but from what he was saying I think it was one of the people from Yamamoto's group."

"And?" I asked.

"What you'd expect. A lot of threats. A lot of rhetoric. There's either a movement to join the militia groups and attack the powers that be, or a movement to wage war on them until they leave the city. I wasn't quite clear on which."

Either would be bad, and I was sure Rio was masterfully inflaming them in *both* directions.

I probably shouldn't have burned my welcome in Yamamoto's group. Then I might know what was going on.

"Is Rio still trying to get you to . . ." Checker trailed off.

"To let Simon fuck with me? Yes."

He opened his mouth, then shut it again and turned back to his monitor.

"Go ahead," I said, without acrimony. "You want to say I should consider it, don't you?"

"I . . ." Checker looked down at his lap. "No. Yes. I don't know. I get why you won't. Just . . ."

He didn't want to see me die.

"Are you?" Checker asked. "Considering it, at all?"

"No," I said. "If I'm going to die, I'd rather die as me. Whoever I am now, at least. I'd rather have at least that."

He nodded, and sniffed a little. "Yeah. Okay."

He didn't try to tell me it was possible Simon might not destroy me, this time. Rio had tried to convince me of that, and I'd walked away.

"If you change your mind," Checker said, carefully, "Arthur suggested . . ."

"Yeah?" I wasn't going to change my mind, but any idea might have aspects we could use.

Checker appeared to be trying to figure out how to phrase things. "Well. Rio. He, um. It's pretty important to him, that you . . . not die. I mean, it's pretty important to all of us, but—"

"You're thinking I might be able to trade," I said. "Myself for Los Angeles."

Checker closed his eyes. "I didn't mean it that way."

"It's okay," I said. I even might have considered it, if I thought it would work. If I was dying anyway, what did it matter how? What did it matter if I got remade entirely, if Rio gave up fighting us in exchange?

"You can't always get your way," a friend tried to tell me.

"Yes, I can. That's the problem."

"Cas?"

I shut my eyes for a moment and breathed through my nose, trying to remember the question. "Rio doesn't work like that," I said finally. "He wouldn't make the trade."

"He did once," Checker said. "With Dawna. For your sake."

He had a point. I'd never understood that, either. Rio's

willingness to trade my safety for the cessation of his violent crusade against Pithica had flown against everything I thought I understood about him—a proof by contradiction that I still couldn't grasp.

Still, I was pretty sure he'd see this as a different case. After all, not going to Simon was my choice; it wasn't like someone else was preventing me or threatening me.

"It's only a thought," Checker said. "I still want to find . . . maybe there are other things we can explore. I didn't know how you'd feel about this, but I was doing research on— well, on conventional medicine."

"What's conventional about this?" I said.

"Nothing. But you know, *nobody* understands the brain very well, at least nobody who's not one of our resident telepaths. There could be a chance some sort of psychiatric medicine would help you. Though I don't know how the hell we'd even guess at the dosage, or which meds—"

"I don't take drugs while I'm working."

"Cas."

I sighed. "I've . . . probably already tried most of them."

"What?"

Did you take your medicine? A thousand voices overlapped over a thousand days.

I pressed my fingers against the desktop, not looking at him, trying to ignore the mental noise. "I've kind of experimented with pharmaceuticals. A lot. There were a few times between jobs . . ." I shrugged. "It seemed like a good idea at the time. Scientific."

"And what happened?"

"I discovered nothing really worked better than recreational depressants. Alcohol's a lot more readily available, and usually made things workable, before."

"God. Cas."

"Stop feeling sorry for me."

He cleared his throat. "Can you . . . um. Can you try any of that now?"

I gave him a half smile. "I don't think it was ever doing anything more than masking some of the crazy. Work does the same thing, and I'd rather do that, for whatever time . . ." I didn't finish, because I didn't want to upset him.

That didn't work out for me, either.

twenty-five

Rio AND I had started having dinner every night. It didn't bother me—in fact, I liked seeing him. I supposed impending death gave me a greater appreciation for everyone I considered a friend.

Even a friend who wasn't really a friend at all, and was also working against me in two different directions.

"I regret my earlier deception to you," he told me, at an outside table of a noodle shop. "Simon had informed me anything that might reignite your memory would only accelerate the undesirable effects."

The sound of thunder, the scent of ink and newsprint.

"He was right," I admitted to Rio.

"It is why he removed himself from your life after causing you to forget him. I do believe his intent now is to help you remain, not to alter you further."

Now that I had some memory of it, most of my nightmares featured Simon reaching out, wiping me clean. Scraping out every piece of who I'd been while Valarmathi screamed.

"You don't understand what he did to me," I said.

"You are correct. I don't." He paused. "He did not prevaricate, however, when he says you would not have survived. I do not know if there might have been some untried way to save your mind, but there was . . . extreme trauma."

"So he, what, lobotomized me?" I laughed harshly. "Nothing excuses him, Rio."

"I did not say it did."

Silence fell between us for a moment.

"Will you tell me anything more about who she was?" I asked. "And . . . what happened to us? My sanity's going anyway; what harm can it do?"

"I will not accelerate the process, Cas."

I hadn't figured he would, really. I twirled noodles around my plastic fork.

"Why don't you want to go?" Simon begged me, somewhere in the past.

"Because I believe in them."

I squeezed my eyes closed for a moment, tried to get a grip on myself. "Maybe she'll come back," I said. "Maybe she's taking me back over, taking back what's rightfully hers."

Rio paused, very carefully. "I do not think that a likely scenario, Cas."

Extreme trauma. Right.

"Hypothetically," I said to Rio, "what would you say if I tried to trade my mind for your war on Los Angeles?"

"You know I could not do so. Cas, you have brainwashed an entire city."

"I wouldn't put it *that* way."

He smiled. "As for your personal decisions, they are yours to make. Regardless of whether I would convince you to make different ones."

Independent variables. His ethical code wouldn't bargain for my consent nor absolve me in exchange for it, and all for the same reasons he would have me stop what I was doing to Los Angeles. Free will, choice, et cetera, and what I was doing was sinful.

I hadn't expected another answer.

"Cas," Rio said. His face had gone serious again. "In that vein. I believe it only fair to inform you. The fact that you have imposed a deadline means I, too, must accelerate."

I blinked. "What?"

"You will not be able to combat me much longer," Rio said calmly. "Nor will you have the capacity to reverse whatever you have done to people's minds here."

"Yeah, I'm *counting* on that," I said.

"Which means I must convince you to do so before you are no longer capable."

"What? Wait, what are you going to do?"

He took a sip of his drink and didn't answer.

I never had a choice, laughed Valarmathi.

I shook her off. "Rio!"

"Reverse this, Cas. Or a great many people will have their blood on your hands."

"This isn't funny!"

"No," he said. "It is not."

"Do you know how much good this is doing?" I argued. "And what's going to happen if we stop? Especially with how much you've been provoking people; I was looking at the stats just today. You're talking about human lives, Rio. A *lot* of human lives!"

Rio didn't move, his eyes fixed on mine.

Then he said, glacially slowly, "'We'?"

I stopped breathing.

"Your friends aided you in this, Cas?"

For some reason it had never occurred to me—every time I'd talked to Rio about what I'd done, it had always been with the arrogance of my own solution. And as far as he knew, I had a long history of working alone.

Oh, *fuck.*

"You promised you wouldn't threaten them." The paper noodle cup from my dinner had crumpled in my fist, the left-over broth trickling over my fingers. "You promised, Rio—"

"And I shall not break that promise," he said.

My fist unclenched. "Good. Thank you."

"Do not thank me, Cas."

Oh, Jesus. His other threat. The deadline. "Goddammit. Please. Don't do this." I swallowed. "What do you expect me to do, fight you?"

"It would not make a difference if you did," he answered serenely. "Things are already in motion. Though I can stop it, if you acquiesce."

"You bastard," I said.

He inclined his head. "Quite."

"How long do I have?"

"Forty-six hours, before events are irreversible."

"Fuck you." I stood up and started back toward my car. I had forty-six hours to find out what Rio was planning and save Los Angeles.

Cold blistered the bare soles of my feet, and a megaphone blared with unintelligible syllables, garbling after me with urgency, urgency.

Go go go only you people will die—

I choked on it. Ducked away as I hurried into the night.

"Consider quickly, Cas," Rio called after me. "I may move faster."

I GOT back to Checker's place to find him just getting off the phone, shaking and pale. "Cas! That was Arthur—he—he just—"

"What's going on? Is he all right?"

"He is, but— Cas, Rio was just in his apartment."

"What?" For a moment I couldn't make a single thought connect into words. "He wouldn't hurt him. Or you. He told me—"

"He didn't hurt him," Checker said. "He just— He came and took his computer. And Arthur said he kept telling him there was nothing on there, not related to what we were doing, and Rio said something like it being too bad he had promised you not to *compel* him to give details—"

I almost choked in relief. "See, I told you he wouldn't—"

"What are you *on*? He *broke in and stole Arthur's computer!* And now he's probably coming here, or to Arthur's office, or—"

"Go back to one of my places, if you're worried about it," I said.

"Because there are any you're sure he doesn't know about?" Checker cried. "Besides, if he promised not to do anything to *me,* then he's just going to come here and raid everything I own whether I'm here or not. My security isn't going to be good enough to—"

"Then stay here, and I'll hang here with you. Listen, we have to start working on—"

"Cas, shut up a minute! He's going after your friends, do you hear me? You have to stop him before—"

"He's not going to hurt any of you!"

Checker's phone chimed. He stared at it, and the blood drained from his face. "Cas, Arthur's driving to the office—he says Pilar's there, says he can't reach her—"

"Rio wouldn't—"

"Get the *fuck* over there!" Checker screamed in my face. "Now! *Go now!*"

I actually backed up a step. If he'd been a different person, I think he would have hit me.

Fists slamming, the grappling of limbs and flesh.

I groped my way out to my car. *Rio wouldn't,* the pieces of my brain that were working kept repeating. *Rio wouldn't*—even if he hadn't promised me, he wouldn't hurt someone like Pilar—would he? Pitting criminals and militias against each other was one thing; if innocent people got hurt in the crossfire it would still be the gangsters' doing. Going after someone innocent himself, just to get to me—

I floored the accelerator.

Walls filled my vision, tile the color of blood.

The F-350 Rio had been driving tonight was parked outside Arthur's office.

Oh, fuck, oh, fuck, oh, fuck—

I pounded up the outside staircase and burst through the door.

Rio stood over Pilar. She was curled on the floor clutching one wrist with her other hand, and he was pointing a .44 Magnum directly at her head. Her little compact CZ dangled from his other hand.

"Rio!" The shout tore out of me. "Rio, *stop*—what in the *living fuck*—" I ducked in front of him and helped Pilar up, hustling her away from him. She whimpered. "You gave me your word, Rio—you *told me*—"

"She has information," Rio explained serenely, lowering his gun. "Your other friends would have been better, but you are correct: I promised I would not threaten them."

I lost the ability to breathe, like someone had smashed a wrecking ball into my lungs.

I hadn't mentioned Pilar by name to him. Holy *fuck*.

"You don't get to threaten Pilar, either!" I made sure I was standing in front of her. "You stay the *fuck* away from her! She's innocent, do you hear me?"

"Not of your project, it appears." Rio's voice was mild.

"*My* project! Mine! You want information on it, you threaten me!"

"I will not threaten you, Cas."

Silver needles and white cloth, and I reached for a syringe and jammed it into my thigh—

I was losing my mind, and Rio had just coolly put a gun to Pilar's head.

"No. No. *No.*" I didn't care how far back we went; there was a line Rio was *not fucking allowed to cross*. I closed the distance between us and snatched Pilar's gun, then marched back and handed it to her.

She raised it in her left hand and pointed it at Rio, her grip shaking.

He tilted his head at her, as if bemused, leaving his own weapon down.

For a moment I doubted my senses. It wasn't as if they'd been very reliable lately. "What are you doing?" I said to Pilar.

"Cas, I think—I think you should move—I think I should shoot him—" Her voice was so low I could hardly hear it, and her hand shook harder, the little CZ vibrating.

"No one is shooting anybody!" Oh, Jesus. "Pilar, put down the gun or I'll make you."

"You didn't hear—what he said to me—what he said he'd do—"

My stomach twisted. "Rio doesn't hurt innocent people," I insisted loudly. "He was just threatening you."

"There you are wrong, Cas," said Rio. "I would have done whatever was necessary to ascertain the information I needed. This must needs be done, and as we have mentioned, she is not innocent of this crime."

Pilar was crying silently, her face soggy with tears. I couldn't blame her.

"What the *fuck*, Rio," I said hollowly.

He gave me a small half nod of conciliation. "I would have released her as soon as I obtained the information I required."

"I'm *right here*!" screamed Pilar. "I am *right here* and I am *pointing a gun at you* and I am thinking about pulling the trigger and you are going to *look at me* and realize I am a human being and take me *fucking seriously*!"

Rio turned his gaze to her, his stare penetrating. "My death will be a great justice," he said. "Perhaps you will shoot me today. I will not tell you it is undeserved."

"Pilar!" I forced myself to take a breath, to moderate my tone. "Pilar. Please. Please put down the gun."

She hesitated for a long moment, then said, "No. Make him leave."

"Pilar—"

"This is my office." Her voice had gone back to that low, barely audible hoarseness, flat and dead and very serious. "Make him leave, or I swear to God I will fire. I swear to God, Cas. Get him out of here."

I could have wrested the weapon out of her hand. I was probably close enough to be able to do it before she could squeeze the trigger. Probably.

Somewhere else, mortar fire thundered through my senses, magazine ammo counts overlapping with probable avenues of safety. Dirt and cold filled my nose and mouth.

I clawed back away from it. Pilar—Pilar—she wasn't really planning to fire, was she?

Shit. Shit.

I needed to take Rio somewhere anyway, drag him somewhere and tear him a new one, loudly, for a very long time.

He'd crossed a line. Some things were fucking *off-limits,* and he should have known. He *did* know—I didn't care how little he understood about human behavior; he knew better.

And he'd done it anyway.

The ice cracked like a gunshot, and the ATV lurched.

"Rio," I choked out. "Let's go."

He paused for a hairsbreadth, his gaze flicking between Pilar and me. Pilar's CZ had steadied, her grip tightened. Along with her jaw. Her face was still wet, but she'd stopped crying.

"If you try to hurt her right now, you'll have to go through me," I said.

Rio gave a little head tilt that seemed to say, *Well, another time then,* and sidestepped to the door. When it swung shut behind us, Pilar still hadn't lowered her gun.

twenty-six

THERE'S NOWHERE in a city that feels truly isolated, but I strode into an alleyway behind a closed and darkened car dealership, clubbing away the encroaching flashbacks of other times and spaces. Rio followed.

When the alleyway got dark enough I turned so fast he would have run into me if he hadn't had Rio's reflexes.

If he'd been anyone else I would have slugged him. I almost did it anyway.

"What the *fuck*!" I ripped into him instead. "I told you, I have friends now. If you do anything like that again, if you so much as *startle* them—" I stopped.

I didn't know what I'd do.

The thought of truly going after Rio physically, actually trying to hurt him—my insides clenched and writhed.

He'll be your ally, a voice said.

Forty-six hours, he'd told me, and then he'd—

"This isn't working." Rio held me down while the world imploded.

What kind of person was I, that I calmly played chess

against him for an entire city, but he went after one woman I happened to know personally, and I fucking lost it?

"Cas?"

I shoved the cacophony in my head away. I wanted to shove Rio, too, but I crossed my arms instead, trapping my hands to restrain myself. "You attacked a friend of mine."

"On the contrary," Rio said. "I promised I would not harm your friends, and I have stood by that. Pilar Velasquez's name was not on your list."

Guilt knifed me with renewed savagery. I'd only just gotten comfortable with the idea of considering Arthur and Checker friends, and I still hadn't been sure what being friends with someone was supposed to mean—figuring out how to fit a third person into that mold had seemed overwhelming. How did someone handle that many obligations?

I supposed it wasn't something that would worry me for much longer.

I wandered. The city was gray. It wasn't a city I knew.

Jesus. Who cared what relationship I had with Pilar? However I labeled it, she was still in the category of people I'd kill to protect. "Anyone I work with, Rio," I spat out. "Anyone I *know*. You can't—"

"I cannot possibly have an awareness of everyone you would likely be familiar with."

"That's a bullshit excuse and you know it. You came after Pilar in the first place *because* she was working with me on this!"

He tilted his head in a nod, acknowledging the fact.

"I'm serious." I didn't know what else to say. Didn't know what else to do. "If I can't rely on you not to—"

Someone put firm hands on my face, turned my eyes into the sun—blazing, consuming me—trust him—

I cried out. I was sitting fallen against the wall of the alleyway, and my back and shoulders hurt as if I'd been hurled into it.

Rio crouched next to me, his hands gentle as he helped me sit up against the wall. "Cas. Are you here?"

"Yeah." My skin was clammy. My throat and chest seized briefly before letting go. "Yeah, I'm here."

"Cas, your condition appears to be worsening."

"Rio," I said, scrambling for my point like a pit bull with a bone, "Rio, I can't trust you if—"

Something blew through my mind like an express train, all noise and light and terrible force. I ducked and clamped my arms over my head and slammed my eyes shut and tried to breathe but I couldn't, because my lungs were squeezed flat.

Dark and pain and blood, fear and betrayal, and Rio reached out as if he would help . . .

Trust him, Cassandra. You have to trust *him.*

"Cas. Cas. Cas." Rio said my name in a rhythm that was almost a chant. "Cas, return here. Cas."

"Stop changing the subject," I growled. I couldn't remember what the subject had been, but I was angry, and rattled, insecurity about—*something*—crawling in roots through my brain, crumbling my consciousness, and I needed to yell at Rio about something but I'd lost my bearings and that made me furious—

Trust him.

The world spasmed again. Neurons crisscrossed and bits of my body went rigid while others collapsed.

"Cas," said Rio, and he might have sounded alarmed, if Rio ever sounded alarmed.

Rio sitting across from me in a small apartment. "That decision is yours, Cas. This life is yours now."

I nodded—

"Cas, I promise you, in the future I will not harm your friends or coworkers, nor threaten them with harm. Respond to me, Cas. Speak."

Breathing became easier. My lungs stopped constricting.

I leaned my head back against the grimy wall. The dim light burned into the back of my eyes.

"Cas?"

I didn't answer.

"Cas," said Rio again, and I wasn't imagining it, there was urgency in his voice. No, that didn't make sense. I had to be imagining it.

"It's good to know all I have to do is have some sort of seizure and you cave in," I said. I felt like my voice should have been hoarse, but it wasn't. Only a little short, like I still wasn't breathing enough. "Now how about you agree *not to fucking destroy Los Angeles*?"

Rio's expression twitched. "On that, I am afraid, I shall stand by my previous imperviousness. Cas, I did not realize this was of such importance to you. I apologize."

"You *what*?" I sputtered. "You didn't realize this was of *importance*? Fuck you, you expect me to believe torturing the people I work with didn't register on your list of human interactions that would *rank*?"

"That is not precisely what I meant," said Rio, after a moment.

Somewhere else, we sat together at a table, at an impasse, while the light changed and the sun rose.

I let the madness in my brain ebb and flow, leaning my head back against the wall behind me while the world passed by.

"Cas," Rio said. "Please reconsider allowing Simon to aid you."

I didn't deign to answer him.

"Is there nothing I can say that would convince you?"

"If I knew of such an argument," I said, "I would already be convinced. Because, you know. Logic."

Rio bowed his head. "In that case, I beg of you to fix what you have done to the city in the next forty-five hours."

He stood.

"Rio," I said.

"Yes?"

I swallowed. Pilar's tear-streaked face danced in my vision again. One woman, and now I had to save all of LA.

"Rio, I don't . . . I don't think I want to see you again."

"If that is your wish, Cas."

Graveyard dirt smelled like any other dirt. I stretched my fingers, pressing into it. It was okay: no one would remember.

Including me.

My eyes were shut. I pried them open to focus on the alleyway. Rio had disappeared. I hadn't heard him leave.

I was cold and bruised, and the uneven brick of the wall was digging into my back. I pushed myself up.

"What do you have for me today?"

"Target practice." A Dragunov was pressed into my hand, its stock smooth and polished.

"I'll try not to have too much fun."

"Fuck you, too," I muttered to Valarmathi. She laughed.

I limped back up to Arthur's office.

When I pushed open the door, Arthur whipped around and drew his sidearm on me.

"Whoa, hey! It's just me. Alone," I added hastily.

Arthur slumped and lowered the gun. "He's gone?"

"Yeah," I said, trying to keep the guilt out of my tone. "Where's Pilar?"

"The hospital, Russell. He broke her wrist."

Considering my brain was rotting me alive, I hadn't thought I could feel worse. Apparently I was wrong.

"Maybe I should end it now," I said.

Arthur's head came up. "What are you talking about?" He asked the question with such controlled evenness that I was pretty sure he already knew.

"Rio gave me an ultimatum," I said. "I don't know what he's going to do. I don't know if I can stop it. But if I'm not here to leverage . . ." I shrugged, trying for careless, but it felt like my blood had gone leaden. "I'm dying anyway. It might be nice for it to mean something."

"Russell," Arthur whispered, and he sounded so broken and defeated I regretted suggesting it.

If I was going to do it, I should have just done it without telling him. That would have been the considerate thing to do.

"You're not telling me not to," I said quietly.

A pounding came on the office door. We both jumped and pulled weapons.

"Who's there?" Arthur called.

"Arthur? Arthur, you here? It's me, it's Justin!"

"Oh, Lord." Arthur holstered his Glock and strode to pull open the door. "Kid, what's wrong?"

"You ain't picking up, I been calling you," Justin babbled, falling into the room—Arthur caught him and helped him to a chair. "You gotta help us. It's Katrina, she OD'd. Arthur, you gotta help—"

"Mary and Joseph, you call 911?" Arthur interrupted. "Where is she?"

Justin kept sniffling, like he was trying not to cry. "Yeah, I called, I ain't care if she hate me for it later. She in the hospital now. They been asking 'bout her parents, I ain't know what to say. . . ."

"How'd this happen?" demanded Arthur. "She was off the stuff—I know she's been struggling this week, but you told me you were keeping her off—"

"Something went wrong!" Justin wailed. "I ain't know what! We was—we was going to meetings, together, and now she say they ain't feel supportive no more. And she ain't inventing it, neither. It all been feeling pointless, the support and shit, just gone. And we been going clubbing, just dancing and shit all night, but this week Katrina said she ain't connecting with none of it no more, said she needed something—something else." He sniffed and dragged a sleeve across his face. "And it ain't just her—I swear I ain't making up no bullshit; my friend said it was sunspots or something, 'cause Katrina, she ain't the only one. We all feeling it. We go out and the music and the lights, they was all the same, but all *flat*—some clubs, they shutting down 'cause ain't nobody coming in no more. And meantime X going through the roof. Katrina, she said she feeling so dead inside, said she needed it, and I tried to stop her, but she ain't listen, accused me of not supporting her neither. . . ."

A kernel of panic exploded in my core. Arthur was trying to calm Justin down, and I didn't know if he'd made the connection yet, but he would—he would—

Support groups who couldn't provide support anymore. The bestial high of clubbing becoming flat and unexciting. Energetic relationships losing their connections. And drug sales skyrocketing as people chased a high they couldn't get any other way . . .

The brain entrainment countered deindividuation. It broke up people's urges to follow each other, to feed off each other's emotions. Deadened those urges.

It dissolved the connections between people.

Oh God. The realization plowed into me like a freight train. I couldn't get enough air, but this time it was reality that strangled me.

Katrina had stood brazen and alive in this very office, just a few weeks ago, and Arthur had been helping her—and then I—I had—

"I have to go," I said to Arthur. He barely heard me, concentrating on Justin.

I ran.

As soon as I hit the alleyway outside Arthur's office, my body rebelled and threw up. I coughed, leaning against the concrete wall.

Just down the block was one of our cell hacking boxes, hidden on the lip of a roof at the end of an alley. I ran, half stumbling, until I reached it.

I barely made the climb. My hands slid and scrabbled, my equilibrium shot. I pulled out my knife and pried the box loose, then half fell back to street level and smashed it under my heel, once, twice, again and again, shattering the components inside.

My hands and feet slapped against wood and ropes and rocks with effortless probability, my course through the obstacles already predetermined. . . .

Not now. Not now!

I'd been so close to considering suicide the perfect solution, to being almost at peace with running out of time, but it was all going wrong, because this wasn't what was supposed to happen, it wasn't supposed to hurt anyone, only give people back their freedom.

It was supposed to *help*. It was supposed to solve everything.

"I disagree with your definition of the mathematical optimum," I said. The wall blew up, scattering tile everywhere, the color of blood.

I picked up the fractured circuit boards and crushed them in my hands until they cut my palms. Even if I destroyed them all, it wouldn't help, wouldn't help at all; my program was already on everyone's phones, all around us, unstoppable . . . I could work with Checker, find out a way to reprogram all our boxes to remove it, maybe—but if we did that—

Los Angeles was poised on the edge of a gang war. Even if Rio walked everything back, I wasn't sure it would be enough to salve the situation. If we pulled the brain entrainment now . . .

We ran through the night and the world burned along with its future.

Don't you understand? Change the axioms, change the world.

My cheek hit the pavement. I'd fallen in the gutter. I blinked my eyes, staring at the curb.

Rio's forty-six hours might have overestimated me.

Hang the fuck on, I ordered myself. *You have to hang on until you fix what you did, or you'll be responsible for a lot more than just what Rio's planning—*

Rio—

I groped for my phone.

I had to tell him it was off. Had to tell him he'd won, that I would take it all down, that he had to stop this.

My senses fractured, stabbing too sharply, numbers everywhere, so many, too many, spiraling into infinite exactitude like a black hole sucking me past its event horizon—

The phone was thick and clumsy in my fingers. I punched the numbers, the 5s and 8s crossing with the 3s and 9s. The wrong numbers. I tried to hit the button to clear it, to dial again.

"We knew this was an experiment," someone said, backlit by fluorescent light. *"Experiments fail."* The curtain drew across my blurry vision, shrouding everything.

I clawed at the curb, trying to get back upright, my fingers imprecise and useless. I had to call him off, and then I had to—to get somewhere. Checker's place. We needed to plan, to figure out how to make everyone stand down, and then we had to undo everything—I had to get to everywhere I'd planted one of the boxes—it had taken a week to plant them; it would take a week to reprogram them—

"A week?" Laughter. "You really think she has a week, in this state?"

I was the only one who knew all the locations. The only one who could reverse it all.

The call finally went through.

"Rio," I gasped. "You win, okay? You win. I'll take it all down. Just *stop this*."

Three tones interrupted me. *"We're sorry; you have reached a number that has been disconnected or is no longer in service. If you feel you have reached this recording in error . . ."*

I tried to focus my eyes enough to see where I'd misdialed,

to call him back, but the outlines of the phone fuzzed in too many duplicates, and my hand wasn't working right.

My last thought before my own brain ravaged me was that Rio and Checker and McCabe and Yamamoto had all been right. Instead of saving the city, I had doomed it.

And that was going to be my legacy.

twenty-seven

I WOKE up in the middle of an empty rave.

At least, that was how it felt. Some sort of bass thumping through my brain, flashing patterns of light and color . . . and I was alone in a dark room.

I sat up. The room was Checker's bedroom—the colored patterns of light alternately flitted over his science fiction movie posters and action figures and bookshelves and gadgets, bringing them to ghoulish prominence before eclipsing them back into shadow. I'd been lying on top of the quilts on the made bed. The blinds on the windows were open, but between the blinds and the glass a heavy black material had been snugged against the wall, blocking all light.

My eyes went to the door. More blacking covered the crack underneath and the edges all around the jamb.

Between the thumping bass, someone knocked, and the door cracked open. "Cas?"

The dim light from the hall felt very bright. Like I had a hangover. I ducked my face away. "What's going on?"

Checker came in and shut the door behind him, the sound

muffled by the blacking. "Are you okay? How are you feeling?"

"I'm feeling like I want to know what's going on." I'd been . . . at Arthur's office. Rio had been fighting me. And—oh God. The brain entrainment. Katrina.

I jumped up, and the room yawed.

"Whoa, whoa, whoa, Cas! Sit down."

The back of my knees hit the bed and I sat, hard. My short-term memory was patchy, confused, like images out of a dream. "What happened to me?"

"You, um—well. We're pretty sure you were—well, you know." He ducked his head self-consciously.

Dying. Going insane.

Come to that, why wasn't I?

I frowned. My thoughts echoed in my own head in blessed silence.

"Checker," I said. "What the hell did you do? What is all this?"

"Brain entrainment," Checker said.

"What?"

"Ha! Now you know how I felt. Not so sanguine when it's you being poked at, is it?" I must have looked murderous, because Checker scooted his chair back a smidge and then raised both hands in surrender. "Sorry, sorry! Um, we didn't know what to do. We argued about whether to get Simon or Rio, but it ended up being a moot point because none of us knew how to find either of them—I imperiled my life by calling the number you gave me for Rio, but he hasn't gotten back to me yet. We did call Doc Washington, though—you know, Arthur's friend who's patched up your bullet holes a time or two? Pilar got the idea to tell her to get her hands on some EEG equipment, because, you know, *data,* and by the time she got here we'd had the utterly fantastic brainstorm of calling Professor Sonya, too. Which is good, because Dr. W. took the EEG but didn't have any idea what to do for you other than possibly a hospital. But we went and got all the brain entrainment math you worked out from that place of yours where we did all the programming, and we shoved it at Professor Sonya, and she looked at your brain waves and came up with this." He waved a hand at the light show. "She says to tell you she basically used your own math on you and you should still consider working with her."

I ignored the last part. So they'd used my own calculations to knock me back into a normal brain state.

Holy shit.

"So, uh—how are you feeling?" asked Checker.

"Fine." I tried to push myself up again and stopped when the wall swayed. "A little dizzy," I amended. "And . . . confused." I remembered Justin dashing into Arthur's office, but not why I'd been there. The brain entrainment—I had to disable it, had to . . . why did I have to?

"Confused how?"

"Not telepathy confused. Head injury confused." It felt like I'd had a raging concussion: my brain didn't want to put together the events leading up to it. There was only a sense of urgency, and guilt . . . I had to do something . . . something important. . . .

But at least I could string together thoughts linearly again, without interference from past lives. I hadn't realized how hard it was to think until I was alone again in my head.

How long would it last? How long would I have? This wasn't a cure—I knew that before I even asked the question. The foundational research on the Signet Devices I'd spent so long immersed in had been clear and mathematically specific: the entrainment could knock me out of an altered brain state, but there would be no way for it to solve the problem that had drop-kicked me there in the first place.

The stupid screwed-up psychology that would mow me down again. And again.

Shit.

I pushed away the inevitability of it, forcing myself to take advantage of my temporary clear-headedness. Trying to get my bearings. The chunks of events fit together like a puzzle missing two-thirds of its pieces.

My tangled sense of urgency deepened.

"What happened?" I asked Checker again.

He frowned slightly. "We used your brain entrainment math to—"

"I heard you the first time. I'm not *that* confused. I meant before this, when you found me."

"Uh. We didn't, for a while. Arthur was caught up in something else—"

Katrina. Right. Guilt pulsed in me, hard.

"—and for the first few hours we assumed you'd taken off to do your own thing, but then I tracked your phone, and after I picked up Pilar we, um, we found you. . . ." He trailed off.

Pilar, I thought. The last time I'd seen Pilar . . .

She'd been pointing a gun at Rio.

The guilt clawed up my trachea, and I shied away from the memory.

"I'm going to ask Professor Sonya to dial it back a bit, okay?" Checker said, and I wondered if he was deliberately changing the subject. "Keep talking to me, and try to tell me if things start going wonky for you. Okay? You promise?"

"What am I, five?"

"No, you're a stupid and stubborn person who doesn't like telling people when something's wrong. But consider this for science. Tell me if you start feeling anything, okay?"

"Yeah, whatever." Now that the brain entrainment had done its work, it wouldn't be affecting me anymore. Checker's concern would be better placed looking ahead to the next time I face-planted in a gutter.

That didn't stop me from feeling a twinge of anxiety as he tapped at his phone's touchscreen and the light and sound both dimmed a little. Checker did something else on his phone, and the room lights came to life in a soft glow behind the color.

My brain stayed silent.

I tried to stop double-checking and dwelling on how long it would last. After all, hadn't Simon said something about how picking at the memories made them worse? Of course, trying not to think about something only made my brain try to think about it more. I concentrated on reading the titles of the books on Checker's shelves, making patterns out of the numbers of letters in the titles, solving for regression equations that gave his paperback collection another dimension.

"Still okay?" asked Checker.

"Yeah."

He tapped at his phone more, and the noise and light dimmed out completely, leaving us in an ordinary room with the windows and door blacked out.

Checker studied me with concern. "How about now?"

"Fine. No voices. I appear to be sane again."

"You were hearing *voices*?"

"What did you think 'going insane and dying' meant?" I said.

"I don't know! You weren't exactly talking a lot about it, you know!"

A startled laugh almost choked me.

"What's going on?" Checker demanded immediately. "Are you all right? Cas?"

"Yeah. Yeah," I hiccupped. "It just, it feels really good to argue with you again."

"Oh, fuck you, Cas Russell," Checker said, but there was no bite in it.

My good humor slipped away as soon as it had bubbled up. Something was wrong. Maybe everything. Why couldn't I think . . .

I pushed myself up off the bed. The floor wobbled, but I kept my balance this time. I did keep a hand against the wall, just in case. "How long was I out?"

"A day and a half, I guess? Well, I don't know how long it was before we found you, so maybe more like a couple days.

By the way, Arthur wants to talk to you—he's switched sides now on the brain entrainment, because one of the kids he mentors—"

"Days?" The wall was suddenly holding me up. "A couple *days*?" That was bad, that was very, very bad—why—why was that so bad—

Forty-six hours, Rio had said.

Rio—Rio—

"Give me your phone; I need a phone right now!" I snatched Checker's mobile out of his hands before he'd fully extended it. My fingers zipped across the touchscreen.

The line on the other end rang. And rang.

Voice mail.

Cold seeped up and clenched my heart. No. This couldn't be happening.

The generic message played out and beeped. "It's Cas," I said. "Call it off, okay? I'm taking it down. LA will go back to normal. So whatever you're doing, *call it off*. Call me as soon as you get this."

"Cas?" Checker said.

I hung up the phone and checked the date and time on the brightly lit screen. Calculated. I hadn't been in the best mental state when I'd talked to Rio, but when he'd given his deadline I'd checked the time—

Forty-nine hours and three minutes. I was three hours late.

twenty-eight

CHECKER AND Arthur and I gathered in the Hole as our war room.

Professor Halliday had wished me well and gone home, declining to become involved in whatever situation we'd embroiled ourselves in—her words. Pilar was noticeably absent. Other than assuring me she was all right, Checker and Arthur avoided my questions about her.

Rio assaulting Pilar. Yet another thing I'd let get out of control. My fault.

I had Checker set up an automated dialer for Rio, with Rio's current phone number rather than with the permanent voice-mail box Checker had originally tried. We still hadn't gotten through to him. I'd tried texting, too, but there had been no response.

Irreversible in forty-six hours, he'd called his plan. Rio didn't bluff.

"Keep checking the news," I said. "The minute we find out anything . . ."

"I said I'm on it, Cas," Checker answered.

"Meantime, we gotta talk about our game plan," Arthur said. He hadn't said much, and he was avoiding my eyes. I'd been too afraid to ask about Katrina.

I didn't want to hear what else I had done.

"Well, we have to abort, clearly." I tried to assuage my guilt by making the declaration as firm as possible, regardless of the fact that it was weeks too late. "We have to. But the minute we do . . ."

The changing variables that had come with the brain entrainment might have thrown all of Checker's statistical programs askew, but every iteration he ran now was telling us the same thing: with the mess of other tensions I had created in Los Angeles—even without whatever hammer Rio was dropping—the brain entrainment was the only thing keeping the city from boomeranging into an exponentially worse state than we'd brought it out of. Ironically, a lot of that would probably come from people's anger over being affected by something they hadn't understood, but they'd only be able to act on it fully once it was gone.

And *with* Rio's provocation, the city would be needing the check more than ever. The same check that was making vulnerable kids lose their support networks and destroy themselves.

Checker coughed. I had the intense impression he was avoiding saying "I told you so." Usually he just would have said it—almost dying must have earned me a small jot of grace.

But instead, he cleared his throat and then spoke quietly, to his keyboard. "You know, if it weren't for . . . uh, practical concerns, I'd sort of like a world where peer pressure and hive minds didn't work."

I jerked to look at him, shocked.

He half shrugged. "*Obviously* we have to abort. But you were also right about there being a certain—that it gave people back their individual freedom, in a way. I . . . there's something that appeals to me about that world. I don't think it's inherently a wrong one, just a—a different one."

"It is wrong," Arthur said.

I glanced between them.

"You don't have to say that," I said to Checker.

"I know," he answered. "Let's figure out how to undo it."

Right.

Now that I had room in my brain to think, an idea had been pushing in from the sides. I absolutely, one hundred percent, and on no uncertain terms did not want to do it.

But it was an idea. And we had less than zero time to start walking this back.

"Arthur," I said.

He looked up.

I swallowed. The echo of Valarmathi's voice flickered, just below the surface. Waiting.

"You suggested something," I said. "That I might be able to . . . give myself up. To save the city."

Arthur glanced at Checker with a frown. "Thought you gave that a go already." The slightest thread of accusation bled through his words.

"I did," I said. "With Rio. He said no. But we all know someone else who can get everyone in the city to step back from shooting each other. Someone who has the power."

Checker got it before Arthur did. His face galvanized into shocked understanding. "What? No. No no no no no no *no*. That is a terrible, horrible, no-good, very bad idea, Cas Russell. In fact, it's almost exactly what Pithica was doing, which is—"

"We're on the verge of a mob war that will take out large chunks of Los Angeles the instant we start removing the brain entrainment," I said. "You really think we should do nothing?"

"I think we should look for a third option!"

"Sometimes there is no third option," I said. "Sometimes there's only one shitty solution and a shittier one."

"Arthur," Checker said. "Help me out here. Using a telepath to solve this—a telepath you most emphatically do not trust, I might add—is not a solution!"

Arthur was looking at the floor again. "You planning on using him to kill people, Russell?"

"No," I said.

"Then we're not Pithica," Arthur said, still to the floor.

I couldn't imagine what he must be feeling. He'd supported this effort, and he held himself to a much higher standard than he did me.

I was still too much of a coward to ask about Katrina.

"Cas," Checker tried again, "*assuming* you can do this in a way that isn't completely and blatantly immoral, and *assuming* Simon agrees to help at all, what can one psychic do against a tide like we're dealing with? What, are you going to march him around to every one of the bad guys and talk to them? Let me remind you that we haven't even been able to find where the militia people are camped out, and considering how badly you've pissed most of the crime lords off, what are the chances they're on the lookout to snipe you before you even get close—"

"There's a much easier way," I said. "You're forgetting there's a radio show that's a poster child for every single person who's mad about this."

"You want *McCabe* to help?" squawked Checker.

"He'll want to help," I said. "Considering it's his cause, and all."

"And, what, you're going to tell Simon to march in there and brainwash *him* into giving us the airtime and then brainwash everyone else into—"

"No," I said. It wasn't like I knew Simon very well, regardless of how thoroughly he haunted my dreams and flashbacks. But his holier-than-thou insistence about not touching people's brains without their consent—me excluded, apparently—had been practically shouted from the rooftops.

I wasn't sure I could get him to talk to anyone, even people who were intent on killing each other. Twisting around the mind of a radio host to give us airtime was definitely going to be a bridge too far.

"No," I said again. "Simon's not going to give us the airtime. You forget who owns half the media stations in Los Angeles—the Lorenzos."

Checker paled. "That's an even worse idea."

I shrugged. "Why? Sure, they've been all passive-aggressive toward me lately, but the Mafia's civilized. Besides, Malcolm only threw me through a door the last time he saw me. I don't think he'd kill me if I asked for a meet."

Checker stared at me. "You are insane."

"Not right now," I said. "But I'm sure it'll swing back around."

"*Not funny,* Cas. Not funny!"

One of his computers chimed.

We all surged forward, Arthur and I coming to scan the screen over Checker's shoulder as he scrolled. "What dropped?" Arthur said. "Am I seeing something about a shooting here?"

Checker flipped through screens full of color-coded data. "Yeah, uh—there was a shooting a few hours ago. It's breaking now—it looks like it was police. They killed someone. The reports are saying he was unarmed."

"Tell me it wasn't a white cop and a black kid," Arthur said softly.

"No, it's—I mean, I don't know. But it's looking like . . . background's still coming in, and nothing's verified, but I think the victim was one of the militia leaders."

Oh. Oh, *shit.* The militia groups had been convinced the government was doing something to the population here.

And now the government had shot one of them.

No. Not the government. Rio.

I wondered how he'd engineered it.

"What's the retaliation gonna be?" Arthur said.

"Are you asking me?" Checker's voice climbed "Because I don't know the answer to that, Arthur. I don't—'

"We have to get on this *now*," I said. "If we get Simon in front of all the rest of them, maybe there won't be a retaliation. Maybe we can stop it."

"You're still talking about using a telepath to—" started Checker.

"How can I help?" said Arthur.

"Arthur, *wait*," Checker said. "I am not okay with this Can we at least discuss it? You're talking about going into the heads of a huge number of people—"

"To tell them to walk away," I said. "To tell them to put down their weapons and not attack each other."

"That doesn't make it right!" cried Checker. "There have been just conflicts—there *are* just conflicts in the world right now. Not everyone who picks up arms is inherently wrong. And I don't even know if they're wrong in this case. If I thought someone had been messing with me the way we did—"

"The way *we* did," I emphasized. "We—I—am responsible for fucking everything up in the first place. All I'm going to do is set it right. Back to the way it was." Minus the militia member who had just been killed, and Miguel, and the other Blood Skulls members, and maybe Katrina, and who knew who else. All of whom had been victims of my catastrophic attempt to fight crime.

"You can't do that!" argued Checker. "You can't say one thing was wrong and then build another wronger thing on top of it and say you're just reverting things—you can't play with people's brains like it's a science experiment and then hit control-Z if you don't like what comes out the other side!"

"What do you think we should do, then?" I demanded. "Seriously. Give me one other choice. You keep talking about a third option, well, find me one, otherwise stop delaying us."

"I don't think we should do *this*! Even if we can't find another way, this is the greater of two evils!"

"Cities've been healed thanks to one leader's charisma plenty of times in history. It can happen again," Arthur said. "I can live with that. Can't live with more folk dying. I'm sorry, son—this isn't intellectual."

"You can't say that." Checker sounded like he'd given up. Hopeless. "You can't say that, Arthur. We *make* the intellectual argument because in the moment, we have to be able to see the larger picture, not the—not the emotional one."

"And that's where we differ, 'cause I think the emotional's just as valid." Arthur turned back to me. "What do you need?"

I braced for more protest from Checker, but he didn't say anything more.

"I want you for the meeting with McCabe, when we get to that point," I said to Arthur. "In the meantime, stay here and keep trying to reach Rio. When you do—tell him I'm calling it off and not to do anything else."

"You think he's got more planned?"

"I'd count on it," I said. "Also, whatever you do, don't tell him what we're trying to do." If there was one thing Rio would object to even more than brain entrainment, it was using a telepath to subvert the free will of everyone in Los Angeles who heard the radio address. I was dreading what would happen when he figured out what we'd done—the best I could hope for was that it would happen after we'd already done it, not in time for him to stop us.

I pointed at Checker. "Don't you tell him, either."

Checker's face twisted like I'd hurt him. "I'm not going to sic Rio on you, Cas."

"Are you going to try to stop us?" I asked.

He sucked in a quick, sharp inhale. "I'm going to keep looking for another way."

"Better look fast," I said.

twenty-nine

I DIDN'T have a way of reaching Simon except through Rio, and we still hadn't gotten through to him. Which meant my next step was clear: prepare everything for when I *did* corner Simon. In other words, get a lock on that airtime we needed, which meant reaching out to the Lorenzos. I tried very hard not to worry about what would happen if I had another neurological collapse in the middle of negotiations with the Los Angeles Mafia.

After making me wait an excruciatingly long time in a cold garage, Malcolm granted me an audience from the other side of a shotgun. He didn't greet me.

"I'm not here to make trouble," I said, raising my hands slightly. It would be ridiculous if I were—he'd directed me to come to the mountain residence of Mama Lorenzo herself, a mansion in the Hollywood Hills that had seriously beefed up security. And since I'd told them I was here on a civilized visit, I'd had to let her people take my sidearm.

Despite my protestations of civility, Malcolm had still met me here, in one of the estate's two enormous garages. This one was empty, with a cement floor that had a drain in the middle of it.

That wasn't ominous at all.

"Good to see you again, too," I said.

"I should kill you," he answered.

"Or maybe I should kill you," I returned evenly.

The corner of his mouth flicked up. "You flirting with me, Russell?"

I gave him a look expressing how funny I thought *that* was. "We want the same things right now."

"Do we?"

"Like you all are always saying. Your boss has a code— she takes care of her city."

"So she does." The barrel of the shotgun stayed on me, as immobile as if Malcolm were carved from granite. I probably also had a dozen snipers trained on me, security I couldn't see.

I tried to ignore it all. "The last thing Mama Lorenzo wants is a war breaking out on her turf. One she doesn't control."

"And you really expect us to believe you're trying to stop such a war? After what you did to Pourdry and the rest of us?"

"Like you wouldn't have shot Pourdry yourself if you had half a chance," I scoffed. "The other stuff was just me trying to keep the peace."

"Funny way of showing it." Malcolm squinted at me. "And yeah, sure, we knew all about Pourdry. Know all about you, too."

My heart started beating faster.

"Now personally, I don't mind you, Russell," Malcolm continued. "Even after your little 'peacekeeping' mission. But we're talking business now, and that means you're dealing with the Madre. Once she got you on her radar, she looked into your dealings. Varga, Thach, Ivchenko . . ."

Oh. Shit.

I'd done a few contracts each for the men Malcolm had named. I knew what he was driving at. "Those jobs were all drugs or guns," I said. "Not kids."

"Well then, our mistake. You're a paragon of virtue."

"So that's why Mama Lorenzo's been blackballing me," I said. It made a breathtaking amount of sense, now that I stopped to think about it. "Not because she's holding a grudge. Because she went and looked into me and then decided she doesn't *approve*."

I couldn't help making the word sarcastic. Mama Lorenzo's usual business might lean toward extortion and racketeering, with blood reserved only for those who crossed her, but we were still talking about a Mafia Madrina.

Malcolm, however, took my statement seriously. "Like you said, she's got a code. She cleans up her town."

Right.

An angry, desperate sort of self-consciousness crept around the edges of my conscience. I'd been trying to *stop* the crime wave. I'd never paused to consider I might be judged on the wrong side of it.

Sure, I took advantage of the jobs that came up, but I was a cog. Replaceable. If I wasn't making money off something, someone else would—the only way to stop the corruption was to behead the hydra, not drive myself to the poorhouse.

General solutions, not particular ones. What I did in the day-to-day had little importance, as long as I fought the bigger evil at its root—right? After all, didn't everyone do that? If I had a plan in place to blow up an evil corporation's headquarters, what did it matter if I'd done some shopping at its local big box store first?

Mama Lorenzo clearly didn't see it that way. She'd probably deemed me too difficult to off, but she could put a serious dent in my income with barely any effort, just a few words dropped into the gossip chain. I'd stockpiled enough cash that money was less than a nonissue, but the work . . . if

Arthur and I hadn't started crusading over the past few months, my brain would have turned inside out on me a lot sooner than it had.

I licked suddenly dry lips. It was hard to have a bargaining position with a woman who viewed you as the dregs of humanity.

"Would Madame Lorenzo be willing to set aside her opinion of me to solve the new crisis we're about to have?"

Malcolm still hadn't lowered the shotgun, and suddenly, without moving, his stance became more aggressive. "What new crisis?"

I swallowed. "The one that's going to break out as soon as I put a stop to what's in the water."

Malcolm was way too smart for a hitman. Or maybe I was just that transparent. He paused for a moment and then said, "So that was you."

"Put a dent in recruitment, did I?"

"You're awfully cocky for someone who just admitted to poisoning everybody."

More like I couldn't help running my mouth off. Fuck. I decided to try for honesty. "It was an experiment. To see if we could turn people from a life of crime. I guess it didn't work on you." He had the grace to look a tiny bit amused. "But we're pulling the plug. The problem is, LA's become a tinderbox. The minute we stop, everyone draws and fires. That's not good for anyone."

I left out Rio. I wasn't sure why—his presence and mission would probably only help my objective here. But for some reason, dragging his name into this felt . . . wrong. I wasn't going to turn the Mob against him any more than they might already be, even if there was justification for it.

Malcolm exhaled through his teeth. "The Madre won't be happy to hear all this. Won't be happy with *you*. And you want our help? After you fucked us all?"

"Yeah." Maybe he'd respect my ballsiness.

"With your mess."

"It is my mess," I said. "And I'm willing to pay. Whatever Madame Lorenzo wants."

"And if it isn't money?"

"What, then?"

"Maybe all she wants is, you run a job here in town, you clear it through her."

"Not a chance," I said automatically. *But why refuse, if you're only going to walk into the lion's den after this, and let the lion sculpt you into an entirely different person?* Still . . . I was already giving myself up to one person. I didn't know if I'd be capable of doing it twice. "Give me something I can work with," I said to Malcolm.

He very deliberately lifted the barrel of the shotgun an inch. "Maybe if you don't agree to our terms, then we don't got a deal. And maybe this being all your doing, there's a different exchange rate for you."

Malcolm probably wouldn't be able to kill me here—probably, though I wasn't sure whether I should bet on the unseen security. Still, it didn't matter. Even considering how hard I was to kill, Mama Lorenzo had the power to make sure people didn't stop trying until they finished the job.

But the fact remained that during this meeting Malcolm hadn't tried himself yet, and that meant there was still room to negotiate.

"I'm not going to be her lackey," I said slowly, more firmly than I felt. "That's a nonstarter."

Malcolm didn't say anything.

"I'll stop taking contracts for her rivals," I offered. "Varga, Thach's people, the Russians. Fuentes and XG44. Turner and company."

"The Grigoryans," Malcolm said. "The cartels. And the Russians will include Dolzhikov."

"Yeah," I said. "Okay." The Grigoryans wouldn't have hired me anyway and the cartels only rarely, so those were no skin off my back. But I'd miss working for Dolzhikov.

NULL SET • 271

Otherwise, the agreement would cut out my employment with all the biggest crime families in town, but I could live with it—I preferred independent contracting anyway. "She quits the blackballing, though. If I stop working for her rivals, I stop hearing other people are afraid to hire me."

"And the water goes clean."

"With your help."

He nodded fractionally. "One last thing. You try any shit like that again in the Madre's town, you talk to her first. Or your name goes on the other list."

I supposed it said something about Mama Lorenzo's character that she would be willing to forgive me for calming criminal enterprise across Los Angeles—even if it had impacted her—but she was making it a priority to stop me running guns into her city.

"Understood," I said.

"Good." He swung down the shotgun to hold it competently at his side. "What do you need?"

"Mama Lorenzo owns Norricom Media," I said. "They fund KHBP radio. I need time on the air with Reuben McCabe."

Malcolm blinked. I'd managed to surprise him. "McCabe? Why?"

"I need to reach his audience."

"Folks aren't gonna stand down just 'cause you ask them to."

"Not because *I* ask them to, no."

Malcolm studied me. "No go without the details, Russell. What's your plan?"

"I've got a friend who has leverage with the militias," I said. "And some of the others. If he can give an indication of that with enough people hearing it, they'll back off. It'll work." Assuming Simon would agree to it. Whatever; I would make him.

"You sure?" Malcolm asked.

"Yeah. I'm sure. Can Mama Lorenzo get me the airtime?"

"She'll get you the meet. McCabe doesn't like being strong-armed."

"I hear Mama Lorenzo's pretty good at strong-arming."

He grimaced. "Free advice, Russell. You want someone's lunch money, you threaten them. You want someone to work with you, you start off by asking nicely."

"Sure," I said.

"McCabe's a political power. You get on his bad side, the Madre won't step in."

"Just get us the meet," I said. "And it has to be tonight. We need to get on air with him first thing in the morning."

It was almost midnight, but Malcolm didn't object. This was, after all, part of the reason it was a favor.

"I'll walk you out," he said, gesturing at the pedestrian door at the front of the garage. "Stay by your phone."

"Thanks," I said.

He paused and turned back to me, his posture relaxing from its militant formidability. "I hope you do succeed. Whispers the past couple days—we've been getting threats. And not from the usual suspects."

I started to put it together then, to make the connection, but too slowly. Far too slowly.

"You pull this off, it could be the start of a working relationship with the Madre," Malcolm continued. "You're not bad, Russell. Stay on her good side, yeah?"

I nodded.

He nodded back to me and reached out. Grasped the doorknob.

Pulled open the door.

The bullet sheared through the right side of his face with so much force it barely spun him, even as it took half his skull with it. His body lost its rigidity a split second later, as if it was only just catching up to the fact that he was dead.

I threw myself to the side, away from the door and any possible lines of sight, just as a rifle report echoed across the mountains. From very, very far away. Security had taken my handgun, but a pistol wouldn't reach the distance the shot had come from anyway—nor would Malcolm's shotgun, lying impotently across his still fingers.

So still. He was one of the most efficiently dangerous men I'd ever met, and now his body lay crumpled, its joints at odd angles.

Someone shouted. Another rifle report rang out. I ran for the back of the garage.

I tumbled through a back door onto a hill at the rear of the property, one that dropped away to reveal a valley of twinkling yellow spread out below me. White lights shone blandly across tennis courts to my right. I wove left, toward the estate house, skidding down the slope to keep my angle below the view of the far-distant sniper. More gunfire echoed, some nearby. A man screamed. Someone else yelled, commands of some kind.

The alarms at the estate blared out into the night, startling and earsplitting, light flaring suddenly from every corner of the building. I ducked and cursed as the freakin' alarms muffled the gunfire and interfered with the data my senses could turn into a numerical re-creation of the scene going on above me.

Still, the numbers had teased out one conclusion, one horrifying, inescapable conclusion: only one person was firing on us.

One man.

My mind had been rebelling against what I already knew was true. *Irreversible. Uncontainable.* The American Mafia had the power of infinite revenge, and no one would be able to hold them back from retribution for an attack at their very heart. Particularly not an attack that assassinated one of their leaders.

If Rio wanted to start a mob war in Los Angeles, Mama Lorenzo was a perfect target. Take her out, and blame someone else—maybe even the militias, or the police, or someone the Lorenzos didn't have a usual agenda for tangling with, someone they couldn't just crush into oblivion.

We've been getting threats, Malcolm had said. It was a setup. The Family would raze Los Angeles to avenge Mama Lorenzo's death.

I ran for the house, every thought crystallizing into the brutal, slim hope that I wasn't going to be too late.

thirty

I DIDN'T know where in the estate Mama Lorenzo was most likely to be, so I beelined for the closest part of the house.

A troop of private security poured out the back, weapons drawn. I belly-flopped into the landscaping, hoping they hadn't seen me. There was no way they'd let me in, and I had to get to her . . . and without killing any of her own security on the way.

The troops dashed by with shouts and tromping. I stayed low and sprinted for the door that had disgorged them. Into the estate, slip out of the way of more troops, down a hall—

I skidded into Mama Lorenzo's study, right into the barrels of a dozen assault rifles.

Thrusting my hands in the air, I yelled, "Friendly!" and turned the skid into a slide, dropping like I was a baseball player just in case. But her troops were good enough that none of them fired. Yet.

"I'm here to help!" I shouted from the floor.

The woman herself rose from behind her polished wooden desk. The head of the Los Angeles Mafia was tall, thin, and perfectly coiffed, and she wore a thousand-dollar cocktail dress like it was armor, but now a gauntness shadowed her elegant maquillage. I fleetingly wondered if she knew about Malcolm yet.

"Miss Russell," she said. "What is happening?"

"You've got one sniper, eight hundred and seventy-six point four meters away at an elevation of eight point four nine degrees. He's to the southeast, bearing a hundred and thirty-one point zero three. Your people aren't going to be able to get him without some serious hardware, and maybe not even then." Almost certainly not even then, but if Rio was watching through the scope and saw someone setting up to fire back, he might abort. "Get everyone behind cover, to the back of the property."

Mama Lorenzo nodded briskly and turned to the bodyguard by her elbow. "It's possible Malcolm would be able to make a shot like that. Get him to—"

"Madame Lorenzo—" I started.

I'd cut in before thinking about it.

Her eyes flickered to my face. I didn't know how to tell her.

But I didn't need to say anything. She read the news off my expression.

"Oh," she said, a quiet, defeated sound, and her hand caught on the surface of the desk. Then she said, very quietly, "Torvald, do you have anyone capable of taking that kind of shot?"

I could have done it, but I didn't volunteer.

"I don't know, ma'am, but we'll put out the word," Torvald answered, talking fast. "We have to get you to the panic room."

"Which way is that?" I said.

Torvald cast me a black look, his hand on Mama Lorenzo's elbow.

"He's trying to flush you toward the front of the house," I said. "Madame Lorenzo has to be his true target, but he's on a timeline. He won't just wait for her to go outside tomorrow. Now which way is the panic room?"

Torvald pointed. "The glass in the front windows is bulletproof—"

"You mean bullet-resistant," I said. There was no such thing as bulletproof, not with enough force. "And are your *walls* bulletproof? Because if he sees her, he knows exactly where she's going to be the next step even if she's behind a wall. Madame Lorenzo, don't follow them."

"Nobody's that good," Torvald said.

I was. Rio was.

Mama Lorenzo turned to me. "Miss Russell. What would you suggest?"

"Ma'am—" started Torvald, but at that moment one of the big picture windows at the front of the house went down in a magnificent crash.

"Out the back," I said. "There's only one sniper, and he's almost a kilometer away. Go out the back and get away from here."

"Ma'am, we don't know there's only one—" Torvald tried, but Mama Lorenzo ignored him. She had a little chrome .32 out on her desk already; she tucked it into a purse and strode through her troops toward me, stepping out of her stilettos. "Someone give me your boots. Men's 8."

A couple of the men started scrambling, and by the time Mama Lorenzo reached my side, hands were thrusting a pair of combat boots at her. "Someone give me a weapon," I echoed her, and Torvald glanced at Mama Lorenzo before signaling the now-bootless guy to pass me his PS90. I slung it on and checked the chamber.

"Let's go," I said.

"Relay the information we got about the sniper," Torvald told Bootless Guy, and then the rest of the security force crowded around us, making a human shield for Mama Lorenzo and covering ahead and behind as we hustled out the back.

Torvald might be an idiot in some ways, but he was decent at his job.

The drop to the northwest of the house was near-vertical, so we edged east before hustling down the slope at an angle. The gunfire and lights faded behind us.

We made it down into a ravine and hiked along the bottom of it. Despite her high-end black sheath, Mama Lorenzo not only managed to keep up with no trouble, but maintained an air of subtle power even tromping through clumps of grass and branches.

A flurried rush through the dark later, the guy who had point stopped us with a raised fist. He gestured to indicate upward—a house, and the distant zoom of cars passing. Torvald made a few more hand signals, and three of our escort broke off to scale the slope and scout ahead.

While we waited, Torvald stripped his own vest and helmet and helped Mama Lorenzo into them. "Do you think this sniper will be able to come around and cut us off?" he asked in a low voice.

It startled me when I connected he was talking to me. "If he realizes which way we went—yeah, he had the time to make it," I said, pacing Rio's ground speed in my head. "And I'm betting he's good enough. But if he went down to the house first, or looped around to the west instead . . ." Rio was good, but he wasn't omniscient. There was no way he'd magically know from the position of his sniper's nest which way we'd gone, was there?

Was there?

I wondered if he knew I'd been at the estate. Probably not—I'd waited on Malcolm for at least forty minutes after arriving, and if Rio had been in place beforehand, wouldn't he have shot Malcolm when he crossed in the open before our meeting? And after that I'd stayed well out of sight by reflex.

Crap, I probably should have shown myself. It wasn't like Rio was going to shoot me, the same way I hadn't exactly been willing to take up a rifle against his hiding place. And knowing I was moving around in his target zone might have made him a little slower on the trigger.

Malcolm's still, faceless silhouette danced across my vision again. Rio had targeted him first on purpose. He would've had intel to know Malcolm was one of the Lorenzos' expert snipers—maybe their only expert sniper. And he'd probably known how much he meant to Mama Lorenzo, too, which meant even if he hadn't nailed the woman herself, he'd probably still accomplished his objective here: inciting revenge.

"I'm sorry about Malcolm," I said to Mama Lorenzo.

She nodded.

Then, a moment later, she added quietly, "He was my brother."

Oh. Shit. "I didn't . . . he never . . ."

Of course, why would I have known? Malcolm had never used any form of address for her that implied she was anything other than the leader of his Family. . . .

I remembered, then, that I'd heard Mama Lorenzo had married in. Perhaps the internal politics of her family were as complicated as the external ones.

"The people who did this will pay," Mama Lorenzo said. She said it simply, factually. Her eyes were dry.

I wondered if Rio had known about the personal connection. Maybe he figured Malcolm was as good a target as Mama Lorenzo, given how it would spur her to bloody vigilantism.

"Madame Lorenzo," I tried. "I have to warn you. Whoever you think did this—whoever, um, the evidence points to, or whoever claims responsibility—I guarantee you it's the wrong target. It's going to be a frame-up."

Her eyes pinned me, a hawk's gaze in the dark. "How could you know this?"

"Please," I said. "Don't go after someone just because . . ." An even more awful thought struck me. Mama Lorenzo was all about appearances—she was the type to go through with crushing someone even if she *knew* they were innocent, just to maintain the appearance of strength. Rio couldn't have chosen a better criminal organization for his scheme. "Give me a day," I said. "Give me a day before you take any action. Before you go for, um. For justice." I would be able to reach Rio in that time, I hoped, and get him to pick apart whatever trail of evidence he'd left to provoke the Lorenzos into firing the next shot.

"And what's your interest in this?"

"I'm trying to stop the, um. What's in the water," I said lamely, falling back on McCabe's assumptions again. "It's bigger than you know. That's what I was talking to Malcolm about; we had worked out a deal. I need airtime from Reuben McCabe, *today,* and I need you to hold off on vengeance for—for your people. I can stop this. Please."

Before she could reply, a shuffle reached our ears from the top of the ridge, and one of Torvald's guys waved us up the slope. The path up was more a climb than a hike, and a couple of the guards helped their boss keep her balance as we scaled the incline.

I slipped in front of them as we reached the top, just in case Rio was watching through a scope from somewhere nearby. But the night was quiet.

An SUV and a sedan hummed in the driveway, the engines already started. I had no idea if they'd been bought, extorted, or hotwired, but whatever family lived here, there was no evidence of them.

I was pretty sure the residents of the house were physically all right. Mama Lorenzo didn't tend to condone her people hurting bystanders. Usually.

Mama Lorenzo and I piled into the SUV among her men, who had her stay curled low on the floor while they covered her. Torvald had taken the driver's seat; he swung us down the sloped driveway at a good clip. "Where to, ma'am?"

"Do you have a safe house?" I asked.

Mama Lorenzo's eyes flickered up to me. "I believe you requested a meeting." She raised her voice. "Make sure we're not being followed, and then drive to the KHBP radio station. In the meantime, Miss Russell, I would like a full accounting of exactly what situation has befallen us here."

Right.

Torvald acknowledged her and took a right, whisking us into late-night traffic at exactly the speed limit. I swallowed. If I didn't tell Mama Lorenzo everything, she might refuse to help . . . but if she blamed me for Malcolm . . .

Flat-out lying to the head of the Los Angeles Family was not an activity with a lot of longevity. Especially considering elaborate lies were not in my skill set.

But even though Malcolm's death may have screwed me with Mama Lorenzo if I ended up on the wrong side of this in her eyes, Rio's attack had also bought me urgency. It could be all I needed to do was convince Mama Lorenzo I'd be helping her get justice for her brother—even though that was about the farthest thing from the truth, considering the people responsible for it were Rio and, well, me.

And now I was going to pretend to be working to avenge Malcolm just to get what I wanted? Maybe because I'd liked him, but that thought made me feel shittier than anything else I'd done that night.

But as I'd told Checker earlier . . . what else could I do?

"I'll give you what I can," I said to Mama Lorenzo, hating myself. "I, um. I owe discretion to some people. But I'm trying to stop exactly the people who killed Malcolm."

That much, at least, was precisely true.

thirty-one

I SENT Arthur a text to get him to meet us at the radio station, along with a terse update, including the attack and what parts of the situation I'd divulged. And then, there in the SUV with drops of Malcolm's blood still on my clothes and Mama Lorenzo crouched between the seats plotting vengeance, I finally got a call from Rio.

I turned away as much as I dared and made sure the volume was turned all the way down. Fortunately, I could measure sound waves accurately enough to deduce the road noise would cover Rio's side of the conversation. "Hello."

"Cas," Rio said, his tone perfectly ordinary. "I apologize for missing your earlier calls. I was in the Hills."

Killing Malcolm. "I know."

"Ah. So you have heard."

In a manner of speaking.

"Your friends just informed me of your decision to dismantle your plan here," Rio continued. "Did they speak truthfully?"

"Yeah." I stared out the window of the SUV, into the dark scenery speeding by.

"Good. I hoped you would return to the way of the Lord, Cas," Rio said.

I wanted to curse him out, but then Mama Lorenzo would wonder. "It'll take a few days, logistically," I said instead, with enforced calm. "Will you . . ."

"I will discontinue the remainder of my activities tonight. I regret the situation came to this."

Yeah, me too. "Take apart whatever . . . anything . . . you've been leaving," I said. Any evidence, any false trails that would put people at each other's throats and make the ensuing violence worse than it was already going to be. "This ends here."

"If I have your promise, consider it done. Although that, too, will take some small time."

"How long?"

"A day. Perhaps two. It will be done as quickly as possible."

He didn't apologize. Probably because he wasn't sorry.

Hopefully I could hold Mama Lorenzo off until then. Her, and the militias, and everyone else Rio had incited tonight.

"One more thing," I said. "I need Simon, or . . ." I had the excuse prepared; otherwise Rio would have suspected my real intent. But the lie stuck in my throat, too close to the truth for comfort. A whisper skittered through my head—the first echoes of Valarmathi waking back up? Or my own paranoia? "I need Simon, or I won't make it to—um, to finish the logistics," I made myself say.

"Understood," Rio answered. "Where shall we meet you?"

I glanced sideways at the other silhouettes in the car. I was sure they were all listening closely. "The same place you met me when you came to town. As soon as possible. I can be there within a couple hours."

"Then we will be, as well," Rio said.

"Good." I hung up.

"Developments?" Mama Lorenzo asked.

"Yes." I scrambled for something to tell her. "That was, um. Someone who's been helping me end this."

"A name you feel you cannot divulge." Her disapproval was severe.

"I'm sorry," I said, a little desperately. "You know if I'd promised not to reveal your part in something—"

She held up a hand. "No need to explain again. I've decided to accept your justifications. For now."

God, this was going to be a tightrope.

Arthur was waiting in the shadows outside the radio station. He greeted Mama Lorenzo deferentially, and she responded with equal respect. It occurred to me to worry about her seeing him working with me—if this went south and she wanted to scorch the particular patch of earth home to Cas Russell . . .

Or whatever your name is.

One of Mama Lorenzo's men had been making calls from the car, and a night janitor was already on standby to let us in. McCabe had been woken at home and was on his way.

"Are your restroom facilities unlocked?" Mama Lorenzo asked the janitor, who fumbled with her keys and led the way to a hallway at the back of the darkened lobby. Mama Lorenzo sailed after her, the armed escort in their wake.

"Let's get away from the windows," I said to Arthur, gesturing at the glass front wall of the lobby. I led the way toward a door to the back.

Arthur cast a glance after Mama Lorenzo and her men before leaning in close to me as he hustled after. "He's called off, right?"

"Yeah. But . . ." Rio was called off, but I didn't know all the ramifications of what he'd done. McCabe's show wasn't exactly on the sidelines—there was the possibility someone would target this place.

Fuck, what a mess.

We flicked on lights in the back and found a small conference room to wait in. I slumped in an office chair with the PS90 across my lap. "I should probably just have you talk to McCabe alone and stay out of it," I said to Arthur. I'd fucked up enough tonight. Navigating another negotiation . . . and then the upcoming one with Simon, with my sanity ready to tip again at any time . . . "It's not like civilized meetings have ever been in my wheelhouse. If I try to punch anyone, stop me."

"You might have to remind *me*," Arthur said darkly.

I snorted. "Yeah right, Mr. Diplomacy."

"Maybe usually. But McCabe and I in the same room, it's a recipe for a fight." He had stayed standing, and his posture was tense, though I'd assumed that was just because of the entire mess—his guilt and mine, and Rio, and Katrina.

I'd finally texted Checker to ask about Katrina. She was still in the hospital but stable. The intensity of my relief had felt selfish—I hadn't wanted her death to be on me.

"Don't tell me the *one person* we need here is the one person in LA you have a beef with," I said to Arthur.

He grunted. "We need him. I'm not a child."

Voices in the hallway. Arthur drew his Glock and slipped to the side; I half raised the PS90 just in case, but I already recognized the blustering ramble of the main talker.

"In here," I called.

The door opened, and another one of Mama Lorenzo's private security slid halfway in. "Identify yourself," he called, over his own weapon.

"We're with Madame Lorenzo," I said. "And, uh, her guys. Torvald and company. She's in the washroom; she'll be here in a minute."

There was a brief shuffle in the hallway as someone went to verify this. Torvald must have sent his own people to get McCabe instead of made men from the Family. Smart—if Rio had been tracking any of the other Lorenzos, this wouldn't have been revealed to them, and in the wake of the attack on her estate, it would keep the internal whispers Mama Lorenzo would have to deal with to a minimum.

Someone called out an "Okay," and the guy on point nodded and pushed the door the rest of the way open, lowering his weapon. Arthur and I did the same. Another group of troops came in, McCabe in their midst. He was a large, ruddy-faced man clearly used to using his size to intimidate people—fortunately, none of us were people who intimidated easily.

"Hey, whoa," he said immediately, raising his hands when he saw our guns. He looked askance at one of his escorts. "You telling me *they're* on our side?"

"Thought you were all for citizen carry," Arthur muttered, holstering his Glock.

"As long as they're the right type of citizens, my man," McCabe said with a jovial grin, all teeth. "If you're defending America, I got no complaint. Hey, ain't this country great? The station owners tell me 'emergency,' and here I am. That's the power of capitalism."

I preferred the power of firearms myself.

"Now, I know Gabby Lorenzo's coming," he continued. The man apparently couldn't stand not to hear himself talk for more than a few seconds. "I don't truck with all her goings-on, obviously. But she has money, and money talks. And I'll admit it, she's a woman with some grit to her, and I respect that. I respect grit."

Jesus, this guy was an idiot. Not to mention I didn't want to know what would happen if Gabrielle Lorenzo heard him call her "Gabby."

"Now you . . ." McCabe lumbered into Arthur's personal space, wagging a finger in his face. "You look familiar. Have we met? Or I could be mixing you all up." He laughed like it was a joke and clapped Arthur on the back as if he wanted to knock him over.

"We met," Arthur said. "Several times. Couple decades ago. I worked with Elinor Hershfeld and Diego Rosales."

McCabe jerked his hand back off Arthur like he'd been burned, his face contorting almost comically. Arthur held his gaze and very deliberately brushed the shoulder of his jacket where McCabe had touched him.

Fortunately, at that moment Mama Lorenzo and her cadre arrived, and everyone shuffled around and went to sit while McCabe made a point of greeting Mama Lorenzo with a loud speech about how good it was to see her again. He kept calling her "Mrs. Lorenzo," which I'd never heard anyone else do, either. I wondered if it was a deliberate insult or if he was just that ignorant.

I sidled up to Arthur during the momentary chaos. "Really starting this off on the right foot, aren't you?" I said, keeping my voice low. "What was that about?"

"Neanderthal," muttered Arthur. "He oughta die or get with the times."

Great. Arthur springing a secret vendetta on this meeting was all I needed. "You're supposed to be the person who's good at talking," I said tightly. "You know what's at stake here. Are you going to fuck this up on us?"

He made a sound that was far too noncommittal for my liking, and we followed everyone else to sit at the table. Mama Lorenzo's security mostly stood behind and around the table, alert set pieces in our ridiculous midnight rendezvous.

"So," McCabe said. "I hear this is some sort of crisis. You need the McCabe Nation on your side. I'll need to know everything, of course, so we can fact-check your data—"

Arthur made a little sound in his throat I hoped McCabe didn't hear.

"—but if it's good, you've come to the right place. I've got true patriots on my airwaves, and tens of millions of listeners across this great country. More than all the other programs in the same time slot combined, as I'm sure you know."

"Uh, sure." I stumbled to find an opening in his monologue. "That's why we came to you. And because, uh, the conspiracy crap you've been going on about." I tried to moderate my wording. "Um, people acting against their own interest, that stuff. We know what's causing it, and we can stop it."

McCabe leaned back in his chair. "Oh, really?" I thought for a moment he was going to let us respond, but then he started in again. "Because let me tell you, I've had investigators out there—"

"Yeah," I cut in loudly. "*Really*. But the minute we do stop it, your militia pals and half the organized crime bosses in Los Angeles are all going to start killing each other. We need a spot on your show to tell them not to. And we need it now. When you go on the air in the morning."

McCabe guffawed.

None of the rest of us moved.

His chuckles died out after a few seconds—he might not really know me or Arthur, but Mama Lorenzo sitting there staring icicles at you was enough to make anybody stop laughing, even someone as weirdly dismissive of her as McCabe seemed to be. "Oh, come on," he said. "I've got a lady of questionable business ethics—no disrespect, Mrs. Lorenzo—and a bleeding-heart liberal activist"—he waved a hand at Arthur, the word "liberal" becoming a sneer— "coming to sit down with me and telling me they can fix everything? Not likely. Where would you have gotten this kind of special knowledge? And why should I grant my airtime, which as you know is a very valuable commodity, to some sort of sentimental plea for goodwill? Real Americans are angry, folks, and they're angry with good reason, because—"

"Well, Madame Lorenzo owns the company that funds

your radio station," I said, my annoyance rising. "So there's that."

"You think you're going to censor me? The McCabe Nation won't stand for it. I'll tell everyone—"

"Whoa, hey," Arthur said, his soothing calm back in full force.

I slumped in relief. *Thank Christ.*

"Nobody's censoring," Arthur continued. "We're giving you a scoop, is what we're doing. As for why a fruity ol' pinko liberal like me would want to give you the goods, well, I don't. I don't like you, Mr. McCabe. But we want the same things for once, and your audience is the folk we gotta reach to stop any fallout when this goes down."

McCabe harrumphed. "An honest lib. Now there's an oxymoron."

"You've got nothing to lose," Arthur went on, before McCabe could start talking again. "Worst that happens is you get a few cooties from other folks' freedom of speech on your air, but even then, you get to point to us as giving a fair hearing to the other side's First Amendment rights. So you win anyway. And best case, this is a coup for you—the leader of the American people who solved it all. Trust me, if I could bring this to anyone else I would, but you're the only one telling the truth to power here. Even I gotta admit it."

God bless Arthur. He really was good at this.

I supposed it helped that all of it was actually true. McCabe *was* the only one. I wondered what that meant for the rest of our news media—or for our opinions of McCabe, come to think of it.

McCabe sat back and folded his hands against his middle. "All right. I'm listening. No guarantees."

Arthur spun a story similar to the one I'd told Mama Lorenzo, one about subtle leverage and coded language we assured McCabe his audience would understand. "It's gonna get 'em all back from the brink," Arthur said. "Then we fix it all, and you get to report on the whole scoop."

"I can give you a sample of the technology, once we get everything removed," I said, adding, "Um, both of you," when Mama Lorenzo turned a burning gaze on me. I'd give them each a mathematically incorrect version of one of the Signet Devices, one no one would be able to make work again. McCabe would report on the truth, all right, but likely nobody would believe him, and somehow we'd figure out a way to convince Mama Lorenzo we'd already brought Malcolm's killer to justice. Everyone else would comment on the strange dip and resurgence in crime as a random happenstance.

McCabe would be a hero, one who would remain unsung except in the echo chamber of his followers, even after he'd saved all of Los Angeles. The status quo would continue. Everything would go back to normal.

Except for Malcolm. And Katrina. And Miguel and his boys. And all the other people who had died or had their lives derailed because of this.

And me. I wasn't sure who I would be, tomorrow. Once I gave myself over to Simon . . .

I didn't want to think about it.

Arthur outlined the plan. McCabe objected to parts of it. Arthur restated those parts in different words until he agreed. It was impressive: he didn't try to talk to McCabe like they were friends, didn't even try to hide his dislike for McCabe's views. He just . . . acknowledged the other man's power, and listened to him bluster and argue where I would have tried to shout him down.

And he got us exactly what we came for.

"You may think I hate people like you, Mr. Tresting," McCabe said, as they stood. "I don't. But I love my country, and I have to do what's best for it."

"Yeah," Arthur said. "Me, too."

"Have your man here at seven," McCabe said. "I want to

interview him. We go live at eight for the morning show, eleven on the East Coast."

Arthur glanced at me.

"I'll get him here," I said.

And I would. Whatever it took.

thirty-two

I NEEDED to hurry. Rio was probably waiting for me with Simon, so the sooner I got this over with, the sooner Rio could rededicate himself to knocking off pieces of the immolating tension he'd plunged LA into.

That *we'd* plunged LA into.

Instead I drove out to the coast.

The ocean at night is a beautiful thing. I parked at the side of the highway and climbed over the guardrail to sit on the rocky tumble overlooking the beach. The surf rolled in out of the darkness with comforting trochoidal periodicity, the depth and wavelength and breaking pattern outlining the contour of the sea floor. The liquid water spun in never-ending circles as the energy of the waves pulsed through it, stretching into hyperbolic tangents before crashing on the shore as if they had never been.

I sat and watched the numbers furl in and out, the fine spray dampening my face. For the first time in my life, I wanted to call someone just to talk.

But I couldn't. Arthur had stayed back at the radio station

to keep McCabe and Mama Lorenzo monitored, and even I could read how he'd been mired in his own guilt since all this had gone south—he'd listen, but I doubted he wanted to, at the moment. Checker was opposed to what I was doing, full stop. And Pilar . . .

I wasn't sure I wanted to know how badly I'd messed up my relationship with Pilar.

That left Rio, who not only *also* wouldn't approve of what I was doing—in the most violent of ways—but who was the one person in my life utterly devoid of empathy.

Screw it. Maybe that was what I needed right now.

I pulled out my phone.

"Hello, Cas," Rio greeted me. "Are you on your way?"

I was so *angry* with him.

"Cas? Are you all right?"

"I'm having trouble . . ." I said. I swallowed. *I don't want to die.*

Rio waited.

"What was she like?" I asked. "Valarmathi?"

Rio considered for a long enough time that I thought he wasn't going to answer, thought he was again going to tell me I couldn't know. "Very different from you," he said finally.

"How?"

"Cas," Rio said. "I am sorry. I am not certain I am adequate for answering these questions."

"Please tell me something."

"She enjoyed books," Rio said, "and animals. Poetry. Elaborate schemes I am given to understand were practical jokes. She found humor in her surroundings, some of it optimistic, some of it cruel. She was a woman of great conviction; she spoke with passion and laughed with startling frequency. She was also competitive, and persistent—traits you share."

The only ones, it sounded like. Rio needn't have worried about my head—his listing was so far off from my reality it sparked no new connection to my misremembered past.

"I really am a different person, aren't I," I said.

"Only God can answer that, Cas," Rio answered. "I do not know if you share a soul."

Right.

"I don't remember much of her," I said. "I remember . . . how hard she fought. How much she didn't want to go."

Standing at the window, pressing one hand to the rain-drenched glass as droplets washed me away.

"I do not believe it will be that way this time, Cas," Rio said.

"But you don't know, do you?" I stared out at the black and endless sea. "If he finds me too . . . damaged, he'll just—reboot me again, won't he? Clean up his mistakes."

The same way I was trying to undo what I'd wrought upon Los Angeles. A hopeless, hypocritical reset button. Erase and try again.

I didn't want to be reset.

"It is a danger," Rio said. "But I do not believe it to be a probable one."

"Would you be able to tell?" I asked.

"Under some circumstances, probably."

"If I start to go . . . different . . ." I stopped.

"Yes, Cas?"

"I want you to end it," I said hoarsely. "Will you do that?"

"You mean kill you."

"Yeah," I said.

The phone was silent. I waited.

"I believe I can promise that," Rio answered at last.

Some tension inside me unclenched. Perhaps it was simply the notion of having some control, some way.

"I'm coming in," I said, and turned my back on the crashing waves.

I ARRIVED back at the apartment where we'd made the phone-hacking devices.

And everything went straight to hell.

Rio and Simon stood up as I came in. And Simon, brilliant people person that he was, took one look at my face and exclaimed, "No! Cassandra, I'm not going to do that!"

Rio glanced between us, in one half second figured out my whole plan, and went for his gun.

I lunged for Simon and tackled him. A shot slammed out over our heads. Rio attempted to adjust his aim but I was in the way now; I kept my body collinear with Simon's and rocketed up at Rio's gun hand.

Rio tried to block me and twist around. He was very, very fast—but not faster than mathematical extrapolation. I lurched into where he was going to be and applied the requisite force to either wrench the gun out of his fingers—or break them, if he didn't let go.

He didn't let go.

I did, a split second before I snapped his wrist.

I stumbled. My breath heaved. I raised my hands, trying to deny the tremor in them. "What the hell, Rio?"

Instead of pressing his advantage, he'd stopped in midstride, weapon still pointed vaguely toward Simon behind me. A slight frown had appeared between his eyes. "Cas?"

I couldn't hurt Rio. In the same way I couldn't seriously hurt Simon.

In *exactly* the same way.

"Did you know?" I asked. My voice shook.

"No, Cas," Rio answered. "I . . . did not."

"You did this," I said, my voice raised to accuse the man behind me. "Or you're doing it, right now." I honestly couldn't tell which, but since the latter didn't make much sense . . .

Rio didn't seem to know what action to take. I stayed standing in front of Simon.

The tension in the room teetered on the point of a needle.

"What?" I yelled at Rio. "You don't want to fight me because—it wouldn't be *fair*?" I didn't even know what I was saying. "Come at me. Come at me!"

"Cassandra, don't—" gasped Simon. I mule-kicked him without looking, and without moving out of Rio's way.

"I am unsure of the proper way to proceed," Rio admitted.

"What else did you do to me?" I screamed, without turning around. *"What else?"*

Simon coughed wretchedly and didn't answer.

"Come on, Rio." I couldn't seem to stop. "Hit me. Shoot me! I have to be able to fight back then, don't I? I have to have some control—"

"I am not going to shoot you, Cas."

"Try!"

Rio lowered his gun. "No."

I wanted to march over and raise it back up, right at me, and force him to pull the trigger.

I wanted to yank it out of his hands and turn it back on him.

I wanted some modicum of power over my own goddamn mind.

"I'm going to use him to fix Los Angeles," I said. "I'm going to convince him. That violates every ethical principle you stand for."

"Yes," Rio answered.

We stared at each other.

"I won't do it," Simon gasped from behind me. "I won't . . ."

"Shut up," I said.

Rio spoke to Simon, even though he was still looking at me. "If you do this, I shall think it meet to kill you."

Hell, he apparently thought it meet to kill Simon at the very *suggestion* I might be able to convince him to break his moral stance. This did not bode well for Simon agreeing to help.

Even if, after fantasizing so many times about his death, I was about to save his life.

"Simon," I said. "Stand up and go to the door."

He hesitated, which made me furious—if he did know me, he should know my skill. He *did* know my skill. Which meant he was hesitating because either he couldn't wrap his brain around it or he just couldn't handle being efficient under pressure, neither of which I had any patience for.

He finally scrambled up and edged for the front of the apartment. I rotated in line with the scuffling of his feet, staying between him and Rio.

"Cas," Rio said. "Do not do this."

"If you want to stop me," I said, "you're going to have to *stop* me." I backed away from Rio until I nearly collided with Simon, and then shoved him out of the apartment behind me without ever turning around.

Rio didn't try to follow us.

thirty-three

SIMON MADE a break for it as soon as we got outside, but I grabbed him by the coat and collared him into my stolen car. He scrabbled at the door handle, but I took off too fast and sped us out and away, running from Rio, zigzagging past any probability he might be able to track us.

"I'm not going to do it," Simon said. Shrilly. He'd wrapped his arms around himself in the passenger seat.

I ignored him. I drove out to the desert, where no one would see us, out where he couldn't get away from me even if he fled, and pulled off the road to bump over rocks and dirt and scrub before I stopped the car.

Simon slumped, defeated, and didn't get out. "Don't try to convince me," he said. "I'm not going to. This is the one thing—I vowed I wouldn't, and I won't. Ever."

I only had one piece of leverage to bargain with. But even here at the end, with no other option . . . Christ on a crutch if I wasn't going to try everything else first.

"Do you know what we've been doing in LA?" I said, without looking at him.

"I've guessed—broadly."

Guessed, my ass. "Brain entrainment," I said. "Technology that knocks people out of groupthink. But we need to dismantle it. Problem is, we're poised on the brink of a gang war." For once I was glad he could read the truth of it in my face and voice, read the severity of the situation off my posture and expression. "We need you to go on the radio and tell everyone to stand the fuck down, or a lot of people in this city are going to die."

He looked away. "You know I don't do that, Cas. I can't."

"Make a fucking exception."

"And then what?" He whipped back around to me. "If I make an exception to help Los Angeles, manipulate everyone here against their will because it will *help,* where does it end? What else do I do to 'help,' Cas? Should I help *you* against your will? Would you like that? I'm not going to start down that slippery slope—"

"The slippery slope is a fallacy!" I got right in his face. "You're a goddamn human being; you're capable of making judgment calls. You don't become a mindless brain-munching zombie just because you decide it's okay to stop a war!"

"Oh, really? I know some other people who make very careful judgment calls about how they use their powers. You know them, too, and you *decimated* them. We wouldn't even be here if you hadn't decided they—"

"Pithica was different," I insisted. I had to believe that. "They were manipulating everyone, the whole world. I'm trying to get you to stop some incredibly violent groups from firing the first shot in a riot that will kill a lot of innocent people. This is clear and immediate."

"And if you have a power that allows you to see many degrees of logic away, it still seems clear and immediate," Simon shot back. "People like Daniela and me aren't the only ones Pithica has. When you have as much power as we do—Cas?"

I groped blindly for the door handle and fell out into the night. The sky reeled above me, stars half–washed out by the city brightness.

"Cas? Cassandra—Cas?" Simon had gotten out, too, but for some reason he wasn't trying to run. He crouched over me, his hands half-raised as if he wanted to touch me but knew I'd try to break his fingers if he did. "Cas, what's going on?"

"Stop talking," I said. "I can't know more about Pithica. She made it so I can't."

"Oh, God, Cas," Simon said, and it sounded like he was swallowing back tears.

"Jesus fuck, shut up," I said.

He folded himself to sit cross-legged on the ground next to me. "I won't say anything more about Pithica, I promise. But you must see why—I can't be the judge of that much power. I can't. Maybe you think *you* could do it, but I'm not—I'm not smart enough, and frankly, I don't think any human is. Or maybe the better way of phrasing is to say my judgment call *is* not to use it. Ever. Not unless people tell me I can, and that's where I'm drawing the line, because I'm not smart enough to be able to draw it anywhere else."

"I have superpowers, too," I said. "I use them."

"Yours are different. You don't . . . unmake people."

"No, they just underestimate me and then I kill them."

He flinched. "Well, then maybe you should think about drawing some lines, too. But that's not for me to say, Cas. Honestly, it's not. I have to decide what I'm comfortable with when it comes to what I can do, and I *have* to draw a line, and I have to draw it here. I'm . . . I'm sorry. I truly am." His face wrinkled at me earnestly.

"You'll let a whole mess of innocent people die, then."

He turned away again, and his jaw clamped shut like he was resisting saying something. I thought I heard it anyway: *Just like you did, when you took down Pithica.*

I wondered if it was an unconscious psychic projection or my own guilt saying the words.

Fuck.

"Maybe," I said. "Maybe I'm just like Dawna, in wanting to do this. I still have to make the decision in front of me. I still have to— I can't live with myself, if I let this happen."

"And I have to make the decision in front of me, too," Simon said, anguished. "And I . . . I can't live with myself the other way. I can't. I'm sorry."

I was down to my last hole card. Every emotion shriveled inside me in rebellion, made me want to get up and run, drive away, flee to another city and leave LA to burn.

That would be the easy solution.

But I'd come here knowing I'd have to. Knowing this was my only shot. I'd made this situation happen from the get-go: I'd caused the crime spike when I'd hamstrung Pithica; I'd set up the brain entrainment to try to combat it.

Maybe it was only fair I had to give myself to fix it.

"You were right, you know." I picked up a stone and dug it into the hard-packed dirt. Cars whizzed by on the freeway thirty meters distant. "You were right that . . . it is killing me."

Simon whirled back around, and whatever he saw, his whole face went wild with alarm. The fucker could read off my expression that I'd had a breakdown, apparently.

At least it saved me needing to tell him.

"Cassandra," he said, my name a breath of relief. "I mean, Cas. I don't know how you're all right, but thank God you are. You— I told you this would happen. I told you . . ."

"Yeah, because of what you did to me," I said. "And that's twice tonight, by the way. I thought you said you didn't read people's minds."

"I explained—sometimes I can't help it. But I only get the sort of . . . overall picture, not details. What happened? Are you truly all right?"

"Never better," I said automatically. Shit. It would only help my case if I told the truth. I opened my mouth to change my answer, but the "no" curdled on my tongue.

Simon saw it anyway. His face creased in worry and pain, as if I'd spoken the word aloud. As if he had any right to worry about me.

"Checker tried to call you," I said. "You're a hard person to find, apparently."

Guilt washed over his features. "I didn't think. I should have been there."

For some reason it made me angry, that he didn't try to defend himself with the indisputable facts: that I'd said no and told him to leave, that therefore no reason existed for Checker or any of my other friends to have his number. I'd chosen his absence. He didn't get to take responsibility for my life like I was some pet he had created in a lab.

He didn't get to feel *guilty* for me, to deny that my own self-destructive decisions had at least been mine to make. Not his.

He winced. "I've upset you. I can't seem to stop doing that."

"Yeah," I said. "Good read there. You know, for a psychic you have terrible people skills."

He wasn't looking at me. I wondered if that was out of consideration for trying to read less of what I was thinking, and hated him for it. I liked being able to categorize him as a one-hundred-percent dick.

"Will you tell me what happened?" he asked, staring out into the night.

"I passed out," I said. "My friends brought me back. With math. We didn't need you after all."

"How do you feel now?" he asked.

"Well, you know. Fewer voices, but I can tell they're coming back."

He jerked. "Cassandra, please consider—"

"I have a different proposal for you," I said over him. "You've got your lines. I want to trade with you for crossing them just this once."

"Cas," he gasped, and I suspected he already saw what I was about to say. But I kept talking anyway.

"I'm fucked. What Checker and the others did to bring me back this time—it wasn't a permanent or practical solution. They can't be around with my math every time I go crazy and collapse. It's also not something that will work until I'm knocked out entirely, which leaves a whole lot of messy gray area fucking me up in between blackouts. And you were right—it's getting worse."

He'd hunched over his knees and dropped his face into his hands. It made me perversely satisfied to see.

"I'm perfectly happy to slide right off the deep end before I let you anywhere near me," I continued, and for the second time I was happy Simon was a human lie detector, because he would know I wasn't bluffing. "I don't trust you or your obsession with me. I'll look for a solution on my own. But since you're so very consumed with wanting to get your fingers in my brain, I'm willing to make a trade."

"Cas," he whispered against his hands. Shredded. Hopeless. "I just . . . I only want to help you."

"Said the spider to the fly."

Yes, I did realize he could do anything he wanted to me anyway, and it was his oh-so-righteous moralism that was preventing him, the very moralism I was arguing against . . .

"You're thinking at me. Stop it," I said.

"I'm not trying to."

"Try harder."

He dropped his hands, but kept his eyes on the distant mountains. "You're saying you'll let me help you. But only if I fix Los Angeles."

"Look at you, drawing conclusions all by yourself," I said.

"You're threatening to kill yourself if I don't do what you want. That's . . . you're emotionally blackmailing me."

"You have a tremendous talent for making this all about you," I said. For Christ's sake, I wasn't suicidal—that was the whole problem with saying yes to him. "I've already found a partial solution. I'll keep looking for a better one until I can't anymore. It's *you* who's so convinced there isn't one."

"Cas, the level of damage you're fighting—"

"You're part of the reason I'm so 'damaged' in the first place. What were you doing that time? Oh, yeah, trying to *help* me. I remember. Except, wait, I don't."

"Cas, I understand why you're angry."

"Oh, goody. Fortunately, I do, too, so you don't have to explain it to me."

"I'm not—God. Cas. I'm not trying to be condescending."

"Well, you suck at it. Are you sure you're really a psychic?"

We sat in the desert together. I stared at the freeway, my eyes unfocused, the headlights zipping through my vision in vectors of light. Simon stared the other way, into the darkness.

"You know," he said, and his voice broke. "You're so . . . you're so different. But every once in a while, you say something, and there's an echo . . ."

"I'm not her," I said harshly. "Don't ever think I am."

His breath hitched. I wasn't looking, but I thought he might be crying. "This is the only way you'll let me help?" he said, the words washed with pleading and failure.

By bargaining with him to break the first principle of his ethical system.

"Yes," I said. "Take it or leave it."

"What about Rio?" he asked. "He . . . he can kill me. He might, for this."

"Then I'll help you disappear."

"What we need to do, Cas—it's not an instantaneous thing. I'm going to have to keep . . . seeing you. Making sure."

Do you realize how complicated the human brain is? Of course it's taking months to get her stable!

How many more months?

I closed my eyes. "Then I'll disappear with you, if necessary."

The cars whizzed by. A light breeze blew against my skin.

"You're letting me save you only if I do what you want," Simon said. "That's obscene, Cas, you know that?"

I knew it.

"Hey, you made me this way," I said. "You've only yourself to blame."

He took a shuddering breath.

"Will you do it?" I asked.

"Yes," he said. "God forgive me."

I'd won. He'd agreed.

I'd won.

If I'd believed in a god, I would have been asking forgiveness, too.

thirty-four

I ARRIVED at the radio station with Simon just after seven. The sun had risen as we drove back into the city, the morning cool and breezy before rush hour and heat. I kept an eye out for Rio, just in case he'd guessed this part of our plan, but caught no sign of him. Likely he was surveilling the people he'd set against each other, expecting us to try to talk to them directly.

Simon and I barely spoke on the way back. I'd explained what I needed from him, and he had nodded. That had been the extent of our communication.

McCabe met us as jovially as he had in the middle of the night, only clean-shaven now and in fresh clothes. He introduced himself to Simon, ignoring me, and ushered him into a back room to "interview" him. I clearly wasn't invited.

I slumped onto a chair in the hallway. I had to trust Simon would do what I asked. As long as he radiated friendliness and confidence at McCabe, I had no doubt we'd be fine. And then we'd get on the radio and calm Los Angeles, I would reverse the brain entrainment, and Simon would go in with a melon baller and scrape out my brain.

Arthur sat down next to me. "I guess you convinced him."

"Yeah," I said.

"You okay?"

Somehow it crushed me, that Arthur was killing himself over what we'd done and still had energy to ask about me. He knew what this was costing me.

I stood abruptly. "I gotta hit the head."

When I came back, McCabe was showing Simon around the glass-walled on-air booth, pointing to a seat and headphones and giving instructions. Mama Lorenzo's security still lurked, fading into the background despite their weaponry, and some of the radio station's staff had arrived, moving about their duties while taking quick glances at all the people with guns.

"Are they vetted?" I asked Arthur, readjusting the sling on the PS90 I was still toting myself.

"Well as we could on short notice," he answered. "It's a skeleton crew; he canceled most of 'em. Only the ones we need."

"And where's *their* boss?" I asked, waving at the nearest of Mama Lorenzo's guards.

"She's around; I— Oh, there." Arthur gestured to the side of the studio, where Mama Lorenzo had just appeared. She'd washed up and changed, too—I wondered if she'd gone to a safe house or her men had brought her clothes and toiletries. Arthur probably would have insisted on the latter, just to make sure she wasn't targeted and followed back here.

Mama Lorenzo swept over and started talking to Simon. I couldn't hear what they said from here, but she was clearly grilling him. His face was tight, but he responded to all of her questions quietly and evenly.

Apparently satisfied, she nodded to him and McCabe and then came out to greet us.

"You are a resourceful woman, Miss Russell, finding a man with his leverage."

I shrugged uncomfortably. "That's what they tell me."

"We shall talk more when this is over," she said. "Your discretion is understandable, but there is one name I will have."

The name of the person who'd killed Malcolm.

"I don't—I'm not sure I know it," I floundered. "I mean, I know who it's not, but—"

"If not, then you suspect," Mama Lorenzo said. "You know how it ties to the situation as a whole. I will have that information."

"Yeah," I said. "Right. After this is over." I'd think of something.

Mama Lorenzo gave me a nod so sharp it was almost a salute and stepped over to station herself watching the booth.

I checked my watch. It was twelve minutes to eight.

I sidled up to watch the on-air booth, too, on the other side from Mama Lorenzo. Simon finished talking to Mc-Cabe and came out while the host made the rest of his preparations, which apparently involved him consulting notecards and talking to himself a lot under his breath with very grand gestures.

Simon came and stood next to me. We watched McCabe's lips re-form the same word over and over as he adjusted his intonation, and then yell at a staff member who came up to talk to him.

"Please don't do this," Simon said suddenly. "Don't make me."

I caught the edges of emotion, empathized with his agony at crossing the moral lines he'd told himself he never would, not since he'd destroyed me. I rode it out. I was getting better at teasing out the foreignness of him pressing at me. "You're really bad at control," I said, instead of answering him.

"No," he said, "I'm not. Have you ever felt an ordinary person walk into a room in a bad mood? This is the same thing, only . . . I can't turn off the strength of it. Not unless I consciously influence you not to feel it."

"No wonder you're such a fucked-up person."

"Yes," he said, without irony.

One of the assistants came for Simon, led him into the glass-walled booth, and handed him one of the pairs of headphones. He looked back at me, and I caught a blast of anguish and guilt.

It's the right thing, I told myself firmly. Or, if not the right thing, the only thing.

Someone shouted out radio lingo, and a bell went off. A red light lit up above me. Across from me, Mama Lorenzo straightened, listening.

"Good morning, my fellow Americans," McCabe began into his microphone. The words played radio-loud from an intercom over our heads. "I'm here today with a very special report on the situation we've been following in Los Angeles. As you know . . ."

He went on for a few minutes, editorializing about the effects, about the mainstream news, about the conviction of the militia leaders who wanted to defend us. "And I'm very pleased to tell you, nation—you are going to hear it here first. Now, I can't reveal everything yet, but I am in the midst of a very delicate operation to bring Los Angeles back to its citizens, and you will be the first to know the truth of exactly what's been going on. The truth, ladies and gentlemen—my fellow Americans. The truth."

He glanced over at Simon, who was breathing shallowly, his eyes unfocused. McCabe frowned up at me, through the glass, and I gestured sharply at him to continue.

Simon would do his fucking job. He had to.

"Now, nation, a part of our current situation I know you are very concerned about—as am I—are the shootings breaking out in answer to the oppression being levied against us here. As we all know, as our Founding Fathers declared, 'rebellion to tyrants is obedience to God,' but God is with the man who can expose corruption and lance the boil on the face of this country without spilling the blood of his innocent countrymen. And that's why I'm going to take a very unusual step, nation, and on today's show, I'm going to counsel everyone listening to have patience and wait. Because tomorrow morning, when you listen to my program, I will reveal it all, and the perpetrators will be forced out of the shadows to face justice for what they have done.

"But today, we must ensure those perpetrators do not start the race and class wars they so desperately want. They will be exposed, nation, I promise you. I promise you as a man, and as an American."

I was impressed. McCabe was doing a good job of building his show up around the mood of Simon's message. He'd drop Simon into a perfectly primed audience and let him talk. And afterward, everyone would put down their weapons, convinced they were doing so because they trusted Reuben McCabe.

"And now that brings me to our very special guest for the hour. As you all know, nation, in this unique situation we've had a lot of people who are rightfully, and righteously, apprehensive about giving us their legal government names. So I'll let our guest make his own introductions, and then he'll talk to you about our situation in this greatest of cities in this greatest of nations. Listen to him, my fellow Americans, and I promise you by this time tomorrow, all will be revealed by yours truly. Now please welcome our honored guest to the one place where you will always get the unvarnished reality of our country."

He turned toward Simon and held out a hand, an invitation for him to begin talking.

Simon's mouth hung open slightly. He wet his lips and leaned in toward the mic. Wet his lips again.

Hesitated.

Alarm bells sounded in the back of my head.

"Our guest," McCabe vamped, "is himself a fierce advocate of the truth, as I know you, McCabe listeners, would expect nothing less."

Simon shut his mouth, took off the headphones, and stood up. Ignoring McCabe's frantic gestures, he turned and pushed his way out through the glass door of the booth.

Directly into me.

"What the hell are you doing!" I hissed, trying to muscle him back inside.

"I can't do it." His face was wrinkled with tension and flushing red. "I can't. It's exactly what I swore I'd never— I can't be this person, Cas. I'm sorry. I'm so sorry. I hope you'll still let me—"

"Fuck you." I wanted to rail at him about all the lives he was wasting, all the people he was killing, and had a sudden, visceral flashback to Dawna shouting those same words at me back when I stopped her. After all my protests, my rationalizations, my insistence that what I was doing was so different—bile and guilt filled my throat.

"Los Angeles is *not* going to go down in flames," I spat at Simon. "I'm not going to *let* it."

"Cas, what are you—"

I didn't know what I was going to do. But I shoved past him and stormed into the booth myself, to the mic he had vacated. The PS90 banged my hip as I took over Simon's seat and jammed the headphones onto my ears.

McCabe, who had been elocuting about patriotism to fill the time, looked up without pausing his diatribe. He made an angry motion at me.

I made one right back.

"Well, it looks like our guest has returned," he segued smoothly, while giving me a fierce frown that I interpreted to mean, *I sure hope you know what you're doing.* "Now we're going to get that real truth I promised you, folks, right now, about exactly what is happening in this town." Barbs spiked his last words, and he jerked his chin at me.

"Hi," I said, leaning into the mic. My voice echoed with me through the sound system.

I didn't know what to say to stop this. I didn't know what anyone *could* say, except Simon. But I'd been willing to give myself up to save the city, and that worked in more ways than one.

"The conspiracies are real." My consonants hit the microphone like popping hailstones. "There's technology all over Los Angeles emitting frequencies for the express purpose of screwing with your brains. I know because I put it there."

I paused for a moment. McCabe was staring at me, openmouthed. Behind him, through the glass, Mama Lorenzo had snapped toward me in fury. Meanwhile, to the side, Simon shook his head frantically, slashing one hand across his throat repeatedly.

I fleetingly wondered if he was right, dismissed that as overflow psychic influence from him, and continued.

"I'm not with the government. I'm working alone. There's no need to storm the military or the police or the CIA. Or each other—whoever you think's been attacking you, you've been misled. It's my responsibility and no one else's. Now, I'd go and disable it all for you, but I doubt you'd trust me, so instead I'm going to go to 697 Norman Street out in Pottersfield right now, in person, and I'm going to give anyone who comes there the information you'll need to start putting a stop to it. Then, if you want a bad guy, you can come after me right there."

I pulled off the headphones and dove to the floor just as Mama Lorenzo fired her .32 through the glass.

The panes making up the wall of the booth shattered and rained to the floor. Arthur drew at the same time every single one of the security guards raised their weapons. McCabe yelled and burrowed under his desk, his headset cord taking chunks of equipment crashing down with him.

I aimed at the ceiling and pulled the trigger on my own

PS90, targeting every single fluorescent light illuminating the place. They all burst and blinked out to darkness at once. The studio room had been built nestled inside layers of soundproofed walls, and had no windows—it went almost pitch black.

I moved before anyone could react. Shouts and flurried movement followed me as I grabbed Arthur's elbow and flew through the side door of the studio. Someone fired after us as the sliver of light appeared, but only once.

We fled out the back, into a parking lot.

"Wait!" someone cried behind us.

My feet stumbled of their own accord. I never stumbled.

Fucking Simon. I didn't know how he'd beaten everyone else out.

I regained my balance and kept up with Arthur, racing toward the nearest line of cars behind a hedge.

"What's your plan?" Simon called after us desperately. "Stop! Cassandra! You don't need to sacrifice yourself!"

I did, because of him. And I didn't have a plan. LA could take out its anger on the brain entrainment and on me, and maybe that would release the pressure valve for the rest of the city.

I jacked into the first sedan we reached, and Arthur slid in alongside me.

"Duck," I said, flooring the car into reverse, and he hunched down immediately. The clap of more gunfire peppered the parking lot, and one of the back passenger windows went.

I peeled away, jumped the curb and a bed of landscaped flowers, and plopped myself down directly into rush hour. Horns sounded as I cut across an intersection on the tail end of a red light, and I veered in front of a bus and through a gas station.

A siren wailed behind me, and then away. Called away from a reckless driver to a shootout at McCabe's radio station, doubtless.

"You're not going to sacrifice yourself, are you?" Arthur said.

"Of course not," I said. "I'm going to make them fight me."

"Russell!"

I wasn't sure if he didn't believe my bravado or he just thought it was a bad plan. "They need a bad guy to blame," I said. "That bad guy should be me. *Is* me."

A Park & Ride sign caught my eye, and I spun the wheel and swung in. Every time I'd been in one of these lots they'd had a section up front for motorcycle parking . . . *Yes!* I slammed on the brake next to the bikes, and our velocity skidded to zero.

An old Hispanic woman yelled an obscenity and flipped the bird at my driving as she crossed in front of us.

I jumped out. Arthur started to follow me.

"No," I said.

"Russell, you can't—"

"In this kind of fight, you'll just be a liability. I can't be protecting you," I said, as harshly as I knew how. It wasn't true, but if I did only one good thing today, not getting Arthur killed would be it. "If this goes south . . . tell Checker it's up to him."

"What now?"

"He'll have to find a way of propagating a . . . I don't know, a virus, or a patch, that will neutralize what we did." Without being able to locate and disable our original signal hacks, it would be maddening work, especially considering he wouldn't have my optimization calculations for the new deployment. He'd just have to figure it out . . . however long it took.

Arthur tried to shout after me, but the open-choked roar of the bike I'd just jacked drowned him out.

Two cops tried to pull me over on my helmetless, speed-demon journey, but I cut between lanes of stopped cars and lost them both.

The address I'd given on the radio was a deserted factory complex, one run-down and abandoned enough that I'd accidentally blown up part of a building there a few months before without attracting any local cops. I wasn't sure if the LAPD would get McCabe's show sorted enough to go to the location I'd specified, but it was outside the city jurisdiction, so I was betting the bad guys would get there first.

For better or for worse.

I hit the right neighborhood—it was more decrepit than the last time I'd been here—and took the bike into a slide in front of the main gate of the factory. I dropped it completely as I punched the engine cutoff, jumping to clear it. I'd scale the gate and find a vantage point as quickly as possible.

I only had the one firearm. I did a quick count in my head—eighteen rounds left. First priority here would be re-arming myself from the first wave. . . .

"Cas," Rio called.

Holy fuck.

Already inside the complex, he strode toward the gate from a banged-up SUV, enough firearms slung around himself over his duster to qualify as a small arsenal.

He'd been listening to McCabe's show.

A rush of gratitude and relief flooded me. My boots gobbled the chain link of the gate, and I rocketed over to hit the ground in front of him.

By the time I landed, he was holding out weapons. "I have more in the vehicle."

Wow. I might live through this after all.

thirty-five

RIO AND I stood back to back on a catwalk above a vast factory floor, one filled by stacks of old cut sheet metal with edges that would slice any careless flesh. We had the cover of several large pillars and chunks of defunct machinery and enough armaments to give us a fighting chance, depending on how many people showed up to kill me. We'd also both geared up with body armor, thanks to Rio's ridiculous-but-welcome mobile supply cache. It was only soft armor that wouldn't stop rifle rounds—other than maybe ricochets—but at least we'd have protection from handgun fire.

"Thanks for coming," I said.

"I am glad you altered your actions," Rio said, "however brash this plan is. The Lord be with you, Cas."

God help me, he thought I had engaged in confession with all of McCabe's audience.

I glanced through our supply of weapons, taking note of them one more time, organizing them in my head like an ordinal number system. I had a rifle ready to go in each hand, and Rio's presence was firm and solid at my back.

Even if we died today, if we took out most of the people angry about this, mopped up those most likely to jump to violence, Arthur and Checker and Pilar could reverse the brain entrainment without much more consequence than going back to where we started. The status quo didn't feel like something to be triumphant about, but at this point, I would take it.

The morning sun gleamed through the factory's high windows. The first shouts echoed from outside. They had found us.

"I miss this," I said to Rio. "Fighting on the same side."

"It is my preference as well, Cas," he answered.

And then there was no more time for conversation, because the doors on the south side of the building blasted in.

RIO WAS good in a gunfight.

I was even better.

The loyal members of Los Angeles's criminal underground along with members of three self-appointed militias burst in on us in waves, with shouts and war cries and overwhelming bursts of automatic fire. But we had the high ground, a lot of ammo, and damn near perfect accuracy.

Through the endless hammering of the gunfire, the smoke, the fire and shouts, I recognized people from almost every faction Yamamoto had gathered. Not the leaders, but their most loyal henchmen and henchwomen, the people who did all the dirty work for their bosses and had been too wedded to the life for my brain entrainment to remove their unwavering allegiance.

Or maybe, in a twist of irony, they were the only people with any kind of integrity. And we killed them for it.

In a gunfight, ten minutes are an eternity, but ten minutes passed, and then another ten. My hands dropped and reloaded, raised and fired, over and over, the world narrowing to metal and thunder and each target only until I'd squeezed a trigger, because by then I was moving to the next one. The mathematical lines of sight and windows of danger spiderwebbed out, saturating the space, each barrel clicking into place in a predetermined probabilistic window.

The roar of the fight was deafening, and the air clogged with the smell of gunpowder. My hands ached and my muscles protested. We kept going.

Then I raised one of the rifles to snap the sights into collinear alignment with the next attacker, and I recognized Torvald.

Mama Lorenzo and her private security had arrived. Delayed—perhaps by traffic, perhaps by the police, but they were here to kill me for betraying their boss, for the attack on the estate, for Malcolm. More of the Lorenzos had to be on their way, too—their whole family. And I was about to wipe them out for the crime of wanting justice.

My finger hesitated on the trigger, and Torvald fired, a three-round burst that flashed against my retinas in slow motion even as I fell out of his aim vector. I grabbed at Rio's duster behind me as I went down, but I wasn't fast enough.

The second and third bullet tore through the air right by my ear and slammed into Rio's back.

He staggered. We fell together.

"Rio! Oh, Jesus—" I knew I yelled the words, but I couldn't hear myself. I tumbled up into a crouch over him and fired blindly behind me. "Rio, talk to me—" My left hand groped, searching for how to help—I didn't see blood yet, but the layers of fiber and unfurling kinetic energy in the body armor flashed through my brain. The armor wouldn't have protected him. It was mathematically impossible.

Oh, God.

Rio grunted. His hand twitched to close around his weapon again.

I'd dropped my left-hand rifle as we went down. Still trying to cover us with my right, I pulled out a knife with my free hand and ripped the blade down the length of Rio's coat. The slugs had mangled his armor just below the shoulder blade. Red bubbled up, as if it had only been waiting for me to be witness.

I smashed a folded layer of his duster against the wounds and got my knee on top of it to apply pressure. I split my attention between the proper vector diagram for keeping Rio's blood inside his body and grabbing for another magazine to reload.

Rio tried to move again, disrupting the equal and opposite forces. "Stay *still*!" I screamed at him, but through the deafening battle I wasn't sure he heard.

I sensed more than saw the wave of humanity below surge forward as I failed to hold them off. Angry silhouettes scaled one of the catwalks to the side, gaining height on me. I shot one of them, but then I had to return my attention to the floor. With half my focus on Rio, I was no longer fending them off—even with the high ground, even with good cover, even with my skills and an accurate rifle.

Inequality of numbers was one of the most basic mathematical concepts.

I still kept going, breathing in gun smoke and decimals, letting mathematical interpolation fill in the data for every blind spot and taking out one enemy per shot.

Rio had stopped moving. Dampness soaked through the folds of his duster.

I heard the ricochet too late to do anything.

The bullet pinged off one of the metal pillars and kicked me in the left side of my ribs. The armor stopped it, but the kinetic energy spun me off Rio, sprawling me on the catwalk.

I struggled to get back up, to protect Rio, to *fight*—the

vast net of data became all I could sense, and I gave myself in to it, squeezing the trigger over and over, but I was only one, and the probability mounted against me, massive and toppling.

Theory argued that when you knew the outcome of a problem, it was immaterial how you got to the end. This fight was over, but I wasn't admitting it. Not until they killed me.

Apparently I was a crappy theoretician.

I crouched over Rio, making my body as small a target as possible—

"Stop!"

The shout was a clarion call above the fray, somehow perfectly audible through the thunder of the gunfire.

"Stop!"

And everyone did.

We stopped.

Below and around me, across the entire factory floor, gun barrels wavered and then dropped to point at the ground. The last shell casings fell in the earsplitting silence, clinking against cement and sheet metal.

I lurched, and had to put a hand down to keep from falling. I tried to raise my rifle to target and fire, but . . .

That was really a bad idea, wasn't it? With the bad guys deescalating, I should deescalate too, shouldn't I?

Rio's arm hitched, and somehow a pistol appeared in his hand, its grip resting on the catwalk. Its sights wobbled in a drunken line. "Let them go," he slurred into the utter stillness. "This is a sin in the eyes of the Lord."

"And slaughtering each other isn't?" came the same voice. It echoed from just down the catwalk, over the heads of those who had come to kill us. "This conflict is pointless. Go home to your families; see to your wounded. Save your lives for a fight with meaning. You can trust that the technology affecting you will be deactivated. Justice has been served here."

Everywhere in sight, weapons slid into holsters or were

slung over shoulders. There weren't many wounded—Rio and I didn't shoot to wound. But the crowd shuffled to retrieve the bodies of their dead and help each other out of the building.

I thought about shooting some of them. But that wouldn't be very sporting, would it? Shooting people in the back as they walked away, after the fight was over?

A tall, lean silhouette slipped in through a side door as the last of the stragglers wandered out. Mama Lorenzo. She'd been outside. She'd probably heard.

She didn't have a gun. Her hands opened and closed by her sides, and she gazed around at the blood-soaked floor with glassy eyes.

"It's over," called Simon, from where he stood, alone and unarmed, on an open catwalk above the empty factory. "No good can come of any more violence. You're done here."

Her head jerked in a nod, and she stumbled against the doorway as she made her way back outside.

The door banged shut behind her.

Simon alone remained, a single living silhouette in a mosaic of smoke and shell casings and blood. So much blood, so much the sharp metallic scent of it overwhelmed everything else . . .

Simon's head bowed forward. He gripped the railing of the catwalk in front of him, and his shoulders began to shake.

"Holy *shit*," I said.

"Cas," Rio murmured. "Are you back?"

He had to know it was a stupid question considering he couldn't trust my response, but I answered by scrambling for my weapon anyway.

Though there was no point in going after them now, was there? Even if I could chase any of them down? And Rio needed help—

"Just let them go, Cassandra. Please," Simon said. Brokenly.

"Let me make the goddamn decision myself," I shouted

back, throwing down the rifle and heaving myself back toward Rio. Moving had opened his wounds further. I pressed back down on them again, ruthlessly, and he let me. I couldn't tell how bad it was.

Simon picked his way toward us. "Would you rather I not have come, then?" he asked, so bitterly I felt it wash through me in a wave.

"Yes," Rio said. "This was not well done."

"Good, we agree," Simon shot back. "I should have left you to die. Or let you murder them all—that would have been so much better." He reached us and stared down at Rio with no sympathy. "Are you going to kill me, if you live?"

"You merit it," Rio answered. "For your sins."

"I'm still the only person who can help Cas. Although why I should, after *this*—"

Rio exhaled slightly in acknowledgement, and let the pistol drop from his fingers.

"Wait just a damn second," I said. "Fuck *that*."

Simon shifted to face me. "We had a deal."

"In exchange for you resolving this situation, which you skipped out on doing," I pointed out.

"It's done now."

Fuck. He might've been late, but he'd crossed every moral line of his to come fix this, in the end. As I'd asked him to. As I'd bargained with him.

I wondered if he was influencing me to think all that. He probably didn't need to.

"If Rio lives," I said, "then you've held up your end."

I knew that wasn't fair—or rather, I could feel Simon thinking it wasn't fair, along with a wave of hatred and anger, for me or the situation or Rio. I wasn't sure. But he crouched and helped me.

"Thanks," I said.

He didn't answer, and I wondered if he regretted saving my life.

Then I wondered if that was my thought or his.

thirty-six

THE FALLOUT was messy and sprawling, but fortunately for us, fell mostly elsewhere.

The police had the recording of McCabe's radio show and the obvious scene of a massacre at the factory, but when they pressed McCabe for a description of me, he apparently couldn't give them anything beyond "short" and "black," which wasn't even accurate. And he'd never asked my name. The detectives did interview Arthur, who managed to spin them a story—again—about being a PI investigating something peripheral who just happened to end up as a witness. He was remarkably good at that.

Mama Lorenzo had a sizeable chunk of the LAPD on her payroll already and turned out to be disinclined to give them any information. Or to come after me. I wasn't even sure she fully remembered all the events after her brother's death—I asked around in some corners, and the word came down that Malcolm's killer had already been declared dealt with.

That should have relieved me. Instead, I was swamped

with guilt and fury, impotent rage with no target other than myself.

Simon and I had gotten Rio to a hospital before he bled out. Between his surgery and when the detectives came to talk to him, he'd disappeared. I didn't much worry about him—Rio could take care of himself. He'd call me if he needed to.

Banking on my mental health stretching just a little longer, I'd told Simon I needed a week before I submitted to my side of our bargain. I spent most of it canvassing the city and reprogramming our boxes to strip the brain entrainment app from any phone that had it. I limped through the process; getting shot had cracked two of my ribs, and my left side felt like one solid bruise. Other bits of intel trickled in from my inquiries—even as the brain entrainment ebbed away, nobody seemed to be taking up arms against each other, and beyond the Lorenzos, no one else was talking about being angry with me, either. Or talking about me at all.

It was as if I'd never been involved.

Even though he'd almost certainly saved my life, the thoroughness of Simon's magic made me resent him all the more. He'd so completely erased a piece of my history right in front of my eyes, a series of events and mistakes that now no one could remember, no one save me and a few friends.

What else of me would he erase, in the name of saving me?

I spent a lot of time wondering if Checker had been right, and we'd chosen the greater of two evils.

I spent a lot of time wondering if *Dawna* had been right, and had only been doing what we had been, on a greater scale.

The morning after I finished spreading our cellular fix, I went to see Pilar at her apartment. The windows were dark, the blinds drawn, but Arthur had said she was taking some personal time, and I knew she was home. I knocked lightly.

"Pilar? It's Cas."

I thought for a minute she wasn't going to answer, but then the bolt slid back and she pulled the door open. She was in pajamas, her right wrist in a cast. I winced.

"Hi," I said.

Her eyes darted behind me.

"It's just me," I assured her quickly.

Her lips pressed together, her face closing in.

"He's never going to hurt you again," I said. "I promise."

"I don't know if you can promise that," Pilar said. Her voice was low.

"I swear to you. He's not." I hesitated. "Can I come in for a minute?"

She turned and walked back into the living room of her apartment, leaving the door open. I followed.

She sat on her couch. I sat across from her, on the edge of a bright rainbow-colored bucket chair.

I didn't know what to say.

"Cas," Pilar said finally. "We're friends, we are, and I've been worried sick about you, and I'm really glad you're okay, and Checker's been keeping me updated and I'm really glad everything else turned out okay, but—fuck you." She started to cry.

I shifted on the edge of the bucket chair.

"And fuck him, too," she added.

Pilar didn't usually cuss. The words sounded wrong in her mouth, like she was searching for something that fit the situation and couldn't find it.

"I promise—" I started again.

"You can't promise that," she said. "You can't, and you *know* you can't!"

"Yes, I can," I said. "I'm absolutely sure. He's not going to come after you again. Ever."

Confusion warred on her face. She sniffed. "Wait, do you mean—what do you mean by that? Did you . . ."

"No! Jesus, of course not. But I told him that if he hurts you again, I—I told him he can't."

"You *told* him. Right." Pilar hunched into herself. "No. This isn't okay."

"It is now," I said. "I'm sorry for what happened, but—"

"No. No, you don't get to—you don't get to *rescue* me by"—her mouth twisted on the word like it was a curse—"by telling a man who, a man like him, by just *telling him not to,* and then tell me it's all okay, because it *isn't* okay. This isn't okay."

I took a breath. "What are you going to do?"

Pilar was too smart. She squinted at me, her brow furrowing. "Is that what you came over for? To make sure I wouldn't—what, go out for revenge?"

That's not fair, I wanted to say. I *had* wanted to see if she was all right. I had. But I'd also wanted to make sure—fuck, I was the one who'd taught Pilar to shoot. Bought her a gun. She wasn't nearly as good as Rio, but if they crossed paths again, which they very well might—and if I wasn't there, or I was . . . not myself, or worse—it would only take one shot, and thanks to me, Rio wouldn't fire first.

Not that I wanted him to kill Pilar, either. Fuck.

Pilar laughed, sudden and hoarse, with no humor in it. "I can't believe it. Two people like *you,* worried about little ol' me. That's like the punchline of a joke." She wiped at her eyes with her sleeve. She'd stopped crying. "Are you going to take my gun back?"

"What? No, that's ridiculous. You need it. And besides, you could just buy another one."

"I guess that's true, huh?" She sat back on the couch and stared up at the ceiling. "I can't believe this is a conversation I'm having. I'm listening to the words I'm saying here and I can't believe it."

"Look," I said. "I got Rio's word on this. I'm asking you for yours. That's all."

"My word. That I won't—what, kill him?"

"Yeah."

She laughed again. It didn't sound like she found anything funnier than the first time.

I waited.

Pilar finally sat forward again and made eye contact with me. "I don't even know if I could, you know? I've never—you know I've never. You don't need to worry about me, as long as he's not trying to hurt any of us again. But Cas, I . . . I need to understand this. You owe me that, at least."

"Understand what?" I said.

"*This.* Him. You. Why you're— If I'm going to see him again I need to understand why I shouldn't call the police."

Her calling the police hadn't even occurred to me. I swallowed. "He does more good than harm."

"That's not a reason. You know that's not a reason. The world can't work that way."

I thought of Pithica. I thought of what we had done, with Simon.

She was right. I did know better.

"Make me understand," Pilar said. "What he almost— And you, you say all you did was *talk* to him, after he— And you say it's okay, and that's *outrageous,* and I know what he was doing to Los Angeles because I was *there,* and I need you to make me understand."

"I trust him," I said. The words dropped in the room, soft and yet too loud.

"Why?"

He'll protect you.

Protection isn't living. Don't pretend it is.

I gripped the edge of the bucket chair. Valarmathi had been surging back again, just as I'd known she would.

"I don't know," I said aloud, to Pilar.

"You don't *know*?"

"You're perfectly well aware of what's been going on with me," I said. "I know I know Rio from before, and I know I trust him, and I know I owe him. And that's enough."

"Not for me, it isn't!" Pilar cried. "I thought you had reason! I knew he was tangled up in all this, with Simo and everything, but I thought you had a history—"

"We do have a history."

"One you can remember!"

She glared at me.

Aren't you supposed to help?

I take a somewhat different view of what it means to help

Yours, or your God's?

"Pilar," I said quietly. "Please. This is the one thing in m whole fucking life I'm sure of. Please."

"You're asking me to trust you on something that— You're asking me to trust you."

"Yes," I said.

"When you don't even know what you're asking me t trust."

"Yes." I paused, and then added again, "Please."

Pilar took a deep breath and blew it out. "Okay," she said "I can't make any guarantees for the future. But, for now . . okay."

"That works," I said.

"What about my family?" she asked.

I opened my mouth to tell her Rio would never, but I hadn thought he'd go after Pilar, either. "I'll make sure," amended.

"Make sure. Or I can't agree to anything."

"I give you my word." I stood up and stopped. "When ar you coming back to the office?"

She gave me a small smile. "When I'm ready."

thirty-seven

APOLOGIZED to Checker, too—both for what we'd done and for Rio. He got emotional and threw an action figure at me, after which he demanded for us please to get drunk together and watch at least fourteen episodes of *Stargate*.

I wasn't sure he'd forgiven me—he never said he did—and our interaction felt rawer around the edges, but I fell asleep on his couch that night and the next day we went to work in the Hole running his statistical programs. Pilar came over, too, a little later in the day. She was quieter than usual, but otherwise acted like everything was normal.

The feelers I'd put out had seemed to indicate everyone was still licking their wounds, but the data hit harder and revealed more. We'd been expecting the crime statistics to rebound to their previous level or higher, but thanks to the massive deadliness of Rio's and my last stand combined with Simon's overwhelming effect, we only saw a slight and gradual elevation in criminal activity. It also seemed like most of the people who had gone straight thanks to the brain entrainment were staying that way—at least for now. I

suspected once the leaders of the various criminal organizations got back on their feet, recruitment would start u
again.

"It wasn't a complete failure," Checker said, his chi
propped on one hand as he studied the line graphs.

"I'm not sure those words mean what you think they do,
I said. "Either 'not' or 'complete' or 'failure.'"

"I'm talking about strictly looking at the numbers." H
pointed. "From a purely utilitarian standpoint, you axed th
crime rate. And I think you were right that most of the peopl
this targeted were the ones who were getting swept up i
peer pressure and indoctrination."

"Most," I bit out.

"All of them, really," Pilar said. "We just didn't conside
peer pressure and indoctrination could be used consensu
ally, for positive stuff."

"It's like computerized doctors, or self-driving cars,
Checker said. "They make fewer mistakes than humans do
but they're different mistakes. What you did helped peopl
make fewer mistakes, but the ones who did made differen
ones."

"Stop trying to make me feel better," I said.

"Don't be so selfish." Pilar spoke more sharply than I wa
used to hearing from her. "We're trying to feel better, too
Did you know the past month was the first time this whol
school year my brother stopped getting beat up? He wa
smiling, his grades skyrocketed, he tried out for the debat
team . . . yesterday he came home with a cut lip again and
wouldn't talk about it. I don't know, Cas. Even after every
thing, I think maybe we *were* doing a good thing." Sh
sniffed. "Until, you know . . . everything else."

"Tell that to kids like Katrina," I said. Justin had stoppe
by to see Arthur. Katrina was using again, and she'd droppe
off the grid. Arthur was devastated.

I'd done that to her. My machines, which had gone in and
knocked her brain around without her consent.

"Not to sound callous, but there are lots of kids like Karina. Cas, wait, hear me out," Checker said, when I tried to growl back at him. "I know this is going to sound really fucked up, but speaking strictly numerically . . . it looks like you helped more of them than you hurt. And it could stick—I don't have enough data to give an accurate prediction. Now don't get me wrong, I still think this was a horrible idea from the beginning, but there's also no denying it took out a good chunk of Los Angeles's worst criminal element—so only castigate yourself where you deserve it."

There were enough legitimate reasons. He was too tactful to remind me.

"I guess it's an argument for the more traditional methods of fighting crime," Checker added. "Low-impact superheroics, and all. Saving people one at a time."

"That would be good," Pilar said. "You save one person a night, that's three hundred sixty-five a year, right?"

"Three hundred and sixty-five?" I tried to keep from yelling. "That's nothing!"

They didn't get it. Didn't get how big the human population was. What Pithica had been doing had been worldwide—a nudge here and a tuck there that had been changing people's lives globally, millions upon millions.

The upper limit of human perception was a ratio of one to seven. If two objects differed by more than a factor of seven, people ceased to be able to compare them effectively: one was "small" and one was "big," and that was it. Similarly, most humans were bad at distinguishing any large orders of magnitude.

But I wasn't.

A few hundred people was a *handful*. An order of magnitude not even comparable to what we'd stripped from the world when we'd fought Pithica. And the change we had wrought here in LA was barely a feather's weight more.

"You guys aren't seeing scale," I said tiredly. "You're trying to convince me we made a positive overall difference, but compared to the global population, what we did here is . . . it's nonexistent. Our actions were mathematically trivial."

The world, as a whole, was just as it had been.

Disintegrating. Collapsing. Because of what we'd done to Pithica.

"Maybe this is as it should be, then," Checker said. "Humanity muddles along, and everyone makes the best of it they can in a chaos of messy, non-optimal Nash equilibria."

"No."

"What do you mean?" Checker asked.

"No. I refuse to accept that," I said. "I refuse to accept that the only two options are either a society spiraling into black holes of entropy or one in which people are murdered and brainwashed to meet the requirements of some self-appointed master puppeteers. There's a continuum. There has to be. To say it's one or the other is—it's a false choice. Just because this didn't work isn't proof nothing else will."

"Cas," Pilar said softly, "we tried this, and it went bad. Don't you think that's a sign?"

"I don't believe in signs," I answered.

I didn't say the other thing I was thinking—that I refused to accept we weren't powerful enough. Because Checker was right, in what he always said half jokingly: between me, and Rio, and—God help me—Simon, we had a terrifying level of both human and superhuman resources.

I just had to puzzle out a way to use them. One that did things the right way.

Whatever that was.

And from what Simon had said—or, well, cagily hinted at—maybe there were more like me. Like us. Pithica had psychics other than Dawna, and Simon was proof more existed outside their influence. If there were other people like me out there . . .

Well. I'd probably have to either kill them or recruit them.

Dawna had an army. Maybe it was time I found one, too.

. . .

THE MORNING my week's grace period with Simon expired, I sat with Arthur on a bench off one of LA's more deserted hiking trails. The old stone seat had been placed where the trail curved up against the lip of a spectacular bluff, and the day was unusually clear for Los Angeles. We could see all the way to San Pedro and the ocean, with the city spread out below us in between.

I drew my knees up in front of me, staring off into the indigo line where the sky met the sea, where my eyeline grazed the curvature of the earth in a graceful tangent.

Silent idleness without the blur of alcohol wasn't usually kind to me. But I wanted this, today, and so far my brain had let me have it.

Perhaps the dread kept everything else at bay—the yawning shadow of the unknown, whispering this might be the end.

My end.

"I don't get scared," I said to the endless blue. "Not easily. Even when I should."

Arthur waited, listening.

"This scares me," I said. "A lot. More than . . . more than anything I can remember." Which was only about five years' worth of fears. But still.

"You know being scared is okay, right?" Arthur said. "It's not a weakness."

"That depends on your definition of weakness."

"Guess that's so."

We sat in silence for a few minutes.

"Scares us, too," Arthur said.

I frowned. "What does?"

"That we're gonna lose you," he said. "That this Simon fellow isn't on the level. That . . . that he's gonna hurt you."

I mulled that over for a while. I was even less used to people being afraid for me than I was familiar with being afraid myself.

"Checker called him," Arthur added.

"He did?" Now that I officially had Simon's contact infor mation, I'd made sure everyone else had it, too. Just in case I . . . unexpectedly worsened again. "What for?"

Arthur chuckled. "To threaten him."

"*Checker* threatened somebody?" My feet thumped down off the bench in shock. "Electronically?"

"Nope. Physically. Think he meant it, too."

"That's not a— It doesn't even—" I'd never seen Checker hit anyone, ever, and he flat-out refused to learn to fire a gun. It wasn't that he was a pacifist; he was just—not violent. "I don't need people trying to protect me like they know what's best," I grumped. That was what had started this whole thing in the first place, wasn't it?

"'Course you don't," Arthur said.

Checker had threatened somebody. For me.

"It's a nice thought, I suppose," I said.

Arthur chuckled again. "If he overstepped, you let him know. But he meant well." He sobered. "Speaking of . . . you want me there? Say the word. We are supposed to be watching each other's brain meats, you know."

"Thanks, but that's okay," I said. "Rio's coming. He . . ."

Rio had called me the day before from wherever he was con valescing, sounding perfectly normal. The gist of the conver sation was that he was staying in LA for a while.

Because of me.

He'd offered to sit in with Simon and me, and I'd said yes, under no uncertain terms. But I had the sneaking suspicion at least half the reason he was staying was to make sure I went in the first place, and kept going. Simon had implied this would be a lengthy process.

Possibly an infinite one, if I kept falling back toward re membering every time I stopped seeing him.

Infinity doesn't exist, sang Valarmathi. *There's always an end.*

"When are you meeting them?" Arthur asked.

I checked my watch. "Twenty minutes ago."

He grinned, and we sat for a while longer, soaking in the sky.

TWO HOURS later, I knocked on a door in Northridge. Rio opened it almost immediately, in a new tan duster, identical to his old one except no bullet holes. He was still favoring his right side slightly, but I doubted it was visible to those whose senses didn't drop out the even functions of symmetry on a regular basis.

"Cas," he said. "Come in."

Simon looked up from where he sat in an upholstered chair. He'd been reading a book while he waited, relaxed.

The fear and loathing swelled in my throat, clawing at me remarkably like panic. I tried to swallow it back. Wistful regret flickered across Simon's face as he read my expression, but for once he didn't say anything.

Rio walked over like nothing was awkward at all and pulled up a chair himself. I tried to mirror him. If nothing else, I still trusted Rio.

And I sat straight, with more bravado than I felt, even if a telepath could see right through it.

"I'm here," I said to Simon. "So. What happens now?"

acknowledgments

IT'S EASY TO MISTAKE writing for a solitary endeavor, but I have never been more grateful for my professional team, the people at my agency and publisher who made this book and this journey a reality. I continue to be terrifically grateful for my agent, Russell Galen, without whom my career would look nothing like it does today—and without whom I would not have my truly fabulous team at Tor. That team is led by my editor, Diana Gill, who brought such a perspicacious eye to this book, helping me push the manuscript until it was punching far above its weight class. I couldn't be happier with the result, nor more thrilled with how thoroughly Diana champions the whole series. And the support I've received from the rest of the Tor crew—my brilliant cover artist, Jamie Stafford-Hill; the incredible Kristin Temple; and the whole team of publicists, production editors, copy editors, proof-readers, editorial assistants, and more—has been nothing short of amazing.

In my day-to-day writing life, my sister continues to be my first and greatest support. From the earliest brainstorming sessions to late-night phone calls when I'm stuck on an edit, and everything in between . . . writing without you would be possible, but so much more difficult and lonely, and I am so very grateful to have you.

So much gratitude also to the invaluable critiquers who helped me shape this book into what it is: Maddox Hahn, Kevan O'Meara, Jesse Sutanto, Layla Lawlor, and Tilly Latimer. And another huge round of appreciation for the people who jumped in during a very short time line to give me feedback during rewrites: MV Melcer, Lani Frank, Debra Jess, Aidan Doyle, and Gwen Phua. I'm unaccountably lucky to know so many generous, talented writers—thank you all so much.

Special thanks to Kevan O'Meara and Sam Schinke for their sharp knowledge and suggestions on baseband hacking for cellular phones—anything I got right is thanks to you; any mistakes are my own. And a big shout-out to Effie Seiberg for holding my hand on this one during a time I really needed it.

Finally, this book has had an evolving journey before it landed at Tor, and I still feel the warmest gratitude for the people who helped me make its previous incarnation a reality, including Najla Qamber, Anna Genoese, and David Wilson. You all rock.

But these acknowledgments wouldn't be complete without mentioning all the other people in my writing communities and in my life who are so vital to me. My friends and family, as always, are my bedrock, and I don't know what I'd do without you. Similarly, I find I am so grateful for all my various writing spaces—where I've met some of the people who've become closest to me—and where, both online and in person, I've found the most incredible support and community.

Thank you all.

Read on for a preview of

critical point

S. L. HUANG

Available now from Tom Doherty Associates

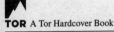
TOR A Tor Hardcover Book

Copyright © 2020 by S. L. Huang, LLC

one

I SLOUCHED in my chair, putting my feet up against the edge of the desk. *My* desk.

I had an office.

The place felt cavernous and stifling at the same time, and massively permanent, as if someone were pinioning me to this spot with a railroad spike.

I had rented the office because I'd lost a bet with a friend. A friend who was, for some unfathomable reason, far too invested in convincing me to stop doing business in dive bars. He was also campaigning for me to get a social security number, but that was over the line.

Even the office made me feel like I'd been brainwashed.

I hunched into myself, the heaviness pressing at me. Getting dragged into mildly more mainstream habits by my actual friends was one thing. But it had still only been months since I'd agreed to let the man who called himself Simon start crawling through my head every week. And I'd only agreed under duress: namely, the implosion of my own goddamn mind.

Telepathy was the closest word for what people like Simon did, and I'd been on the verge of refusing his help even if it had killed me. No matter how much he swore he would never take control of my thoughts, someone I didn't trust should never have that much access.

Unfortunately for me, it wasn't like trustworthy telepaths were thick on the ground. Better Simon than the ones who wanted me dead. The shadows of conspiracies and killers slithered through the back of my mind, strangling me. Conspiracies that involved my past. Killers who had forced me not to move against them.

And me, stuck in a city I hadn't even managed to save from my own actions, and struggling just to tread water on my sanity. Losing ground while the psychics and ghosts recovered their power.

The room loomed, and I hunched farther into the chair. The walls weren't claustrophobic, I told myself. The office was roughly twelve feet by ten, though I could see the long side was a little more than two inches shy of its stated length. The ceiling was four feet, nine and seven-eighths inches above where I was slouched in my chair. Or 1.47 meters. Imperial was stupid.

Before I could stop myself, I'd calculated the volume of the small room, minus the space taken up by desk, chairs, and me. I multiplied and estimated the number of oxygen molecules. Moles and moles and moles. Not the least danger of suffocation, I told myself. The math wouldn't lie.

If only my bizarre computational ability could fix my brain.

I thought of the bottle of cheap vodka in the bottom drawer of the desk. No, I had a client meeting in a few minutes. The promise of work to distract me was the only reason I was here. However flimsy and trivial a job this was, I needed it. Treading water. I felt sick without even drinking the vodka.

Someone tapped on the door outside, the timid sound barely making it through the wood.

Early. Small favors. "Come in," I called, swinging my feet down and trying my best to look professional. I probably should have worn a clean shirt.

The African American girl who pushed the door open was tall, but clearly young—probably not older than sixteen, and with the beanpole thinness and awkwardly long limbs that come from unexpected growth spurts. She was dressed smartly but not overly fashionably, wearing a jean jacket and various braided bracelets and necklaces that looked home-made, and had her hair plaited tightly back against her head.

And she wasn't my client. The message requesting this meeting had been left by a babbling man with an Aussie accent.

She was probably lost or something. "Can I help you?" I asked with an effort, and was pleased with managing some tact. Kids bring out the best in me.

"Are you Cas Russell?" She said the words hesitantly, and one of her hands gripped the cuff of her jacket like she needed it to anchor her.

"Yeah, that's me. Retrieval expert." Also known as thief, mercenary, and soldier of fortune who could punch a guy in the face as hard as the relationship between impulse and momentum allowed, but I didn't add that. Or the part about being a woman without a memory, someone else's living weapon until my old self had gotten sliced out of my head. I wondered how she had gotten my name. "Do you want to sit down?"

She stepped forward as if she were about to walk the plank and perched herself on the edge of one of the client chairs in front of my desk. "I need your help."

She didn't say any more. I suppressed a sigh. "What's your name, kid?"

"Tabitha."

More silence. "Okay," I said. "Tabitha. Do your parents know you're here?"

"Well, that's what I'm here about," she said, fidgeting. "My dad, he—he's not answering his phone."

"He's not answering his phone?"

"He *always* answers his phone."

I tried to speak delicately. "He may have lost it temporarily, or been busy—"

"No. He always answers when I call." Her face was tight and tense, and her voice quivered slightly. "And he warns us beforehand if he thinks he might be out of touch—and other than that, he's only not answered once, and it was 'cause he was in trouble, and he called me back right after. Now I haven't been able to reach him in two days, and I think he's in trouble again, and his message on his other phone said to come find you—"

My thoughts smashed to a halt with the grace of a car crash. "Wait, what? He said to come find *me*? Kid, who's your dad?"

"Arthur Tresting."

The bottom dropped out of my stomach.

"Are you a friend of his?" Tabitha asked.

I turned away from her, grabbed out my phone, and dialed Arthur's cell. Voicemail. I hung up and tried his office number, the one he listed online as a private investigator. The message informed potential clients he was away from the office for a few days, and sure enough, advised any current clients with an emergency to contact me, complete with the address of the brand-new office Arthur himself had only recently strong-armed me into renting.

Well. Nice of him to tell me. "I'm not even a PI," I growled into the speaker, and jabbed at the button to hang up before tossing my phone on the desk.

Then I turned to face Arthur's daughter.

Arthur had a daughter. I'd known Arthur almost two years now, and I didn't know he had a daughter.

For all the enemies I had been expecting to come feinting out of the dark, this was a sucker punch.

"I'll track him down," I promised her, finding my voice. "Do you have a number where I can contact you?"

She gave me her mobile number, the beginnings of relief sketching her features.

"Did he tell you anything? Or, uh, anyone else in your family?" Was Arthur married? Wife? Ex-wife? I had no idea.

She shook her head. "My sister and brothers don't know anything. Dad never wants to involve us in his work; he won't talk about it. They keep telling me not to worry, but . . ."

"Better to be safe," I agreed, trying for comforting. "I'll find him." A sick worry had started squirming in under the shock. "What about your mom? Would she know anything?"

"My other dad," Tabitha corrected. "I have two dads. No, they don't—they don't really talk anymore."

So Arthur liked men. In the name of everything holy, how had I never known that he had what sounded like an ex-husband and a family? These seemed like pretty basic things for friends who regularly saved each other's life to know. Forget the shock and worry, I was settling on pissed off.

"I'll find him," I vowed to Tabitha again, even more firmly. *So I can punch him.* "Are you okay getting home?"

She nodded. "I'd better go. My dad will miss me if I'm home too late."

Her dad—Arthur's ex. I seethed with curiosity, but forcibly behaved myself in front of Tabitha. "Go home. I'll call you as soon as I know anything."

"Thank you, Ms. Russell," she said solemnly, and hitching what looked like a school bag on her shoulder, she ducked awkwardly out of my office.

I picked up my phone.

I knew exactly who my next call would be.

"Hey, Cas!" said the voice of the best hacker I knew—who also happened to be Arthur's investigative partner and information broker. "Did you hear David Tennant is doing an event in Los Angeles next month? *David Tennant*. I might have to leave the Hole for that."

"Checker, have you heard from Arthur lately?" I interrupted.

"Uh, yeah, talked to him last week. We don't have any cases right now, though. What's up?"

"Have you talked to him in the last two days?"

"No, why?"

"Me neither. And guess who was just in my office worried she can't reach him? His daughter."

Long pause.

"Checker, did you know Arthur has a family?"

Another long pause. Then Checker said, "Yes."

"And did you find this out through Internet stalking, or am I justified in feeling shafted right now?"

"It's not like that," Checker said a little desperately. "I knew Arthur before everything went down. Before he lost— while he was still with them. Nowadays he never . . . he got private about them afterwards. His business, Cas," he added severely. He cleared his throat. "Which daughter?"

Great. He knew them all by name. "Tabitha."

"I, uh, I think we should be worried. Maybe very worried. Arthur wouldn't ignore one of his kids, ever."

The squirming in my gut got worse, enough that my anger faded a bit. "Do you know what he was working on?"

"Not a clue. I didn't even know we had a case on."

"I'm going to head to his office, then. See if I can find anything."

"Sounds good," said Checker, and I could already hear the quick clack of his computer keys. "I'll see if I can find anything on my end. Does Diego know?"

"Who's Diego?" I was proud of how calmly and precisely I managed to speak.

The clacking of the keyboards stopped for a moment. "Uh, his husband. Never mind, I'll call."

"Still in touch, are you?"

"Stop it." The clacking had resumed, and a thread of annoyance joined the worry in Checker's voice. "You can be petty after we find him."

He was right, but that didn't mean I had to concede it. "I'm capable of multitasking," I snapped. "I'll let you know what I find at his office. And after that I'm going to his apartment. Are you going to give me grief about respecting his privacy on that too?"

"Just find him," said Checker, sounding tired and concerned, and hung up on me.

I grabbed my coat, steadfastly resisting any urge to feel guilt about my snippiness. I checked the Colt in my belt and made sure the hem of the coat covered it completely, shoved a few spare magazines in my pocket and, feeling in a better-to-be-safe-than-sorry mood, a revolver in another pocket. Part of me hoped to find Arthur snoozing at home, but a strong sense of foreboding in my chest warned of how unlikely that was.

Wherever he was, he'd better be alive. He owed me about a thousand damn explanations.

two

SHIT. I'd forgotten about my client meeting. I pulled out my cell as I locked the door of the stupid office behind me, punching in the contact number I had. It was already seven minutes after the hour; maybe he was a no-show anyway.

The phone rang out without a voicemail message. That was weird.

"You're not supposed to be leaving," said a voice with an Aussie accent.

I turned. It took me three scans of the decrepit parking lot to find the person who had spoken. My client—well, I assumed—was scrambling toward me over the gravel: an unkempt Asian Australian man, with shaggy black hair, greasy stubble, and a torn shirt beneath his leather jacket that was even dirtier than mine. "Sorry," I said insincerely, waving my phone at him. "I was just trying to call. Something's come up."

"No. No!" He whipped his head in a frantic headshake. "No, you have to stay!"

"Look, we can reschedule for—"

"No!" he cried, and launched himself at me.

His movement translated into mathematics, clumsy Newtonian mechanics with his mass and velocity throwing themselves forward with no regard for efficiency. He might be bigger than I was, but still, it was insulting. And I was in the mood to hit someone.

I twisted and struck my palm against his hip, building the perfect fulcrum. His body flipped over in a spin an acrobat would have been proud of, and he landed on his back, wheezing.

I stepped into the afternoon sun so my shadow fell across his face. "Hi," I said. "I'm Cas Russell. *Our meeting is rescheduled.* Is that underst—"

My office exploded.

The concussion roared outward through shattering glass and splintering wood and slammed across the lot. The blast flung me into the air, the noise overwhelming everything else. I flailed against it and managed enough of a partial solution to twist and hit the ground hard on my shoulder before rolling out back to my feet.

The explosion had shredded the front wall of my new office, bits of boards hanging by mere splinters against crumbling mounds of plaster. Nothing was on fire, but I didn't want to know what it looked like inside. The small, grimy parking lot had only a few cars in it, but their windows had all shattered, and I could hear car alarms wailing from some distance away. My lungs twinged in the aftermath of the sudden pressure differential.

My would-be client, who had escaped the worst of the blast by being flat on his back, tried to scramble to his feet and dash away. I snatched up a piece of wood rubble from the explosion and threw it.

And *missed*.

What the hell? I never missed. One hundred percent accuracy was one of the perks of having a freakish mathematical superpower. I picked up another piece of debris, concentrated, and tried again. This time the board smacked him against the back of the knees, and his feet flew up, landing him on his back for the second time in thirty seconds.

"You!" I shouted, bearing down on him. My voice sounded strange and tinny. Also, my head hurt. "You just tried to get me killed!"

He mouthed something at me.

I grabbed him by the neck and slammed his head into the gravel. "Who are you?"

His jaw worked frantically, as if he were trying to form words, and he stabbed one finger repeatedly at the side of his head like a jackhammer.

Ears. Right.

The car alarms I was hearing weren't from far away. They were right next to me.

I yanked the guy to his feet and levered one of his arms behind his back to force him along with me. His face contorted in pain as he stumbled to keep up. I brought us to a car that wasn't mine and shoved him to the ground while I jacked it open; glass showered down onto the seats. I shoved my new friend into the back, brushed the glass off the driver's seat, and pried open the dash to touch the right two wires together.

The car thrummed to life beneath us. I couldn't hear it.

Neighbors were starting to poke their heads out. An Armenian guy in an apron who was probably the owner of the car came running, waving his arms, but I was already pulling out, skidding in a 360 to squeal out of the parking lot. At least, I was pretty sure we squealed. My head felt like it was wrapped in wool, muffling all sound to almost nothing. A high ringing phased in over it, as if trying to prove the point.

Christ, I'd have to start tracking my hearing damage. Between firefights and explosives, I was pretty sure some of it was becoming permanent.

We had to switch cars fast; it wasn't like we could stay under the police radar with all our windows blown out. I swerved into an underground garage beneath a run-down apartment building, and within minutes, we were driving back out in a much less conspicuous sedan. In the chaos I'd almost forgotten to haul my prisoner along in the car swap, but he'd tried to run again and I'd clotheslined him into the front passenger seat.

I texted Checker with one hand as I drove:

OFFICE BLEW UP
ON THE RUN
BURNING THIS PHONE
IN TOUCH SOON

Then I popped the battery out, dropped the phone out the window, and lost us in the summer heat of Los Angeles traffic.

My prisoner moaned next to me, reminding me again that he was there. He tried to reach for the car door handle, but I punched him in the throat.

"No, no," he wheezed between bouts of coughing. "You don't see me!"

"Of course I do," I said. "You blew up my office!"

Come to that, where the hell should I go with him?

Aside from my office, I exchanged monthly cash payments for plenty of shabby little apartments around LA which doubled as both safe houses and interchangeable living spaces. Arthur had also tried to get me to stick to a semipermanent address, but I absolutely had never seen the point to that.

I had to get to Arthur's office and home and check them, but what if those were rigged too? What if the explosion had to do with his disappearance? How likely was that? After all, I had plenty of enemies who'd be more than happy to blow me to kingdom come, and they had nothing to do with Arthur.

The grasping hands of my past reared up again. Flashes of fragmented memory had given shape to doctors and drugs, training and cruelty. Someone had been honing me—honing a lot of us—but I still didn't know who or why. Only that they had been frighteningly similar to the people who called themselves Pithica, the mind witches who'd eventually claimed themselves puppet masters of the world until I'd been dumb enough to throw a spanner into their works.

Or maybe it's closer to home. Maybe someone in the city found out about you *screwing them all in the head.*

That was a troubling thought. As of four months ago, almost all of Los Angeles had owed me a broken skull, but my mistakes had been psychically erased in the most discomfiting way possible, and most of them appeared to have forgotten. I doubted the telepathic sweep had gotten everyone, though. Some people seemed to have dismissed the rumors of my involvement, given the ultimately bizarre and seemingly inconsistent sequence of events, but I suspected there existed others—people who'd recognized a voice on the radio and now nursed perfectly rational grudges even as their cohorts laughed them off.

Then there were all the people I'd screwed over directly by breaking into their secure lairs and threatening them. I was pretty sure Yamamoto wasn't the only crime lord still taking my rampage as a personal insult, and I hadn't even pointed a gun at him.

But even with all the lurking threats, I still didn't believe in coincidences, or at least only believed in them when they fit the relevant probability distribution. And for my office to blow up *exactly* after Arthur had gone missing . . . especially considering he'd left a message on his voicemail about being connected with me . . .

"You're not supposed to *see* me," moaned my passenger.

I blinked.

Somehow I'd stopped paying attention to him. Weird. Especially considering he was currently my most likely source of answers. The ringing in my ears had died down enough to hear the very loud rap music in the car next to us; it was past time to run an interrogation.

"Yeah, I've heard blowing people up is great for stealth," I said back to him. "In fact, we're going to have a nice little conversation now. Talk and you'll live."

"I don't know anything," said the Aussie man. The emphasis on the words was odd, as if he wasn't used to speaking aloud. "You were supposed to stay. You were supposed to stay and not see."

What?

"Nobody sees," he continued. "I'm *not here*." He started giggling.

Oh. Oh, shit. This guy was . . . not all there. Someone else must be taking advantage of him.

Fuck.

I thought for a minute and then drove to a four-story apartment building where I kept a one-bedroom place on the top floor. The Aussie man whimpered about hidden secrets and invisible friends all the way up.

I didn't want to hurt him again—I wasn't opposed to hurting people in general, but in this case, it didn't seem fair—but when he wouldn't get out of the car, I had to hustle him out with a grip on his jacket. I got him up to the apartment and sat him down in the bedroom. There wasn't a bed, only a couch with one of its cushions missing, but hey, I didn't run a Hilton.

"What's your name?" I tried.

"People don't talk to me," he said. "And I don't talk to people."

"A man after my own heart." I sighed. "Who told you to blow up my office?"

"They told me to do it," he agreed. "And they were right."

"*Who* told you?"

"The one who makes the music," he said. "Playing the songs when you ask."

"Does this person have a name?"

"I'm not supposed to tell anyone. How did you know it was me?"

"You basically told me," I said. "I do tend to notice when people try to kill me."

"No, you don't. It wasn't me. You're wrong."

I gave up.

He had access to the bathroom, and I opened some cans of overly processed food and left them in the room with a spoon and a few bottles of water. Then I locked the door to the bedroom and shoved a wedge under the outside door to the apartment for good measure. The windows in the place were painted shut and four stories up—the only danger of him getting out was if he started making noise and someone investigated. But this building was mostly empty units or people who spent their entire days high, so I didn't think it likely.

Two years ago, I probably would have tied the guy up and gagged him, or at least considered it. "Fuck you, Arthur," I muttered.

Are you sure it's all Arthur?

I stomped down the stairs. No—Arthur had been trying to convince me to have a conscience long before I'd had a telepath in my head regularly. I wasn't going to go there.

Wasn't going to start second-guessing myself.

I'd repeated the same words so often over the past four months that I was sick of them.

Besides, I reminded myself, it was bad enough if it *was* just Arthur pushing at my morals—pretending to be my friend, trying to fix me up to be a model citizen, and not even telling me the basic facts of his own goddamn life. He knew the most personal details about me, after all. He'd been with me all through fighting a worldwide organization of psychics who were only too ready to kill me if given half a chance, and knew all about Dawna Polk, Pithica's telepath who'd clawed into my brain and almost destroyed me. He knew about my amnesia—that I was mired without any memory more than five years back, aside from hellish remnants best forgotten. And he knew about Simon, who I had to keep letting erase me once a week or I'd fragment and blow away on the wind . . . even after I'd found out he was the one who'd obliterated me in the first place. A past I couldn't look at, the capacity for ruthless mathematical violence with no explanation behind such an abnormal skill set . . . whispers of words and images and nothing more to tell me who had made me . . . Arthur knew all of it.

I'd saved Arthur's life so many times now, and he'd saved mine.

He'd never once mentioned he had a family.

TOR